What splendid words her mother had written!

"Here in the theater we wear beautiful clothes.
Tonight my green satin dress is garnished
with gold lace, and tomorrow I will wear
one of silver tissue."

Lorena sighed with content. She could not know how her mother Lenore had embroidered on the truth, that the gold lace was tarnished, the silver tissue threadbare —costumes to be worn onstage. Still Lenore's beautiful violet eyes had darkened wistfully as she penned the words. It sounded so much better that way. And she wanted young Lorena, the child she had not seen since babyhood, who had been so cruelly torn from her arms by fate, to love her, to think well of her.

The letter had wrought much more than that. Lorena went to sleep starry-eyed with dreams of the glitter of London shaping her own hopes for the future. Would life be fraught with the pain and passion that swept her mother from love, to adventure, to fame?

Lenore and Lorena—their names are so alike—
their beauties so dissimilar.
Yet each is bound to reap the rewards
and the troubles of love won by

Her Shining Splendor

Novels by Valerie Sherwood

This Loving Torment
These Golden Pleasures
This Towering Passion
Her Shining Splendor

Published by
WARNER BOOKS

Her Shining Splendor

Valerie Sherwood

WARNER BOOKS

A Warner Communications Company

WARNER BOOKS EDITION

Cover art by Elaine Duillo

Warner Books, Inc., 75 Rockefeller Plaza, New York, N.Y. 10019

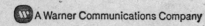 A Warner Communications Company

Printed in the United States of America

First Printing: August, 1980

10 9 8 7 6 5 4 3 2 1

Dedication

In loving memory of Sherry, my long-haired silver tabby cat, who was with me for sixteen years and who was as beautiful and as gallant as any of my heroines.

Author's Note

Although this novel is entirely a work of fiction, and all the meetings of my characters with actual historical figures are of my own invention, the Cotswold "Olimpick Games" were real and, except for a hiatus during England's Civil Wars, were held on Dover's Hill near Chipping Campden during Whit week from 1612 until 1852. The infamous Hellfire Club also was a reality—and a terrible one. And Nell Gwyn and Lady Castlemaine and Louise de Keroualle, Duchess of Portsmouth—three of King Charles II's seventeen acknowledged royal mistresses—were all certainly real enough. But for the purposes of this story, some dates and names and places have been changed—all, I hope, without violating the spirit of these stirring and turbulent times.

Valerie Sherwood

WARNING:

Readers are hereby specifically warned
not to eat or drink or otherwise use
any of the unusual items mentioned herein
without first seeking medical advice.
For example, the cosmetic "ceruse,"
so popular for whitening the face in the
seventeenth century, contains white lead
which is lethal and undoubtedly
caused many deaths in its day.

Contents

Her Shining Splendor

BOOK I:

Lenore–
Too Desperate

London 1662

Chapter 1

Lenore Frankford's soft, excited laughter floated out into the moonlit night. Only moments ago she and Geoffrey Wyndham, riding double, had raced across London Bridge and lost their pursuers in the narrow winding streets of Southwark. They had tumbled from the saddle in the courtyard of the Tabard Inn on Borough High Street, a tall cavalier and a radiant woman in low-cut black silk, and waited in the shadows while the pursuit thundered by.

Now on light feet Lenore matched the pace of her black satin, red-heeled slippers to the stride of Geoffrey's wide-topped boots. She was still giddy with amazement that he had appeared, naked blade swinging, to save her from Wilsingame's devilish crew, who had kidnapped her from in front of the theater where she worked as an orange girl. They had meant to have cruel sport with her this night—she had almost driven a pair of scissors into her white bosom to escape them. Then, miraculously, Geoffrey had arrived and whisked her away.

Now, he swung open the door to the deserted common room, and Lenore stepped inside, waiting while Geoffrey impatiently demanded of the innkeeper the best room in the house. A goodly room they would have, the sleepy landlord promised, one with a fine view of the courtyard. He called, "Eliza!" and a sallow serving maid in white apron and cap scuttled in. She seized a lighted taper from a table, snatched up her homespun skirts and lighted their way up the wooden stair.

Spurs clinking, Geoffrey strode up beside Lenore. He smiled down at her.

"Thomas Dekker says High Street is now one continuous alehouse," he told her lightly.

She caught her breath, for his gray eyes were subtly telling her something else—how beautiful she was, how much he wanted her.

"At last count there were some twenty-three taverns and inns along it. If Wilsingame's slimy crowd attempts to search them all out, the sun will have risen and set again before they've done!"

The warm timbre of his resonant voice coursed through Lenore. The tall shadows cast by the candle wavered along the whitewashed wall. She laughed deliciously. "Faith, they're too drunk for that! They'll go back to Wilsingame's house on London Bridge and play at cards—and fight, most like."

She saw Geoffrey's gray eyes flicker dangerously.

"Should any one of them even so much as leer at you again, by God, I'll hunt him down and skewer him on this!" He touched the serviceable hilt of the blade by his side significantly.

Lenore thrilled to that truculent note in his voice. This was the masterful Geoffrey she had never forgotten, the reckless cavalier who—on that long ago day when she had found her handfast lover dead on the field of Worcester after the battle and refused to leave him—had swept her up and galloped away with her, and saved her life, then, as now. This was the redoubtable Geoffrey

Wyndham she had fallen hopelessly in love with as they fled across England pursued by Cromwell's men; wanted Royalists in a Puritan land. This was the romantic Geoffrey she had lived with in Oxford and planned in her heart to marry.

She remembered with a catch in her throat how she had stood on her high heels for seven long hours in the Strand and watched King Charles II's triumphal procession wend its way toward Whitehall—all in the hope of seeing Geoffrey, who she was sure would return from overseas with the king, now that he had regained his throne.

But Geoffrey had not ridden in the procession, and she had gone home to her lodgings bitterly dejected, believing him dead.

Oh, so many terrible things had kept them apart— lies, misunderstandings . . . their pride. But now, miraculously, he had returned to save her! She went up the stairs so lightly, neither foot seemed to touch the surface of the wooden steps.

"I watched for you two years ago, Geoffrey, when the king's procession rode in across London Bridge. I looked at every face, expecting to see you. Why did you not come with him?"

"Had I known you waited for me there, I would have led the procession," he said ruefully, smiling down at her. "I have been about the king's business in Somerset and Dorset, Lenore. Ned's been helping me. His Lavinia died of the childbed fever and he's married to Lally now."

"To Lally?" Lenore smiled brilliantly at this welcome news of her old friend. Now *she* was reunited with her lover—and Lally was too! "How wonderful, Geoffrey! She loved Ned so much."

"When Lavinia died, Ned went seeking her. He found her ill in Southampton. But now she is well and they are expecting a child next month at his home in Somerset."

Lenore reached up and touched his dark face with gentle fingers. "Not only do you bring me the gift of yourself—you bring me glad tidings!"

They had reached the top of the stairs.

"This room, sir." The white-aproned serving maid swung wide a door to her right, her pale eyes losing their sleepiness at the sight of the gold coin Geoffrey carelessly tossed her.

"A bath for me," he decided. "And—you look just risen from a bath, Lenore, like Venus from the foam. Do you desire a bath also?"

Lenore was indeed recently risen from a bath—at Wilsingame's, with a coverlet held up by the maid to hide her white form from Bonnifly's lascivious inspection! She nodded vigorously. "I'd like to wash away the touch of Bonnifly's dirty fingers as he tried to shove me downstairs into the arms of that evil pack!"

"And so ye shall. Two baths, wench. We'll take them here."

The serving girl repressed a giggle, and adopting the seriousness that Geoffrey's large tip demanded, she lit a candle by the bedside with her own taper and scuttled away.

"You've shocked her," Lenore reproved him, but her violet eyes sparkled with laughter. "But tell me, what lucky chance brings you from the West Country to London, Geoffrey?"

Geoffrey hesitated. "The king has given me an estate in Kent, Lenore. 'Tis named Claremont Court. I found it very run-down and much in need of supervision. This is the first time I've been to London since I returned from overseas, for usually I've contrived to see the king when he was visiting in the country, to avoid that great press that always surrounds him at Whitehall."

Lenore's arched brows elevated. "You chose a monstrous good time to arrive," she marveled.

"In truth I rode in seeking you. A friend stopped by and dropped word that the king had mentioned seeing the

'Angel of Worcester' in London. Such is your fame, that I thought I had only to ride in to find you—and I was right!"

"I've been called other things since. In the theater they called me the Iron Virgin. They said I wore a chastity belt beneath my chemise."

A knock sounded on the door and Lenore hushed Geoffrey's possibly ribald response. The serving maid edged into the room, carrying a big pitcher of hot water. She was followed by another girl similarly laden.

"One tub will be enough," Geoffrey announced coolly. "Just so it is a capacious one."

"But we've none big enough, sir!" stuttered the girl. "For the two of ye, that is!"

"Two tubs will be fine," said Lenore with a reproving look at Geoffrey. "And lots of towels. And scented soap if you have any."

"Oh, aye, Mistress," the girl declared eagerly.

"Good." Geoffrey's tone was bored. He struck an indolent posture, leaning against the footpost of a massive fourposter. "And be quick about it. We've no mind to wait until the water cools!"

"Can I help ye undress, Mistress?" the serving girl asked Lenore doubtfully, once the two metal tubs were brought and filled with steaming water. "Ye've many hooks down the back of that dress."

"I'm here to assist in that," Geoffrey said outrageously. With a genial smile he tossed the girl another coin. "Ye did not see us here tonight—remember that!"

"Aye, sir—I've forgotten already!" The girl giggled and ducked from the room.

"Faith, you've grown very broad in your language," Lenore's violet eyes challenged him. "Assist me indeed!"

Geoffrey locked the door. He drew off his leather gauntlets and tossed them aside, flung his plumed hat after them, and stripped off his sword and baldric. " 'Tis exactly what I have in mind," he said hoarsely. "Lord,

Lenore, ye can't know how many times I've undressed you in memory! 'Twas all that kept me going sometimes, remembering you had loved me."

Lenore's luminous eyes shone with tears. "I have taken no lover since you left me," she said in a husky voice. "You ruined other men for me, Geoffrey—I'm yours alone."

He gave her a sharp look. "Not even the King? There are rumors . . ."

She smiled at his jealousy. "Not even the King. Although he did give me a ruby ring," she added lightly.

"'Tis not like Charles to miss such a sweet parcel—methinks he may be around yet to collect you!"

Lenore's indifferent shrug was its own answer. "Oh, Lady Castlemaine rushed in and dragged him away from me—'twas her ring he gave me. He tore it from her finger!"

"Barbara let him do that?" Geoffrey's uproarious laugh filled the room.

"She struck at us both with her riding whip," Lenore recalled. "They tussled."

"I don't doubt it." Geoffrey was unhooking the back of her dress. "Must you wear so many of these?" he demanded testily as they resisted him.

" 'Tis the fashion. I could take the dress off faster by myself," she teased.

" 'Tis a reward I've promised myself for too long, that I'll let it elude me now!"

Lenore closed her eyes. Every tiny touch of his fingers as he unhooked the black silk bodice, no matter how light, made her senses reel. Her pulse raced from the warmth of his quickening breath on her white shoulder.

Those gentle, competent hands—now expertly working the hooks—how well she remembered them. How often had she waked from blissful dreams where she was in his arms again—and wept that she was not.

"Oh, Geoffrey," Lenore murmured, "don't ever

leave me." She turned, just as her dress was pulled down to her waist, and threw her arms about him.

"God willing, I'll not," Geoffrey whispered against her long, perfumed hair. "Lenore, whatever is in store for us—we have this night."

"Yes," she agreed, her voice muffled against his broad chest. "Even if we were to be found tomorrow and cut down, we would have had tonight!"

"Ye need fear them no longer, Lenore," he said tenderly, easing down her delicate lace-trimmed, black silk chemise. Her exposed breasts trembled under his hot gaze. Geoffrey lowered his head and planted a nuzzling kiss on one rosy nipple. "Ye are under my protection," he added significantly.

Half mad with longing at his touch, Lenore stood entranced and let him remove her silks, so that they fluttered softly to her feet and lay there in a gleaming midnight pile. Now she stood proudly before him, her alabaster flesh gleaming gold in the candlelight. Her glistening shawl of red gold hair, her black satin red-heeled shoes and sheer black silk stockings and silver tinsel garters were her only garments.

"God, you're beautiful," he said hoarsely.

How long she had yearned to hear those words from his longing lips, to see the hunger for her alone in his gray eyes.

She shook her head, the gleaming mantle of long hair rippling and falling away like heavy silk, revealing again her rounded, rose-tipped breasts.

Fired with passion by the embodiment of his dreams, Geoffrey lifted Lenore in his arms and carried her to the bed. There he set her on his lap and slowly removed her dainty shoes and tinsel garters, and last of all her sheer black stockings. She caught her breath as the black silk rasped down her bare legs, and Geoffrey's warm hand brushed the smooth skin of her thighs, and came to rest on that silky triangle of blond hair between them.

The tension that had built between them was too much.

"If I hold ye here longer, ye'll get no bath," he warned.

Lenore laughed shakily and spun away from him, to step into her bath as gracefully as a water nymph—only to withdraw her foot hastily. " 'Tis too hot!" she protested. "I'll be red as a lobster if I bathe in this!"

"Then you can help me undress while your bath water cools," he said, unperturbed. As he spoke he was stripping off his coat. With a lazy smile, he sat down again on the bed to pull off his wide-topped boots.

"I'll help you off with those," she offered, making to straddle his long leg in order to tug off his right boot.

"Nay." He pushed her round white bottom away with a gentle pat on its satin surface. "I've no mind to put a boot sole on *that!* I've something else in mind!"

Lenore laughed self-consciously and busied herself with playfully helping him out of his russet trousers. She marveled that it seemed as if Geoffrey had never been gone at all! The years had fallen away and this roof at the Tabard Inn had magically changed into their bedroom in Oxford, where they had undressed each other as eagerly as they now did.

"Oh, Geoffrey!" Leonore's voice broke, and she swayed against him. He swept her up tightly against his lean, naked body, held her for a moment as if to protect her from harm. Then she felt herself lifted from the floor, and he carried her to the tub and tested her bath with a careful toe.

"About right now, I should say. What think you?"

He lowered her gently into the tub. Her bottom struck the water first—and quivered. Then the soles of her feet were immersed. Then her whole body settled down in the tub, and the water came up around her waist and knees and lapped at the base of her round breasts, giving them the sheen of a seashell.

Geoffrey watched her, smiling for a moment, then tossed her a bar of scented soap. Whistling, he strode naked across to the other tub. She watched as he lowered himself, folding up his lean body tightly to accommodate it to the tub. His hard ropy muscles were just as she remembered, that light furring on his broad chest just the same.

She turned her head quickly so that he would not see she had been watching him, for she suddenly felt as shy as a young girl with her first lover. Her cheeks a little redder than even the hot water demanded, she soaped herself and eased down into the water as far as she could. She swept her hair up, coiled it atop her head with a practiced hand, then made a turban of a linen towel to keep her hair dry. Then she bent over and scooped up a handful of the hot water, letting it trickle through her fingers over a white shoulder, rinsing off the soap. And then again. And again.

Geoffrey, watching Lenore luxuriate in the bath, thought her neck was swanlike, her body a miracle, her face the loveliest he had ever seen. The very sight of her spurred him to finish his bath quickly. He rose from the tub with a shake like a big, wet dog. Roughly, he toweled himself dry so that his sinewy muscles gleamed in the candlelight.

The very hairs of his chest and the back of his neck prickled as he looked at Lenore, and his groin gave a sudden lurch as she rose dripping from the metal tub. She stood, letting little silver rivulets of water trickle down into the cleft between her breasts, along her stomach and down her sleek thighs.

She stretched—and Geoffrey was lost. With a low moan, he seized a towel and strode toward her.

"I'll dry you," he offered. Lenore watched him through her lashes, as slowly, sensuously, he stroked her with the fresh linen until her skin tingled and glowed pink. She gave a little sigh—it was pure, delicious, torture!

"Stop it," she told him huskily. "I can't stand it. Geoffrey, I must be twice dried already!"

He laughed and tossed aside the damp towel, took

both her hands and swept her arms up and apart and, taking his time, surveyed the naked length of her. She felt a shiver go through her as those gray eyes traveled up and down.

The smile had left his eyes now to be replaced by something akin to awe. "I was not wrong," he murmured with heartfelt joy. "How often have I told myself that no one could be so beautiful as I remembered you—but you are even more lovely than I pictured you, Lenore."

Lenore glowed with pleasure. She tossed off her turban with a careless gesture and let her bright hair cascade down her back. She smiled at him and smoothed gentle fingers against his heartbeat. His big chest muscles contracted suddenly beneath her touch and he looked down at her, his gray eyes dark and deep.

"Lenore . . ." His voice ended in a kiss as his lips closed over hers, and he folded her in his arms. Dizzy with desire, Lenore hardly knew it when he swept her up and carried her to the big fourposter. Tenderly, he laid her down and lowered his naked body upon her. In the dim light it seemed their discovery of one another had made their bodies shine.

They had no need of words, these reunited lovers. Their endearments were only broken murmurings, but their locked embraces spoke eloquently the timeless language of love. Lenore felt Geoffrey's hands caressing her and she was glad, glad she had not taken any of the many offers that had come her way, glad she had waited for Geoffrey; enraptured to be back in his arms again.

She ran her hand lightly across his groin and heard his soft groan. She nearly sobbed with happiness as he entered her, moving with authority, yet silkily, expertly, holding her at his ease. Heart to heart, they embraced and tingled and tormented with joy. Deftly he caressed her pliant body, and soft explosions of passion flowered within her on vibrating notes, like music rising to a crescendo. His questing fingers moved down her spine and their tingly feeling rippled along her skin like a scale of music.

Never before had she felt such tigerish power in Geoffrey—as if he would devour her. Never before this controlled violence with which he turned and twisted her slight body to his own. She shared this wild desperation, for she had thought never to feel these sinewy arms about her again, never to feel the leanness of his long body as he possessed her. She had thought never to have her soul bursting with this ecstasy, as fierce as she remembered it. Her every sense shattered like crystal—the sparkling shards left to fall on sand, on silk, on velvet. Within her, the rhythmic throbbing sang and rose in waves to the thunderous, overwhelming, not-to-be-denied finale. Then, together they floated down, their senses whirling slowly back to the soft, gentle caress of their love. Lenore lay quietly beside Geoffrey as he slid away from her and smiled down into her eyes.

"Lenore."

She looked up dreamily, her head nestled in the crook of his arm.

His voice had a wrench in it. "How *long* I have wanted you."

"As I have wanted you, Geoffrey." Her sigh was deep-drawn, blissful. "And now we need never part." She pressed closer against him and threw her naked leg lightly across his lean hard-muscled one.

"Don't talk," he said huskily, aroused again beyond his senses. He took her again . . . this time the highest heights were scaled, the farthest stars seemed but milestones on their road to ecstasy. Space seemed limitless and time without meaning as they murmured soft, wonderful things to each other in the age-old language of love.

By morning they slept a little, happy and exhausted, and smiling in their sleep at the miracle of belonging wholly to each other again.

Geoffrey was dressing when Lenore awoke. She sat up and leaned on one arm and looked at him as he pulled on his trousers. A thousand things she might have asked him at that moment, but all the intervening years seemed unimportant when she saw his back muscles ripple as he adjusted his russet trousers.

"Come back to bed," she said, smiling wickedly.

He turned and gave her a look of indecision. His gray gaze was speculative. "If I do, I'll not rise again until time to sup."

"I care not if you don't rise till tomorrow morn!"

"I had thought to go out and buy you a fine gown, a plumed hat, a necklace of brilliants," he demurred.

"That can wait. What need have I of fine gowns?" Lenore threw back the coverlet and opened her arms. Lying there, she had a lustrous seductive beauty that Geoffrey could not resist. Quickly he divested himself of the clothes he had just put on.

"I am yours to command, Mistress," he said, looking down on her with a smile.

"Then I command you to love me, Geoffrey."

"I have always loved you," he said slowly. "Whatever happens, remember that."

"Be not so serious!" she teased, pulling him down so that the dark, silky dusting of hair along his powerful chest brushed her rosy nipples, causing them to flinch in delight. "We are eternal lovers, like Will Shakespeare's Romeo and Juliet, save that we will end up well, of course!" She gave a rich low vibrant laugh and pulled his body down to hers.

"If I could but save you from the blows of life," he murmured. But Lenore hardly heard. She was straining against him, her smooth hips thrusting against his own narrow ones. In a night, in a day, she would make up for all those years apart. She would possess him completely, as her towering passion for him had possessed her mind, her body, her very soul—all those empty years without him.

The Cotswolds, England 1662

Chapter 2

Like a red ball sinking into a sea of misty blue, the sun dipped behind the Cotswold Hills. Candles were being lit in the village of Twainmere as Lorena Frankford, swinging an empty basket, strolled home to the vicarage through the unseasonably warm autumn dusk. Past ancient trees and houses of honey-colored Cotswold stone with low stone walls over which red roses spilled their fragrance, her light step took her.

As she neared the village green, Lorena heard laughter and excited teasing voices egging each other on. She peered forward, and her brilliant sapphire eyes, dramatically fringed by thick dark lashes, sparkled. In the shadow of the big oaks that dotted the green, teenage village maids were playing hide-and-seek with the husky local lads. Full skirts were being lifted, petticoats artfully displayed—and flying ankles and shapely calves too—as giggling girls sped to the shelter of the oaks or ran to crouch in nearby hedges or under yew trees, waiting for some promising lad to find them and steal a kiss—or perhaps a bit more—beneath the sheltering branches.

Pretty and precocious, young Lorena—although she was already late for supper at the vicarage—promptly hung her basket over a nearby branch and joined in the game. Still a child, though tall for her age, Lorena had already been noticed by several of the older boys who had given her long thoughtful looks. It was hard not to notice Lorena. Anyone looking into that appealing heart-shaped face, framed by long thick almost hemp-white blond hair, was instantly struck by her loveliness. Her sheer complexion, with the color coming and going softly in her peach bloom cheeks, the curve of her slender white neck, invited one to touch. Her figure, still slender as a boy's, gave little hint of the lissome beauty that would one day be hers, but her wide blue eyes held a challenge—some said an invitation—and her smile was reckless. She had the face of an adventuress and everyone in Twainmere predicted that that face would get her into trouble.

Joining heartily in the game, Lorena's soft mouth curved into swift laughter as Harve Meadows rounded an oak, pounced on saucy Jane Frye and bore her to the ground in a laughing shrieking heap. Lorena's laughter faded as Jane gave Harve a sudden hard slap and scrambled up, pouting and blushing. Something . . . had happened there. What had Harve done to rate a slap?

Now it was Jane's turn to close her eyes and count while the others hid. Lorena was concentrating on the game, but big Harve was now concentrating on Lorena. Her fair hair, moonlight pale, beckoned to him like a flickering firefly winging through the rapidly deepening dusk. He noted where she was running off to with her light skirts flying. Why, she was going to hide in the hedge beside the cottage in which he lived with his parents—almost against the side window. There was a candle burning in the cottage kitchen, but the side of the house Lorena had chosen for her hiding place was dark.

Moving silently over the soft grass, Harve circled about and stole up behind her quietly.

Harve was grinning. He'd had his eye on Lorena for some time. Not yet ripe, but getting there. He saw that Lorena's slender form was bent over as she peered through the leafy hedge, her full attention centered on the wild activity taking place on the green. Her saucy little bottom was turned in his direction, almost quivering as she gauged whether the hunt was coming *here*. For a moment Harve stood appreciating the sight of that slightly wriggling mound of gray cambric—for as the vicar's foster daughter, Lorena was always soberly dressed. His eyes traveled down the backs of her slender gray-stockinged legs, revealed below a laceless white lawn petticoat.

"Gotcha!" Harve leaped forward, leant down over Lorena's crouched form and seized her in an enveloping hug. His sturdy arms tightened round her waist and as Lorena straightened in shock, her buttocks collided with his hard thighs.

The startled shriek that rose in her throat was muffled before it was half out, as Harve spun her around and his laughing mouth closed down over her soft parted lips. But the noise was enough to attract Jane, the seeker, who was looking for someone to catch. Now Jane ran forward, her soft slippers making no sound on the grass, and pushed aside the hedge and peered through.

She might not have seen them, though she would certainly have heard Lorena panting as she fought valiantly to be free of Harve, had not a candle been at that moment brought into the side of the house toward them. Its sudden light picked out the slender gray-clad girl struggling in the arms of big Harve.

Jane drew in her breath, and her shriek as she crashed through the hedge and pounced on them both was one of anger and dismay. Harve was *hers!* How dare this little snippet from the vicarage entice him? She twined both her hands in Harve's shoulder-length brown hair and gave a yank. Harve's lips left Lorena's with a howl as his head was jerked viciously back.

At the noise, the casements nearby swung open and

an arm holding a candle in a dishlike holder, followed by a gray head, poked out.

"You there! Why, 'tis Harve!" cried his mother. "What are you doing there, Harve, fighting with those two girls?"

"He wasn't fighting with us, Mistress Meadows," cried Jane in a passion. "He was kissing *this* one, and I'm trying to pull him off."

With his stern-eyed mother beaming a candle at him, Harve did not have to be pulled off. He let Lorena go as if she were a hot poker and assumed an innocent expression. "We were but playing, Ma."

"Playing?" cried a voice from behind Mistress Meadows, and another head—this one with a cap on askew—was thrust forward through the window. Harve winced. It was their neighbor, Goody Kettle, who was the biggest gossip in the village and frequently advised his father to "thrash him."

Lorena, flushed and trying to adjust her disordered hair, gave Goody Kettle a rebellious look. "We were but playing hide-and-seek," she said resentfully.

"Why, 'tis Lorena Frankford from the vicarage!" shrilled Goody Kettle, scandalized. "Wait till the vicar hears about *this!*"

Lorena sighed. She was sure Goody Kettle would make haste to tell him. And then she'd be on bread and water again, or forced to stand on a stool in the corner facing the wall for hours. "I have to get home," she muttered.

"I would think so!" Goody Kettle's strident voice followed her as she moved away from them through the hedge. "I will tell you, Mercy Meadows, that child is as wild as her mother. I wouldn't have a son of mine . . ."

Lorena didn't hear the rest, for she was running to retrieve her basket and race home before anything else untoward happened. But she could guess what Goody Kettle might be saying, for she was well aware of her wild heritage. It was impossible to live in Twainmere and not be aware of it.

Her beautiful mother, Lenore Frankford, had been, they said, the wildest girl ever to grow up in Twainmere. With her flaming red-gold hair and violet eyes and vivid smile, she could have taken her pick of Twainmere's ardent swains.

But Lenore was a flirt and had found herself a playboy, Jamie MacIver, who'd had no mind for marriage. Oh, they had called it a marriage, those two, when they lived together in his sister Flora's house, but the town knew different. *They* had called it living in sin.

And Lorena had been the result.

Jamie might have made an honest woman of Lenore, the more charitable insisted, might have taken her to the kirk at that point for a wedding and a christening on the same day, had he not died in the battle of Worcester—fighting on the wrong side from the villagers' point of view, for Scottish Jamie had taken up arms on the side of the king. But they'd let that pass now, for King Charles was back firmly on his throne again and that long rebellion had been put down. But Jamie's death had caused Lenore to flee the victorious rebels' wrath, and many were the wild stories told of what she'd done while on the run. She had come back to Twainmere with her babe in her arms, and except for the sooty lashes inherited from her young mother, the child Lorena had had the young Scot's coloring exactly.

Flora, Jamie's sister, now married to Robert Medlow, the vicar, had taken in Lenore and her child. And when the law closed in, Lenore had fled, leaving Lorena with Flora.

Lenore Frankford's daughter growing up in the vicarage! Twainmere expected the worst.

As she neared the vicarage, Lorena—busy adjusting her bodice—could hear angry voices raised. This was not unusual, for Aunt Flora was a hot-tempered Scot and Uncle Robbie a most determined vicar. Usually the quarrels were about *her*.

Lorena flung open the front gate that breached the low stone wall and paused—but not to drink in the overpowering sweetness of the last of the roses that cascaded over the wall. She frowned thoughtfully. The voices were much louder than usual. Plainly a stormy scene was in progress in the dining room.

Cautiously Lorena turned and moved past the clipped boxwood into the rose garden, where again her senses were assaulted with the sweetness of the late-blooming flowers. She pushed aside a branching rose, winced as a thorn tore at her hand, and peered through a mullioned window into the dimly lit room.

Across the long oaken board with its two tall pewter candlesticks, gaunt Aunt Flora and tall Uncle Robbie stood facing each other. They were both soberly clad, and their faces looked angry. The lighted tapers illuminated a letter clutched in Aunt Flora's bony hand. As Lorena brushed aside the rose branch, the vicar's fist struck the oaken dining table a blow that made the candle flames flicker wildly.

"How can ye expect the girl to amount to anything if ye subject her to letters like this?" he roared. "Ye know her wild blood! Her father—God rest him, for he was your brother—died fighting on the wrong side, and the whole world knows her mother is wanted for murder!"

Lorena winced and her hand nervously rubbed against her gray skirt, staining it with blood from the thorn scratch. It was true, what Uncle Robbie said about her parents. All the village knew these things, and Lorena was often the butt of scornful jokes. Her fair head turned as she studied Aunt Flora, waiting to hear her answer.

Flora's hair was as pale as Lorena's, though it was bound up tightly instead of cascading down. But in no other way did she resemble her niece. Tall and bony and with a naturally intimidating mien, her long body now went rigid, and she leaned across the oaken table and thrust out her head on her long neck in a way that would have made a strong man flinch.

"Ye know the murder charge is false!" she shouted, her voice with its Scots burr hot with indignation. "Lenore killed no one."

"She *said* she killed no one," said the vicar heavily. "And you chose to believe her."

"I thought ye *liked* Lenore when she lived with us, Robbie." Flora looked ready to strike him.

"Aye, I liked her well enough, but always I knew her for what she was." Having said it, he was convinced it was true. He *had* seen through her, had he not?

Flora decided to adopt a more placating manner. "Even though we've not heard from Lenore before, she's often sent gold buttons and coins in pincushions to help pay for Lorena's keep," she reminded him. "Besides ye know not what's in the letter, Robbie, so how can ye pass judgment on it?"

Not heard from her *before*—Lorena's fascinated gaze flew to the letter clutched so firmly in Flora's competent hand. She hardly heard the vicar's scathing response.

"Have ye forgotten how Lenore flirted with all the men before she moved in with your brother Jamie? Then I'll remind ye! Her Lorena has that same wild look about her. Hers is a face that will tempt men sorely."

"She's but a child yet, Robbie," protested Flora.

"Even so, heads turn in church to look at her. I can see them from the pulpit. There's naught we can do about her beauty, but we *can* train her to keep her eyes properly downcast, her skirts well down, and to walk a straight and narrow path."

Flora sighed. Train Lorena to keep her skirts down, they might do, but she doubted that any daughter of Lenore's—or Jamie's either, for that matter—would ever keep her eyes downcast. "I will open it first if ye insist, Robbie. But we *must* let Lorena read the letter—'tis from her mother!"

"No! I say burn the letter unread and be done with Lenore for all time!" Robbie leant across the table to seize the letter from his wife's hand and Flora swiftly retreated. "Lorena would be better off without such a mother!"

Burn the letter? Her first letter ever from the wild young mother she had never seen?

35

"No!" Lorena wailed.

In astonishment, the pair turned to see her white face, beautiful and appealing as her mother's had been, at the window. Now she reached a slender arm beseechingly through the open casement. "Please don't burn the letter—I want to read it."

With a sound that in another man would have been called a curse, the vicar darted around the table to swoop down upon the letter, but Flora snatched it away, eluding him and putting the letter safely behind her back.

"What are ye doing spying on us from the garden?" she shrilled, turning her anger on Lorena. "Come in here at once!"

Lorena collided again with the rose thorns, this time tearing her dress, as she made haste to do Aunt Flora's bidding. She hurried inside, her heart in a tumult.

"Where've ye been?" demanded the vicar irascibly. " 'Tis way past supper time."

"I was at the Godwin's," Lorena mumbled, holding her empty basket in front of her as she edged toward Aunt Flora and away from the angry vicar.

"The Godwins, is it?" he snarled. "I doubt not ye were. For they've two stout young lads for ye to ogle! 'Tis like your mother ye are, more's the pity!"

"*I* sent her to the Godwins," interposed Flora, "with a basket of cakes for Mistress Godwin, who's been ailing these past three weeks."

"And did she stay long enough to eat them all?" he asked heavily. "Or perchance did she stay to supper? Is that why she is so late?"

"Lorena, I *told* you not to stay for supper, even if they asked you," Flora said severely. "They've little enough to eat these days as it is."

"I didn't stay for supper, Aunt Flora." Lorena gave the tall vicar a nervous look. "As I came back, they were playing hide-and-seek on the village green and I—I joined in." Color rose in her cheeks as she recalled how she had been *found* by big Harve.

To the vicar her flushed face was the very picture of

guilt, as she turned in appeal to her aunt. "Oh, Aunt Flora, do let me read the letter, do!"

"Hide-and-seek, is it? Dark as it is?" The vicar was almost frothing at the mouth. " 'Tis more than hide-and-seek they play on the village green after dark! First a kiss, and then a roll and a toss on the grass, and the next thing we know, ye'll be pregnant!"

"Hush, Robbie," chided Flora. "The child's innocent yet. Don't fill her head full of—"

But Robert Medlow was too filled with a sense of outrage to stop now. "Innocent, ye say?" he roared. "Look at her dress there—torn! How did that happen? And—" He stiffened as he saw the blood on her skirt. "Lord preserve us, has some young buck pierced her maidenhead out there on the grass?"

Flora's gaze flew to the spot of blood on Lorena's skirt. "Lorena," she began, frightened.

In confusion, Lorena followed their gaze to her skirt. How—? Ah, the roses!

" 'Twas the rosebush," she babbled. "I tore my hand on the thorns when I came up to the window just now, and I must have brushed off the blood on my skirt. Oh, Uncle Robbie, I've done nothing wrong, I swear it!"

His face was mottled. He took a step forward with hand upraised to strike her, but Flora's gaunt form glided between them.

"Robbie, ye're angry now," she said in a voice gone suddenly calm. "Ye should do nothing in anger."

For a moment the tall soberly clad form of the vicar swayed uncertainly. Flora had always had the power to calm him. He respected Flora the way he respected the bell tower of his church. It was sturdy, it was always *there*. He made a valiant effort to contain himself. Still his teeth ground slightly as he turned away.

"I will be in my study," he said hoarsely. "I want no supper. Nor should *she* be given any." At the door he turned. "I will pray for your soul, Lorena. As should you."

The door shut and Lorena took a deep breath and

turned her anguished blue gaze on Aunt Flora. "Oh, Aunt Flora, you *will* let me read the letter?"

"You'll to bed, Lorena." Flora's voice had gone loud and severe as she studied the closed study door; it carried to the vicar inside, as it was intended to. "But first we'll wash that blood from your dress lest it stain, and see how bad ye've pricked your hand. Come along."

She led a disappointed Lorena to the kitchen and ordered her to take off her dress. Lorena did so, standing there in her simple white chemise and petticoat, her slim white shoulders gleaming in the candlelight. Flora took the gray dress from her silently, ordered her to exhibit her hand. With a sigh, Lorena displayed her right hand, palm up, and Flora inspected the thorn mark which was still bleeding a little.

" 'Tis but a scratch," she announced, "and will heal of itself. Wash it in the basin here, while I get the blood out of this dress. 'Tis fortunate it's fresh. There, it's coming out."

Lorena plunged her hand into the bowl of water Flora indicated, then dried it off. "The letter, Aunt Flora?" she breathed.

Flora rubbed her hands dry on her apron and silently picked up the letter. She handed the folded parchment to her niece, watched indulgently as Lorena broke the red wax seal. She loved the child so. Silently she prayed that Lenore had not broken her long silence to tell them something dreadful. There had been so many catastrophes in Lenore's tempestuous life.

"Tell me what she says," she told Lorena. "For though she's sent coins, I've not heard from your mother since she left Twainmere."

Lorena was bent over the parchment, reading avidly. When she looked up, her smile was blissful. "Mother's in London," she said. "And she's an actress now—she's playing parts in the theater before the king himself!"

"What?" Flora snatched the letter from her, read it in consternation before returning it to her niece's hand.

"Let not Robbie hear that," she muttered. "For he'll say acting's ungodly. There, child, take the letter with you and run to bed. Here's a candle, and an apple for your supper, for Robbie will banish you from the table for being naughty if ye sit down to eat."

Lorena snatched up the apple and gave Aunt Flora a sudden impulsive kiss. "Isn't it wonderful?" she said. "To hear from mother at last? Maybe she'll come home now. She says the king has pardoned her."

Flora swallowed and gave Lorena's fair head a pat. Hearing from Lenore after all these years seemed indeed a minor miracle. But even with the king's pardon, if Lenore returned it would certainly be a mixed blessing, for the rebellious beauty stirred passions to flame wherever she went.

"To bed with you," she told Lorena gruffly. "I'll just spread this dress out over the bench to dry. Mind the candle now."

Clutching the precious letter and the apple to her bosom, with the dish-type candleholder hooked around one finger, Lorena tucked up her petticoat and chemise and ran with legs flashing up the ladder and through the trapdoor into the loft above the kitchen where she slept. It was half storage room, but Lorena did not care. It was *her* bedroom and private, and now she set the candle down on the low wooden bench that served her as a table and flung herself down on her pallet and read her mother's letter. And reread it.

When at last she blew out the candle, she lay on her back and munched the apple and looked up at the light of the white moon that filtered through the rustling leaves of a giant oak into the window and onto her rapt face. The precious letter was still clutched to her breast as if someone might try to wrest it from her, but she could remember it almost word for word.

Such splendid words her mother had written! Among all the concern for Lorena's welfare, the good wishes to Flora and Robbie, the grateful thanks, the admonishments to Lorena to be good, some phrases stood out, for they epitomized the life Lenore must be leading in London.

"Here in the theater we wear beautiful clothes. To-night my green satin dress is garnished with gold lace, and tomorrow I will wear one of silver tissue."

Lorena sighed with content.

She could not know that Lenore had embroidered on the truth, that the gold lace was really tarnished bronze and mended, and that the silver tissue was threadbare and had been given to the theater by a duchess who refused to wear it any longer. Anyway, Lenore owned neither; they were but costumes to be worn onstage. When she went home to her tiny lodgings, she wore mended stockings and run-down shoes.

". . . . and I do perform before the King in Whitehall. He has noticed me."

He had indeed noticed her, but it was Nell Gwyn who had got him, and the performance in Whitehall had been a disaster, with Lenore nearly breaking her ankle. Still, Lenore's beautiful violet eyes had darkened wistfully as she had penned the words—it sounded so much better this way. She wanted young Lorena—the child she had not seen since babyhood, who had been so cruelly torn from her arms by fate—she wanted Lorena to love her, to think well of her.

The letter had wrought much more than that. Lorena went to sleep starry-eyed, imagining her mother's triumphs on the London stage, the glamour of her life there. Why, she must have all London at her feet!

But the letter's news was stale. It had been a long time coming, for the bearer was a chance friend of Lenore's journeying to Bath, who had promised to post it nearer the Cotswolds to defray part of the high cost of receiving a letter (postage at that time being paid by the receiver of a letter, not the sender). The journey to Bath had been interrupted by a bout of sickness, after which there had been a need to work to earn enough money to push on to Bath.

So the letter was months late. And while Lorena imagined that Lenore had spent those intervening months in a triumphant march toward becoming at least a duchess, nothing could have been farther from the truth. She had lost her job in the theater, she had become a mere orange girl selling China oranges in the pit. She had been brought low, indeed.

At the very moment that Lorena closed her eyes in the Cotswold Hills with a sigh of content, Lenore, kidnapped from the theater by Wilsingame and his friends —Lenore, beautiful and desperate, her black silk dress cut ravishingly low, was standing proud and erect on a London stairway. Below her glittered the lustful eyes of a dozen hard-faced men. Her white arm was upraised, and she held high a pair of scissors to plunge into her white breast and end it all.

But then, at the base of those stairs, she heard a voice she had never thought to hear again. . . .

London

Chapter 3

Downstairs in the common room at the Tabard Inn, the candles were glowing when Lenore and Geoffrey roused themselves and sent for supper to be brought up. It was served by the same serving maid, who now looked at them enviously, for their happiness showed on their faces. She served them a supper of roast chicken and chops and peaches and wine, which they ate sitting companionably in the big bed and sharing a tray, their bare thighs touching and Geoffrey's arm around her shoulders. Sometimes he pressed on her a tasty bite of his chicken or a sip of his claret. Sometimes he stopped eating altogether and cupped a warm hand around one of her tempting bare breasts, kneading it with his fingers, or stopped to present an admiring kiss to a quivering nipple.

Lenore caressed his sinewy arm with a loving hand. Her fingertips wandered up to his muscular shoulder, roved down his breast to his stomach. She felt his muscles jerk a little in response to her touch as her hand moved lower.

"Ah, Geoffrey," she sighed. "There's so much we haven't said, so much to tell."

"Hush, Lenore." He pushed aside the tray and gathered her to him. "There'll be time enough for all that. 'Twas an evil fate kept you from me, and a merciful providence that restores you to me again. I've a mind to give thanks—in my own way." He buried his strong, dark face in the rumpled torrent of her hair, smelled its faint perfume, and sighed.

Lenore, reaching up loving arms to twine them around his neck and hold her beloved Geoffrey to her once again, found her voice trembling to silence. Her violet eyes, dark now as royal velvet, glittered with unshed tears like stars across the Milky Way. Her Geoffrey, returned to her at last! Who would not give thanks? With a barely perceptible sob, she swayed against him.

Yet . . . there was one thing she must bring up. They had so far, in the glory of their reunion, ignored the subject of her daughter, born in Oxford—that child Geoffrey had claimed hoarsely was not his own. Lorena was the reason he had flung away from her. She must know how he felt about Lorena now.

"Lorena is with Flora," she murmured, tensing.

"Flora?"

"Jamie's sister. You remember the Scot whose handfast bride I was?" A slight hardening of his muscles told her better than words that he remembered all too well. "Flora recognized the child as Jamie's at once and was more than willing to care for her niece since she has no children of her own."

He lifted his head and she saw that he was regarding her keenly. "But would you not prefer to have her with you?"

Lenore tried to shrug nonchalantly. "Flora has brought her up for me—and done a better job of it than I would have done, I imagine." Suddenly her voice broke. "Oh, *yes,* Geoffrey. I would prefer to have her with me. How can you ask?"

"Then we will bring her to London," he said huskily.

"Lenore, I am sorry for all those things I said to you the day I first saw her. I was half out of my mind with disappointment."

"Hush," said Lenore, "I know. By count, I truly thought she was yours. How I could have made such a mistake, I do not know."

"It matters not who her father was," he burst out. "She is *your* daughter and I will give her my protection!"

"Oh, Geoffrey!" How long she had yearned to hear him say that! They would be a family yet, the three of them. Blinded by happy tears she reached out for him, felt herself borne backward into the softness of the great bed, and deeper into another night of joy at the Tabard Inn.

Morning came all too soon. Sleepily, Lenore opened one eye. She saw that Geoffrey was dressing, stealthily as if he would slip away from her.

"Wait for me," she said drowsily and sat up. "I'm coming too."

"Nay, back to bed. I'm but off to buy ye a dress. Something that will not remind ye of Wilsingame."

Lenore stretched. "If you want to buy me a dress, be good enough to let me select it!"

He laughed, but his gaze was wary. "Are you sure you'd not rather stay in bed while I bring back an armload of gifts?"

She shook her head, her tousled red-gold hair flying about, and climbed gracefully out of the fourposter, paused to stretch again—and saw his gray eyes kindle at the sight of her lissome body so luxuriantly displayed in all its feline beauty.

"I do believe you lust for me, Geoffrey," she murmured lazily.

"Aye. As would any man." His voice grew husky as he reached out and ran his fingers down her shoulders, then down her smooth neck past the hollow between her round breasts to her navel. He straightened up with a groan. "Dress if you must!"

Lenore was already bent over, sliding her sheer stockings over her pretty legs, fastening her silver-tinseled garters, slipping into her black satin slippers. She straightened up and stepped into her chemise, pulled it up and reached for her rustling petticoat.

"You haven't told me how you spent the time since you left me in Oxford," she reminded him. "Did you really go to France then?"

"Yes."

"And were you with the king all that time?"

"No." There was a reluctance in his tone. "Not all that time."

Her black silk dress was on now. She beckoned him to her. "Help me with the hooks, Geoffrey. Where were you then, if not with the king?"

Geoffrey bent his attention to fastening the hooks before answering. "I was—with Letiche, Lenore."

Her body froze to stiffness. Even though he had gone to France, somehow she had not expected that. "With . . . Letiche?" she whispered.

Before she had gone to live with him in Oxford, he had told her that his marriage to Letiche was over. That it had never been anything more than a marriage of convenience between two fortune hunters with no fortune between them and no love on either side. That he had fled France, fled Letiche, and would never return. She remembered how they had planned to change their names and go to live in the American Colonies.

Now she turned and faced him. Her large violet eyes beamed into his and his shoulders moved restively under that glittering surveillance.

"Aye, with Letiche. I returned to find her in bad case. Her family were disgruntled that I had not died and conveniently left her a widow so that they might repair their failing fortunes by marrying her off again. They had all but cast her out—she needed my protection."

She was entitled to my protection, his tone said.

"Yes, of course," she agreed colorlessly. "She is your wife. Where—where is she now, Geoffrey?"

"Home on my estate in Kent."

All Lenore's bright hopes came crashing down. Letiche was here, in England. That tall white ship that was to carry them away to the Colonies dipped over the horizon, lost forever. She drew a deep ragged breath. "You brought her with you then when you came back from France?"

"Yes."

Her voice was deceptively gentle. "And what do you propose to do now, Geoffrey?"

She saw him take a deep breath. His hawklike face was stern. Only his eyes suffered. "I propose to find you good lodgings, a house of your own here in London, a staff of servants. I would already have been about it, had you not waked."

"And I will be your mistress in London, and she your wife in Kent?"

He flinched at the sharpness of her tone. "Do not think of it that way, Lenore. We always knew—"

"What other way is there to think of it?" cried Lenore, her voice wild. "*I will not do it, Geoffrey!* Oh, God—and I thought you had come back to me! And now I find myself trapped with half a man—and that half on the wrong side of the blanket!" She flung away from him, black skirts swirling.

Geoffrey caught her by the wrist. He was white to the lips. "What else can I do?" he cried. "She is my wife! None of this is her fault. It is not her fault that I do not love her as I love you. I met her first, wed her first. She has borne me two children since, Lenore."

She winced at that and turned back to stare at him coldly. "*Two children* and yet you've spent the last two nights with me? Faith, you must be pleased with yourself!"

"Twins. Both died near the same time of a fever in Bordeaux. Letiche was beside herself with grief; she nearly died herself. Now you see why I cannot leave her. She has no one."

46

Lenore's lips twisted. So poor Letiche had no one? *She* had had no one *all these years!*

His voice rang out. "I will care for your child, Lenore. *Think,* Lenore! Is it not better that I who love you provide for you than some—"

"Some passing fancy?" she finished for him ironically. She could feel a pulse beat in her forehead, and she felt as if she might die of the gripping pain in her chest. "But *I* am a passing fancy for you, Geoffrey. We met and loved for a season—and then you went back to Letiche. For whatever reason, all these years you have spent with Letiche. I will take care of myself—as I always have."

"But the child, Lenore!" He seized upon the argument he felt might sway her. "Ask yourself, does not your child deserve all that I can give her?"

Lenore gave him a cynical look and threw back her red-gold head arrogantly. "The daughter you say is not your own? No, my child has no claim on you, Geoffrey—as I have none. I decline your offer for myself, and for Lorena also. We will get out of your life altogether. I'll not go through it all again!"

Geoffrey seemed to rise to a great height and his sigh rent the air. "It may be that I deserve all you have said to me, but . . . should you ever need me, should you ever need for aught, you have only to send for me, Lenore—I will be there."

A sort of summer madness came over Lenore. Need? *Need!* She had no need of anyone! She would not be used as he proposed to use her—as a perpetual mistress! She who had thought to be his wife!

She chose her words carefully, to draw blood.

"I have no need of you, Geoffrey. I can have a *royal* protector."

He flinched at that taunt. She saw on his face that he believed her and felt an angry satisfaction.

"Or if I choose . . . others." She let her voice slide away negligently and shrugged her shoulder. Let him suffer! *She* had suffered.

"But if you would share the bed of others out of wedlock," he began passionately, "then why not with me, who loves you?"

"Why not you?" Her innate honesty burst through her wall of pride. "Because I cannot be second with you, Geoffrey." *I love you too much for that. It would tear me apart, having you leave and knowing that you were going—to her.*

His quick ear, sensitized to her every thought, caught the sadness in her voice that she could not hide.

"Lenore." He seized her by her slender shoulders. His voice was husky. "Let us not quarrel. Love left my life when you departed."

She shook her black silk shoulders from his grasp— and what it cost her harshened her voice. "Then love has left your life again, Geoffrey, for I am leaving." She reached for her long black gloves.

His expression hardened as he saw her determinedly pulling on those gloves, refusing to look at him. "Perhaps I was wrong about you," he said with slow deliberation, for at that moment he meant to hurt her as her rejection had hurt him. "I was stunned when I saw you coming down the stairs at Wilsingame's, apparently ready to entertain a horde of men."

She flung him a resentful look. "I told you Wilsingame kidnapped me from the theater."

"The theater," he drawled. "I had forgot ye were an actress. So perhaps 'twas an act that ye seemed about to plunge the scissors into your breast, perhaps 'twas but a bit of playacting meant to sharpen the senses of the moment."

Lenore drew a deep ragged breath. That he should accuse her thus!

"And your clothes." Suspicion roughened his voice, and he studied her gown as if he had not seen it before. "And is the theater how you came to be so richly gowned?"

"I have been . . . successful," she said in a tight voice. She would not let him know the truth, that she had been forced to don these seductive clothes at Wilsingame's, that her own clothing was in rags. She knew he was trying to hurt her, but she would not let him know his barbed remarks had struck home. "Believe what you like of me," she said tersely, determined at all costs not to let him pity her. At least she would leave this room with the scraps of her pride!

"Lenore!" There was apology in his tone but she ignored it. With a violence that almost split the seams, she finished tugging on her gloves, and brushed past him.

At the door she paused and turned about, for she must have one more look at him, one more chance to fill her eyes with the sight of the man who had brought her more joy than anything, before she left him . . . forever.

He stood before her, tall, brooding, every inch the handsome cavalier he had been when first they met. Not a dandy but a man with a distinctive dash to his clothes, a sense of style that transcended fashion, from the sweep of frosty Mechlin at his throat to the russet velvet coat that spanned his broad shoulders, the wide rakish boots at the base of long lean legs. In an age of wigs, Geoffrey's thick shoulder-length dark hair was his own and swung about a dark and restless face.

Just looking at him had always made her heart beat faster, and today was no different. Even though she tried to harden her heart against him, she knew she would remember him this way.

"Good-bye, Geoffrey." The look she gave him was a stony one.

His dark face was haggard, his angry eyes studied her in alarm.

"I will not say good-bye to you," he growled. "When you have thought this over, you will come to your senses."

"That may be," she taunted him in fury as it all washed over her again, "but I will come to my senses in somebody else's arms!"

"Lenore!" The words were torn from him. "I admit

49

I was wrong to leave you in Oxford—but I did come back, only to find you gone. Run off with Michael, Gilbert said. I thought you gone to America, long ago married and better off without me. Had I known you were still in England, unmarried—"

"You would not have gone back to Letiche?" Her bright cynical smile flashed suddenly to hide her hurt. "Ah, I believe you, Geoffrey. But now that you have done so, there is no turning back, is there?"

His white tormented face told her this was so.

"Then it is over, Geoffrey." Her words tolled like a bell. "I cannot be second in your heart. I must be first. As you were always first with me."

"You were never second with me!" he said roughly.

She gave a short disbelieving laugh.

"You will come to grief," he warned angrily. "I like not the look in your eyes, Lenore. Remember there is not only Wilsingame's pack out there who may do you a mischief while I am not at your side. London teems with others equally bad."

His belief that she could not take care of herself stung her.

"You think I have no money?" she taunted. "No resources? No friends of my own? I will show you, Geoffrey! No! Stay where you are, and you will see me ride by in my own coach drawn by my own coachman!" Lies came easily to her lips in the face of his patent disbelief. She wanted him to see her as wealthy, as Letiche was wealthy. Valued, as Letiche was valued! Respected, as Letiche was respected. "Stay and you will believe!" she screamed at him and slammed the door behind her, running downstairs and out of the inn into the courtyard.

Geoffrey made no move to stop her. In two strides he could have been beside her, dragged her back, but he did not. Still, his tormented face told the story as he watched her go, this woman for whom he had hungered all these years. So she had not gone with Michael as he had thought in Oxford, but was here in England all this time. Now he cursed himself that he had been so quick to believe her faithless—now that it was too late. Life, he realized, had changed her, hardened her. She would seek royal favor now and—so great was his love for her, so blinded his eyes by her sumptuous beauty—he felt she would surely get it, for where in his kingdom would the king find such a woman?

But Lenore was *his* woman! Geoffrey's balled fist came down on a small wooden table with such a blow that the top gave way and the timbers split. He flexed his bruised knuckles, hardly aware of the numbing pain, consumed by a pain far deeper.

He blamed himself, only himself. He had taken the wrong road long ago, a dishonorable one, before he had met Lenore—long ago in France when he had married Letiche. Letiche was not to blame, nor was Lenore. Both had a claim to his protection, but . . . only one held his heart. And that one, he now felt certain, he would never hold in his arms again.

By God, he *would* hold her! He would not let her go back into that cursed theater world that had brought her almost to her death at Wilsingame's! He would seize her, he would carry her away with him!

He charged through the door and down the stairs, almost knocking off the black hat of a Quaker who was just rounding the newel post. Through the courtyard he ran and out into the cobbled street.

And came to a stop in chagrin, for Lenore was nowhere in sight.

He looked about, he inquired, but he could not find her. One or two people had seen a lady dressed in black run out, but none had noticed the way she went.

Just as she had vanished from his life once before in Oxford, Lenore had once again disappeared.

Heartsick and haggard, Geoffrey paid for his lodgings—and, scrupulously, also for the table he had broken in his despair. The landlord gave him a sharp look as he left, wondering if this could really be the dashing gallant who had swept in with the lustrous lady two nights before. The landlord shrugged—a lovers' quarrel, perhaps.

It was a grim-faced Geoffrey who went out into the courtyard and mounted his horse, brought by the same lad who had stabled it last night. He tossed the lad a coin as he left. Faith, he would attend to the business that had brought him to London and then devote all his time to looking for Lenore.

Time, he reasoned, would cool her hot temper.

Geoffrey had not counted on the depth of the wound he had dealt Lenore. As she ran from the inn, it seemed to Lenore that she had waited a lifetime for Geoffrey, faithful even when she had believed him lost to her. Then to have him come back—and at such a moment!

It had been as if the heavens had opened and poured out a shower of gold. All her prayers had been answered, all her fondest dreams come true. She had accepted it all without question. She had believed, in her fool's paradise, that Geoffrey had come back to make their old dream come true—they would sail away to the Colonies and live as man and wife as he had promised.

No more would she be his mistress in London, than he would be her husband in America!

She guessed he might be following her and darted down an alley, into a shop, and out through the back door, into another winding alley awash with slops. She had to thread her way carefully here, but it was hard for her to slow down since anger drove her on.

By now she had lost herself in the maze of alleys that lay between her and her lodgings. So stormy were her violet eyes, so violently did she toss back her red-gold hair that an old gentleman passing by on a cane hopped nimbly away from her. Why, the wench in black silk looked as if she might attack him!

Near bursting with rage at Geoffrey's perfidy, Lenore hurried home.

She had a little money—and she was consumed with

making good her lies about having her own coach. She would show him! All the money that she had she hastily spent to rent a coach and hire a coachman for the day. On credit she snatched up a huge wig and a plumed hat displayed in a shop window, and a great swirl of costly lace to drape across the top of her gown—from outside the coach it would seem that she had changed her clothes!

Back and forth before the Tabard Inn she rode in her coach that day. Whether Geoffrey saw her or not, she could not be sure. Finally she sent her coachman inside to find out if the tall gentleman who had lodged there with a woman in black silk two nights ago had left. The coachman came back to report that the lady had left first and shortly afterward the gentleman. They knew not where either had gone.

That brought Lenore to her senses. The madness that had drenched her with impotent fury and the desire to strike back left her, and she was sane again, back on her feet. Deserted again, alone again.

She dismissed the coachman and the coach. The hat and wig and costly lace she tried to return, for all they had been bought on credit. But the shop refused to take them back, insisting they be paid for. Lenore promised to do so. She would find a way. After all, had she not attracted the notice of a king?

She told herself resentfully that she had not *wanted* to be faithful to Geoffrey all these years. It had been like sorcery, as if she were under some great spell that had never been lifted. All this time, through all that had happened, her towering passion for Geoffrey had sustained her.

Now the spell was shattered. She must go on alone.

Claremont Court, Kent

Chapter 4

In Claremont Court, Geoffrey's brick and timber manor house in Kent, a great commotion was taking place. Across the handsome red Turkish carpet that graced her sprawling second floor apartments, Geoffrey's French wife Letiche was walking tensely back and fro. Her froufrou violet taffeta petticoats rustled as her short form circled about the room. The brilliants scattered in her deep red hair (liberally hennaed to keep it at its flaming best) flashed as did her eyes and two bright spots in her cheeks stood out against her milk white skin. Now the corkscrew lovelocks that fell on either side of her face spun violently as she whirled to face the Marquis de Vignac, who had brought her this bad news.

"So now Geoffrey is a scandal all over London?" she cried in her slightly rasping French accent. *"Mon Dieu!* It is not to be borne!"

De Vignac took snuff from a blue enameled gold box and studied that pert angry face, the snapping auburn eyes that almost matched her hair, before he answered. "I said only that your husband is searching London for the woman he took by force from Lord Wilsingame's house on London Bridge."

"Andre has already brought me word of that affair at Wilsingame's. Disgraceful! A woman of the streets, a—"

"I would hardly call her that," de Vignac corrected mildly, shifting the position of his rose satin-clad legs as he leaned against a gilt chair, one of a dozen Letiche had recently ordered from Paris. "Her name is Lenore Frankford and of late she has been an orange girl. But before that she was of Killigrew's Company, the King's Company of Royal Players. And 'tis said—though not confirmed—that the king himself invited her to Whitehall and sent her to Killigrew."

"The king—bah! How many mistresses had *he* at last count? Seventeen? Or thirty? I wonder he can keep track of who is in his bed!"

"If gossip is to be believed, Mistress Lenore Frankford has never wakened in the royal bed."

Letiche sniffed. "Who has *not* wakened in the royal bed? That whore Nell Gwyn, and that slut Louise de Keroualle, and God knows how many others!"

"Louise de Keroualle," said de Vignac warningly, "has just been created Duchess of Portsmouth. I would not inveigh against her if I were you. Rumor has it that you have said too much already, and that that is why you are not at court today, that the king himself suggested to Geoffrey that you stay away until your tongue has lost its sharpness."

In her excitemeent, Letiche was clutching a delicate white lawn handkerchief, embroidered and trimmed in finest point. At his words the fragile point lace and the handkerchief parted company as she twisted her hands in fury.

"And that is another thing," she raged. "That arrogant Barbara Villiers may say what she pleases anywhere, whilst I—"

De Vignac regarded her sternly.

"Barbara, Lady Castlemaine, has long been a love of the king's. If he does not allow his barren little queen to denounce her, he will hardly allow you, the wife of a mere friend—and a foreigner to boot—to say aught against her!"

Once launched into her tirade, however, Letiche could not stop. This was the main reason Geoffrey kept her here in Kent and excluded her from his excursions into London town. Her barbed tongue, even with its delicious rasping French accent, managed to make enemies everywhere. She had almost had a shoving match in Whitehall with Louise de Keroualle, and had called Nell Gwyn a whore to her face.

Still smarting, Letiche recalled both incidents. "That Nell Gwyn!" she shrilled, her purring voice rising. "Why, she has had her picture painted by Sir Peter Lely with both breasts entirely exposed, even to the nipples!"

"Nay that is another painting," de Vignac objected. "And it is only one nipple that peeps out, and shyly, caressed by a dainty curl." He sighed, thinking of those small round globes thrust so attractively forward. "The portrait by Sir Peter exposes but one bare shoulder and an expanse of white bosom."

"You are defending her! You know that she is being painted right now completely in the nude!"

"Yes, yes," de Vignac agreed, remembering another nude painting of the lustrous Nell at which everyone had leered.

"And this, this—Lenore Frankford! *She* is no better! An orange girl—and Geoffrey makes a fool of himself by chasing all over London trying to find her!" She burst into a flood of angry tears.

The Marquis de Vignac bethought himself of the current quip of a Whitehall wag over which all London was chuckling: that Geoffrey Wyndham was caught betwixt two redheads, one from each side of the Channel, and he well might be driven to plunge himself into that

Channel before his affairs of the heart were set straight. But the marquis remembered his duty as a guest and confidante, and hastily proffered the lady a fresh handkerchief with which she dabbed fiercely at her auburn eyes.

" 'Tis not as if ye loved Geoffrey," he ventured politely.

"Oh, what signifies that?" Letiche snapped pettishly. "Marriages—in France at least, as you well know—are not made in heaven, they are *arranged*."

Certainly the marriage of Letiche d'Avigny and Geoffrey Wyndham had not been made in heaven. De Vignac remembered well the stories he had heard: how Geoffrey's friends, hoping to mend his fortunes when he was self-exiled in France at the side of his prince, who had yet to ascend the English throne, had found for Geoffrey a great heiress—Letiche d'Avigny. To make the tall Englishman acceptable to the d'Avigny family, they had concocted clever lies about his holdings, his prospects.

When she found out he was as penniless as she, Letiche had promptly left him, and Geoffrey had returned to England to fight beside his prince all the way down from Scotland until Cromwell had defeated Charles's forces decisively at the Battle of Worcester in 1651. Gossips told that it was in his flight from that crushing defeat that Geoffrey had first encountered the beautiful Lenore Frankford. 'Twas also said that she had borne a child by him in Oxford and that she had left him for another.

Well, he had snatched her from a debauch and she had left him once again. And now he was combing London for her, alley by alley.

De Vignac would not tell the sobbing Letiche that.

"Do not cry too long and redden those pretty eyes, *ma petite*," he said absently. "Malraux told me in London he'd be down to Claremont Court today in time for supper. He'll soon be riding up."

Letiche stopped in mid-sob. "Andre—Andre is coming here? *Today?*"

"Oui, oui, ma petite." De Vignac nodded his handsomely periwigged head. "And you will wish to look your best for him," he added meaningfully.

A slight natural flush rose in Letiche's lightly rouged cheeks, for hers was the pink and white complexion of the true redhead. There had been something insinuating in his tone. Did de Vignac, who was an old friend of her family's—although he had been sadly absent when she had first met Geoffrey and thus had not been able to warn her of Geoffrey's true circumstances—suspect that Andre was her lover?

"I would wish to look my best for any guest," she asserted.

"But better yet for Andre?" De Vignac's sardonic smile told her that he knew everything: about the trysts she and Andre had shared in the latticed summerhouse on the east lawn; the occasional hasty trips to London with a vizard mask disguising her face; the boating on the river when they had put in at that little island downstream and made passionate love beneath the branches of an overhanging willow.

She hesitated. "I would not wish you to think that Andre and I . . ."

De Vignac's cynical gaze had been passing over—and toting up the value of—his hostess's handsomely embroidered mauve satin overdress, cut daringly low and tucked up above her rustling froufrou violet petticoats. One violet satin slipper with an amethyst buckle peeked out from below those skirts like a little mouse. Through the half open door of a large gilt and green armoire, he glimpsed pastel gowns in rich brocades and lustrous satins, trimmed with gold embroidery, encrusted with seed pearls, garnished with silver lace. This handsomely furnished manor house in Kent and the lucrative lands that went with it had been the gift of a grateful king to a friend who had shared his exile and his battles—the redoubtable Geoffrey Wyndham. What matter that Geoffrey had so long been poor? He was rich now.

De Vignac wondered briefly how Letiche, having a man like Wyndham by her side, could not but prefer him to a man like Andre Malraux. Alas, he thought. De Vignac was, after all, a Frenchman, and most diplomatic in matters of the heart. Indeed, his diplomacy had won him many a warm night in the arms of other men's wives. Now he chose his words carefully, not desiring to offend this arrogant daughter of France.

"Letiche, what you do with Andre is no concern of mine. Andre is a handsome fellow—and he is *French*. 'Tis easy for me to understand that you might prefer him to some grim Englishman who settles his arguments with a sword."

Letiche squirmed. That this was hardly a fair assessment of her husband did not at the moment concern her. Everyone knew that Geoffrey was a dangerous duelist who backed down to no one.

"Geoffrey considers Andre a simpering fop," she burst out resentfully. "He told me he'd be relieved to see less of him here at Claremont Court!"

De Vignac leant over his snuffbox to hide his sympathetic grin. He too considered Andre Malraux a simpering fop, even though he knew the wiry, curly headed Malraux was reputed to be a very devil with the rapier, that lean needlelike blade so fashionable just now among the gallants of both nations.

Letiche dried her eyes and said impulsively, "It is so good of you to bring me down the news from London—else I would never hear it!"

De Vignac hid another smile, this one behind a lace kerchief and a deprecating cough. He usually found the elegant Letiche as well informed as he was himself—and from a variety of sources, mainly French hangers-on who had trailed over in the wake of the restoration of the English monarchy after years of Commonwealth rule and civil war. His interest in the lady was not amorous, but political. There were hotbloods aching for revolution in France, and if revolution actually came, de Vignac meant to be in the vanguard of power. Among his set, there were those who were being mentioned for the throne. De Vignac had no royal aspirations. He was a kingmaker, not a king. His side was not definitely chosen as yet. Mazarin was dead, Louis XIV had married Maria Theresa of Spain—who knew which way the wind would blow? De Vignac was an opportunist by nature. He did not enter into intrigues as passionately as Andre Malraux or Letiche; he meant to listen and wait and—if it came to that—accompany the winner all the way to Versailles.

Letiche Wyndham, little fool and coquette that she was, might be a valuable link in the chain of power he was forging. Her husband was rich and formidable, a friend of the king, who had rewarded those friends from his days in exile.

His fingers drummed lightly on his satin knee. "Ye would do well to hold your tongue and quieten down your views of these court ladies," he advised Letiche, thinking that his own ends would be better served if he could have another listening ear—even the heedless one of Letiche—at Court. "For then the king might relent and let Geoffrey bring ye back to Whitehall."

"To sit among his whores?" Letiche tossed her dark red curls resentfully, and the scattered brilliants flashed as sharply as her angry eyes. "I'll not do it! I am a daughter of the aristocracy of France and I'll not be brought so low!"

"The people of England love Nell Gwyn," he warned her. "For though her beginnings be humble, she is an *English* whore—which Louise de Keroualle is not."

"Bah! I'm told she was born in a brothel, sold fruit and herring in the very streets, and a whore before she was thirteen!"

De Vignac sighed again. This conversation was getting him nowhere. He dusted a bit of snuff from a satin knee and straightened up to go.

"Wait, you cannot leave! There is so much I would know. Tell me of this woman, this Lenore Frankford. I would know of her appearance, her hold on my husband!"

"She is beautiful," admitted de Vignac, sinking back into the gilt chair. *Outrageously beautiful,* he had almost said, but checked himself. "I saw her once in a breeches part at the theater in Vere Street. Her hair is of a light shimmering red-gold and her eyes are a deep violet shadowed by thick dark lashes that fall upon a cheek of pink and white—what one would call a sheer complexion."

Letiche glanced involuntarily into the gilt-encrusted oval mirror nearby. She saw a complexion that was whitened with ceruse, a mixture of egg white and white lead, which her maid applied with a brush as if she were whitewashing a barn wall. Her cheeks, which had grown a bit pale lately, were reddened with cochineal or, as now, with lake, a crimson dye from which shellac was made Her survey of her own rather piquant face was distasteful, and she determined she would send at once for some of the "Spanish paper" which, when wetted, could rub a red dye onto cheeks and lips. Perhaps she should dye her hair black as well. A friend of hers had obtained ebony tresses by dissolving a groat in *aquafortis* and sponging it onto her graying hair. Unfortunately, *aquafortis* was nitric acid and the friend who had used the resulting nitrate of silver had nearly lost her scalp from the corrosive liquid. No, on second thought Letiche decided that she would keep her red tresses as they were and use more face patches to attract attention to her features. A tiny black diamond at the corner of her mouth, a half-moon upon the cheek— alrhough last week she had seen an enchanting new patch consisting of a coach drawn by four horses and designed to be worn across the entire forehead.

De Vignac, realizing himself forgotten for the moment in that intensive study of Letiche's own face, coughed delicately. Only if he brought her tidbits of information could be hope to remain in Letiche's favor, and her favor—now that Geoffrey had become rich and powerful—was a thing to be desired.

"'Tis said Mistress Frankford committed some crime in Oxford or Banbury—I forget which—and that she was later pardoned by the king."

Letiche stopped studying her small face in the oval mirror and swung round. "Ah, a criminal!"

"Perhaps. But then there are many stories about her: that she rode naked into the Battle of Worcester; that she humbled Lord Wilsingame before half of London; and in the theater I am told she was called the Iron Virgin and slept alone. Who knows what to believe?"

"Humbled Lord Wilsingame?" From this diverting mishmash of information Letiche had plucked that which interested her. "Have I not heard something about Lord Wilsingame lately?"

"You might have. His star was eclipsed at court by his own excesses—and doubtless finished by this affair in which your husband snatched the Frankford woman from his house on London Bridge. Since that incident, I understand he has attached himself to the circle of Lord Faltrop and has entered wholeheartedly into Faltrop's scheme to convert a ruined abbey on the Thames into a debauching place for a group of young rakes of high degree."

"Yes, I have heard of the Hellfire Club. Is not that what they call it? Wilsingame is connected with that?"

De Vignac did not see fit to tell Letiche that many others were connected with the scheme as well, though perhaps she already knew it. Faltrop was pouring in his money. Indeed, there were to be expensive lewd statues carved from marble, and licentious mottoes writ into stone tablets, and a chapel of sorts—some said to worship the devil. But there were also plans afoot with an assortment of pimps and those well-known London madams, "Mother" Moseley and "Lady" Bennett, for the procuring of young virgins, as well as handsome experienced strumpets from their establishments, for the debaucheries to be held there when it was finished.

" 'Twill be for members only," he said cautiously, for there were rumors that certain court ladies planned to mingle with the strumpets, disguised by vizard masks and wigs.

"And their guests."

"Oui, and their guests."

"Raoul," she said, using de Vignac's given name. "We are very old friends, are we not?"

De Vignac steeled himself. Whenever Letiche used his given name, she wanted a favor—usually one he could not grant.

She minced toward him and plucked at his satin sleeve, giving him a dimpled winning smile. "Could you not find her for me?" she coaxed.

"Find who?" he asked, startled. "Surely you do not mean Mistress Frankford? Your husband has prowled every London alley and still has not found her!"

Letiche pouted. "Well, she may have left the city, and if she is gone for good, then I will forget her. But if she returns—if she *ever* returns, Raoul, will you notify me at once? I think—I *really think"*—and now her dimples deepened—"that Mistress Frankford should be returned to this Lord Wilsingame, from whose house you say she escaped, so that he might escort her to his Hellfire Club. Do you not think so, Raoul?"

A tiny sliver of ice seemed to be finding its way down de Vignac's satin spine. He shifted his shoulders uneasily in his gold-embroidered coat.

Letiche, he knew, would not hesitate to do it. To turn over the wench Geoffrey had snatched from one of those mad orgies for which Lord Wilsingame was famous —orgies from which women were reputed to have emerged sometimes raving mad, and sometimes dead, their bodies dropped from a window of his house on London Bridge to sink into the Thames—to turn a wench who had escaped back to Wilsingame? Even coldhearted de Vignac shivered at what might be her fate.

Abruptly he reminded himself of his own self-interest. What was the fate of some English girl to him, even if she were beautiful to behold!

"I will let you know at once," he promised Letiche, and this time rose to go for another reason: he had an appointment back in London for which he would be very late—an appointment in a duchess's lavender-scented boudoir. The duchess was eager for him, and he could have kept her waiting still longer, but he could no longer stand Letiche's pettiness. She had come a long way since they had picked little green apples together in the orchards of her uncle's stately home near Boulogne, or smelled the lilacs as they strolled along the river's edge, or stolen away to dance incognito around some peasant village's maypole.

He had liked her better then.

Now he took his leave with a courtly bow and clattered down the broad stairway with the spurs on his fashionable, wide-topped boots jangling. Then out to mount his hastily brought horse, and canter away down the wide driveway.

At the tall iron gates he met, just entering, Andre Malraux, the younger son of the Chevalier. Andre, whipcord-lean and with a mass of golden curls—his own, carefully pomaded and perfumed—rode a sleek, white horse and saluted the departing marquis with a languorous wave of one handsomely gloved and gauntleted hand.

De Vignac raised his whip to return the greeting, but did not stop to talk.

As he passed Andre Malraux and went on through the iron gates, de Vignac turned once and looked back. Behind him in the gathering dusk, a great Tudor structure with dark heavy timbering and clusters of small leaded panes glittering in the last of the light, Claremont Court rose up in testimony to the new-won power and grandeur of the man who lived there: Geoffrey Wyndham.

But de Vignac's cynical gaze passed over the building's imposing front and sought out one bank of second-floor windows alone, where recently lit candles glittered from several massive crystal chandeliers. One of those windows had been opened and a mauve satin arm recklessly waved a white lace kerchief toward the lesisurely advancing Malraux.

Letiche Wyndham was welcoming her lover.

London

Chapter 5

Seated pondering in her room, Lenore started at a knock on her door. She seized a poker before she demanded in a fierce voice, "Who's there?"

" 'Tis me, Lenore. Let me in." Mistress Potts' aggrieved voice came through the panels.

Hastily, Lenore unlatched the door and Mistress Potts bustled in. So great was her girth that her gray tabby skirts fairly bounded as she waddled. Her round face was hidden by a vizard mask.

"To think that ye now live so far away!" she wailed. "I near smothered in the sedan chair that brought me. Why can ye not return to the George, Lenore? 'Twould be so much more convenient for me!"

"I can no longer afford the George, as you well know," said Lenore crisply. She put down the poker and lifted her new plumed hat from a bench, so that Mistress Potts might sit. "I see you're still covering your face with a vizard mask when you go out—even in warm weather," she added pointedly.

" 'Tis proper for a lady in public to wear a mask," chided Mistress Potts. "*You* should wear one, Lenore."

She sank down, panting, upon the wooden bench and removed her mask, fanning her perspiring face with a plump gloved hand. She was very vain of her small hands and her gloves were always marvels of workmanship. Her shrewd glance took in the shabby room furnished with only a cot, a rude table, two benches and a cupboard; then lighted in astonishment on the plumed hat and Lenore's low-cut black silk gown. "Tut, tut!" she exclaimed, amazed. "How come ye by these fancy clothes, Lenore? I thought ye were selling oranges in the theater, not play-acting again!"

"No, my career as an actress is over," said Lenore dryly. "Nell Gwyn saw to that, when she contrived for Killigrew to fire me. And my career as an orange girl is over as well, for Wilsingame and his friends kidnapped me from the theater, and now I dare not return there lest it happen again. These clothes belong to him."

"To Lord Wilsingame?" Mistress Potts' eyes grew round. "Ah, the stories that go round about *him! His* clothes, you say?"

"Fine garments he forced on me so that I might disrobe in public—for his guests' entertainment."

Mistress Potts, whose private world was haunted by would-be rapists, nodded her head in satisfaction. " 'Tis no more than I would expect of him!"

Lenore gave her friend a weary look. For Mistress Potts to imagine herself in imminent peril of rape was a kind of parlor sport, but for Lenore it had been real—*she* had been facing a dozen hard-faced men. "I escaped," she said shortly.

"Of course, of course!" agreed Mistress Potts, for in her own happy imaginings, one always escaped un-scathed. She put one fluttering gloved hand to her large bosom and leaned forward. "I was in almost the same situation," she confided in a conspiratorial whisper, de-spite the fact that they were alone in the room. "Last night a gentleman in a claret coat *accosted* me on the stairs at the George. I can imagine what he had in mind. Ah, he was much the worse for drink, I can tell you!"

Lenore managed to still the smile that was playing on her lips. The gentleman must have been deep in his cups indeed to have accosted stout, elderly Mistress Potts.

"I gave him a good scolding," Mistress Potts said energetically, "and struck him with my fan, which nearly sent him tumbling headfirst down the stairs, so unsteady was he."

"At least you fought him off."

"Yes, yes, I did, didn't I?" Mistress Potts bridled, and her cheeks flushed with pride. "But that's not why I'm here, Lenore. I've not been feeling well lately and I don't like to hire a nurse. What I need is a friend to stay with me for a while. You liked staying at the George, remember?"

Yes, she had liked staying there . . . in the days when she had hoped that when the king returned triumphant to reclaim his throne, Geoffrey would be with him. But now . . .

"Has something happened?" puzzled Mistress Potts. "I mean, *besides* Lord Wilsingame? You look so—sad, Lenore."

"No," said Lenore slowly. "Nothing has happened actually. I am right back where I started. Just a little wiser." Her voice was listless. "But I will go with you and take care of you, for we have been friends ever since I first came to London. But do not be surprised," she added with some irony, "if the bailiffs come and take me away to debtors' prison, for while the dress and chemise I'm wearing were forced on me at Wilsingame's, I bought the hat and wig and lace in a moment of madness—do not ask me why."

"Well, I'll pay the shop for them myself," said Mistress Potts sturdily. "So that ye may be free of debt and not afraid to open the door when ye move into the George with me."

Lenore gave her a grateful smile. Mistress Potts had

always stood by her. She determined that she would stay with the older woman as long as she was needed.

"And your lodgings, Lenore, are they paid up? Else they will not let ye take your things."

"Paid up till Thursday next."

"Good. Then gather up what goods ye have and we'll have them sent round to the George."

Lenore hesitated. "I have little enough. 'Twould be an easy load to carry. And I do not want it known that I have gone to the George." Her jaw hardened, for she was thinking of Geoffrey as well as Lord Wilsingame. "I want no one to be able to find me."

"Of course! I did not think of that! Then we'll just go out carrying our bundles and then send word by some boy in the street that your lodgings are now for let. Come, Lenore, we're to the George!"

Once outside, Mistress Potts entered with enthusiasm into what to her was an enchanting game of hide-and-seek. She insisted on hiring a sedan chair and announced with a wink at Lenore and a dig in the ribs with her elbow as they climbed into the suffocating boxlike interior, "With the curtains drawn, that dreadful man will never be able to find us!"

Stifling behind drawn curtains in the swaying sedan chair, Lenore was carried back to the familiar George, where she had lived when she first came to London.

Mistress Potts was thoroughly enjoying her role as co-conspirator.

"Hist!" She drew the landlord aside when they arrived. "The lady with me—whom ye well know—is in hiding." The landlord blinked at Lenore, whose face reddened at this bald-faced pronouncement. "She's to stay with me." Here Mistress Potts fished for some coins. "But I'll count on ye to warn your staff to keep quiet about it."

The landlord shifted unhappily on his feet. " 'Tis not the law that's seeking ye, Mistress Frankford, is it?"

Mistress Potts gave him a reproving look. "Pish, the

law! Of course 'tis not the law! 'Tis a gentleman. He's been harassing her, and he kidnapped her from in front of the theater where she worked—"

"Mistress Potts!" cried Lenore in a strangled voice.

But Mistress Potts pushed her aside and leant forward to whisper something in the landlord's ear. He straightened up and gave Lenore an understanding look.

"The gentleman who did that will learn nothing about Mistress Frankford from me," he promised between his teeth.

Nor did Geoffrey learn anything from him, when he included the George in his search. But from the description the landlord gave her, Lenore knew who it was, and though her voice was colorless as she thanked him, her knuckles were clenched white.

Geoffrey was seeking her! He had been here. Had she been looking out the window she might have seen him leave!

It shook her more than she cared to admit.

She did not go out for three days.

At the George she devoted herself to caring for Mistress Potts, who really did seem to be ailing. She was very short of breath and complained a great deal. Lenore stayed in the room, read to her, and talked to her for long hours.

She told herself she must not go out, for she might meet Geoffrey, and she could not trust her treacherous heart.

Each dawn an increasingly haggard face greeted her in the mirror—violet eyes like great suffering pools, beautiful arching brows that gashed a white face, and riotous unkempt beautiful hair she had not bothered to comb.

Her feelings for Geoffrey were at war with her overwhelming pride, and the turbulent battle was destroying her.

On the afternoon of the third day, she went out. Her face was concealed by a vizard mask she had borrowed from Mistress Potts and her hair by the large black wig she had bought. She was despondent and did not fear recognition. She walked to the banks of the Thames, considered casually hurling herself into the water, letting the weight of her billowing skirts drag her under—but she sighed. She was a good swimmer, and whenever death came near, the urge to live rose strongly within her.

No, suicide was the coward's way out. She could not do it. She must drag out her life somehow . . . without Geoffrey.

Surprisingly, the way out was again furnished by Mistress Potts.

When she returned home that day Mistress Potts announced that she was feeling worse and had summoned the doctor. When he arrived, Lenore found herself banished from the room. The doctor came out, shaking his gray head and hurried away.

Alarmed, Lenore hurried past him into the room where Mistress Potts' ample form was bent over, rocking with grief. She was crying into her linen kerchief.

"What did he say?" cried Lenore.

" 'Tis dropsy," Mistress Potts sobbed. "Ah, I knew it all along, but he said—he said this could well be my last illness, and that if I did get better, 'twould not be for long!" She burst into a fresh flood of tears and Lenore, inwardly cursing the doctor for his bluntness, tried to comfort her.

By suppertime Mistress Potts had developed a sudden longing to see her old home in the north of England.

" 'Tis where I was born and grew up," she confided wistfully to Lenore, "and I'd see it again before I die."

"But you're not going to die, Mistress Potts. Let's get another opinion. Perhaps another doctor—"

"One barber surgeon is as good as another," Mistress Potts scoffed. "Sometimes these last days I *have* felt death stealing over me, Lenore, smothering out my life. And 'tis then that I miss Northumberland. Ah, ye'd like it there, Lenore. So peaceful and quiet. My family home is called Wallham—ye'll see why, if ye go with me, and I do wish ye would. Indeed I don't think I could make the trip without you!"

Lenore was touched. "But you'll have family there, Mistress Potts. You'll have no need of me."

"Ah, but I will, Lenore. They're all men there, except for servants. My brother Amos lives there now. You should see the place, Lenore. The house is stone with great slanted roofs and it overlooks the moors. Many's the time I've lain in the meadow grasses and looked up to the old Roman wall that skims the peaks and seen the summits lost in the clouds."

Lenore hadn't known that Mistress Potts could wax so poetic over a place. Mainly she saved her flights of fancy for large well-cooked dinners and that legion of men she was always sure were pursuing her.

"But what of your brother's wife?" she asked the older woman gently. "What will *she* think if you bring me along?"

"My brother has no wife. He's a bachelor and his two nephews, both grown men, live with him." Mistress Potts began to sniffle. "My brother's the last of my kin in the world, save for a cousin in Cambridge, and I don't know whether she's alive or dead, for she never writes. Ah, Lenore, 'twould be a terrible journey for me to make alone. I fear I've not the strength for it! Besides," she wheedled, "they were *all* bachelors there the last time I heard. Perhaps one of them will fancy you, Lenore!"

"Perhaps." Lenore tried not to think of Geoffrey. Once she had thought she recognized his lean, broadshouldered form and swinging gait as she looked through the window into the street below. Her heart had skipped a beat, and she had tried without success to tear her gaze away from that jaunty approaching figure. But as he drew closer, she had seen that she was mistaken and had turned away from the window, telling herself that it was ridiculous to feel so sick with disappointment. After all, *she* had cast *him* out!

"Anyway, 'tis no good staying in a city where women outnumber men thirteen to one, Lenore—not that you couldn't find one anyway with your pretty face," Mistress Potts amended hastily.

Lenore gave her a tortured look.

"And remember, there's always that vicious Lord Wilsingame who might kidnap ye again, if he knew where ye were living!"

That decided her. Lenore agreed to accompany Mistress Potts north and even went down to make the arrangements, for they had best leave hastily before winter closed in and made the roads impassable. She came back to report soberly that the stage coach to Durham would leave tomorrow morning, and would cost fifty-five shillings per person with no time of arrival guaranteed, and had not Mistress Potts best rethink such an expensive journey?

Mistress Potts shook her head vigorously. She seemed much restored to health at the thought that they were both about to be off on such a great adventure. Quickly she counted out a hundred and ten shillings and bade Lenore hurry down and arrange for seats to Durham. There they would arrange transportation to Newcastle-on-Tyne and thence to Wallham.

Lenore drew a deep breath after the money was paid, for now the die was cast. She was really going.

She wrote a letter to Lorena, addressed it to the vicarage at Twainmere in the Cotswolds. The following morning, attired in a fustian cloak she had borrowed from Mistress Potts and the plumed hat she had bought to taunt Geoffrey with, she accompanied a puffing Mistress Potts into the dusty innyard of the George, doubtfully eyeing the mountain of luggage they were taking north.

"Hurry along, Lenore. Don't dawdle." Mistress Potts was anxious to be off. She thrust at Lenore the sharp-cornered little leathern chest which contained her valuables and panted as one of the stableboys boosted her into the coach. Lenore followed more gracefully, but she was hardly inside before she heard the stage driver's loud, "Here, here! We can't take all this stuff!"

Lenore had been afraid of that. Now she peered out to see the stage driver standing, arms akimbo, glaring at the monstrous pile of Mistress Potts' luggage. He opened the door and caught a glimpse of the sharp-cornered leathern chest on Lenore's lap.

"And that chest, Mistress," he cried. "Why, that will jump off your lap the first time these wheels hit a rock. 'Twill fly up into the face of the gentleman sitting across from you! That happened on my last trip to Durham and near cost the eye of one of my passengers, but 'twill not happen again, by the Lord Harry! Here, give me that chest. We'll put it on top."

"No!" Mistress Potts reached over and seized the chest, clutching it dramatically. "It cannot go on top. This little chest contains my valuables, and it rides inside with me or I won't go!" She thrust out her chin in truculent fashion and Lenore sighed. They were off to a bad beginning.

"Then go ye will not!" shouted the stage driver in a rage. "Out! Out of my coach, the both of you!"

"But we've already paid for our journey," protested Lenore, catching hold of Mistress Potts' arm to detain her.

"Ye shall have your money back! For there stand two students on their way north, seeking to take your places. Out!" He reached in and fairly scooped up the now enraged Mistress Potts, and set her firmly on her feet in the courtyard. Ignoring Lenore's protests, he reached into his capacious pocket and began to count out a hundred and ten shillings into Mistress Potts' plump gloved hand while the two students seeking a ride north nudged each other and grinned.

Lenore gave them a baleful look, and as a tribute to her beauty they wiped the smiles from their faces. One of them even stepped forward gallantly to give her a hand and help her down from the stage she had so recently boarded.

Lenore alighted with a rustle of her black silk skirts

beneath her fustian cloak, and her plumed hat, not tightly secured, promptly tumbled off. To her exasperation, the two students charged into each other in their efforts to retrieve the hat from the dusty courtyard and began to wrangle over who should restore it to her.

With cursory thanks, she snatched it from them and bent anxiously over Mistress Potts, whose round face had gone pale as she slumped down on one of her numerous pieces of baggage. She looked woefully up at Lenore.

"I've already given up my rooms at the George," she quavered. "And a new gentleman's moved into them already! Oh, what are we going to do?"

"If you were not so determined to take all this luggage," began Lenore, "we could climb back aboard this stage."

"Nay, ye are too late to go with me," called down the angry driver, now seated high above her head. "For I've already accepted the money of these two young gentlemen here"—he indicated the students—"who sensibly travel with a box apiece, and we're off this minute. Climb aboard, young sirs. 'Tis a long way to Durham!"

Lenore gave him an angry look, and he spat, just missing her hastily pulled-aside skirts. She jumped back as he cracked his whip and was off, leaving them choking on the dust as the stage rolled away.

Mistress Potts began to wring her hands.

"Well, I will see if I can find us a private coach," sighed Lenore. "But 'twill be very expensive," she warned.

"Oh, bother the expense." Mistress Potts was already looking more hopeful. She peered up at Lenore like a fat little bird. "Think ye can find one?"

"I will try," said Lenore grimly. She settled her plumed hat more firmly on her head and marched back into the George. Before the hour was out she had negotiated with a coach driver to take them as far as Cambridge. "From whence we must make our own arrangements," she told Mistress Potts.

"That will suit me even better," said Mistress Potts, brightening. "For 'twill give me plenty of time to look for my cousin in Cambridge."

The coach was brought round and Mistress Potts counted out the money into the driver's big callused hand.

Still doubting the advisability of this journey north in the face of advancing winter, Lenore climbed into the hired coach, laden with Mistress Potts' luggage. She cast a look back at the George as they thundered away and wondered for a fleeting moment if she'd ever see London again.

This small hired coach was not so roomy as the big stagecoach had been, yet at least they had all the space to themselves, and Mistress Potts became quite jolly. Their jolting way led them through the brisk fall weather into the great university town of Cambridge. But Lenore scarce had time to see the sights, for Mistress Potts embarked at once on a frenzied search for her cousin, who had moved twice since she had heard from her. Their search ended with a house draped in mourning, for the cousin had died a week ago. The event so saddened Mistress Potts that Lenore half expected her to turn around and head back for London.

But she did not. Seemingly quite reconciled after a night spent at an inn where roistering students spotted Lenore and noisily toasted her health, she announced herself ready to leave.

"Are you sure?" asked Lenore. "After all the eels and quince pie you ate last night, I would think you'd take to your bed for a day to digest it!"

"Nonsense. Find us a coach. I'm quite ready to travel."

This time Lenore was lucky. She found an excellent coach which belonged to a north country lord whose son had been sent down to Cambridge to study; the coach was returning empty and the driver, on the lookout to make himself a bit of money on the return trip without his employer knowing, agreed to take the ladies as far as Lincoln—and for a good price.

Mistress Potts beamed. "Ye drive a good bargain, Lenore. Fancy—a gilded coach!"

"Pray that the weather holds," warned Lenore. "For it looks like rain and that will mire down the roads, gilded coach or no!"

But the weather held. Through the coach window Lenore looked back at the spires of Cambridge as they rolled away and remembered other spires that had risen abruptly at the juncture of the Cherwell and the Thames—Oxford, where she had lived with Geoffrey, and where she had borne Lorena.

She smiled wistfully as she thought of Lorena. Lovely little Lorena with her hemp blond hair and blue, blue eyes . . . the daughter she had never been able to claim.

It had been wise of her to leave Lorena with Flora, she told herself. Of course it had. In Twainmere Lorena could grow up as a lady in the vicarage under Flora's supervision. By letter, Lenore could spin tinsel tales of her fame and success, and young Lorena need never know the seamy side of her mother's life.

Lenore's face softened, there in the jolting coach, as she thought about her daughter, imagining her to be as sweet and ladylike as she herself had been wild and flirtatious.

Nothing could have been further from the truth.

Twainmere

Chapter 6

It was a lovely fall afternoon in the Cotswolds. From an azure sky the sun beamed down on the die-straight Roman roads that bisected these gentle limestone hills formed from an ancient seabed pushed up eons ago to form a great escarpment. In the high open land of the wolds, the sun shimmered on grazing flocks of sheep, called "Cotswold Lions" because their fleece hung to the ground. And in the green valleys called "coombes," in the slate-roofed villages with their quaint houses built of the local gray-and-honey-colored stone, women—as they had for centuries—carded the unbleached Cotswold wool, spun it expertly into yarn and wove it into woolen cloth of a quality unmatched in all England.

In the little village of Twainmere the cottage women were busy weaving, some with children clinging to their homespun skirts. Their men were mostly out tending the sheep, though few enough of them owned their own flocks. The memorial brasses that graced the pinnacled

Cotswold churches attested to the fortunes of wool merchants and not of shepherds.

In the lazy heat of an unseasonably warm afternoon, the village seemed to slumber. Young Lorena was in the kitchen garden, Aunt Flora was in the kitchen picking a chicken for their supper, and Uncle Robbie worked over his sermon in his study, his quill pen scratching busily on the thick parchment over which he was bent.

"Here, child," Flora called, "Take this pigeon pie over to Mistress Cardwell," she said hastily. "We did not see her or her family at church this Sabbath, so I fear she may be ailing again, poor thing."

Lorena brightened. She loved going to the Cardwells' little croft. It was a long walk up a steep hill, down through a hollow, and up another forested hill. Then around a bend you suddenly came upon it, a glistening stone-roofed cottage of gray lichened stone, nestled in the mossy vale below. There was a scant patch of land for a kitchen garden, but somehow the Cardwells made it. Jonas Cardwell tended sheep for a rich wool stapler from London, on whose estates this tiny croft was located. Jonas was always away and his harassed wife Jane—always pregnant and with seven little mouths already to feed—spent all her waking hours washing, mending, cooking, and cleaning, in her spare time carding and weaving wool. It was no wonder that at twenty-seven she was but a shell of a woman, old before her time and always sick.

But it was not the absent Jonas nor his hard-driven wife who interested Lorena. The eldest daughter Maude, although she worked almost as hard as her mother from morn till night, was a fresh-faced, chestnut-haired country girl, bursting with lusty good spirits like her father before her—that father who as a dashing country lad had attracted young Jane to this life of drudgery.

Three years older than Lorena, Maude had gotten to know the vicar's "niece" when Lorena had brought some barley broth to her mother on the birth of her latest child.

The two girls had taken an instant liking to each other, and ever since had contrived to talk in the churchyard after services or at market when Maude swung in from the croft carrying trussed-up live chickens or a basket of eggs to sell, and Lorena strolled down from the vicarage with an empty basket to fill with country produce.

Maude couldn't read and was endlessly amazed that Lorena could. But Maude was vivacious and cocksure, and when the dazzling letter from Lenore arrived, she was almost as thrilled as Lorena. Together they had schemed to procure a copy of a play. Lorena had been dying to read a play ever since that first glowing letter had come from her mother, announcing that she was an actress in the King's Company in London. She had chosen Will Shakespeare's *Midsummer Night's Dream* as the first play she would read. But where to get a copy? Uncle Robbie had given her another religious tract to read when she mentioned it to him.

It was Maude, with her ripening young body, who had found a way. She had tossed her chestnut hair and paid a passing peddler in kisses to bring her a copy of a play on his next visit to Twainmere.

The peddler had hoped for more than kisses from buxom Maude on his return journey, for her young body had been sweet to hold, and it was few lasses who came to his arms now that he'd lost three front teeth in a fight in Cirencester. So he'd detoured by way of Twainmere on his next trip even though he usually swung farther south at this time of year.

From the vicarage garden, where she was cutting late-blooming roses for the table, Lorena had looked up to see him trudge by, leading his tired, overburdened horse, its back heaped high with pots and pans and cheap baubles and wooden spoons. He must have passed by the croft on his way into town! Could he have brought the promised play to Maude?

She couldn't wait to find out. It was providence smiling down on her that made Aunt Flora give her this errand. She rushed inside and stuffed the roses unceremoniously into a cream crock, forgetting to fill it with water first.

Flora smiled fondly at the girl and handed her the basket. Shrewdly she guessed it was really young Maude that Lorena wanted to see. And why not? It was natural for Lorena to enjoy going to the Cardwells' croft which was full of life and children's laughter.

"Fill the rest with rolls. Jane Cardwell will be glad to get them. And mind you, don't stay to supper—we're having guests."

"I'll remember," promised Lorena. She was wrapping the rolls up in a big linen square as she spoke.

Flora watched her leave, cautiously tiptoeing past the study where the vicar labored over next Sunday's sermon. She frowned. With his rigid ways, Robbie was making Lorena afraid of him. He was restricting the child too harshly, and that meant she would break out—as her mother had done.

Once she had cleared the vicarage gate, Lorena swung along, light-footed. She was humming a little tune, and indeed she would have sung aloud but that her Uncle Robbie forbade it. She was almost skipping as she left the village and walked down the main road, passing several small farms on her way. In a grove of trees she left the main road, taking the almost indiscernible path that led to the croft. She was running as she climbed the first steep hill that lay between the croft and the road. Twice she tripped over roots and nearly dropped the basket she carried slung over her arm. Panting, she gathered speed in the hollow below, then up another wooded hill.

At last, at a turn in the path, the croft came in sight and Lorena paused to catch her breath. She stood looking down upon the stone-roofed cottage in the vale below, and now her sharp eyes spotted Maude. Maude's brown skirts were gathered up and she was plunging forward, chasing a chicken to cook for supper. With a wild squawk the chicken became suddenly airborne and disappeared into the low branches of a tree. Panting, Maude came to a halt, tossed back her damp chestnut curls and looked up to see Lorena waving from the wooded hilltop.

A smile broke like sunshine over Maude's scowling face. Forgetting the chicken, she raced up to meet her friend.

"Maude, did you get it? The play? Did the peddler bring it like he said he would?" cried Lorena.

"Oh, didn't he now?" Maude laughed. "*And* tried to get me to roll in the hay with him for it! But I let him give me a pinch or two—and then my ma called me and I said I had to go, and he said he'd catch me next time!"

"But you *did* get the play from him!"

"Aye." Maude nodded, her eyes dancing. "And next time he comes by, I've a mind to ask him for earbobs!"

"Oh, you wouldn't!"

"I might. He'd ask a price for them, o'course—and if the earbobs were good enough, I might be of a mind to pay it!" Maude tossed her head recklessly and laughed. Only recently had she come to a realization of the power of her young charms. The peddler's greedy gaze upon her round torso had spoken volumes.

Lorena was breathless at Maude's daring, although she guessed that her friend was only half serious. Maude wouldn't really give herself to a broken-toothed peddler for a pair of earbobs!

"I didn't want Ma to know he give me the play," said Maude. "For she'd have boxed my ears for me. I hid it stuck under the eaves of the cote. Come along, we'll get it."

"Won't it be ruined?" worried Lorena, for a cote was a sheep shelter, and she feared for the precious play.

"Naw." Maude shrugged. "Twill be nice and dry there. What's that you got in the basket?"

"Oh, I almost forgot. Aunt Flora sent these—a pigeon pie and some rolls. She thought your mother might be sick," she added, "since none of you were at services again last Sunday."

"Oh, she weren't sick! Pa were home for two days,

and he and ma spent all their time in bed." She winked broadly at Lorena. "Guess we'll be havin' another little 'un come next summer!"

Lorena wasn't quite sure how that would come about, for the vicar had kept her sheltered from the "facts of life." But she'd no time to ask, as she followed Maude into the clean-washed cottage, where Jane Cardwell was scrubbing the floor.

"Why, 'tis Lorena from the vicarage." Jane Cardwell came to her feet with a slight stagger, pressing one hand into the small of her aching back. Her tired face broke into a smile as she took the basket from Lorena's outstretched hand. "Thank 'e. 'Tis a good woman your Aunt Flora is." She almost had to beat her way to the table, for at sight of the well-filled basket, she was besieged by her younger children, who all clung to her homespun skirts, demanding a "taste."

"You, Walter, and you, Jack—move along there and stop botherin' Ma!" Maude aimed a good-natured cuff at the two little boys, which they dodged with practiced skill. "Come on, Lorena," she cried above the children's shrill voices, "and I'll show you the new settin' hen Pa brought us!" She gave Lorena a wink.

Lorena stepped carefully over a bowl one of the children had dropped and followed Maude out of the cottage. As she accompanied Maude out to the cote, it occurred to her that Maude's haggard young mother must have looked very like Maude at her age. Now she looked older than Methuselah! Did marriage do *that* to a woman?

They reached the cote and Maude stepped inside, plunged her arms into the hay, and felt around. After a moment she dredged up a pamphlet, which she dusted off on her apron.

"Here. You can see 'tis not damaged," she said proudly, offering the pamphlet to Lorena.

Lorena took it reverently. *"A Midsummer Night's Dream* by William Shakespeare," she read in a breathless voice.

"Gramp says his plays were banned when Cromwell ruled England," Maude said, grinning. "Gramp" was Maude's widowed grandmother, who lived alone in a hut hardly big enough to turn around in, just over the hill.

"*Banned!*" Lorena was thrilled. She leafed through the pamphlet. ". . . her womb then rich with my young squire," she read, puzzled. "What does that mean, Maude?"

"Don't ye know *anything?*" Maude railed at her.

Lorena, who had grown up in the repressive atmosphere of the vicarage—Uncle Robbie had even locked her in her room the night the cat had kittens—realized, scarlet-faced, that she did indeed know very little.

At her friend's embarrassment, Maude relented. She giggled and whispered in Lorena's ear. Lorena's face turned bright pink. Her eyes widened, and she hastily turned the page, looking for a safer topic.

"No, don't stop to read it now," urged Maude, seizing her arm. "I've been practicing my dancing and I need a partner. Lottie's hurt her foot and my brothers won't dance with me."

Maude grabbed the play pamphlet and tossed it onto the straw. She grasped Lorena's hand and swung her around, launching into a leaping, stamping country dance.

Lorena, who had been sternly forbidden to dance by the vicar, was as eager to learn as Maude was to teach her. With more energy than grace, they enthusiastically practiced their steps while the sun moved lower and the air took on a hint of chill. They were both exhausted before they stopped and threw themselves down panting onto the hay that had been spread out for sheep bedding in the cote.

"I won't be left standing like a stick-in-the-mud, watching the others dance around Saint John's fire next Midsummer's Eve!" Maude boasted. "I mean to be the best dancer there—and have the most partners."

Lorena's heart kindled. Next Midsummer's Eve she'd be dancing too. Somehow she'd persuade her Uncle

Robbie. And she'd dance around the big bonfire even as her lovely mother was dancing with the King's Company between acts on the London stage!

She reached again for the play.

Maude saw her reach for the pamphlet and jumped up and stretched. "I've got to catch that fool chicken or 'twill be rabbit stew again."

"No, I brought a pigeon pie, remember?"

"That's right, you did. Oh, well." Maude glanced up at the slanting sun. "You'd best get back to the vicarage or your Aunt Flora will wonder what's happened to you."

Lorena stood up and brushed the straw from her gray skirts. She proffered the play to Maude in some chagrin. She had hoped to be able to stay and read it.

"No, you take it." Maude pushed the play away impatiently. "Just mind you mark all the hot passages. Be sure not to miss a one, for I'll want you to read all those to me. The peddler said 'twere a hot one!"

Lorena promised and trudged home. She stopped to read a page or two and arrived at the vicarage shivering, almost at dusk.

"What took ye so long?" demanded Flora, thinking uneasily that Lorena grew prettier and more like her reckless mother every day.

"I was just passing the time at the Cardwells," said Lorena truthfully.

"And how's Jane Cardwell?"

"Oh, she wasn't sick," said Lorena innocently. "Her husband was home and they spent the day in bed."

Flora gave her a disapproving look. "Did Maude tell you that?"

Lorena saw she'd made a mistake. "He was home from his herding, and I guess he was tired," she said.

Flora hid a smile. Lorena wasn't so grown-up after all. It was just as well. She hoped not to have another Lenore on her hands!

"I stopped to gather some herbs on the way home,"

put in Lorena hastily, as a diversion. Actually, she'd hurriedly picked them to cover up the pamphlet in the bottom of her basket.

"Good. Take them out to the kitchen and then set the table. We've company coming. Mistress Plimpton and old Mister Oakes. They're both alone in the world with neither kith nor kin, and Robbie hopes to make a match between them by throwing them together over a good supper."

Lorena's heart fell. She'd forgotten there was to be company for supper. That meant she'd have to sit with her back straight and ankles demurely crossed, and listen to a lot of boring conversation about the price of wool and whether the weavers in Cirencester would riot again if their wages weren't raised. Oh, well, perhaps she could slip to bed with a candle and peruse the play.

But that didn't work out either. Thick-bodied Mistress Plimpton and stooped old Mister Oakes ate heartily of Flora's good food, but they disagreed on every subject the vicar brought up and eyed each other with suspicion over tankards of cider after supper.

Lorena had whisked away the festive roast goose and the shield of brawn with mustard, the numerous vegetables and coarse bread, and brought forward the "dowsets." Now, having served everybody cider, she was spooning up her own dowset.

The vicar's gaze passed over her, and it occurred to Lorena that Uncle Robbie was thinner lately, that his eyes held a more fanatical gleam. She was suddenly certain that he would never let her go dancing. Never.

She laid down her spoon. For her the custard had suddenly lost its flavor.

Mistress Plimpton was leaning forward heatedly, brandishing her tankard of cider as if it were a weapon. "I say to you that London is a sinkhole of sin now that the king's been restored to this throne," she declared in her squeaky voice. "And ye should preach about its evils next Sunday!" All her chins quivered with indignation.

Lorena stared at her jowly face, wondering if it was

true what they said—that Mistress Plimpton sprinkled white wine over powdered myrrh on an iron platter and heated it and leant over it so that the fumes would fill in her wrinkles. To *her* critical inspection, the wrinkles seemed to be still there!

Across from Mistress Plimpton, dour old Mister Oakes belched his first assent of the evening. "Plays and loose women and tennis matches and bearbaiting!" he roared. "We didn't have *that* under Cromwell!"

Plays! Lorena sat up straight and opened her mouth to protest.

Flora saw her and said abruptly, "Ye'd best to bed, Lorena, if ye've finished your dowset. I'll light ye up myself. If ye'll excuse me?" she said, with a nod to her guests.

That meant no candle! Lorena knew Flora guarded her candles because tallow, even in this sheep-producing corner of the earth, was expensive.

Flora gave her a warning look and Lorena was silent as she took the dowset to the kitchen and followed Aunt Flora up to her loftlike room.

"There's nothing wrong with having plays," she told Flora defiantly.

"I was afraid ye'd say that." Flora's face was grim. "That's why I sent ye to bed. And I came along to tell ye that 'twill do ye no good to go babbling that your mother's gone on the stage. I've kept it from your Uncle Robbie, and there's no reason he should learn it now. Ye must remember there are those who don't consider the theater a decent place."

Like that pair downstairs! Lorena sniffed. If the theater was good enough for her mother—her *real* mother, although in truth the only mother she'd ever known was kindly Aunt Flora—it *must* be a decent place.

"Good night," she said stiffly, as Flora turned to go.

Flora gave her a fond look. "Be sure to say your prayers," she said in a gruff voice. "And ask God to forgive ye for what ye've no doubt been thinkin'!"

Lorena started. Aunt Flora always seemed able to read her mind. Aunt Flora was a Scot, and Scots were said to have "the sight." For hadn't Aunt Flora told her she'd dreamed of oceans of blood spilling over England long before the Battle of Worcester that had claimed Lorena's father? She hoped Aunt Flora hadn't guessed she had a play hidden away under her pillow!

Flora had not. Hoping ruefully that she could turn fiery young Lorena into some semblance of Robbie's godly mold of what a vicar's daughter should be, she went back downstairs to her once-again quarrelsome guests, leaving Lorena in darkness upstairs.

Wistfully, Lorena touched the pamphlet hidden under her pillow, and wondered if she'd ever develop the sight, like Aunt Flora.

It was late the next afternoon before Lorena got a chance to read the play.

Tiptoeing over the carrots she was supposed to be digging, Lorena slipped away to the stable. In the warm dimness a low whinny greeted her, and she went over and threw her arms around the neck of an old, but still beautiful, white stallion. The horse nuzzled her playfully and tossed his white mane proudly, lifting the young girl from her feet with the gesture. This was Snowfire, Lenore's horse. Years ago Lenore had ridden in from Oxford on Snowfire—and when she had left, she had left behind both the horse and her daughter. The horse was as beautiful and gentle as ever, and Lorena had learned to ride on that white silky back. The affection between them was forged with strong bonds of summer rides into the peaceful countryside around Twainmere; of soft-hooved trots down snow-covered lanes through a world frosted with ice; of long happy hours of currying in the warm little stable which Snowfire shared with the vicar's sorrel mount and the two soft-eyed dairy cows that furnished milk and butter and cream for the vicarage throughout the year.

The vicar had been doubtful about their keeping the horse. But then, the vicar had been doubtful at first about their keeping Lorena. The horse, he had reminded Flora, would unceasingly remind the gossips of Twainmere that Lorena was wild Lenore Frankford's daughter. Best that Lenore come back and take them both. But Flora had declared passionately that Lorena was a bairn laid on her childless doorstep, her dead brother's only child, and none but the Lord God himself would take Lorena from her.

"Or her true mother," Robbie had countered sternly.

"Aye, her true mother," assented Flora sulkily. "But can ye not see, Robbie? Lenore will not be comin' back for she's a wanted woman, even if the charge be false. We have us a bairn, Robbie! A bairn!"

Her face was aglow and Robbie turned away, half blinded by the light in her fierce blue eyes. Perhaps 'twas well that Flora should have a bairn, he told himself resignedly. Even such a child as Lenore's and Jamie's offspring might turn out to be!

And if they were keeping the child, they might as well keep the horse, he supposed.

Now, in the dimness of the stable, Lorena winced as she thought of the many arguments Uncle Robbie and Aunt Flora had had about her. She leaned her face against the horse's neck, feeling the ropy muscles beneath that rippling white mane, and brooded about that. Uncle Robbie seemed to think there was something inherently bad in her. Even though Flora did her best to change his mind, the shadow of her wild beautiful mother hung like a cloud over her childhood. She would turn out badly ... because she was Lenore's daughter. Everybody said so.

As she led Snowfire out of the stable into the bright sunshine, she shook off these thoughts. Mounting the sleek white back, she let Snowfire pick his dainty way down the dusty street that led through the double row of stone cottages that made up the bulk of Twainmere.

As she rode past the bootmaker's house, she could see the bootmaker's wife carding wool. And on the other side of the street through an open window, the wainwright's wife busy at her loom whilst he labored outdoors, fitting a huge wagon wheel to a wooden wagon. Now she was passing the cottage occupied by the miller's widow, Mistress Piper, and her nearly deaf sister, who had once been renowned for her skill in crimping ruffs with a goffering iron, but now those ruffs were as out of fashion as her farthingale. Both women were outside, snipping the late roses.

"Who's that riding by?" demanded the deaf sister in a loud fretful voice.

" 'Tis Lorena Frankford," said Mistress Piper, looking up from the roses she was cutting.

"Who? Speak up, Madge, I can't hear ye."

"Lorena Frankford," shouted Mistress Piper.

"Riding astride," observed her sister disapprovingly.

"Aye. 'Tis sure the vicar did not see her mount, else he would have reproved her for her boldness," Lorena heard Mistress Piper say.

She did not care. She rode sidesaddle only when Uncle Robbie was looking—the rest of the time, bareback and astride. Aunt Flora did not mind. She herself had grown up riding astride in the wild Highlands to the north. That this was prim, recently Puritan, England, did not matter to her Scottish way of thinking.

Now Lorena was passing by Tom Prattle's cottage with its overgrown yard. Sprawled out unkempt on the long wooden bench by the door, big Tom glowered at the girl on the white horse and muttered. Tom Prattle was Lorena's uncle by marriage, for he'd married Lenore's older sister Meg. Lenore had lived with them until Meg died and even for a while after, till Tom in drunken anger had driven her screaming from the house. Now Lorena gave Tom a cold look. Never once had the surly oaf given her so much as a "Good morrow!" and she his very own niece! Ah, well . . . She tossed her head. Tucked into her gray kirtle, along with two shiny red apples, was the treasured play. Her mother might have appeared in it before the king himself!

Leaving the last of the stone cottages behind her, she

nudged Snowfire with a lazy foot, and the horse ambled into the overgrown patch of land that had once been Jamie MacIver's smithy and was still owned by his sister Flora, although she lived in the vicarage.

Through a yard tall with weeds Lorena guided Snowfire beneath the big spreading chestnut tree that had once shaded the forge. There she seized a low-hanging limb and pulled herself up off the horse's back. Snowfire looked up at her tolerantly, for he was used to this unladylike behavior. Lorena crawled along the branch and settled herself into the crotch of the tree, letting her legs dangle over into the green leaves. Lorena often came here to the old smithy when she wanted to hide and daydream.

"Go on, Snowfire," she called to the horse. "You can graze awhile."

As if he understood this lighthearted command, the white stallion strolled back over the familiar ground to the overrun remains of Flora's old herb garden behind the deserted cottage where Lenore had once lived as Jamie MacIver's handfast bride. Contentedly, Snowfire began munching the tall grasses that now grew up through rosemary and thyme and onions and garlic.

Eagerly Lorena thumbed the pages, thrilled, as she imagined her mother playing a "breeches part" in the play. She was concentrating so on the pages that she did not notice the sudden dampness in the air or the sky's rapid clouding.

She *did* rouse with a start, however, at the sound of voices below her and feet scuffling through the tall grass. She peered down through the leafy branches.

Why, it was Warren Bixby, whose young wife was always ailing, and who came to church alone and always sat in the front pew staring unblinkingly at the vicar throughout the sermon. And that was one of the Malvern girls with him—from above she couldn't tell which one, but that high squeaky voice with the uncontrollable giggle was unmistakably Malvern. They came to a halt almost beneath her perch, and now she saw that the girl's hair was fiery red. It must be Floss Malvern, who sang hymns in a high breaking voice and always lifted her head to give Lorena a haughty stare as she left the church.

Lorena saw that Floss was simpering and giggling, and now she was leaning back with her hands on her hips and an arch expression on her pointy face. Big Warren's sandy head was bent and—Lorena closed the play pamphlet and looked down with interest at this real life drama unfolding below her—they were *kissing*.

Lorena considered making herself known, dropping down lightly from the branch above their heads and giving them a good scare. But even as the thought crossed her mind she saw that Warren's big calloused hand had now uncovered the girl's shoulder. He was tugging her dress down!

"Watch, Warren, ye'll tear my bodice!" Floss protested, flouncing away a step.

"Then why don't you take it off, Floss?"

"Well, I might," she pouted. "If ye'd turn that big head of yours away!"

Lorena watched in surprise as Floss slipped out of her separate bodice, and stood in a tempting pose in her chemise and kirtle. And to think this same Floss had hurled taunts at her one rainy day about her mother being a brazen wench! Grimly, Lorena decided to stay and see just how brazen Floss was.

She wasn't long in finding out. Warren turned and swooped down on this inviting baggage. There was a rip and an "Oooh!" from Floss as her chemise tore and her bare breasts flashed impudently.

Now Warren was dragging her down to the ground beside him, one arm pinioning her narrow waist. With his other hand he was tugging at his trousers.

Apparently Floss had not meant to go so far.

"No, Warren, no!" she wailed, flapping her arms and legs about like a fledgling bird. "The devil will get us, Warren. The devil gets them as lies together unwed—the vicar says so!"

"Oh, come on, Floss. 'Twon't be any different from

last time in the barn loft. 'Twill be better, the air's fresher here!"

"I shouldna done it then. I shouldna." Floss shook her red head but without much conviction. "You know 'tis a sin for a man and a woman to lie together out of wedlock."

Warren sighed impatiently. He was playing with her skirts, flipping them up. And each time Floss reached out to pull them back down, he tossed them higher until at last they displayed her plump legs to the hips.

Lorena knew she shouldn't be watching, but the scene below fascinated her. Besides, there was no way down except past Floss and her lover.

"And you a married man!" Aggrieved, Floss stuck out her lower lip.

"Aye, I'm married," he muttered.

"But not to me!"

"Ye knew I was married, Floss, when we done it the first time—and I'd marry ye, Floss, truly I would, were it not for that."

He'd marry you, Floss, if only his wife would let him! thought Lorena derisively. Could Floss be so stupid as to really believe that?

Apparently Floss was. "Well . . ." She sank back relaxed upon the ground, ignoring her raised skirts. Suddenly her head shot up. "But suppose I have a babe?" she wailed.

"Then ye'll name him after me," roared Warren, and wrapped his muscular arms about her.

Floss's arms went around his neck. "The devil will get us, Warren. The devil . . ."

Her words were lost in a kind of throaty gurgle as Warren thrust deep within her. From the branch overhead Lorena inched out a little farther. The pair below were rolling on the grass. She could see Warren's broad back flopping up and down rhythmically over Floss, with Floss's arms locked tightly about him to keep him on target. She could see Floss's striped cotton-stockinged legs flailing about between Warren's worn breeches.

This, thought Lorena excitedly, was what Maude had been talking about; this was what Will Shakespeare had been talking about in his play! She slid down the branch and craned over to see.

Below her, on her back, lay Floss, with a glazed unfocused look in her brown eyes and an unidentifiable expression somewhere between pain and delight on her pointy face. Her lips were parted and she was muttering, making a kind of gurgling sound. All Lorena could catch was "The devil . . ."

So this was how it was done!

There didn't look to be much to it, and she couldn't understand why Floss's eyelids were fluttering, why her eyes were rolling blankly up to heaven until the whites showed, or why she was gasping now and moaning, culminating in a kind of high keening wail.

All that noise was undoubtedly why Warren Bixby had chosen the isolated and deserted smithy for his tryst.

Their tempo increased. Warren's powerful back rose and fell faster. Suddenly Floss made a strangling sound as if she were choking and Warren bellowed, and at that moment Lorena leaned out too far and the bough broke with a terrible snap as she was catapulted with a wild yell to land asprawl on that broad heaving back.

In the gloom, Warren had no idea what had hit him. A wildcat, or perhaps one of those monsters that roamed the night woods and about which tales were told by hearthsides after dark. As her body struck him and skittered off, rolling along in the grass, Warren gave a wild half-human howl.

Floss saw his expression change from lechery to terror and she gave a loud shriek: "Yowr! 'Tis the devil, he's come for us!"

She dug her fingers into Warren's back with such force that, coming up bleary-eyed from his thunderous joining, he could not rid himself of her.

As they wrestled, howling, there on the grass, Lorena scrambled up and raced through the brush for

Snowfire, who was still contentedly grazing in the over-grown garden.

Just as she leaped onto the horse, the first lightning bolt of the approaching storm rent the sky, and thunder rumbled deafeningly.

"Oh, Lord!" cried Floss. "He's throwin' lightnin' bolts at us!"

It was too much for Warren. He rose with a shout, his lady clinging to his broad body like a squirrel to a tree, and began to run.

Snowfire had always feared lightning. As Lorena vaulted onto his back and the lightning bolt struck, he bolted, thundering for home and stable by the back way. Rain began to fall in heavy pelts. They were already out of sight of the smithy through the trees, and the pande-monium behind them was dying away as Floss let loose shriek after shriek that faded into the distance, as horse and rider sped for home.

Shaken, Lorena felt ashamed. She was sure neither of them had seen her, but—she should not have watched.

Not till she reached the vicarage did Lorena realize she had left the pamphlet containing Mister Will Shake-speare's play. It must have fallen out of her hand as she fell. She dared not return for it. Not only was it raining hard, with Aunt Flora calling her in to supper, but War-ren might have figured out what had happened to him and be waiting vengefully in the brush to pounce on whoever came back for the pamphlet.

She returned next day and searched the area around the chestnut tree thoroughly, but the play was gone.

Lorena stood beneath the chestnut tree wondering if she dared ask Floss for the return of the play—for cer-tainly either she or Warren must have it. She decided reluctantly that she did not dare.

But she could not forget that raptured look on Floss's face, her glazed unseeing eyes, her peculiar ex-pression. What could have been happening to Floss of sufficient import to make her look like *that?*

She would have to give it some more thought. And perhaps ask Maude.

For a whole month Warren Bixby was a changed man. He went about muttering to himself that the devil had took out after him, had descended on his back whilst he were sinnin'—and had left him a tract to prove it. That the pamphlet was neither a religious tract nor a manual for devil worship but a play, illiterate Warren had no way of knowing. Floss had shrieked and refused to look at it, insisting it smelled of brimstone. Night after night, Warren Bixby sat looking at the pamphlet, mesmerized—looking at this concrete evidence of a devil who had come after him, thumping down out of a tree and letting loose lightning bolts. Finally he set fire to the "devil's tract" and went down on his knees and repented at the top of his voice. His next-door neighbors heard him and decided he was drunk again.

Floss he shunned as he might have the plague. It was just as well. Poor Floss had decided for herself that the devil had been after *her* with his thunderbolts. Not for lying with half the boys in the village; oh, no, *they'd* all been single. He had sent down his bolts only when she had lain with a married man! When a shepherd from north of Cirencester came by to visit relatives and took a liking to her, Floss promptly married him and departed from Twainmere forever.

At first Maude was furious at the loss of the pamphlet, but when Lorena told her how she had come to lose it, she laughed so she almost split the seams of her worn bodice.

"You *fell* on Warren's back?" she whooped, with another gasping shout of laughter. "Oh, lor', I wish I'd 'a been there to see it!"

In Twainmere, despite the vicar's efforts, young Lorena was getting a liberal education.

Cambridge to York

Chapter 7

Fortunately unaware of her precocious daughter's problems or the machinations of Geoffrey's French wife, Lenore watched the countryside change as their gilded coach rolled north toward Peterborough. Mistress Potts' constant chatter depressed her and the coach wheels seemed to toll out "Geoffrey, Geoffrey" in a melancholy way as they rolled along, every mile taking her farther from her lover. It seemed a lifetime, yet in all they had been gone from London only six days when Peterborough's beautiful Norman cathedral hove in sight.

In Peterborough, Mistress Potts suffered a stomach upset (Lenore was sure it came from eating too many eels, a great favorite with Mistress Potts), so they stayed over a day while the coach driver scowled and muttered over how his lordship would have his hide for being late. But Lenore's smile won him over and while Mistress Potts rested in her room, Lenore spent the day sightseeing. She loved this town on the western border of the fens, which two hundred years before had been such a great center for weaving and wool combing. But she was brought up short when she saw how the lovely cathedral had been damaged, the tomb of Catherine of Aragon desecrated by Cromwell's soldiery. It reminded her bitterly of the days when she had fled through southwest England with Geoffrey and seen everywhere crossroads markers that had stood for centuries now broken and vandalized by Cromwell's men. She was so sad on that journey up the Great North Road, rousing herself as a limestone ridge loomed ahead. "Listen!" Lenore cried, for Lincoln's Great Tom Bell, a leviathan of five tons, was tolling.

"I care not for bells," declared Mistress Potts fretfully, ignoring the sonorous peals. "My bones are all aching. I do hope our next inn has a soft bed with no bedbugs!"

Lenore hoped so too, for bedbugs were a hazard of the road for travelers and she'd had no sleep at the last inn, for fighting them.

At Lincoln they turned into a good inn and bade the driver of the gilded coach good-bye. Lenore had expected Mistress Potts to want to lay over and rest, which would give her a chance to see something of Lincoln, fabled city of the north. But to her disappointment, as Mistress Potts alighted with some difficulty from the coach, she announced that they must at all costs get on to York.

With raised brows, Lenore sprang down from the coach without assistance. Leaving the driver to attend to their luggage, she hurried into the cozy half-timbered inn and made arrangements for a coach to York even before she washed away the travel stains. The driver whom the landlord recommended had a mean expression and a bristly beard. He was muttering over his ale when she found him, but since he agreed to leave on the morrow at six, she had no choice but to put aside her misgivings.

She was tired, and disappointed that there would be no time to see Lincoln. She hurried upstairs, clutching Mistress Potts' little leathern valuable chest, poured water into the washbowl from the pitcher, and washed her face and hands, grateful at last to be free of the road dust. Before she had finished, Mistress Potts was waiting by the door to go down to the common room for supper.

"You're sure you're up to leaving for York without resting a bit?" Lenore demanded at supper as Mistress Potts gloomed over her marrowbone pie.

Mistress Potts looked up with a start, as if interrupted in the midst of some unhappy reverie.

"Aye." She nodded her head vigorously. "We must hurry, Lenore. Did ye not note today how the air grows colder? The winter weather is closing in."

"Your gloves aren't warm enough for cold weather." Lenore glanced at the thin, delicately embroidered leather gloves Mistress Potts was wearing, for it was fashionable to keep one's gloves on—like one's hat—even at meals. "And a woolen hood would help to keep you warm. I could try to procure some tonight. There might be a shopkeeper who'd open up to make a sale."

To her surprise, the older woman's faded blue eyes filled with tears. "Ye're my only friend, Lenore," she burst out.

"Nonsense, you have a host of friends. How many do you correspond with?"

" 'Tis not the same," Mistress Potts sniffled. "We exchange gossip, true, and I'm more than glad to hear from them. But there's not a one of them would make this long hard journey with me, Lenore. Ye're more like a daughter than a friend."

Lenore flushed with pleasure at this heartfelt compliment, half whispered in the noisy common room. She ducked as a serving girl carrying an enormous tray filled with roasted capons hurried by. "Your marrowbone pie's growing cold," she told Mistress Potts kindly. "And it's your favorite."

"Aye." Mistress Potts passed a kerchief over her eyes and launched into the pie. Somewhat restored, she finished off her supper with Florentines. Indeed, she was so much her old self after that, that she leaned over roguishly to Lenore. "See that man in the corner over there!" she hissed. "He's been staring at me all through supper, did ye not remark him?"

Lenore, whose mind had been on other things—notably memories of Geoffrey—turned to observe a soberly dressed individual who was staring gloomily at nothing at all. "He looks like a parson!" she laughed.

"Ah, they're the worst kind," Mistress Potts insisted, bridling a little. "Why, I remember a parson in Bath who had *three* wives and not one of the three knew about the others! There was a merry to-do, I'll tell you, when they all found out!"

Lenore, who had been ignoring several admiring gentlemen throughout the meal, grinned. "I think we'll be safe from him if we remember to latch our door." She rose to leave and assisted Mistress Potts in rising also, for the stout lady was pinned between table and wall and could hardly squeeze out.

"Aye, probably," agreed Mistress Potts. She waited for Lenore to dive beneath the table and seize the little chest on which her feet had been propped, then puffed along beside her through the crowded common room where many wistful eyes followed the tall beauty with the red gold hair. Her good humor was back in force, and after they reached their room she even insisted on summoning a serving maid to bring them a snack of raspberry sack and sausages "in case we become hungry later."

Lenore hid a smile, for Mistress Potts fell upon them at once.

"It reminds me of Wallham, Lenore," she confided in a sentimental tone as she munched. "My father always loved his raspberry sack and sausages in the evening."

"I am surprised you have not returned to Wallham before," Lenore said frankly, "since you obviously love it so. Yet you never mentioned the place to me until you decided to return."

Mistress Potts frowned and took a large swallow of sack. "That is so," she admitted, "but 'twas always in the back of my mind."

"Tell me about your brother," Lenore pursued. She

bent to take off her shoes as she made ready for bed. She was trying to discover what drove Mistress Potts so relentlessly northward.

"Half brother," corrected Mistress Potts absently.

"*Half* brother?" Lenore shot her a keen look as she slid out of her dress. This hotly pursued relationship was growing more remote!

"Ah—yes." Self-consciously the older woman resettled her voluminous skirts and pushed away her empty trencher. "My father married twice. I am the only child of his first wife. After my mother died of a fever, he married again—a woman from Lancaster." Her voice showed her distaste. "When I was old enough to marry, I left."

Now down to her chemise, Lenore gazed at her friend thoughtfully. "And this second wife, how many children had she?" she asked as she slipped into her dressing gown.

"One son—Amos. 'Tis he who owns Wallham. My father left everything to Amos when he died."

"What is your brother Amos like, Mistress Potts?"

"Amos?" Mistress Potts settled into her bed. "Why, I scarce know, Lenore. I haven't laid eyes on him for more than thirty years."

"Thirty years!" echoed Lenore, aghast. "Won't he be awfully surprised when we descend on him? For you decided so quickly, there was no time to write!"

"Well, 'tis really the *place* I want to see," defended Mistress Potts. "I spent my girlhood there, after all. And Amos has written many times asking me to come back for a visit," she added hastily. Mistress Potts' voice grew a trifle petulant. "Lenore, if we are to start early in the morn we must be abed and not sit up talking all night!"

But Lenore lay awake puzzling for some time in the smothering softness of the big feather bed. She wondered what else Mistress Potts had not told her.

It was just starting to snow as they set out the next morning. They traveled slowly but surely, following the ancient road the Romans had used.

By the time they reached York, the snow had stopped falling, the weather was sharp and clear, and all the countryside around was breathtakingly lovely. But as they entered the city gates they were greeted by a hard frost and a cold, searing wind that reached in around their woolen hoods and struck icily through their gloves, even though they each wore three pair, one pulled on over the other. The driver looked relieved to have got through and found himself the center of attention in the snowy innyard of the Fox and Bow, as other drivers crowded around, inquiring of the condition of the roads to the south.

Lenore opened the coach door and looked about her. Another coach, with winded horses blowing heavily, their breath sending up clouds of steam in the icy air, their backs and heads and manes frosted with snow, had pulled into the innyard just ahead of them, and now a young girl flung open the door with a glad cry. She was clad in sky blue velvet trimmed with beaver, and she was waving her beaver muff at a young fellow who burst out of the inn door crying, "Eliza, ye got through!"

As he skidded to a halt below the coach door, the girl in blue velvet plummeted down into his arms and there in the snowy courtyard they embraced, the girl laughing and crying at the same time. Then the boy scooped her up triumphantly and carried her into the inn, shouting merrily back over his shoulder, "Ye may bring my lady's luggage in speedily, for her bridal chamber awaits her!"

A bride and groom! Lenore smiled to see them but the sight tugged at her heart. She remembered a snowy night in Oxford long ago when Geoffrey had fought his way through a blizzard to seek her arms.

Her soft mouth hardened. She had been faithful to Geoffrey for so long—*too long!* And all that time he had been with Letiche!

Now, on their high pattens, she and Mistress Potts clambered down into the icy courtyard. They were helped by the sturdy postilion, who handed down their baggage to a boy from the Fox and Bow. In the biting wind—for she must oversee the removal of all the luggage—Lenore found herself staring up at the old black timber-and-wattle inn that must have stood in King Harry's time or before. Beside her Mistress Potts sneezed.

"Go on inside," she told the older woman. "I can see to this."

Gratefully, Mistress Potts trudged forward, clutching the arm of the boy who was carrying in the luggage, and disappeared inside. As Lenore was about to follow the last of the boxes, the coach driver shouldered his way to her and bade her good-bye, shaking his head when Lenore said they would probably continue on to Durham despite the snow.

She found Mistress Potts warming herself before the blazing hearth in the common room, and hastened to join her. As she stood beside the pile of luggage which had not yet been taken to their rooms, Lenore blew on her half-frozen fingers from which she could barely extract her gloves and asked herself why in heaven's name she had attempted such a journey at this time of year!

Her answer was as bitter as the wind-driven sleet that had lashed her face. She had to get away from Geoffrey, from London, where any day she might run across him. She had to be away from that possibility, so she could think, and plan, and try to make something of the rags and tatters of her life.

"We've a room ready for ye now," the landlord said heartily behind her. Lenore turned to follow him. She moved instinctively, not seeing where he led as her heart forced her thoughts to confront the truth.

I have run all the way to York and still Geoffrey follows me. I take him with me everywhere, in my heart. Is this to be my curse?

Their room had a slanting ceiling and a heavy oaken floor that tilted a bit, causing the table to sit slaunchways and the heavy chest to tilt forward alarmingly. But it sported a huge feather bed big enough for four travelers! Lenore sighed with relief and her despondency lifted. Solid comfort at last!

The boy who brought up their luggage built a fire on the cold hearth, which drew the chill off the damp room. But even with the fire blazing, Lenore noted that Mistress Potts was still shivering.

"There's time for a nap before dinner," she suggested. "Why don't you climb into bed, Mistress Potts?"

Mistress Potts gave her a doubtful look. "Well—if ye'll go down and arrange for a coach to take us and our goods to Durham, I'll rest a bit."

Lenore cast a glance out the window where it was again snowing hard.

"Mistress Potts," she entreated. "What is this terrible haste to get north? You heard the drivers in the courtyard just now say that nothing is moving on the roads. We were the last coach in!"

Mistress Potts looked up from removing her pattens and gave Lenore an owlish look. "The haste is that we get to Wallham before winter closes the roads." With a groan she eased out of her shoes. "Seek a coach, Lenore!"

"Very well," Lenore sighed. "I'll bring you up a hot posset if I can find one."

"Never mind that." Wearily the older woman tossed aside her cloak and hood and crawled, fully dressed, into the big feather bed which closed around her comfortingly. "Call me in time for supper," she murmured drowsily, and was instantly asleep. Eyes closed, round cheeks still red from the cold, she looked like an elderly cherub as she lay there.

Lenore gave her a fond, if exasperated, glance. The poor, foolish woman—didn't she know that if they ventured out into this weather, they might become stranded in some snowdrift? Why, they could freeze to death by the roadside!

Nevertheless, she went downstairs to inquire among the drivers about a coach. They thought she was out of her wits to consider leaving so soon. Stay a week, at least, the landlord suggested, or "until the weather breaks."

"My traveling companion is adamant," Lenore said

flatly. "She is obsessed with pushing ahead. At least to Durham."

"Sit a while in the common room," he urged. "I'll ask about and see if there's anyone as will attempt the journey."

Lenore crossed the long, narrow room with its rude furniture and low ceiling crisscrossed by heavy, dark beams. She leant upon a deep windowsill and peered out through panes clouded with hoarfrost.

Out there the city beckoned. She could see the houses winding away through an alley across the street, the timbered buildings leaning out and nearly meeting in their upper storeys. Below such spots the snow was light—only blowing snow had reached the cobbles. As she watched, a group of children in brightly colored woolen stockingcaps raced by, shouting and throwing snowballs at the tall icicles that hung down from the buildings. A snowball knocked one large icicle from the overhanging roof of the inn with a musical tinkle. An old woman in a gray apron ran to the door and called to the children to go away; they'd break the windows! The children scattered and ran away, laughing.

Lenore smiled. The inn was hospitable, the proprietor merry, and the atmosphere of the common room warm and friendly. Wistfully, she considered asking this pleasant innkeeper for a job, and staying on in York.

She was musing over a cup of hot chocolate and wondering if the flirtatious broad-hipped barmaid would succeed in sweetening the expression of a sour-faced gentleman she seemed to fancy, when the landlord returned.

For a price, he told her, he'd found a sturdy fellow willing to take them north. His name was Elias Plum and he had a high-sided cart pulled by four large plough horses. Elias was not staying at the Fox and Bow, but at a cheaper hostelry down the street. He was reliable, the landlord assured her, and willing to take them all the way to Durham and beyond, even in this weather. Wallham lay in far Northumberland in the shadow of Hadrian's Wall.

Lenore hesitated, but she was sure Mistress Potts would agree to any price, and the landlord beckoned to the driver.

He sauntered over, a ruddy giant of a fellow with a big gusty laugh and twinkling hazel eyes. His back straightened when he saw Lenore, and he surreptitiously brushed some crumbs from his leather doublet with hands thick-callused by the reins. All the time they were talking, he never took his eyes from her, and the landlord grinned.

"Elias'd have driven ye anywhere," he whispered with a wink as Lenore, having completed her arrangements, passed him a few minutes later on the stairs. "To hell, I think, if ye'd asked him!"

York

Chapter 8

The candles had been lit, and stranded travelers were beginning to assemble in the common room as Lenore went upstairs. She paused on the landing and looked down at them, frowning. Her blood was stirring rebelliously in her veins tonight. She tried to shake off this treacherous mood which could land her in trouble, telling herself she'd do better to learn more about the people at Wallham, where the tall-sided cart, God willing, would be taking them.

"Tell me, Mistress Potts, what are the nephews like?" she asked, when she breezed into the room where Mistress Potts, already up and refreshed from her nap, was combing her hair with a heavy gilt comb.

"I'm sure I don't know, I've never seen them." Mistress Potts winced at a tangle. "Did you find us a coach, Lenore?"

"I've found us a high-sided cart pulled by draft horses. 'Twill be a rough passage north, I'm afraid, but the driver seems sure he can make it. It will shake loose our teeth, and the luggage may shift and crush us," Lenore warned. At Mistress Potts' indifferent shrug she said, "But surely Amos has written you about his nephews?"

"No. I know only that their names are Sedgewick Robb and Caleb Apperton, and that they reside at Wallham with Amos. Lenore, could ye open that box—no, that one there. I've a mind to wear something different tonight."

Lenore got the heavy box open after a struggle and clothes seemed to burst out of it. She wondered how they'd managed to pack so much into it and whether they'd ever get it closed again.

So Mistress Potts was going to wear something different tonight. Lenore looked down at her own plain woolen dress. Well, she'd wear something different too! She had ordered a bath, and after it was brought and she'd bathed, on a sudden whim she took out her black silk dress and delicate black chemise, her silk stockings and black gloves—even the big hat with plumes that she had bought to torment Geoffrey.

Letiche Wyndham doubtless wore such finery every night . . .

"You'll wear that for supper?" Mistress Potts' eyes nearly bulged from her head. "One would think ye were meeting a gentleman downstairs!"

Perhaps I will! Lenore thought, her violet eyes flashing with a reckless glint. For what was the cure for one man? *Another!*

Aloud she said, "I'm tired of being dowdy and travel-stained. Unless it clears—and that isn't likely— we'll be going nowhere tomorrow, so there's no need to rush to bed early. I think I'll sit a while in the common room after supper and enjoy a glass of wine."

"Well, if you're going to dress up, I will too!" cried Mistress Potts. "I'll wear my wine silk with the scarlet petticoats and dangle my red lace fan, if I can find it!" She was delving into the big box Lenore had opened as she spoke.

"Ah, there it is!" She came up with the fan and quickly arrayed herself as handsomely as Lenore. Peering into a small mirror by candlelight, she began to rub her cheeks and lips with "Spanish paper" to make them redder.

"Don't you want to use it?" She proffered the bit of paper to Lenore.

Lenore hesitated a moment. She had used such things in the theater, of course, but close up in the candlelight she preferred her tissue-sheer complexion untampered with. "Perhaps another time," she smiled.

"Aye, ye're probably right." Mistress Potts clacked her tongue. "For I'm told," she added impressively, "that if men want to learn if your face is painted, they do eat a mountain of garlic and then they breathe in your face. And 'tis said the painted color will vanish—like that!" She snapped her stubby fingers.

"So would I—vanish," said Lenore dryly.

"Well, at least ye'll take a patch to show how white is your complexion!"

Lenore thought wryly that her complexion was not half so white as Mistress Potts', who had lacquered her face with ceruse, which gave her an eerie dead look in the half-light. But to please the older woman, she accepted a small diamond-shaped patch of black taffeta and placed it near her mouth, like a dimple.

"So many ladies are using patches now to cover up pimples or warts," Mistress Potts remarked contentedly.

Lenore promptly removed the patch. "On second thought, I think I'll go down as I am." She picked up the little leathern chest and followed Mistress Potts down the stairs.

"As she was" was sufficient to turn all heads as she came into the common room with her white bosom gleaming above the lustrous black silk and the plumes on her hat floating gaily above her now intricately arranged red-gold hair. In the noisy room conversation ceased in tribute to her beauty.

Mistress Potts was enjoying the sensation their arrival created. "Did ye see that gentleman in the dark green velvet?" she demanded hoarsely of Lenore who bent to slide the little leathern chest under the table they had selected. "I declare to you he *winked* at me!"

Lenore sat up, straightening her hat. She had noted the old gentleman's wink, which had been aimed at a likely serving maid bouncing by. But she had no wish to dampen Mistress Potts' good spirits.

"I'd ignore him, were I you," she advised with a straight face. "One cannot be too careful."

Mistress Potts looked daunted. She stole another look at the gentleman in dark green velvet. His back was now turned away from her as he jested with the impudently smiling serving maid. "I guess I gave *him* a set down, ignoring him!" she told Lenore virtuously.

So that she would not have to discuss that, Lenore asked hastily, "Would you prefer the eels or the capon?"

"Both," said Mistress Potts promptly. "And I see they've sallets and fricasees as well," she added, peering at the trenchers on the next table.

"Aye, and I spy meat that's been grilled over hot coals," Lenore said indulgently.

"Carbonadoes?" cried Mistress Potts. "Why, this is a very passable inn, Lenore! Let's have the carbonadoes too. And olive pie, if there is any."

Lenore sighed. Sometimes she had had the feeling on this journey that England was one vast cheese and they, like scurrying little mice, were busily eating their way through it to Northumberland!

"You'll be sick again," she warned.

"Pish!" scoffed Mistress Potts. "It does a body good to eat well! Ye should follow my example, Lenore."

But Lenore ate lightly of the heavy repast that was brought. While Mistress Potts dove with relish into the hot breads and rich conserves, the array of meats and sallets and fricasees, she ran her eyes over the assembled company: most of them stranded travelers like themselves.

They were gentlemen of means, for the most part, she saw, for this was an expensive inn. The room was atremble with plumed hats and starched lace, and from numerous strong hands jewels of price sparkled. That one there with the long ermine-trimmed cloak could be a banker, that frowning gentleman whose taffetas were shot with gold braid, who kept returning his food as either "underdone" or "overdone," was perhaps some titled lord, passing through. That trio of young bucks who kept raising their tankards and smiling at her, and whose spurs jingled as they stamped their feet and laughed at each others' jokes—they would probably be wastrels, perhaps younger sons of the nobility. It was a scene that could be duplicated any night in inns all over England.

So then, why was all this comfort, this good food, not enough for her?

She would not answer that, even to herself.

Foundered at last, Mistress Potts staggered off to bed exhausted, but Lenore lingered in the common room. Several gentlemen, observing that her "chaperon" was retiring, eyed her speculatively across the rims of their tankards.

Meeting look for curious look, Lenore sipped her wine and gazed back at them. Her old resentment toward men had come back, that resentment born of an unloved childhood, all the bitterness that had made her a fabled flirt in Twainmere. Now she eased into a graceful posture that showed her resplendent figure to best advantage, lifted her chin defiantly and let her violet eyes sweep the room again.

She had been humbled in London—by a man. And she would make these strangers pay for it! She would taunt them with her beauty, she would amuse herself by the lust she aroused! Not a man there but had noticed the reckless tilt of her lovely head, the challenge that flashed from those long-lashed violet eyes.

Mistress Potts had hardly cleared the room before two of them—from opposite ends of the room—gained their feet.

One was the large gentleman clad in rosy taffetas shot with gold braid, who had found nothing "fit to eat" all evening and had filled the air with his complaints. Now his great russet periwig shook and his chair creaked as he reared up and marched toward her with a measured tread. Rather as if he were marching to battle, Lenore thought—off in pursuit of an easy conquest.

She studied him. He had a hard yet somehow flaccid face and a lax, cruel mouth. It was easy to imagine him in Whitehall, exchanging nasty jests about the court ladies, or in the pit at the theater buying a China orange from an orange girl and carelessly raking her ankle with the rowel of his spurs . . .

From the other side of the room one of the group of young wastrels knocked over his tankard in his haste to be up and to arrive at Lenore's table first. Lenore turned to consider him. He was almost a head shorter than her other "suitor" and was wearing a creamy brocade doublet which he had just splashed with ale in his surge forward. He was a bit unsteady on his feet, his eyes bloodshot from too much drink, but he had a merry and determined look to him. He was wearing a sword that looked as if it had seen use.

Lenore could have stopped either of them merely by turning a disdainful look in their direction. But she did not. A devil had been loosed in her tonight.

Let these two squabble over her, let them fight. She could cast her look of haughty disdain at the victor!

They arrived at her table simultaneously and Lenore looked questioningly from one to the other.

"Allow me to present myself. I am Charles Revercombe," drawled the large man in rosy taffetas.

"Indeed?" The boredom in Lenore's voice matched his own. "And have we met before, sir?"

He frowned slightly. "I do not believe we have. However—"

Lenore looked past him at the flushed young man in the cream doublet. "And you, sir, do I know you?"

"You do not, my lady!" he cried in a slurred but enthusiastic West Country voice. "But indeed I'd be proud to make your acquaintance. Alan Barnsdale is my name and—"

"Be silent, you young puppy!" roared the large gentleman. "Can't ye see I'm in conversation with this lady?"

"Conversation, is it? Ye know her no better than I do! Ye're trying to make her acquaintance the same as I am!"

The large man flushed. He reached out a heavy hand and gave his opponent a shove. Much the worse for drink, the young buck in the cream doublet staggered and almost fell. He caught himself against a table and lurched unsteadily back toward them, pulling at his sword. "I'll not take a blow from ye, sir!" he cried drunkenly. "If 'tis a fight ye want, let's have at it."

A moment ago Lenore had been ready to let them fight, just as she had stood flirtatiously by a bonfire at Twainmere long ago and let two young men beat each other to the ground just for a dance with her.

It seemed so long since two stout blades had battled for her favor. But now she saw it would be murder. For the big man now pawing at his own sword was sober and the boy facing him half his weight, a head shorter, and wholly drunk.

Nearby chairs were scraping hastily back as men scrambled out of the way of the combatants.

She half rose, intending one way or another to put a stop to this before the younger man lay bleeding on the floor.

But before she could speak, a robust masculine voice intervened. "What, cousin, not even finished your drink and already half the bucks of the county are fighting for ye? Dispose of them at once, cousin, for I've not come half across the country at your behest just to watch a duel between your ardent swains!"

Three pairs of dangerous eyes turned to focus on this jaunty newcomer.

The man who lounged indolently before them was tall. His golden hair spilled carelessly to his shoulders, but his golden Van Dyke beard was carefully trimmed. A pair of laughing crystal eyes were looking into Lenore's from a young but weathered face. Now he insinuated his wine velvet shoulder between the combatants and stepped forward. He reached over and seized Lenore's hand. In astonishment, she surrendered it and he bore it to his lips.

As he did so he spoke, a wisp of sound that reached only her ears. "D'ye not remember me?" he murmured. "I'm the man who tossed ye the whip that day at Wells."

Wells! Memory flooded back to Lenore, of the day she had raced Snowfire against Hobbs' big roan at the fair, and Hobbs had tried to run her headfirst into a wagon tongue that stuck out onto the course. Only by smashing her whip into Hobbs' hard face had she caused his powerful horse to break stride. *And that whip had been tossed to her by a man with crystal eyes and a golden Van Dyke beard—this man!* It had been years, but she had not forgotten him, the stranger whose careless gesture had meant for her the difference between life and death.

She gave him a swift shadowed look and turned to meet two frowning faces. "I cannot let this contest between you go forward," she said in a tone of appeal. "This gentleman is right—I was to meet him here. 'Twas why I was sitting here alone, woolgathering."

The large man in rosy taffetas looked discomfited. He shifted his shoulders, half a mind to fight anyway, but the man from Wells gave him a winning smile.

"He is indeed my kinsman," Lenore lied sweetly. "And we've a deal to discuss for we've not seen each other for years. Indeed I was afraid he'd not make it to York in this weather!"

The young man in the cream doublet shrugged and

returned his sword to its scabbard. After a moment's hesitation in which he wrestled with himself, the large man's hand left off hovering over his sword hilt, and he whirled on his boot heel and stalked out. His color was very high and he was muttering. His departure was followed by a slight ripple of laughter.

Lenore sank back down. With a careless gesture, the man from Wells threw a lean leg over the bench and joined her, calling to the barmaid to bring more wine.

Lenore gave him a humorous look. "I'm beholden to you but now the score is even." To his suddenly quirked eyebrow: "I've saved your hide for you this night. For that large man in rose-colored taffeta looked to me a most dangerous opponent."

"Saved my hide for me, ye say?" He looked shocked. "Faith, I'll go after the taffeta brute and bring him back and we'll have a go at it here and now!"

He was half on his feet before she reached out and took hold of his wine velvet sleeve and urged him back.

"There's a whole roomful watching our reunion," she laughed. "We would not want it to seem we had met only to quarrel and part!"

"So long as 'tis clear who saved who," he grumbled. "For neither the large bully nor the young puppy were worthy of you!"

"Am I not to know my kinsman's name?" she teased. "It could be awkward, should I be asked!"

"I'm Christopher Dorn," he supplied promptly. "Late of Sussex, late of Lincoln, late of his majesty's horse."

"You're a soldier then?"

"I was but I sold my commission." He was smiling at her. "For my debts. Always my debts. And you?"

"Lenore Frankford, late of the London stage."

"An actress?"

"And orange girl."

"We rise, we fall!" he laughed. "And to think ye should turn up here!"

"Everyone turns up somewhere," she said ruefully.

"I meant to track ye down that day at Wells," he remembered.

"Everyone did, but we left in a hurry as you'll remember!" She was thinking back to the pell-mell flight through the crowd after she was recognized. "We rode our horses into a church and waited there while the pursuit thundered by—and then the church steeple was struck by lightning and we had to leave lest people come to investigate."

Christopher Dorn laughed. "I was in that crowd thundering by. But not to catch you—I meant to help ye effect your escape."

She gave him a wary look, noting that his crystal eyes were just now roving from her softly curving mouth to her softly curving breasts, so temptingly displayed in the black silk gown. "And why should you have done that?"

"Can ye not guess? 'Twas your beauty that took me. I meant to wrest ye away from the tall fellow at your side—" He looked around him. "By the way, where is he?"

The "tall fellow" had been Geoffrey.

"Long gone," sighed Lenore.

She thought Christopher Dorn looked pleased. "Then am I to understand that the Angel of Worcester has flown into this inn with only an elderly lady to accompany her?"

The Angel of Worcester . . . so long since anybody had called her by that name.

"We did not fly, we *floundered* through the snow to this inn. And 'angel' I am not. Yet the sound of the name was good and won me a king's pardon."

"Did it now?" His crystal eyes kindled, sparkled like prisms. "And with what were ye charged?"

Lenore was cursing herself for having said that. What good to dredge all that up now? "With killing a man," she said lightly. "Among other things."

"Ah, and did ye do it?" His lively interest was sparked.

"I think so," she admitted, studying her wine. "But not the one they charged me with."

He threw back his head and gave out a peal of laughter that caused heads to turn. "I knew ye'd be a wench after my own heart! From the moment ye threw away your saddle and kicked off your shoes at Wells and announced ye'd ride bareback."

Lenore finished her wine. "I was lightening the load. I was riding against a heavier bigger horse with a great length to his stride—and Snowfire was tired, we'd been riding all day."

"Well, ye certainly evened the score!" He beckoned the barmaid again. "More wine here."

Lenore allowed her glass to be refilled. She was aware that around the room significant glances were being exchanged, as if to say this was no tryst with a kinsman but with a lover!

The wine was beginning to go to her head. It had been a long time since she'd had so much to drink.

"We'd only pennies in the purse we wagered against Hobbs' gold," she remembered. "I had to win. Had the race gone against me, Hobbs' friends would have killed us."

Christopher Dorn choked on his wine. "Better and better! But where did ye go? The whole countryside was out beating the brush for ye."

"We hid in a cold cavern." *But Geoffrey's arms had been warm around her. How they had made love that night!* Her eyes grew lustrous, remembering. She had been so sure then that they would marry.

"I'd have given much to have spent that night in the cavern with you," Christopher Dorn said softly.

Lenore cast a startled look up at him. For a moment she had forgotten him. But this man who had saved her life once was still there, strong and masculine and with a look on his weathered smiling face, a gleam in his crystal eyes that was unmistakable: Christopher Dorn meant to have her.

She felt a sudden, uneven fluttering in her breast and gripped her wine glass tighter. "The amazing thing is that we escaped from Wells at all," she said hurriedly. "I had half expected big Hobbs to overtake us. His roan was powerful and our mounts had ridden hard that day."

"And who did you think unhorsed the rider of that big roan and bore him to the ground?" he asked a trifle haughtily. "Otherwise you'd have been caught for certain!"

Her violet eyes widened in surprise. She looked very lovely with her lips curving into a sweet smile. "I didn't know you did that," she said softly. "I owe you my life twice, it seems."

Christopher Dorn flashed her a sunny smile. " 'Tis a debt easy paid." His bold gaze traced her lovely body from chin to ankle, and Lenore flushed and dropped her eyes before that hot, insolent look.

Her blood was beginning to race. There was something about this audacious stranger that caught at her senses, zinging them like harp strings. Breathless little wicked thoughts tinkled in her ears. She lifted her head and returned his look.

Here was her chance to banish Geoffrey from her mind, her soul, from her very heart. Here, at last, was her chance to make a new beginning.

York

Chapter 9

"I am accompanying a friend to her old home in North-umberland," Lenore heard herself say. She was looking down so that she would not meet his eyes, lest he see surrender in hers. " 'Tis near Newcastle-on-Tyne."

"The old woman in red who left earlier, looking as if she'd not make the stairs?"

His reference to Mistress Potts as "old" broke the tension that had built up between them and made Lenore laugh. "Mistress Potts would not be pleased to hear herself called 'old.' She would rather say she is 'tired,' having come all the way from London."

"Indeed, if she's come all the way from London, she must be exhausted! Our Mistress Potts needs rest." His tone was insinuating and now he downed his wine and again called for their glasses to be refilled. "Look at it snowing outside! How much better that tired Mistress Potts stay snug in this inn than risk the icy roads!"

He meant how much better *she* stay. Lenore gave him a smile of pure witchery. "And how would you suggest Mistress Potts spend her time until the roads clear?"

Christopher grinned at her, his lighthearted meaning as transparently clear as his hot crystal gaze.

"In bed," he said promptly. "Resting. While Mistress Potts' young companion jaunts about York with an experienced guide."

His offer was very tempting.

"It grows late," she murmured, hating to spoil this witching mood by announcing that their arrangements were already made, that they would leave York as soon as it stopped snowing.

Christopher Dorn cast a look around him. The common room was indeed emptying out as sleepy travelers sought their beds. "I've a fine bottle of French brandy in my room upstairs," he said casually. " 'Twas smuggled in for me from France by a friend, and I've yet to open it. Would ye not like to try it?"

The openness of his frank gaze robbed the suggestion of any hint of seduction.

"We would disturb the others who may already have retired," objected Lenore. For rooms in crowded inns like this one were rarely occupied by just one traveler. If the bed was large enough, two, three or even four travelers often occupied it.

"I took the room a week ago," he told her off-handedly, studying her face in which a slight flush was rising. "For I was expecting a friend who owes me money. I'm still expecting him, but he's not likely to arrive tonight, with all this snow."

So they would be alone in his room—a heady thought.

The wine—or was it the wine?—sang through her head. Outside all was still; here in this inn was the only reality, the only life.

From the hearth a dry twig blazed up, like a small explosion, sending out a bursting shower of sparks.

As if mesmerized, Lenore rose.

"Yes." Her voice sounded distant to her ears,

dreamy, as if somebody else were speaking. "Yes, I will try your brandy."

"Ye'll find it warming." Hastily, lest she change her mind, he pulled back her bench, hefted the little chest on which her feet had rested, and escorted her up the stairs. The gaze of the late-staying gentlemen followed their progress wistfully.

Lenore felt light-headed.

"I must put this chest in my room first," she said. " 'Tis not mine but belongs to Mistress Potts."

"She is lucky to have you," he said caressingly. But he surrendered the chest and Lenore slipped quietly into their now dark room where she could hear Mistress Potts' rhythmic snoring.

Christopher was waiting for her in the hall. *Lest I change my mind!* she thought on a suddenly hysterical note. Then, as if she had no will of her own, her feet carried her with swaying grace across the hallway into his own chamber, and she stood still while he bent to light a candle from the hearth where a fire burned low.

"I ordered the fire built earlier," he said. "To knock off the chill."

He thinks of everything, she thought. Now he will say, *It is very warm in here. Let me take your hat.* And then—

"It is very warm in here," he said. "Wouldn't you be more comfortable without your hat and gloves?"

She tossed her plumed hat to a chair and began to ease off her black gloves. It was a long, slow, seductive process. Christopher Dorn thought her white arms gleamed with a special light. He thought Lenore a perfect woman standing there—tempting, desirable . . . within reach yet somehow remote . . .

Lenore could feel with an increasing physical intensity the pressure of his steady, admiring gaze.

She had felt an instant flash of attraction toward the dashing Christopher Dorn from the moment he had impudently placed himself between the combatants below stairs. Back in Wells—his face had attracted her even then, she realized with a flush from the memory. The man had strength and wit and humor—and a casual recklessness that appealed to her own reckless nature.

He would fill for her a desperate void.

Yet somehow, despite her attempt to destroy his ghost, Geoffrey's tall shadow lay like a spell between them.

Geoffrey has ruined all other men for me, she told herself bitterly. *Even this one, who entices me so. It is as if I am bound to Geoffrey by invisible ropes!*

She turned, picked up her gloves. "I—I cannot stay." Her voice was unsteady, blurred.

Christopher Dorn surveyed this beautiful bird about to take wing with glittering, acquisitive eyes. He was not a man to go down to defeat easily.

"Well," he cried heartily. "At least since ye are here, let me offer ye a drink of the brandy ye came to sample. 'Twill make you feel better, I promise."

Yes, she owed him that, this man who had tossed her the whip in Wells.

She nodded, moved restively to the window, and stood looking out. What had possessed her to come to his room, she asked herself. She who had been so faithful to Geoffrey that she had been called mockingly "the Iron Virgin" of the London stage? She, the flirt-gone-faithful, ready to fall like a ripe plum into the arms of a stranger!

Behind her, as she stared out through the small frosted panes, she could hear Christopher Dorn pulling a bottle and a pair of silver cups out of his saddlebags. There was a small clash as the cups bumped together, then the sound of liquid splashing down into the cups.

Before her was an empty, snow-covered landscape, the houses burdened with snow and long icicles, the road a white deserted ribbon.

No, not quite deserted. To the south a lone horseman was struggling through the drifts on a big dark horse, making his way north toward the inn. His hat and the shoulders of his cloak were as heavily encrusted with snow as was his horse's mane. He would be the last traveler to get through this night, she guessed as she watched his horse's labored approach. Indeed it would take a good mount to make its way over these roads tonight—the gentleman must be a judge of horseflesh. But to her it was a melancholy sight, for she remembered another night and lodgings on Magpie Lane in Oxford and the sight through frosted panes of Geoffrey slogging home, snow-covered through the tall drifts, to reach her in time for Christmas.

The gentleman approaching down the road had the same breadth of shoulder. Though his body was bent against the whipping wind, he rode with the same assurance as Geoffrey did. He *looked* like Geoffrey.

For a moment she tensed and strained forward. Then she bit her lip. *Of course, this was not Geoffrey!* Geoffrey was in London—or Kent. More likely Kent. But even when they had passed through Stamford, she had seen a man, booted and spurred, striding down the srteet, and she had not been able to look at the houses Mistress Potts pointed out for leaning out to gaze at him—because he looked a little like Geoffrey.

She would lose her mind if she went on like this! For now she was beginning to see him everywhere. Even in this stranger fighting his way through the snow toward the comforting warmth of the inn.

Well, she would put an end to this madness! She would eradicate Geoffrey from her memory, blot him out here and now, in the arms of the man from Wells!

She whirled and Christopher Dorn found himself looking into a lovely and rebellious face. Her white bosom heaved slightly with her quickened breathing, and her stance was feline, tigerish. Like the fire in the hearth belowstairs, she seemed to be sending off sparks.

He could not account for this mercurial change in her, but he regarded it as a lucky sign.

"A bit of brandy, my lady." He proffered her the cup with courtly grace.

Lenore took the silver cup, sipped it, considered him dangerously across its rim.

Christopher sensed the tumult in her. He was almost afraid to approach her in this mood, lest she bolt.

But of a sudden she set down her cup.

"You do not like the brandy?" he asked, for she had not finished her cup.

"It is excellent brandy, Mr. Dorn."

"Christopher."

"Christopher."

"Better yet—Chris."

"Chris." She spoke the name caressingly. Abruptly she reached up and loosened her hair, ran her fingers through it so that it tumbled down over her shoulders in a bright rippling cascade.

Dorn caught his breath. He gave her a sweet smile and set down his own cup, admiring the sudden gleam of white skin or black silk that showed through those long ribbons of red gold hair, turned to flame by the glow from the hearth.

" 'Twas not your brandy I came to sample," she murmured in a low rich voice.

A moment later she was in his arms.

A moment after that her body was bent back from the waist and Christopher was kissing her closed eyes, her hot cheeks, her gasping parted lips.

As his mouth found hers, a great shudder went through Lenore, and she gave a throbbing sob of surrender. Christopher felt her resistance melt and gripped her lissome body the tighter. One of his arms encircled her narrow waist, the palm of his hand pressed against the small of her back—and she lay against that arm languidly. With his other hand, he cradled her head, his fingers caressed the nape of her white neck. Now that hand moved slowly down her back. He was neatly unfastening the hooks that held her bodice, she knew, and moving with a speed that suggested experience in such matters! Lenore did not care. She pressed against him, every pliant motion of her body telling him that she was his—his to enjoy.

Now his warm tongue was probing between her parted lips and she was giving him back a fiery response. Dimly she was aware that her bodice had slipped down from her white shoulder and a familiar warm feeling raced through her veins as her senses came alive to a man's fierce tender touch.

With a swift jerk, his impatient fingers brought both her black silk bodice and her lacy chemise down to her waist. Her arms were pinioned by the sleeves but her breasts had surged free. She gasped as Christopher's lips left her mouth and traveled a scorching path down her pulsing throat and wandered across her bosom. A little involuntary cry escaped her ripe lips as his mouth paused to toy with a quivering rosy nipple. Her eyes were closed, lashes a dark fluttering line against her cheeks. Her head was thrown back, giving a swanlike line to her white throat. She felt the soft rasp of his silky golden beard against her bare skin, felt the tickle on her naked breast.

But even at that wild moment, her heart was flooded unbidden with memories. Rapturous memories. With her eyes tight closed, it was Geoffrey she kissed. Tense as a drawn bowstring, her treacherous body was responding to a memory—the memory of another man who had been her love, her life: Geoffrey Wyndham.

So rapt were they, neither of them heard the unlatched door open.

"I—I be sorry, sir!" babbled the startled voice of a chambermaid. "I thought ye were still downstairs and since ye were alone in this room, I thought ye'd not mind sharing it with another gentleman on such a fierce night, but since ye are not alone—"

No one heard anything she was saying because suddenly a hand grasped Christopher Dorn by the back of his coat and yanked him away from Lenore. A hard cuff against the shoulder blades with a swung saddlebag sent Christopher into a corner where his foot slipped and he went down on one leg, falling awkwardly.

The chambermaid screamed.

Lenore, cast adrift, staggered to retain her footing and her violet eyes flew open.

"Geoffrey!"

Before her, his dark fur-trimmed cloak covered with snow, and seeming to tower in his rage, stood Geoffrey. Snow-covered boots wide planted, he leant forward threateningly, angrier than she had ever seen him. His light gray eyes glared at her from his dark face, windows on a burning hell.

"Is this how ye greet me?" he snarled, his saddle-bags hitting the floor with a thump. "Half naked and in the arms of another man? All these weeks I've been searching for ye—and to find ye thus! I should kill ye for what ye have become!"

Lenore shrank back before his unleashed fury, but from the corner where he'd been flung, Christopher Dorn picked himself up and staggered forward. Apparently indestructible, only the chambermaid noticed how drunk he was.

"Why," he said pleasantly, his voice slurred. " 'Tis the tall gentleman who won a wager at Wells. 'Tis a bit late for ye to try to claim this lady for as ye can plainly see, she now prefers—"

The rest of his words were never uttered for Geoffrey turned on him. With his left hand he grasped the froth of lace at Christopher's throat, twisted it, spun him around by it, and with all the anger that was in him, his big fist smashed against Christopher's golden-bearded jaw, lifted his boots from the floor and sent him hurtling through the open doorway into the hall.

"Lor!!" squawked the chambermaid, as Dorn's flying body plummeted past her and struck the unlatched door across the hall. She gave another strangled shriek as the door flew open under this assault and Christopher sprawled inside, to lie senseless, his bloodshot eyes gone blank, in an inert heap upon the oaken floor.

"You have killed him!" cried Lenore. She was tugging futilely at her sleeves as she spoke. She fought dazedly to get her bodice up to cover her nakedness but it would not seem to obey her. One sleeve was caught on one of the hooks of her bodice and the material held firm.

"Nay, I've not killed your lover—though I should have, and you in the bargain," growled Geoffrey. He rubbed his bruised knuckles and thought she had never looked more beautiful, more desirable, this devil-woman who confronted him. Her breasts moved with rippling temptation as she struggled with her gown, her bright hair was tumbled, and a pulse beat in the hollow at the base of her throat.

All the way from London, after he had learned from a groom at the George how the pair of women had been put off a coach bound for Durham and had made private arrangements for their trip north, he had imagined her standing before him like this: her red gold hair spilling down over her white shoulders in a fiery shower, her soft lips parted, her violet eyes deepened with desire, her pale naked breasts gleaming in the golden candlelight—but for *him!* He had imagined her thus in *his* arms, not in the arms of some other man! And he had imagined them alone together, not with some chambermaid squawking, "Lor', sir, don't you kill her too!"

Your lover! He had called Chris her lover! Lenore drew herself up like a spitting cat. She had loved Geoffrey, dreamed of Geoffrey, kept herself free of entanglements with other men until this moment—and he dared accuse her!

"*Yes,* he is my lover!" she flashed, determined to hurt him even if it must be with a lie.

Geoffrey's face turned gray. For a moment he swayed there, like a great forest oak buffeted by some northern gale. Disgust and grief and the fierce hatred born of thwarted desire burned and fused in his gray eyes.

Had she but supplicated, had she but hung her head in shame, had she but pleaded with him to forgive her! But no—her head was lifted defiantly and that defiance was reflected in her eyes. In amazement, he saw that she even dared to look angry, this lustrous woman! As if *she* had been affronted—not at all as if she had just been caught in the very act of betraying him! His teeth ground.

And then, some latent devil in him awakened. All his life this woman had bedeviled him. She had worried his waking hours, robbed him of sleep, haunted his dreams. He had loved her, lost her, found her—only to lose her again.

And now at the end of his long search, to find her taunting him *with her lover!*

But was she not here? murmured that devil within him. Beautiful, desirable, unrepentent—*and within his grasp.* His body burned for her, his loins ached for her. What did her treachery matter at this moment? He wanted her, by God he would take her!

Now!

He flung aside hat and cloak.

Lenore caught that wicked gleam in Geoffrey's gray eyes and was aware of the flickering danger of that moment. Geoffrey aroused was a formidable adversary. He well might kill her.

But Lenore had never lacked for courage. She tossed her head. "See to Mr. Dorn—to *Christopher*," she instructed the chambermaid, with spiteful emphasis.

Christopher!

At this flaunting use of his rival's first name, all the blood in his body seemed to rush to Geoffrey's head and to ignite like a torch. He viewed his lady through a reddish haze.

"Get out!" he snarled at the chambermaid. She left with a bleat, and another "Lor!!" as he kicked the door shut, latched it and turned to face Lenore.

Lenore retreated warily to the other side of the room. She was still struggling with her bodice and the caught sleeve. She was tempted to rip the hook free, but it was her only good dress, she could not afford to tear it. Still she must be fully clothed if she was to regain her dignity. "You might at least help me with these hooks, Geoffrey!" she panted.

"Oh, I'll help ye with them!" He crossed the room at a bound, his heavy boots as he landed shaking the bare boards, and spun her about. She gasped as she felt his hard knuckles graze the small of her back, felt his long fingers forced down below the waistline of the black dress. There was a sudden yank and she felt the breath leave her body as the waistline was jerked inward, tightening like a vise around her. And then a sharp tearing sound as the material of both bodice and skirt was ripped away from the back and the entire dress tossed into a corner.

Lenore cried out in angry protest, but before she could turn she was grasped by her luxuriant hair and propelled stumbling toward the bed, helped onto it by a none too gentle swat on her naked bottom.

Flushed and sputtering, she landed on the bed in a furious heap, tangled in the remnants of her chemise. She had tumbled face downward into the smothering softness of the featherbed. She felt herself being buried in feathers although her arms and legs were flailing. With a choked cry, she managed to turn over and found herself looking up into a fierce, dark countenance. There was no comfort in the merciless smile that curved Geoffrey's lips and for a moment even her stout heart quailed.

"Damn you!" she cried, rallying. "You've torn up my only good dress!"

She heard him laugh, a nasty sound. "Doubtless your numerous lovers will provide you with others."

The words caught her like a blow, and she struck at his face with a choked sob, felt her wrist snatched up and held in a paralyzing grip.

From outside came the sound of running feet, and now there was a pounding on the door. The chambermaid had gone to fetch the landlord. She heard his voice, slightly atremble, demanding to know what was amiss.

Geoffrey tore his gaze from Lenore's vibrant form and lifted his big head. "I'm teaching my lady a lesson," he roared. "And ye'd be well advised to go away from that door, innkeeper, for I've a short temper and a long

129

pistol and I'll put a ball through it if ye do not heed me!"

"Whist!" sputtered the voice outside. "I did not know she was your lady!"

Lenore opened her mouth to refute that, but Geoffrey divined her intention. His hard mouth crushed hers and she felt the very breath sucked suddenly from her lungs. She thought he would desist but he did not. He was deliberately preventing her breathing.

Her eyes flew open in sudden terror, and she struggled impotently against him. An eternity passed. Now her senses were reeling. Just as the world blackened he lifted his head, gazed down at her menacingly.

"There are many ways to kill a faithless woman besides the knife," he murmured. "She can be smothered or"—his strong hands found her pulsing white throat, kneaded it threateningly—"strangled. Or I could just"—his smile was nasty—"toss you out of that window to freeze to death in a snowbank."

Lenore's breath and her courage came back in a rush together. "Someone would take me in!" she choked haughtily.

A flicker of admiration that she remained undaunted at such a moment played momentarily over the murk of his gray eyes.

"Ah, that's true," he muttered. "Off with your chemise," he snapped. "Obey me!"

"I'll not," cried Lenore in righteous indignation. "You do not own me, Geoffrey."

"Do I not?" His hands closed about her narrow waist with punishing pressure. "When I could snap your spine with a flick of my wrist?"

"Then be about it!" she stormed. "For I'll not submit to you!"

He gave a short brutal laugh and reached out and tore from her the last vestiges of her chemise.

Angrily she clawed at his face, felt her hand brushed aside as if it had been a feather—and then he was on top of her, the weight of his hard body sending her down farther into the smothering softness of the down mattress, which closed around them like a warm cloak.

Lenore was panting. Her pulse beat furiously, and her whole body was tingling with excitement—and fury. And something else, the climax of a great longing, a dream come true.

Here was Geoffrey at last! A raging Geoffrey, true, but—she had imagined him here in her arms and her vivid dream had become reality. There was no tenderness in him tonight but Lenore gloried in his touch. Anger forgotten, her whole body thrilled to him and with a little moan she gave herself up to joy.

A tremor went through Geoffrey's taut muscles at this sudden evidence of surrender in his rebellious lady. But the fierce passions unleashed in him would know no abatement until he had taken her, until he had made her fully his. Under his insistent rhythmic assault, her senses wavered Then her whole body seemed to catch fire, and she was caught up in the heat of his passion, lifted by it, exalted. She was spinning out of control toward some unknown destiny that shimmered before her in the high wild peaks of ecstasy.

With all the fierce concentration of lovers, they swayed and murmured and touched and loved and were overcome with the vastness of it, this powerful emotion that turned the featherbed in that plain room into a place of enchantment, and the room into a palace, and melted anger into joy.

Floating down from the heights at last, Lenore felt a deep bubbling of the spirit, as if some new spring had been plumbed and the snowy world outside their window had turned to flowering green.

"Geoffrey . . ." she murmured. On a long-drawn sigh she reached up and lovingly caressed his neck.

To her astonishment he pulled away. He was rising, pulling together his trousers. His dark face was haggard, spent— but resolute.

"You're—you're not leaving?" she whispered in disbelief.

For answer he gave her a hard look, bent to sweep up his plumed hat in one big hand, his saddlebags in the other.

"Where are you going?" she demanded in alarm.

"Away from you," he muttered, heading for the door. "Ye can go back to your lover, now I've done with ye."

Lenore sat up. She brushed at her eyes, as if to strike away cobwebs. Looking down at her legs, she saw bruises along her calves. Dazed, she realized that he had taken her like any whore—with his boots on.

"Get out!" she cried brokenly. "Get out and don't come back!"

His voice flicked over her like a whiplash on a raw wound. "Have no fear," he growled. "Ye've seen the last of me."

That he was fleeing from her witchery lest it seduce him into forgiving her, she could not guess.

Wide-eyed and sorrowful, she watched him throw open the door and charge into the hallway, almost toppling the frightened chambermaid, who had been hanging about anxiously near the door and now stepped back against the corridor wall with a screech, flinging up her apron to shield her face as if this charging madman might do her bodily harm.

As the door slammed, Lenore's anger melted. Even though he had left her with words that fell on her like a striking whip, she no longer had any doubt what she wanted. It had rung out in her mind like a gong, with the slamming of the door. She wanted to be his again, only his. Wife or mistress, what did it matter? She could not bear to lose him.

"Geoffrey!" Her voice was a wail. Impatiently she thrust her feet into her slippers, snatched up the remnants of her black silk dress and wrapped them about her. With the material flapping around her she surged forward after him. But his long booted legs were already taking the stairs three at a time.

"Lor!!" cried the chambermaid as Lenore flung past.

Geoffrey had already reached the bottom step, and now he was plunging through the outer door, but Lenore followed him anyway, running down through the now almost deserted common room—deserted except for one or two velvet-clad gentlemen who were sleeping off the night's drink with their heads on their velvet arms, snoring loudly, and one late-stayer, drowsing and smoking, who jumped to his feet and dropped his long clay pipe at the rousing sight of her.

Unmindful of her disheveled appearance, the wide expanse of naked skin, Lenore swept forward in her rags of black silk and ran after Geoffrey. She struggled with the heavy inn door which he had banged shut behind him—and then she was through it and out into the blowing snow.

The wind caught at her hair and whipped it over her face, blinding her. The cold caught at her throat and seared her lungs. Uncaring that she was not wearing her pattens, that the snow was closing around her ankles with an icy grip even where it had been earlier brushed away, she waded through the dark innyard to the stables.

There a surprised stableboy, just about to unsaddle Geoffrey's horse, leaped aside as the saddlebags were tossed back on and Geoffrey seized the reins.

"For your trouble." Geoffrey tossed him a coin and led the tired horse to the stable door.

"Did they not have room for ye?" cried the stable-boy. "For 'tis warm here in the hayloft."

"Thank ye, I'll find accommodations elsewhere," was the terse answer.

"Geoffrey!" From the open stable door, Lenore's wail reached him, and he flinched as if he had been shot.

As if he did not see her standing there, he marched the big horse past her into the innyard, vaulted to the saddle.

"Geoffrey!" Lenore surged toward him, grasped the nearest boot, clung to it. She could not let him go without telling him that she had no lover, that she had lied, meaning to hurt him. "Wait—oh, Geoffrey, let me explain!"

His harsh laugh rang out. "Explain, is it?" he mocked. "And how can ye explain away what I saw with my own two eyes? Let go of my boot, ye lying strumpet!"

He reached down and thrust her away from him and was off through the courtyard on his winded horse, his dark cloak flapping in the wind.

Lenore had slipped as he pushed her, and now she crumpled up in the snow, weeping. When she looked up, he had gone. The wind was freezing the tears on her lashes and her toes felt numb as she staggered to her feet. Looking down, she saw that a scratch from the rowel of one of Geoffrey's spurs had drawn a trickle of blood down one bare arm.

Half-frozen, she stumbled back to the inn, where the same chambermaid waited, big-eyed, at the door.

"Give me your apron," said Lenore, for the gentleman with the broken pipe hovered fascinated in the background. And when the girl had untied her apron and Lenore had covered herself with it, she asked wearily, "The gentleman upstairs, Christopher Dorn, how does he fare?"

"He is not dead, Mistress. He gave a great groan as I left and asked who had struck him."

"See to him." Lenore tore off her ear baubles. They were cheap but they were all she had. She pressed them into the girl's eager hand. "And tell him—tell him I left with the gentleman who just rode away."

The chambermaid looked startled but she bobbed her head and hurried back upstairs.

Her fingers pressed against her throbbing temples, Lenore declined the proffered help of the gentleman with the broken pipe and somehow made it up the stairs to her room. For a shuddering moment she paused, leaned dizzily against the wall and tried to comprehend all that had taken place in such a short space of time. Then with a sob she made it blindly into her room and managed to latch the door before she crumpled up into an agonized heap on the floor, hugging her knees and rocking with agony.

Geoffrey had come for her, as she had wanted him to come for her, as she had dreamed in her treacherous heart he would come for her. And found her—thus! She who had always been so faithful!

She told herself dully that she had set her foot on a road that was trod by men like Christopher Dorn, and now there would be no turning back.

Bitterly she wept for a world that was gone.

Morning brought with it a kind of harsh sanity.

Stiff with cold, she stirred at the sound of pots and pans being banged belowstairs as the kitchen help moved about. She lifted her head and saw a grayish light stealing through the frosted panes.

Geoffrey, she told herself, would not have left York on a winded horse last night. He must have turned in at some other inn, roused the landlord, demanded a room. If she hurried, she could still find him, reason with him. Surely by now his anger would be cooled enough that she could explain!

Without disturbing Mistress Potts, who still slept heavily, her tired body probably still trying to digest last evening's heavy supper, Lenore rose to her feet. She pulled off the black silk dress, hating it, feeling somehow that the beautiful seductive dress had cost her her lover. And then the lacy chemise. Shivering, she put on the sober traveling garb in which she had arrived, slipped into her pattens, threw on her cloak and woolen hood, and hurried downstairs to ask the location of nearby inns.

There were three, she was told.

The first had been full since yestermorn and had taken in no overnight travelers at all last evening. The sun was risen now, but the story was the same at the second inn.

At the third they remembered a gentleman who, though they had protested they were full, had announced he'd stretch out by the fire in the common room for the night, could they but provide him with a fresh horse in the morning, for he was a mind to push back to London, snow or no snow.

That gentleman was Geoffrey Wyndham.

He had ridden south with the dawn.

Her face had gone pale as she heard this, and Lenore sagged against a table of the common room. Geoffrey was gone. He would hear no explanation from her now.

The alarmed landlord called out for a hot posset, some rum, anything—he'd a lady here about to faint.

But Lenore struggled back to an upright position. "I'm all right," she said hoarsely, and ploughed back through the heavy snow to the Fox and Bow. There she made it up the stairs and leant against the wall outside her room and closed her eyes.

But even then she could still see Geoffrey's accusing face, his gray eyes burning with a kind of devil's light flickering in them. She could still hear him say, *Ye've seen the last of me . . . let go of my boot, ye lying strumpet!* Could still feel him push her away.

What a fool she had been! She had let her yearning for Geoffrey trap her into kissing a stranger, so that she might enjoy the luxury of imagining herself once again in his arms.

She had lost him—again. And she was bitterly certain that this time it would be forever.

Someone was walking down the hall. She did not want to be seen leaning against the wall, dissolved in tears. Lifting her head, she dashed away those tears and straightened her back, turned slightly so that the gentleman passing might not see her tear-stained face.

For of everything she had lost along the way—and she had lost so much: her virtue, her good name, her daughter, her lover, her home, her childhood friends—she had not lost her pride. Pride, in a woman like Lenore, would be the last to go.

BOOK II:
Lorena–
Too Beautiful

The Cotswolds

Chapter 10

The green, mystic hills of the Cotswolds, which darkened almost to black where the forest thickened, were covered now with snow. Ice had frozen over the ponds, and the scraping of skates rang out in the crisp cold air. Soon great drifts of snow would be piled in the valleys that cut deep gashes through rolling uplands walled with stone. The sparkling trout streams would freeze over and the footprints of little woodland creatures would lead to hidden lairs concealed deep in the brush. Even now snow was flung like a bridal veil over all the rounded hills, and the Cotswolds slumbered, a white enchanted world, waiting for the bursting thaw and the coming of spring.

Icicles hung from the eaves but the chimneys of Twainmere smoked merrily as bright fires blazed from the big stone hearths. Throughout, the village kitchens were filled with a spicy aroma as the late fruits of the fall harvest were cooked in big iron or copper pots.

In the vicarage kitchen young Lorena, demurely garbed in a dress of village-woven gray homespun, was skillfully skimming cream from the top of a large crock of milk with a wooden spoon. Around her the copper pots sparkled, for she had just scoured them.

The vicar was away making calls, and she and Aunt Flora would have the house to themselves till after supper, for the vicar would doubtless accept a supper invitation from one of his flock.

Now over her shoulder Lorena flung a question: "Aunt Flora, do you believe the Five Knights were once alive?"

With her arms around the round wooden butter churn as she moved it to a better position, Flora hid a smile. Lorena was so precocious and at the same time so naive! Last spring, at Robbie's request, Flora had accompanied elderly Goody Caldwell to join her equally ancient--but much richer—brother who could take care of her. It had been an overnight trip and she had taken Lorena with her.

On the way, they had stopped to see one of the sights of the Cotswolds—the famous Whispering Knights, fifty-eight gray megaliths that rose in a rough circle, the tallest standing more than a foot above gaunt Flora's head. Lorena had never forgotten the King Stone which rose in solitary grandeur, and near it the Five Knights which seemed to bend together as if whispering. Round-eyed, the girl had listened to the legend which another visitor at the stones told them: that these five stones had once been men of blood and fire and vigor—but when they had turned against their king, a witch had turned them all to stone. The king and his army likewise were turned to stone, but the witch herself had turned into an elder tree.

Flora had grown up on legends like this in Scotland, where the ghosts of ancient warriors haunted the age-old hills, but to Lorena it had all been fresh and new.

When they came home, Lorena had touched the big elder tree that grew behind the vicarage with awe, and asked Flora if this tree too had once been a witch.

Flora had laughed and given the child an offhand

"no," but now she turned sober at the question, for she knew that Robbie would be angry if he knew Lorena harbored such heathen thoughts.

"I don't think they were ever alive," she said meditatively, "but there are ignorant people who believe such things, Lorena. Ye must learn to sort and sift what ye would believe and not put your faith in fancies. There, ye've taken enough cream from that milk," she added energetically, glad to be on firm ground again.

Lorena sighed and pushed aside the earthenware crock. Wistfully she licked the cream from the wooden spoon. In her secret heart, she *wanted* to believe in the legend of the Five Knights, that they had once been real men, great warriors who had sat there leaning upon their swords and plotting. She had hoped that Flora too would believe in the legend.

Flora set her to peeling russet-skinned apples for their supper, and Lorena worked for a while in silence, wielding her small sharp knife. Then she turned and asked Flora a question that had increasingly been troubling her of late.

"Aunt Flora." Her voice was hesitant, for some instinct deep within her made her dread the answer. "Why does Kate Tilson hate me so?"

It was a question that had been long in coming. At first she had thought it just a childish enmity, this fierce animosity of Kate's. After all, they were the same size and near the same age and evenly matched in the village games. Kate, with her better clothes and freer ways, Lorena had discerned, had wanted feverishly to win out, to best the cloistered vicar's ward.

But no, it was more than that, and Kate's attacks had intensified of late.

Last week at market, she had noticed Kate spitefully whispering behind her hand to two other girls and giving Lorena significant looks. When Lorena had passed by, they had turned away, giggling maliciously.

Lorena had ignored that, as she had ignored so many other things where Kate was concerned.

Last Sunday in church, Kate had reached out a silver-buckled shoe into the aisle and tripped Lorena as she followed Flora's straight back up to the vicar's front pew. Lorena had sprawled forward on old Goody Kettle and knocked her cap awry. Blushing and stammering apologies, Lorena had made it to their pew. But when she had looked back, she had seen Kate's blue eyes, that mirrored the color of her own, gleaming in triumph.

The vicar had punished Lorena for making a spectacle of herself in church. For three hours she had had to stand on a stool in the corner facing the wall, and later had to commit to memory a whole long passage of the Scriptures.

Kate, of course, had escaped scot-free, though several of the boys—the more sharp-eyed ones, such as Benny Trent, who never missed much, and Tabby Aylesbury, who never missed *anything*—had observed the incident.

Ever since, Lorena had been spoiling to "have it out" with Kate. Actually she had yearned to knock her down. Kate left right after church with her mother, the Widow Lizzie Tilson, so there was no chance then. But the next day Lorena had been carrying two fresh wheaten loaves Flora had baked, in a basket to Mistress Potter, who was down with the ague again, when she had come across Kate strolling by.

Lorena had come to a full stop on the icy street as she confronted Kate. "Kate Tilson." Her breath steamed in the cold air and her young voice held a warning. "If you *ever* trip me again—in church or anywhere else—I'll black both your eyes!"

Kate too came to a stop in the street. Her woolen-gloved hands came to rest on the saffron wool kirtle that covered her slim swaying hips. Arms akimbo, standing tall on her pattens, Kate gave Lorena an insolent look.

"Who says *I* tripped you?" she challenged.

"I say it!" cried Lorena. "For you know you did!"

Kate swaggered a step closer to Lorena—they were standing now about ten feet apart—and her blue eyes burned with hatred. "You're a liar!" she hissed. "But that's not surprising since your mother was a harlot and you were born on the wrong side of the blanket!"

Lorena's face turned white. "That's not true! None of that's true and you know it!"

"You're not good enough to speak to me!" Kate lifted a haughty shoulder and, having delivered her parting shot, turned to go.

Hardly aware of what she was doing, Lorena reached down, seized a heavy clod that had been kicked up by the wheel of a passing cart, and hurled it at the departing Kate. The icy clod caught Kate squarely on her saffron bottom and gave her a whack as solid as the toe of a boot.

Kate gave a yelp and whirled about, glaring at Lorena. She bent down and seized a clod of her own and flung it at Lorena's fair head. Lorena ducked and the clod struck harmlessly against a low stone wall behind her, breaking up against the gray-gold lichened stones.

Still angry, Lorena picked up a big piece of ice and hurled it at Kate. Kate deftly danced aside and the clod knocked off Tom Prattle's hat as he staggered unsteadily toward home.

With a roar Tom turned to pursue Lorena, who dropped her basket as she fled and had to circle back for it. Tom was still running after her drunkenly, shouting that the wicked wench had attacked him in the street, when the vicar happened along.

For that, Lorena had been put on bread and water for three days and switched painfully with a willow switch.

Her problems with Kate had gone on for so long, she couldn't even remember when they had begun. Now when Flora didn't immediately answer, she felt suddenly frightened. She almost wished she could take the question back.

Flora turned from her butter churn and studied young Lorena's beautiful troubled face. *Kate Tilson . . . Lizzie's child.* How to tell Lorena: *Kate is your father's child, that is why she hates you. She knows it, Lizzie knows it, the whole town knows it. But Kate was born in wedlock because when Jamie was killed at Worcester, Lizzie promptly married an old man to give her child-to-be a name. Your reckless young mother wasn't so lucky, Lorena. Oh, they called their handfasting a marriage, but Jamie died before I could boot him to the kirk. And so ye were born out of wedlock, does she taunt ye with that too?*

Ah, but the child wasn't ready to hear all that. She'd told Lorena such merry tales about her carefree young father—and indeed Jamie had had so many good qualities: he'd been generous, kind. But she couldn't bear to see that sweet young face fall with the realization of what Jamie had really been—a playboy who loved them and left them.

Her own voice was hesitant as she answered, giving the lie to her words. "Kate doesn't hate you, Lorena, you mustn't think that."

"She does!" cried Lorena passionately. "She said I was born on the wrong side of the blanket, and that my mother was a harlot—and that's when I threw the clod at her!"

So that, no doubt, was how Tom Prattle's hat came to be knocked off—he got caught in the middle of a battle between Kate and Lorena. Flora's mouth tightened. "Lenore was no harlot. Wild she was, and gave her heart without thought of gain—but never a harlot. Remember that, Lorena—and don't be throwing clods. 'Tis unlady-like."

"I missed her anyway after the first one," sighed Lorena. "But *why* does Kate hate me so, Aunt Flora?"

"Tomorrow we'll dip candles," Flora said, changing the subject. She knew that was a task Lorena enjoyed. "We have enough tallow now."

Lorena sighed. Candle-dipping was fun, but answers were better. It was always like this with Aunt Flora—no answers on the important things.

But the town was beginning to provide her with answers. Even though she lived at the vicarage, yesterday at the market she had heard Mistress Warder, who lived down the street, mutter, "Illegitimate little snip! She has that same look her mother had. Well, she won't grow up to marry *my* son, I'll see to that!" She'd been looking right at Lorena.

"People say I look exactly like Kate," she muttered in a disgruntled voice.

"Well, ye're both fair-haired and fair-skinned with blue eyes."

"So is half the village!" protested Lorena. "Why do people have to say I look like *her?*"

Because you do. You have the same coloring, the same look, the same size. Wayward! You can't help it, but it's there. Everyone sees it.

Aloud she said, "Hand me the butter paddle, Lorena."

Her shoulders drooped as she handed Flora the paddle, and Flora said kindly, "You haven't used your skates lately. 'Tis cold enough that the ice should be very good on Sutter's Pond."

"Oh, Aunt Flora," breathed Lorena, looking guiltily at the butter churn. "Could I?"

"Aye, but be home before dark."

Glowing with happiness at this unexpected outing, Lorena flew to get her skates. She threw her dark woolen cloak over her gray dress and affixed her thick fleecy forest green hood above her shining hair. With her skates slung over her shoulders, she walked jauntily through the vicarage gate and down the snowy main street of Twainmere.

Long before she reached Sutter's Pond, she could hear the ringing skates striking the ice. As she topped the little wooded rise just above the pond, she could hear laughter and happy, shouting voices.

Lorena stood for a moment atop that rise beneath the snowy branches of a big beech tree and studied the

145

scene. The pale winter sun diffusing through a milky white sky illuminated an irregularly shaped pond on which a number of figures glided and danced on shining blades. Most of them trailed long bright woolen scarves or wore colorful hoods. On the snowy bank below her someone had lit a small bonfire and a group were warming their hands there. Their laughter floated to her over the ice.

Lorena headed down the slope toward the bonfire.

As she approached, she was disappointed to see that they were all older, and with the diffidence of the young and alone she sheered off, walked on farther and sat down on a little hillock of snow to put on her skates. Across the pond, she now saw with distaste, was Kate Tilson, dressed in brilliant green and swirling in big figure eights. Kate was surrounded by a laughing group of boys who swooped in and out on their skates. Kate, whose mother never bothered to chaperon her, was always surrounded by boys.

Her skates on, Lorena stepped onto the ice and glided toward the center of the pond. She was a good skater, but she felt self-conscious, for everybody there knew she was the vicar's ward. None of the boys glided forward to take her arm to dance on skates as they did so lightly with the other village girls. They felt shy in Lorena's presence although she had the same wild look as Kate Tilson. But with Kate, who had easy ways, they felt entirely comfortable.

Alone, yet feeling less awkward now that she was swirling about on the ice, Lorena swung and circled on her flashing skates. Now she spun into a wide figure eight, and then another and another. She had forgotten the world and was now enjoying the cold wind on her face and the white glitter of the ice beneath her feet, listening with joy to the ring and clash of her skates across that shining surface.

In her inattention, she had swung too close to that part of the pond just now controlled by Kate Tilson and her admirers. Lorena looked up to see Kate flashing by, her bright skirts billowing. Kate had a sneer on her pretty face, and Lorena tossed her head and looked determinedly away. She wasn't going to let Kate Tilson spoil *her* day. Kate didn't own the ice!

"Watch this," murmured Kate over her shoulder to one of the boys who clustered about her admiringly. She waited until Lorena glided by again, and went into a turn which brought her face to face with Lorena.

"Hepworth!" Kate called piercingly. "Hepworth!" One of the group skating nearby snickered.

Hepworth? Lorena gave her back a puzzled stare. Hepworth was the name of those people who lived on a small farm just out of town on the way to Maude's house. Martin Hepworth was nearly forty, a widower who had six months ago remarried a comely young woman from Cirencester. She kept to herself and nobody knew much about her. Three months ago, Martin Hepworth had fallen out of his barn loft and landed on the cutting edge of the big scythe he used to mow his hay. The scythe had been rusty, and though the wound had not been deep, it had festered. Now it was anybody's guess whether he would be up to next spring's planting, for he had become a semi-invalid. The vicar often went over to pray with him, for Martin Hepworth had always been a confirmed churchgoer, a man of God-fearing ways—and now he was in pain much of the time. The vicar usually took with him a basket of hot cross buns or a pasty and came back with the basket filled with oat cakes by Hepworth's young wife.

Lorena didn't even know the Hepworths!

But she knew and understood the taunting look on Kate's face, the insulting note in Kate's voice.

Kate, having made her point, tossed her head and grasped young Abner Ferris by the arm, skating away with him.

Lorena drifted on by, turned with a clang of skates on ice and skated back, making a big lazy circle. That circle again brought her past where Kate was making showy figure eights that showed her striped stockings for her appreciative audience.

"Oat cakes!" Kate hissed at her as she passed, and behind her there was a nervous titter.

Lorena's skates came to such a fast stop they cut up the ice. She didn't care what gibberish Kate was spewing, she didn't like her tone.

"If you've something to say to me, Kate Tilson," she drawled, lifting her head in a disdainful gesture, "try to use entire sentences. I realize that may be a little hard for you, since you don't read and write as I do, but if you really *try*—"

With a screech, Kate tore free from Abner, for the fact that she couldn't read and write while Lorena could had always been galling to her. Green skirts flying, she sprang for Lorena and sent her sprawling across the cold ice. Lorena, almost knocked out of breath by this sudden onslaught, rolled over in time to avoid a kick from the metal runner of Kate's skate. As Kate whizzed by, Lorena reached out and grasped her by a striped ankle, and Kate came down on the ice with a satisfying crash beside her.

Kate gave a sob of fury and gained her knees. Lorena slashed at Kate's face with her gloved fingers. Kate took a bite at her hand and missed.

Moments later their fingers were locked in each others' hair. They were surrounded by a cheering crowd of boys, egging them on. Lorena felt Kate's knee jab painfully into her thigh and retaliated with an elbow gouge in the upper arm that caused Kate to grunt. Kate's head was being pulled back by Lorena's relentless grip upon her blond hair, and now Kate bent her knees and brought them up, meaning to bring her skate runners down upon Lorena's legs. Lorena guessed Kate's intention and gave a cruel twist to the other girl's hair that caused her to roll over in pain. At that point Kate let go of Lorena's hair, and her long fingernails—she had already lost one fur-lined glove in the tussle, just as Lorena had already lost her hood—raked over Lorena's face.

At that point, Lorena too let go of her adversary's hair, and both contestants began to flail at each other with real fury, but not much damage until big Tabby Aylesbury, just arrived with his skates, pulled them apart.

"Here now!" He grasped Lorena around the waist and tugged her away as with a none-too-gentle straight arm he skidded the other combatant away across the ice. "Little girls don't fight—they call each other names!"

On her knees a dozen feet from them and just scrambling up, minus a glove and with her skirt torn, Kaze did just that. Her hair, pale as Lorena's, was tumbling down and she was sobbing as she called Lorena all the names she could think of before she stumbled to the bank and sat down.

In Tabby's restraining arms Lorena was shaking and fighting back tears. This skirmish with Kate had been coming for a long time, and it had felt good to find her fingers locked in Kate's hemp white tresses, yanking away while Kate yelled. There was even a pale strand or two caught in her fingers still.

She made a last valiant attempt to struggle back toward Kate and renew the battle, but Tabby's arm held her like a vise.

"Simmer down," he said sternly, but his gray eyes looked worried. "There's blood on your face, Lorena. D'ye want me to take you home?"

Ordinarily Lorena would have been flattered by all this attention from one of the older lads, but she was so humiliated by her recent encounter and all the things Kate had called her and the way the group around Kate had snickered, that she just wanted to get away by herself.

"No," she said, muffled, relaxing at last against Tabby's strong arm. "I can get home all right by myself." He had eased her over to the bank by now, some distance from Kate and her admirers, and she reached down to take off her skates. Her hand shook a little.

"I'll take you home." Tabby's voice was kind. "Here let me do that." He dropped on one knee and gently removed her skates, then stood her on her feet in the snow. "I've seen Kate lash out at ye before," he said cheerfully. "But then I guess sisters always fight."

"*Sisters!*" Lorena stared at him, thunderstruck. "Kate's *not* my sister!" she shrilled.

"Half sister," he corrected himself, and her jaw dropped. Tabby frowned, his dark brows coming together uneasily. "You mean you didn't know?" he asked, puzzled. "But the whole town knows!"

"No, I didn't," she said in a sulky voice. "But I guess you're going to tell me, Tabby Aylesbury!"

Tabby meditated about that, drumming his big strong fingers against his lean thigh. "I guess you ought to know about it," he said thoughtfully. "Though why the vicar didn't tell you—!"

"Go on!" she almost shouted.

"All right!" Irritated by her tone, Tabby pushed her to a seated position in the snow, glaring down at her from his considerable height. "Your father had another girl besides your mother—several other girls, but Lizzie was the main one. After he got killed at Worcester, she got married real quick to a man near ninety. And had a baby—Kate. Premature, they said. Living picture of your father—just like you."

Lorena jumped up. "It's a lie!" she shouted. "I'm not related to *her!*" Forgetting her skates and hood, she stumbled off rebelliously through the snow.

Tabby sighed and watched her go. They were both little beauties, Kate and Lorena. Kate had money and pretty clothes—she was wilder. But he liked Lorena better. Though Tabby didn't know it, it was her mother's fiery nature that he admired in Lorena, her reckless spirit. Lorena was every inch Lenore's daughter.

Lorena was crying by the time she reached the vicarage. She didn't want to be Kate's sister. It was bad enough that people said she was born out of wedlock, that handfasting wasn't a real marriage, but this was worse!

Blind with tears, she exploded through the front door of the vicarage and into Flora's arms.

"There there! Look at you! However did you get your face scratched like that? Let me wash it off before Robbie gets home. And your cloak's torn! Lorena, where is your hood, where are your skates?"

It was all too much. The whole story came pouring out between sobs, and Flora stroked Lorena's hair and held her. "I suppose I should have told you," she sighed. "But I thought it would only hurt you, and that you'd learn all about it soon enough. 'Tis all so long ago, Lorena. What can it matter now?"

"It—it matters," gasped Lorena, dashing away her tears with her knuckles. "Now I know why Kate hates me!"

"You're the living proof that her mother wasn't a virtuous woman," said Flora ironically. "And I guess it rankles. Poor Kate."

"Poor Kate!" Lorena was indignant. *"She* has friends, and red and green petticoats, and striped stockings! She can do anything she wants, her mother doesn't care where she is or who she's with!"

"While you are cooped up here in the vicarage practicing your penmanship and wearing gray dresses. I know. But you're growing up, Lorena. The world is opening up for you."

There was a knock on the door. Lorena turned away lest some visitor see her scratched face, but it was Tabby's cheerful voice at the door.

"Here's Lorena's skates and hood," he said, handing them to Flora. "She took a fall on the ice," he added tentatively.

Flora smiled. "Thank you, Tabby. I know how it happened. Lorena has told me. Come in and have some hot chocolate with us."

He shook his head with a grin and his white teeth

flashed. "Thank ye, but I'll be getting back to the pond. I had a mind to take a turn or two on the ice." He hesitated. "I'm afraid I spoke out of turn, told Lorena some things about Kate." He cast a worried look at Lorena's stiff back.

"It was time someone did, Tabby. I should have told her myself."

Their eyes met. They understood each other, the tall lad and the gaunt Scotswoman.

Tabby turned to go. "Doesn't matter who your sister is, Lorena," he called back to her as he left. "You'll grow up to be the prettiest girl in town!"

Lorena turned and stole a look at his tall form as he went whistling out the gate.

"I like that boy," said Flora, closing the door. "He reminds me of Jamie when he was that age. Carefree. Lighthearted. And no meanness in him."

Perhaps, she thought, *Tabby and Lorena . . . some-day . . .*

York to Newcastle

Chapter 11

Lenore had hardly arrived back in her room at the Fox and Bow, before Elias Plum's big knuckles were pounding on the door.

"It's stopped snowing and the sky looks to be clearing," he announced merrily. "We'd best be off for 'twill be slow going over these drifted roads."

"What? What?" cried Mistress Potts, lurching awake with a start. Seeing that Lenore was fully dressed for departure, "Oh, is it late? Have ye let me oversleep?"

"No. There's time to dress—and breakfast too." Lenore went to the door, opened it a crack. "We'll be ready shortly," she said in a low voice, for she did not want Christopher Dorn—if he was awake—to hear her voice and know that she had not ridden away with Geoffrey.

She could not face Dorn this morning, she would not know what to say to him. Now, she realized that Christopher Dorn *had* attracted her, that she had been drawn to him, held as by the sudden crackling of a fireplace log when it sends out a shower of sparks. But she had not really admitted this honest attraction; instead she had been thinking of Geoffrey when he took her in his arms. She was ashamed of herself. It was best she not see him ever again.

She bestirred herself. Elias Plum was speaking to her. "I'll be waiting for ye downstairs." His wide grin was admiring "But try to move smart, ladies, for there's a long day ahead."

There was a long life ahead that must be got through as well. a life without Geoffrey, but Lenore did not want to think about that. She would live out her future, day by day, she told herself. She would not look back.

Today the problem was to get Mistress Potts off on her difficult journey northward. Quickly Lenore packed up their things fought back a desire to rip to shreds the black silk dress that had brought her no luck at all, and went down to supervise the removal of their baggage to the cart while Mistress Potts finished powdering her face.

Lenore came back shivering into an almost deserted common room, for in a day when stage coaches left with the dawn or before, the snow-stranded travelers at the Fox and Bow were taking advantage of this rare opportunity to sleep late. She found Mistress Potts, who had puffed downstairs lugging her little leathern chest, already seating her plump form on a bench and calling for her breakfast.

"A roll and a cup of chocolate will be enough for me," Lenore said. To Mistress Potts' indignant protests, she assured. "I'm not really hungry."

Breakfast was, for Lenore, a nerve-wracking experience. With each creak of the stairs she expected to see Christopher Dorn's accusing face. She was so jumpy, her face was so white and set, that Mistress Potts remarked on her "distemper" and innocently offered Lenore a bit of her "salts."

Lenore wished that what ailed her could be cured by "salts"!

"I'll be fine," she said mechanically, to forestall any

other proffered medications. Then in a weary attempt to get her mind off Geoffrey and her savage self-recriminations, she shifted her thoughts to Wallham. "You told me you'd heard from Amos often, Mistress Potts. When was the last time?"

The older woman did not answer. Instead she brushed aside a third helping of pancakes and rose. "Don't dawdle, Lenore," she said on an imperious note. "We mustn't keep the driver waiting. 'Tis a long hard way to Durham."

Lenore's senses were too dulled by heartache to realize that her questions were being dodged.

Once settled in the cart, which cut off her view of all but the bright blue sky overhead, she turned to look at Mistress Potts, crouched down among the baggage. The older woman was so bundled up she looked more like a bale of goods wrapped for shipment than a woman, and now she staggered up, clutching a chest for support, and reseated herself with a groan beside Lenore among the mountainous luggage.

"If this stuff shifts too much, we'll be bruised black and blue," muttered Lenore.

"Don't talk," admonished Mistress Potts. "The cold wind will make your throat hurt as we travel. Here, wrap your woolen scarf over your mouth as I do."

"Are ye all right back there?" called Elias Plum. He was affixing the leathern covering of the cart which blacked out the sky. Through a crack where the leather top met the wooden cart side they could see his eyes peering at them. "Sure ye've brought everything?" When Mistress Potts bobbed her swathed head vigorously and Lenore said, "Yes, Mr. Plum," the eyes disappeared, and the body of the cart lurched as Elias clambered up. Then they heard the whip snap smartly over the huge plough horses' patient heads, and they shambled off on what turned out to be a miserable journey. For past York, and the great Roman Way that had led into it, the roads became almost impassable.

The luggage swayed perilously and listed, tumbling

down and sliding against them bruisingly as the heavy cart bounced and lurched over the road. Mistress Potts was well padded against these onslaughts and only grunted or gave an occasional complaining "Oof!" But Lenore, in her borrowed fustian cloak, soon felt that all her bones were broken and that she must be a mass of bruises. Even Mistress Potts was in a bad way when at midday they stopped at a roadside inn for a hot meal, and Lenore had already decided that she would ride up beside the driver for the rest of the way, after wedging Mistress Potts in between the bounding luggage as best she could.

Mistress Potts, however, showed remarkable powers of recovery, for she seemed completely revived by roasted mallard and teal washed down with tankards of ale. The inn was deserted of travelers. There was only one long board in the low-ceilinged common room, so Elias ate with them. He wolfed down his food and kept shifting his position, somehow managing to nudge Lenore's thigh with his knee from time to time. Lenore, to elude him, edged toward Mistress Potts, who drummed her fingers on the table, giving the impression of one lost in thought. Lenore was about to chide Elias, who had just painfully nudged a spot on her thigh already bruised by falling luggage, when Mistress Potts spoke up sharply.

"The road is too mired with all this soft snow," she announced. "Today was a bit warmer than yesterday. If only it would turn colder!" She sank back again, biting her fingers as she meditated.

Lenore forgot Elias's encroachments and gave her companion an astonished look. All the older woman's remarks since the cart had started out this morning had had to do with the cold and now she was wishing it would turn *colder*? Puzzled, she turned to Elias, who was nodding his big head in agreement.

"The lady be right," he told Lenore. "If the roads would freeze over, so there'd be hard-frozen ground under the snow instead of soft mud in the ruts, we'd have an easier time of it."

"Sled runners!" Mistress Potts snapped her fingers.

"We'll have to affix sled runners. And we must lie over here until they're attached, for we'll never reach Durham over these roads on wheels."

"Removing the wheels and putting on sled runners will cost money," Elias demurred. He frowned—and mercifully removed his bony knee away from Lenore's bruised thigh as he fidgeted. "I'd not thought to be put to that extra expense when I made ye my price."

"Here then." Mistress Potts was busy feeling about in her velvet purse. "Here's extra money, enough to affix the runners and more. And 'tis all yours if ye get us to Wallham before winter closes in."

Lenore considered privately that winter had already "closed in," but to northern-bred Mistress Potts apparently it had not. Elias's hazel eyes brightened as he leaned forward to scoop up the coins Mistress Potts had put upon the table. " 'Twill be enough for the runners," he declared. "And maybe enough to buy a gift for my new sweetheart." His roguish glance lingered on Lenore.

Lenore busied herself spooning up her custard and pretended not to understand. She had had about enough nudging. When Elias made no move to go, she rose. "If we're staying over, I'd best see about a room for us for the night, Mistress Potts."

As she walked across the hard-packed earthen floor toward the landlord, bent over his wine kegs in the corner, Elias's big cheerful voice followed her ringingly. "I'll get ye to yer destination, ladies, never fear, or my name's not Elias Plum!"

A bare little room under the eaves was secured. Elias himself would sleep downstairs, sprawled out beside the fire, for he refused to pay the cost of a room. The cart was again unpacked. A hastily sought-out smith labored into the starry night on the runners. And the next morning, which dawned clear and cold, they were off across the Yorkshire Moors of the North Riding on makeshift sled runners.

Lenore sat, muffled against the freezing wind, on the driver's seat beside a beaming Elias. He was delighted with her presence there and took it as a good omen for better things to come. Prudently she had wrapped not only her legs and feet but her whole body in blankets—as much against Elias's questing fingers as against the stinging wind. Behind her under the leathern covering, Mistress Potts—even more heavily padded with blankets—was wedged into a small enclosure among her various boxes. Among its contents the cart now sported, besides Mistress Potts' voluminous luggage, four great wagon wheels. Under these circumstances, only a shouted conversation between them was possible, and this was usually limited to, "Are you all right back there?" when the leathern top was lifted after a particularly resounding shift of the luggage from the rear, and Mistress Potts' muffled, "Aye!"

They made it into Darlington in bitter cold weather and could not go farther, for a great fall of snow held them there a week. Great drifts were piled halfway up the first-floor windows of their inn and long icicles hung glittering from the eaves. Mistress Potts, rested and loquacious again, was eager to talk about everything but Wallham and what awaited them there. Lenore, in her efforts to avoid Elias, who lay in wait for her in the common room with his big boots propped on the board and who sprang forward to attend her every time she came down the stairs, found herself trapped upstairs with an alternately talkative and brooding Mistress Potts. They ate all their meals together, and now Lenore was shrewd enough to place Mistress Potts' broad form squarely between them. She had thought that enough of a barrier, but to her annoyance one night at supper Elias let his big hand trail down across her back as he leaped forward to pull back her chair.

"Don't do that, Elias!" she said sharply, for he had insisted that she call him by his first name and sulked if she did not.

Elias looked so crestfallen she almost wanted to laugh, and the next day at breakfast he appeared with a peacemaking gift of a cheap pair of gloves. Lenore feared she would hurt his feelings if she did not accept them, so she gave him a bright smile, remarked on the beauty of the gloves, and fled back upstairs to Mistress Potts.

Desperately tired of their cramped smoky quarters and the inability to get out without Elias's company, Lenore had begun to wonder if their journey would ever end, when she awoke to the tinkle of a long icicle breaking and falling into the innyard. She opened her eyes and saw that the sun was shining.

Almost at the same moment came a rat-tat-tat knock on the door.

"Up, ladies!" called Elias's cheerful voice. "I think the roads be passable for us now!"

The women dressed hurriedly, swallowed their breakfast almost at a gulp and clambered once again into their makeshift sleigh.

"Careful!" cried Mistress Potts. "Careful with my boxes there!"

Elias winked at Lenore and set a heavy box down with elaborate care. And then they were off. Floundering through great drifts, behind near-winded horses, they negotiated the icy roads into Durham. There Elias, who was fond of his big gentle horses, insisted they stay for another three days, for his lead horse had cut his right foreleg when his hoof broke through the ice on the road and went down sharply into a deep rut. When Mistress Potts opened her mouth to protest, Elias told her sharply that he could not afford to lose the beast, and if the horse died she must pay for it.

Lenore, who guessed that threat was a bluster to give his horse time to mend, expected a great uproar from Mistress Potts, but none was forthcoming. Mistress Potts' wild anxiety to get on seemed abruptly quenched. She bit her lips and muttered, but she did not demand that another horse be furnished.

Still scowling at the suggestion that his horse go forward with an injured leg, Elias swept away and was gone through supper, which they ate early. Lenore hoped that one of the lusty lasses of Durham had taken his fancy, for he was becoming more difficult to handle every day. She was glad to have at least this one relaxed meal without surreptitious nudges beneath the table. But the exchange between Mistress Potts and Elias had made her thoughtful.

"Our driver, Elias, fancies you, Lenore," observed Mistress Potts as she polished off a great pasty, enough for three people.

" 'Twill do him no good," retorted Lenore. "For I don't fancy him."

"Tut, tut," chided Mistress Potts. "I think ye should consider him, for he's a fine strapping lad—and ye'd always have transportation."

"I am not that eager to travel," said Lenore ironically. "But now I understand why you did not immediately dismiss Elias and demand some other driver to take us to Wallham. You've taken a fancy to him yourself!"

"Of course I have not!" Mistress Potts' plump face flushed with indignation. " 'Tis just that—"

"Just what?"

But the older woman turned away, avoiding her eyes.

Lenore leaned forward. "Mistress Potts," she said severely, "I think you have been less than frank with me. But now you must tell me the truth or else I will refuse to go on to Wallham with you."

With a large bite of pasty halfway to her mouth, Mistress Potts paused and looked at her in alarm.

"Did your brother *ever* write you asking you to come to Wallham?"

"Why, he—" Mistress Potts' aplomb was fast wilting She looked around the common room in a hunted fashion. finding no help from the few shabby travelers intent on wolfing down their food.

"Mistress Potts," said Lenore sadly. "The truth is you have not heard from him for years, isn't it?"

Looking entirely miserable, Mistress Potts nodded. "I was afraid to write to Amos," she admitted, "for fear he'd say not to come."

Lenore sighed. "Then we may not be staying at Wallham," she said grimly. "And you'd best alert the driver to that fact, so that he does not leave without us. For I do not know how we could get transport back to Durham if your brother will not receive us."

"Oh, he'll receive us, Lenore. He has to!"

Mistress Potts spoke so eagerly that Lenore turned a puzzled face to her. "What do you mean, he 'has to'?"

"Why, why—family ties," sputtered Mistress Potts. "Blood is still thicker than water, Lenore! And he's my father's son, just as I'm my father's daughter, even though we had different mothers."

Lenore shook her head tiredly. "I know that you are still keeping something from me," she said. "And I won't question you about it, since you seem so upset. Go on and eat your pasty. We won't speak of it again."

Mistress Potts looked vastly relieved and attacked her pasty with renewed vigor. Lenore watched her, troubled. It occurred to her that Mistress Potts, for a dying woman, had stood this journey extremely well. There were spots of color in her cheeks, and she spoke almost gaily as she called for another glass of malmsey.

But Lenore was tired and pushed the thought aside. Lying over in Durham would give her time to explore this city stronghold of the north.

The next morning she eluded Elias by the ruse of dawdling and suggesting Mistress Potts go down to breakfast alone, and then rushing down the stairs and giving them a lighthearted wave as she ran out through the inn door. Elias tried to rise, but he was blocked by Mistress Potts' girth. By the time he could get up without knocking over the table, Lenore was already hidden in a shop across the street, peering out and enjoying his discomfiture as he looked up and down the snowy street for her. Finally it came to him that he had left his cloak inside and that his half-eaten breakfast—for Elias was a hearty eater—remained on the breakfast table where he had left it. He stomped back in, shaking his head as he stamped the snow from his boots. Lenore clutched her fustian cloak around her, adjusted her woolen hood, gave the amused shopkeeper her laughing thanks and scurried down the street.

From the shop she climbed the icy way up to the great Norman cathedral which stood hard by Durham Castle on a snowy bluff above the River Wear. Entering the cathedral by the North Door, she saw the famous Sanctuary Knocker which a chambermaid last night at the inn had told her not to miss. "Long ago any hapless lad who'd committed a crime, if he could but reach this ring and clutch it, was given sanctuary by the church," she'd told Lenore, giggling. "Would it were still true today, so my Jack could stagger up and grab hold of it!" Lenore had gathered that "her Jack" was a hopeless drunkard, who spent more time in the stocks than he did with his sweetheart. And now she looked at the knocker—a demon's head with a ring set in its mouth—and wished whimsically that she too could grasp it for sanctuary and not have to continue this trek into the frozen north country.

Elias was sulky when she returned famished. He spent all his time at supper surreptitiously feeling for her slippers with the toe of his boot. Lenore's feet kept up a rapid dance under the table as she ate her herring and grouse, ignoring Mistress Potts' questioning looks at her "fidgeting."

The next morning at breakfast she announced sweetly that she was off to the shops and that anyone who accompanied her would have to pay the bill! Elias backed away warily at that, and Lenore, who had no money for shopping anyway, spent another pleasant day strolling through the snowy streets enjoying the sights.

All the next day she spent in bed, having her meals sent up, for she had had little rest and she knew that the last lap of their journey could well be the hardest. They might get stuck on these roads and have to walk out. Or be frozen in by a swift-moving blizzard. She might need to call on all her strength.

Feeling whimsical, she sent down word to Elias that

she was tired and thought she'd just stay in bed until the horses were again in shape to travel—and then came down to breakfast the next morning looking fit and beautiful.

She was not surprised to be met with an eager, "The horse is looking pretty good now," from Elias. "Healing good, and if I wrap the leg well, he should be all right. You going back to bed after breakfast?" he finished with a wistful look.

Lenore gave a slight yawn behind a delicately lifted wrist to indicate that she might. "Unless of course, we could start for Wallham?" she suggested.

"Aye," agreed Elias fervently, for he missed her company. " 'Twas what I was about to suggest."

Lenore hid a smile. At least they'd be on their way again!

So with the big horse's leg heavily wrapped—indeed Elias had carefully bound all the horses' ankles against the cutting ice—after breakfast they found themselves moving once again on silent runners.

North to Newcastle-on-Tyne they sped. The weather was clear and cold, but the roads were difficult and Elias had no time to pester Lenore as he drove—he needed his full attention on the road ahead.

At Newcastle-on-Tyne, that town renowned for grindstones and salt and shipping, Elias reluctantly gave up Lenore's company beside him and hired a boy for the journey to Wallham "because I hear the road is bad and we might need him in case we get stuck in the drifts."

From Newcastle-on-Tyne they swung west. Conscious that they were now approaching their destination, Lenore struggled up. Ignoring the blows that thudded against her calves and thighs from the luggage, she held on to the wooden side of the wagon so that she might peer out of the slit between its high side and the leathern top that shielded them from the weather. Tiring of that, she pulled back a part of the leathern cover. It flapped relentlessly in the wind.

That same wind blew back her hood and loosed her

glorious red gold hair. Elias, looking back at her, smiled. A bonny lass, this one! He'd a mind to bed her, he had!

Lenore gave him back a cool, violet look and once again turned her attention to the landscape, ignoring Mistress Potts' groans as one box or another lurched against her. She leaned down toward the older woman.

"Don't you want to see out?" she asked. "After all, this is the country you've longed for."

Mistress Potts nodded, and Lenore called to Elias to stop and remove the leathern cover. He did so, managing somehow to brush against her hip in the process and give her a knowing smile. He was so obvious and persistent that Lenore didn't know whether to laugh or to cry. She turned her attention to Mistress Potts, steadying her so that she too could hang on to the wagon side and look out.

Thus it was in the wide snow-covered Tyne Valley that Lenore, looking up at the ragged escarpment that rent the gray winter sky, got her first glimpse of the vast Roman Wall that stretched for seventy miles from the North Sea on the east to the Irish Sea on the west. Her eyes widened. Rising and falling along the sheer basaltic cliffs, lying like a twisting stone serpent along the very edge of the precipice, the dressed gray stones stretched as far as the eye could see. Hadrian's Wall.

Lenore exclaimed at the sight of it.

"Aye," came Mistress Potts' voice, muffled by the big woolen scarf that covered the lower part of her red wind-whipped face. " 'Twas built hundreds of years ago. 'Tis eight feet thick and so tall that a man standing on another man's shoulders cannot reach the top of it! It reaches clear across England, they say, from Newcastle-on-Tyne to Solway Firth. There are mile-castles all along the way and turrets and great forts—all falling down now, of course."

Lenore, who had often ridden the Roman Way to Cirencester in the Cotswold Hills, was struck dumb. She could not keep her eyes off that great soaring wall that seemed to leap from crag to crag above them.

"That's why the house is named Wallham," shouted Mistress Potts into the biting wind. "For the Wall." She leaned forward to shout directions to the driver, then turned back to Lenore, her blue eyes beneath her woolen hood looking hunted. "We'll be there soon."

But so difficult was the going, even for the big draft horses. that dusk was falling, turning the snowy landscape blue-gray when at last they arrived at the desolate place called Wallham.

Twainmere

Chapter 12

Lorena was having a poor time of it. Uncle Robbie had put her on a diet of bread and water for ogling the boys in church on Sunday. She had, specifically, turned to look at Tabb Aylesbury, who had come jauntily in, spurs jingling, in the midst of service and set himself down as innocently as if he had not minutes ago risen from a bed of sin with giggling Angie Batts, the new barmaid at the tavern.

All the girls had heard those spurs jingle and had turned to look at Tabby, whose sleepy gray eyes and flashing grin lit up a strong, handsome face. Aware of this bright feminine surveillance, Tabby had reached back to run long fingers through his thick russet hair as if to give it a surreptitious combing—which it had not had this morning due to his rapid rise from a shared featherbed in the loft above the tavern.

All the brightly turned heads had swung back demurely to the vicar. But Lorena, who told herself that she alone among the young set had not succumbed to Tabby's masculine charms, had giggled.

It was for this she was being punished, and she felt it was vastly unfair. Tall Tabby, with his swinging gait and swift, amused whistle of appreciation, cut a striking figure in Twainmere. He was a constant object of attention among the girls. They whispered to each other that he was sleeping with this girl or that one—Lorena gossiped about him no more than the rest. Every little town had some dominant young male like Tabby who stood out head and shoulders over all the others. Why should *she* be singled out for punishment because she had seen that quick surreptitious combing motion, imagined where he had just been and *why* he had not yet combed his hair, and giggled?

No one else had noticed, but the vicar had. All the way home from services, he had thundered at Lorena that she would become a veritable "whore of Babylon" if she did not change her ways. Afterward Lorena had pored over the great Bible on Uncle Robbie's oaken desk until she found the "whore of Babylon." Having read, she doubted not only her present ability to emulate her, but also she felt the setting of Twainmere was entirely inadequate to such talents.

Twainmere was not without its vice, but it was mostly of a straightforward variety—couples gone a-Maying and being carried away, and nine months later something to show for it; bright-eyed young wives who sometimes slipped out of their houses to some meadow rendezvous and later innocently presented their unsuspecting husbands with children who "didn't look like either of them"; and an occasional full-scale scandal.

Lorena's mother had presented Twainmere with a full-scale scandal, and people never tired of talking of Lenore Frankford and her wild ways. Lorena supposed that was why Uncle Robbie babbled so much about the whore of Babylon—he didn't want to admit he was really talking about her mother.

"But mother *isn't* a whore," she told Aunt Flora sadly.

"Robbie knows that. He isn't talking about Lenore, but about a woman in the Bible who was very bad and lived long ago."

Lorena gave Aunt Flora a level look. She sensed it was the remembered image of her wild young mother that was behind all that pent-up fury with which Uncle Robbie switched her, the kind of frothing-at-the-mouth satisfaction it gave him to lock her in her room, or banish her from the table.

And now—bread and water.

She wasn't exactly locked in her room. The trapdoor of the loft still opened, but Uncle Robbie had taken the ladder away so that she was trapped up there, staring out through a tiny window at the icicles that hung down from the eaves. Aunt Flora, under Uncle Robbie's watchful gaze, had hauled the ladder back and was bringing her up a slice of brown bread and a pitcher of water, which was to be her lunch.

"It's cold up here," Lorena protested, shivering as she pulled her gray shawl around her. She gave a look of distaste to the meager food Flora had brought. "And besides," she added plaintively, "don't you need me downstairs to help? It's butter-churning day."

Flora sighed. "Yes, I do need you. And if you'll swear not to eat anything but bread and water, you can come down."

"Bread and water for how long?"

"God knows!" Flora was growing impatient with Robbie. Lorena was a growing girl, she needed sustenance.

"No, Uncle Robbie knows," Lorena said bitterly, her stomach churning a bit at the thought of the sweet fresh-churned butter, the aroma of the big pasty that would soon be baking, the wheaten cakes and steaming sausages. She turned angrily on Aunt Flora. "Why doesn't my mother come and take me away from here?"

Flora started. She loved Lorena like her own, but Robbie—Robbie had changed so lately and he was building a high wall between her and Lorena. "Your mother can't come for you," she said haltingly.

"She doesn't love me," Lorena cried. "That's why she doesn't come!"

"That's nonsense. Lenore left here with a murder charge hanging over her head. It was *for your sake* she brought you to me and I,"—her blue eyes misted over— "I was so glad she did."

"Oh, Aunt Flora, I'm sorry!" Penitent, Lorena flung herself at Flora, hugging her impetuously. "You've been the only mother I've known. It's just that I never seem able to please Uncle Robbie anymore."

Flora patted that fair head. "Lenore loves you very much, Lorena."

Lorena tossed her head. "But if she loves me so much, why does she only write letters? Why haven't I ever seen her? I don't even know what she looks like except from what people tell me!"

Flora sighed. It was true. She had guessed the reason Lenore never came to visit: having written how wonderful her life was, she could hardly come back in rags and tatters to be laughed at. For Flora had correctly guessed the state of Lenore's finances. She knew it by a simple deduction. When she was in funds, Lenore always scrupulously sent gold coins or gold buttons stuffed inside pincushions to help with Lorena's keep—and no pincushions had arrived for a long time.

"Lorena," she said gently, with a look at that single slice of bread. "Do as your Uncle Robbie wishes. Swear."

"Very well," sighed Lorena, who was tired of being cooped up in this loft when the sun was shining on the snow, and there was the sound of sleighbells and laughter going by. "I swear I'll eat bread and drink water."

Flora noted she hadn't said, "only bread and water." She gave Lorena a thoughtful look and went to the trapdoor. "Robbie," she called down, "Lorena has sworn."

"Then she can come down," called a stern voice from downstairs.

Munching her slice of brown bread, Lorena climbed sullenly down the ladder after Flora. She saw Uncle Robbie's disapproving figure, rigidly upright in the study doorway, and she curtsied to him as she had been taught to do, before following Flora into the kitchen. But her blue eyes were snapping angrily, for she felt ill-used.

"You can put these things away in the pantry first," directed Flora. "That ham. And the cheese there. Oh, and don't forget that bit of leftover pasty."

Their eyes met and Lorena gave her aunt a startled look. Calmly, Flora turned away to see to her butter churn. Grateful at this chance to eat, Lorena snatched up the ham and cheese and "bit of leftover pasty" and charged into the pantry. She was eating fast when she heard Uncle Robbie come into the kitchen, and she nearly choked when she heard him ask, "Where's Lorena?"

"Doing her chores," said Flora.

"Where is she?"

"Lorena," called Flora, in her voice a note of warning.

Lorena swallowed, hastily shoved the food under a large linen napkin, passed her sleeve over her mouth and came out. Her blue-eyed gaze was innocent. "Yes, Aunt Flora?"

"Your Uncle Robbie wants you."

The vicar gazed at Lorena with distaste—and something else, something he did not care to identify even to himself. Her swaying walk always reminded him of Lenore. Lenore, who had turned the head of every boy in the village—and most of the men. Lorena was not to grow up to be another Lenore! "When you have finished your chores, Lorena," he said heavily, "you will read three chapters of the Bible and discuss them with me afterward."

"Robbie," Flora cut in, "that will have to be done later. I have a great deal to do today and I must send the girl on errands for I have not the time to go myself."

"Very well, but the Bible study must be done." Stiff-backed as always, the vicar turned away. He wanted to escape before there were tears—he hated tears. Not that Lorena ever actually cried. He told himself that was unnatural, a young girl never crying.

Robbie had underestimated the cool pride that Lorena had inherited from her mother. Lorena would have died rather than let Uncle Robbie see her cry!

Now she gave Aunt Flora a bleak look.

"Go back to the pantry, Lorena," Flora said gently. "I'm sure you haven't had time to put everything away. When you've finished in there, put on your pattens and your cloak and hood and your warmest gloves. I've several errands, but first I want you to take a basket of apples to Jane Cardwell, she's down again. Snowfire's ankle is acting up again, so you'll have to walk. It might take you all day, going there and back."

Happiness flared in Lorena's eyes. She'd get to see Maude! "Not if I got someone to drive me partway there on a sleigh! I heard two of them going by a minute ago," she added eagerly.

Flora hid a smile. "After you've finished in the pantry, Lorena. I want *all* the apples to get there!"

Back to the pantry Lorena raced. She finished her breakfast with a gulp of water to wash it down. She told herself she wasn't breaking any oath. She had sworn to eat bread and water. And indeed she had. She hadn't sworn *not* to eat ham and cheese and pasty!

When she came out, she gave Aunt Flora a spontaneous hug. "I didn't mean it about wanting to leave you," she said earnestly. "I *never* want to leave you. It's just that Uncle Robbie is so hard on me."

"Go along with you," said Flora huskily. She wasn't a demonstrative woman but just at this moment she was fighting back tears. "Bundle up, be sure to deliver the apples and—have a good time." She didn't add, *Don't let Robbie see you having a good time,* but she thought it. "Be home before dark, Lorena."

Robbie's too hard on the child, Flora told herself as Lorena skipped away, giving a wide berth to the study door. *She's young and 'tis only natural for her to be high-spirited. This is the third time he's punished her this week and it's only Wednesday!* For besides the bread and water and the extra Bible reading, Lorena had been forced to stand in the corner with her face to the wall for three hours because she had waved to a passing sleigh from the window of her loftlike room—and from the front gate Robbie had seen her.

Normally Flora let Robbie's punishments stand. But now she sensed that he was going too far, that he was alienating the sensitive young girl. She loved Robbie, in spite of the fact that he never took her to his bed, indeed, treated her like a saint. Flora sighed. She hated being treated like a saint, being told humbly that she was "too good" for carnal passion. She supposed she'd never have married Robbie if she'd known he felt like that about her. Still it was fortunate she had, for Robbie had proposed in the nick of time during the Rebellion when the Puritan fever was at its height. If she hadn't married Robbie, the people of Twainmere might well have lashed her out of town tied to the tail of a cart, in retribution for her brother Jamie's going off to Worcester to fight for the king.

Jamie . . . Wistfully she thought of her wild young brother and of the lovely young handfast bride he had brought home to share his bed. What a golden couple they had been—Lenore with her fiery red-gold hair and quick laugh, and Jamie with his hemp-white shock and easy ways. Laughing, fighting—indestructible they'd seemed.

If only Jamie could have lived to see his daughter. Flora considered the best day of her life was when she'd opened the vicarage door and seen Lenore standing there—and then seen Lorena and known instantly that this was Jamie's daughter. Holding little Lorena in her arms had made up for so many things: for the tragic death of her first husband in Scotland, for whom she'd borne no bairn; for Robbie's strange sterile love for her; for the alien English ways that sometimes tore at her wild Scottish heart.

Lorena had made up for everything, and—Flora's strong jaw hardened—she wasn't going to let Robbie come between them. She knew it was sinful to go against the wishes of one's husband. Ask any parson in England! It was even illegal, for a husband could beat a disobedient wife with a stick and still have the approval of the community. Not that anyone was likely to beat *her!* Flora's blue eyes glittered at the thought. For hadn't she stood off Tom Prattle with a broom when he'd pursued Lenore to Jamie's smithy? She'd stand off anyone, and everyone—for Lorena.

Lorena, her heart again singing as she slipped into her tall pattens and demure gray woolen cloak and hood, knew how Aunt Flora felt about her and rejoiced. It was Flora who had given her life its stability. Once it had been both Flora and Robbie, but gradually Uncle Robbie had changed. At first the change had been so subtle that she had not noticed it except as a rumbling undercurrent in the way he treated her. Then it had suddenly exploded into the fanatical passion with which he now punished her—sometimes unmercifully—for the smallest infractions.

At first bewildered and hurt, Lorena had grown sullen and angry. She might have run away but for Aunt Flora, for it was to Flora she had given her love. It was Flora who'd washed her small wounds when she—daredevil that she was—had ventured too far in playing the rough village games, or barked her shins climbing trees. It was Flora who'd nursed her through the fever when she was nine years old; Lorena remembered waking hot and frightened in the darkness—and it had been Flora's face she'd seen by candlelight, watching her raptly, sponging her forehead, murmuring soothing words, lifting her lolling head with gentle fingers so she could sip broth. It was Flora who'd been a mother to her all these years. Lorena didn't know it, but she'd have died for Aunt Flora.

At the sound of sleigh bells approaching, Lorena

grasped her basket of apples and left the vicarage. She slipped on the icy front step and almost fell but she righted herself quickly enough and plunged through the gate. Picking up her skirts with one hand, she ran along the low wall that fronted the property and came to a skidding halt beneath the snowy branches of an old yew tree. She raised her arm and waved at the oncoming sleigh.

She had hoped it would be a crowd of jolly young people in the sleigh, but to her disappointment it was only Alfie Wattle, who would go out of his way any time to ride past the vicarage. Alfie was fourteen, built like a grasshopper, and had large protruding eyes that opened even wider at the sight of Lorena Frankford standing there in cloak and hood and pattens with her cheeks as red as the apples she carried—and waving at *him*. Alfie had long worshiped the gorgeous Lorena from afar; he brought the sleigh to such a smart stop that the surprised horses reared up.

"Oh—Alfie." Lorena tried not to show her disappointment in her voice; what she needed, after all, was *transportation*. "Would you happen to be going anywhere near Mistress Cardwell's?"

"Why—why, Mistress Lorena, I'd be *proud* to take you there!" stuttered the inept young suitor. He leaped from the sleigh so energetically that when his leading foot hit a slick spot he skidded and sat down in an undignified heap. Lorena gave him a pained look. It occurred to her suddenly that Tabby Aylesbury would never have done that.

Embarrassed by his clumsiness, Alfie sprang up, dusted the snow from his rump, and took the basket from her. Having deposited it in his sleigh, he handed Lorena in like a queen. Lorena cast a quick glance back at the vicarage, hoping Uncle Robbie was not watching. Although Uncle Robbie approved of Alfie Wattle—he always approved of the milk-toast sort of lad—he definitely would not approve of her riding alone in a sleigh with *any* boy.

Having settled her in, Alfie leaped to the driver's seat and cracked the whip showily over his horse's head. Obediently it ambled forward.

"Uh—no, Alfie." Lorena touched his arm and Alfie, electrified at the touch, almost lost the reins. "Don't drive past the vicarage."

"But 'tis the best place to turn the horses around, Mistress Lorena!"

"I know that, Alfie, but—but Uncle Robbie has a headache and he's sleeping now, and the sleigh bells might wake him."

All liars went straight to hell, Lorena knew that. But was this really a lie? Uncle Robbie *looked* like he had a headache, and he often took a nap around this time. She tossed her head. Oh, well. . . .

Doubtfully, and with some difficulty, Alfie wheeled the sleigh about at this narrow place in the street, sending his sled runners over their neighbor's rose vines. Lorena winced. Uncle Robbie would hear about that, no doubt!

Beside her, Alfie brightened. He'd just swing through town and show off the lovely girl beside him. How the other lads would envy him, for Lorena Frankford was seldom allowed out, and the town's young bucks were eagerly awaiting the day when Lorena would shake free of her constant chaperonage. For wasn't she Lenore Frankford's daughter? they declared. Gossip told them that nothing had ever held Lenore back!

How wrong handfasting was or how bad Lorena's blood, Alfie couldn't say, but he knew he'd give anything if Lorena would turn her pretty face toward him and kiss him on the mouth. Just thinking of it made his cheeks burn and his heart pound.

Beside him Lorena sat straight-backed and prim. "Oh, there's Tess Willet," she cried, turning at the sound of tinkling sleigh bells behind them. "Hello, Tess!"

The other sleigh passed them smartly and Tess, a buxom girl older than Lorena, waved indifferently. She was lying back looking very luxurious in a new embroidered butterscotch wool cloak and fur-lined hood. Tess was the only child of a retired wool merchant who had left Cheltenham and purchased an old farm outside town and was proceeding to renovate it. Among Twainmere's young crowd, Tess was the fashion, for she had been to London and spoke French—at least a few words—and she had a Pomeranian dog.

"I see Tabb Aylesbury's squiring her," remarked Alfie.

"Yes." Lorena's soft lips compressed. Tall russet-haired Tabby, the innocent reason for her diet of bread and water, was indeed driving the light sleigh, his strong hands easy on the reins. Ever since the day when he'd broken up the fight on the ice between her and Kate, all he'd had for Lorena had been a nonchalant nod. But it had taken him no time at all to single out Tess Willet! The Willets had been here a scant three weeks! Lorena tossed her head. She had no idea her cheeks were burning resentfully.

"You sure look pretty with the wind whipping up your color like that," Alfie said, surprised at his own temerity.

Lorena gave him a stormy look. "Do you think you can pass that sleigh, Alfie?"

Alfie was startled. "Well—I don't know, Mistress Lorena. That horse of Tabby's is pretty fast."

"Yes. but you've a lighter load. You don't weigh half what Tabby does and I"—she ignored the fact that exaggeration was said to lead to hellfire as well as lying—"I couldn't weigh but a *third* what Tess Willet does. Pass them, Alfie. I'll kiss you if you do!"

Alfie sat straighter. His lady had asked him to do something—and for such a golden reward! Grimly he gripped the reins, and fate smiled on him for at that moment Tabby Aylesbury, under the guise of leaning over to rearrange the blanket around Tess's waist and legs, had just reached up under her cloak and pinched one of her resplendent ripe breasts. Tess gave a delighted little jump and slapped halfheartedly at Tabby. Sensing the tumult he had caused, Tabby let the reins go slack, the better to concentrate on Tess. His horse, noting the change, slowed to a gentle walk, and Alfie and his lady shot by in triumph.

As she had known he would, Tabby's head shot around to see who was passing him at such a pace. At that exact moment, Lorena, watching Tabby out of the corner of her eye, seized Alfie's long thin face in both hands, turned it toward her and pressed a sudden kiss on his startled mouth.

That Tabby saw that kiss, she had the satisfaction of knowing, for he gazed at them in a kind of fixed fascination as they careened onward.

"Mistress Lorena," gasped Alfie, "I've lost the reins!"

He had indeed and Tabby, still watching, doubled up with laughter as Alfie struggled vainly to regain them and finally leaped off the sleigh and ignominiously picked them up from where they glided along over the hard-packed snow. Lorena turned to see Tabby laughing. Red with embarrassment, she slouched down in the sleigh and when Alfie, still atingle, climbed back up beside her, she hardly looked at him.

Out of town they rode along a white road lined with big trees whose snow-covered branches nodded over them, occasionally dumping a load of snow which they must hastily dodge. Past the Whitleighs, the Hepworths, the Bensons. Lorena was quiet, Alfie told himself, because she was enjoying the scenery. For himself, he was tongue-tied. He could hardly wait to noise it around that Lorena Frankford had kissed him! He guessed that would settle his big brothers, who considered him backward for having reached the advanced age of fifteen without having seduced one of the plump dairymaids (Alfie's father owned a small dairy) out behind the milking barn! Alfie would rather have a kiss from Mistress Lorena than the warm embraces of any number of dairymaids.

"Here, Mistress Lorena." Alfie brought the horse to a stop and jumped from the sleigh. "I'll carry your basket for you."

They had reached that place in the road from

whence a narrow path led through the woods to the Cardwells' croft, a path so narrow it could not be negotiated by horse and sleigh.

"Never mind, Alfie. I can carry it, and besides I want to spend a while with Maude Cardwell."

He was being dismissed! Alfie gaped at her. "But, Mistress Lorena!"

"Thank you for the sleigh ride, Alfie." Lorena swung away from him through the snow, holding up her cloak and skirts so that her slender ankles were revealed to his gaze.

Disappointed and not knowing what to do about it, Alfie stood and watched her glumly until she disappeared into the trees. Then he climbed back onto his sleigh and headed for home, shaking his head and muttering, like many a man before him, that he would never understand women.

At the Cardwells the apples were welcome, and Maude especially was glad to see her. This snowy weather irked Maude, whose pattens were old and worn. It was easier for the young fellows with sleighs to get to houses that lay conveniently along the roadside than to out-of-the-way crofts. She said as much.

"I know." Lorena's voice was bitter. "We passed Tabby Aylesbury taking Tess home in his sleigh."

"Now there's a la-di-da wench for you! Did you know she never even speaks to me when we meet at market?"

Lorena had little doubt that this was so. "I think Tess only speaks to *me* because Uncle Robbie's the vicar!"

Maude laughed, but her low estate rankled with her. "I hope Tabby breaks a runner, and they end up in the snow on their backsides! Come on, Lorena, come out to the barn loft. It's warm there and we can't hear ourselves talk in here!"

It was true enough. In the shabby room the younger Cardwells were playing hide-and-seek—mostly trying to hide in their mother's voluminous skirts—amid shrieks of laughter. But Lorena cast a wistful look back at the uproar as she accompanied Maude on the slippery well-trodden path to the barn. The vicarage was never noisy like this. It was quiet—and lonely.

"Now then." Maude led her through the big double barn doors into the interior smelling sweetly of hay and climbed a rickety wooden ladder to the loft. There they plumped down on the soft hay. "Can you stay overnight?" asked Maude.

"No chance." Lorena shook her head. "Uncle Robbie would never stand for it. He called me the whore of Babylon again."

Maude shrieked with laughter. "*You?* But you're such a goody-two-shoes! I'll bet butter won't melt in your mouth!"

Color stained Lorena's face. Was *that* why Tabby Aylesbury had only nodded nonchalantly to *her,* while he was *squiring* Tess? She must enliven her reputation!

"You wouldn't say that, Maude, if you knew what I was doing when we passed Tabby's sleigh!"

Maude stopped laughing and leaned forward. "Tell!"

"I was kissing Alfie Wattle, that's what!"

Alfie Wattle, that string bean! Maude was tempted to laugh again but she saw that Lorena was serious. "In front of God and all the people, aye?" she grinned. "And what will your precious Uncle Robbie say to that?"

"He won't hear about it. Nobody was looking." Except *Tabby,* Lorena thought guiltily.

"Oh, well, even if he does hear about it and makes Alfie marry you, at least Alfie's father owns a dairy and Alfie'll inherit part of it one day," Maude encouraged her.

"Make him *marry* me?" gasped Lorena. "Maude, it was only a kiss on the lips!"

Maude shrugged. "You know your Uncle Robbie!" she grinned.

"Yes." Lorena's shoulders drooped. "He's put me on bread and water, Maude. For giggling in church."

"Wait, I'll get you an apple!"

"No, thanks," said Lorena hastily, for she knew the Cardwells were near starving this winter, and she had no intention of eating any part of their little hoard. "I've already eaten. Some ham and cheese." She hadn't meant to say that but it slipped out.

"Good for you." Maude grinned at her.

"Maude." Lorena rested an elbow on her knee and leaned her chin upon her hand. "Mistress Plimpton says London is a sinkhole of sin, but Uncle Robbie is always holding up 'Lady this' or 'Lord that' as models of behavior to me. Do you think the court ladies and gentlemen are really so good?"

"Listen, them at court—them's no better than us," stated Maude with authority. "You should've heard what the peddler told me when he give me that play. He'd just been to London and he said a coach shot by him coming out of Whitehall with a tipsy half-dressed girl falling out and two cavaliers bawling out a song he couldn't even *repeat* for my"—Maude giggled—"tender ears. He said the coach horses were wearing tassles and they were staggering too!"

True or false, Lorena was thrilled. *"Even the horses were drunk?"* she echoed, enthralled.

"Aye. Why, in London, half the women don't even know who's the father of their children! Take on three or four cavaliers in one night, the peddler said. Lorena, your mother must have flirted her skirts real high to get onto the stage. The peddler said young girls—*virgins,* mind you—would sell themselves just to become *orange girls* in the theater!"

Unaware that her mother had been reduced from actress to orange girl before she had quit London, Lorena drew herself up. *"My* mother would never sell herself to be an orange girl—or an actress either!"

"Of course, it was her beauty that caught them," agreed Maude instantly, realizing she'd come close to angering her friend. "But who's to say what's right and what's wrong in a crowded place like that? Why shouldn't folks lie around the streets and drink gin? They're doing the same thing at Whitehall, only they're lying about on marble floors or Turkish carpets. Even in the old queen's time—only o'course we shouldn't call her a *queen* because *she* was a man!"

"What?" cried Lorena, forgetting all about sinful London. "You can't mean Queen Elizabeth?"

"Good Queen Bess herself," nodded Maude. "'Course, she *started out* as a girl but she *ended up* as a boy."

"How could she do that?"

"Well, listen and I'll tell you." Maude leaned over and lowered her voice. "*Everyone* over at Bisley knows all about it, and Gramps was the one that told me. When Princess Elizabeth was just a young thing—seven, I think—her father, old King Henry the Eighth, sent her to Bisley to visit some aristocratic folks there and she caught a bad cold *and died there*. And them she was visiting was terrified he'd blame them."

"But," protested Lorena, "I thought he didn't like to have her around. He was always having her declared illegitimate."

"Just so," agreed Maude. "But he swung like a pendulum, and the folks she was visiting couldn't be sure that once she was dead he wouldn't decide he liked her after all and *blame them* for not taking better care of her—and maybe he'd kill everybody in the town for vengeance. So they looked around real quick and they found this seven-year-old boy who looked a lot like Elizabeth and he'd studied Latin, same as she had. And they promised his mother a pension for life if she'd give him up so he could become a princess—"

Lorena was staring at Maude, aghast. "But that couldn't have happened! I mean, too many people would know her. know what she looked like. And besides—"

"But it *did* happen. And Gramps said sure, plenty of people noticed but since Elizabeth—or the boy *pretending* to be Elizabeth—was the only hope of the Protestants. they kept quiet about it. Her older sister Mary was a Catholic and burned the Protestants as heretics, and her brother Edward were too weak to live long, so *she'd* be the Protestant Queen—I mean *he* would be."

"But her father—!"

"Old King Henry hardly ever looked at her, so *he* wouldn't notice the difference! No, Queen Elizabeth was a man—and he came from right over there at Bisley."

Lorena trudged back through the snowy vele and up into the trees with her head abuzz. She never quite trusted Maude's information, which was always startling, but it made fascinating listening. And suppose it was *true?* She shivered delightedly. But then some other problems a man posing as a woman would have occurred to her. What about the ladies-in-waiting who accompanied her—him—to the royal bedchamber and disrobed her—him? She determined, as she broke through the trees and headed for the road where Alfie had left her and driven away in his sleigh, to confront Maude with *that* when next they met.

She had almost reached the road when she heard the sound of sleigh bells and paused. Surely Alfie hadn't waited all this time, or spent two hours driving his poor horse up and down the road!

At the roadside she stopped and peered down it. The tinkling bells were coming closer.

As the sleigh rounded a turn and came into sight, she stiffened. It *would* be Tabby Aylesbury returning alone after taking Tess Willet home—and probably bedding her down in one of the Willet's big featherbeds too, if her parents weren't home to stop him!

Hoping he hadn't seen her watching for him, Lorena whirled about on her high pattens and started mushing along by the side of the road, heading back toward town.

The sleigh came to a neat stop beside her.

"Care for a ride, Lorena?" Tabby was looking down at her, his gaze languorous. He had the attitude, she thought, of a fully surfeited lover, a purring tomcat just stretching out on the warm hearth after licking his fur.

But a ride *would* be nice. Lorena hesitated.

"I'll drop you down the street so the vicar won't see you consorting with a rake like me!" he offered.

A shadow of irritation crossed Lorena's countenance. She had been put on bread and water just for looking at him in church! Still, that sleepy gaze mesmerized her. and she felt her will turning to water.

"It *is* messy out," she said, daintily offering him her gloved hand so that she might leap aboard the sleigh. If it had been Tess. she thought resentfully, he'd have jumped out and swung her up into the sleigh; he was treating her like a child!

"You're growing up, Lorena." Tabby turned to gaze down thoughtfully at her as he flicked his whip in the air and the sleigh sped off, the runners moving smoothly over the snow. His gaze passed over the top of her head where the woolen hood had fallen back to display the silky beauty of her white-gold hair, roved questingly down over her snapping blue eyes and flushed face, down her now-exposed throat where a pulse beat uncontrollably, and came to rest meaningfully on her bosom and budding breasts. "Funny I hadn't noticed before," he murmured.

"And how did you leave Tess?" Lorena asked pertly.

In point of fact—her father being gone to Cheltenham for a fortnight and her mother having gone to Twainmere to hire a sempstress—Tabby had left Tess entirely naked and flailing angrily about in her big featherbed. beating the pillows with her fists in rage that he should take his leave of her so soon. As he had fastened up his breeches. he had paused to enjoy the spectacle, although it was no new thing for girls to pout when he left them. Though he never made them any commitment, they all seemed confident that they could instantly extract one from him as soon as they made their bodies available. It was a conceit that hadn't worked with him yet.

"I left Tess having tea," he lied pleasantly.

"Ha!" said Lorena.

Tabby turned and gave Lorena a sharp look. She was indeed a beauty, but her manners needed mending.

"How does Alfie kiss?" he asked calmly. "I mean, in your opinion as an expert, how would you rate him? Good? Fair? Or not-so-good?"

In her heart Lorena considered Alfie a complete dud. In his excitement at the sudden unexpected pressure of her lips he had not responded to her at all, and she had somehow managed to crash against his front teeth. Her lips were still bruised from the contact.

At Tabby's blunt question, her face flushed crimson, but she was determined not to be bested. "I'd say he was—oh, about average. Among those I've known," she added carelessly.

Tabby's eyebrows elevated. "Oh, and have ye known so many then, Mistress Lorena?"

Lorena tossed her head so that her bright hair rippled in the sunlight. "A few," she said recklessly.

Tabby stopped the sleigh.

"Then let's see how you rate *me*," he murmured, and swung around and seized her. It was lucky he did, for as she divined his meaning, she jerked away and would have toppled out of the sleigh but that he caught her with a long arm. "What's this?" he mocked. "Reluctant? For one so experienced, that's strange!"

Wrathful at this mockery, Lorena lifted her clenched fist. "You let me alone, Tabby Aylesbury!"

For answer he laughed and pulled her to him in an enveloping bear hug. Lorena found herself pressed against his fleece-lined leather cloak. One of his fur-lined leather gloves was holding her head upturned, while the other pinioned her angrily clenched hands. She felt his lips rove down her forehead, over her eyebrows and eyes, brushing her lashes, and wander down her soft flushed cheek to her mouth.

She gasped and closed her mouth as his lips closed over hers, immediately to open it again in protest. Tabby was quick to seize his opportunity. Lorena stiffened in shock as his hot tongue pushed impudently past her lips to nuzzle about in her mouth. A kind of warm frenzy overcame her, and she tried to beat at him with her pinioned fists. But the surging feelings that were welling up in her were new and strange and wonderful. Leisurely, Tabby's lips left her mouth and traveled down her neck. She quivered as she felt his teeth trying to unbutton the top of her bodice—and failing, pass on to her fast-beating breast.

At that point she gave a great virginal jerk and Tabby let her go. He took a quick look up and down the white road to make sure it was still empty, then back at the girl. She stared up dizzily into his laughing face.

"Well, how do you rate me, Lorena?"

Lorena's face was white and shaken, but she wasn't downed yet. "Average," she gasped. "*Almost* average."

Surprise washed the smile from Tabby's face. Anger glimmered in his eyes. "*Almost* average!" he echoed.

Lorena saw she had punctured his smug composure and was fiercely glad. The dizziness was receding now although her heart was still beating madly. She gave Tabby a slanted critical look through her long lashes. "Perhaps you'll improve. After you've practiced a bit, I may give you leave to kiss me again sometime," she added airily.

Tabby stared at her, open-mouthed. This saucy virgin, barely more than a child, was mocking him. Mocking him on a subject on which he considered himself an expert—sex!

"And now you've taken me far enough, Tabby!" Lorena sprang lightly down from the sleigh with her empty basket and Tabby made no move to stop her. "'Twould not do for Uncle Robbie to see me riding through town with you. He knows your reputation and he'd make me marry you!"

Tabby leaned forward. "And would that be so bad?"

"Terrible!" Lorena laughed. "I intend to try out *all* the men before I choose one!" she called back over her shoulder as she skipped away. "Marriage would hold me back a bit!"

"It might at that," muttered Tabby, who had often had the same thought himself. But that was a thought for a man, not a wench! With narrowed eyes he watched young Lorena picking her way jauntily through the snow, swinging her basket, her cloak and skirts drawn up a trifle higher than was necessary to clear the snow but showing to advantage her dainty ankles and the rise of her pretty calves.

He had never really thought about Lorena before, considering her merely a pretty child. Ripe young damsels ready for bedding, who reached out for him, were his game. But the touch of Lorena's sheer skin, the sweet, innocent, almost joyous response of her newly budding body, the soft gasping indrawn breath that had met his encroaching tongue, all bore promise that the child was soon to become the woman. And what a woman she would be!

Lorena, he swore to himself, his sleepy eyes aglitter as they watched her dainty retreating figure. *When cherry-picking time comes, 'tis myself will shake the tree!*

He started the sleigh and rode up beside her. "Climb back in." He bent over and offered his hand. "I promise to be a perfect gentleman."

She laughed. "You don't know how!"

"I'll learn," he said shortly. "There's no need for you to get your feet wet out there. Besides, it's turning icy. You could slip and fall."

Lorena gave him a wicked look. Tabby was looking down into her eyes with an intentness he usually reserved for older girls. She had gained a degree of mastery over him after all—and it was only the beginning!

Her spirits soaring, she took his hand, let him boost her up, and seated herself primly in the sleigh beside him. From time to time she noted that his sleepy gaze shot in her direction, but she continued to look straight ahead, letting him study her fine profile.

A short distance from the vicarage, Tabby let her off. "Fly away home now, Lorena," he said with a grin. "And don't tell the vicar you've spent your day kissing all the boys!"

Lorena gave him an uncertain look. That momentary power she had felt she had over him seemed to be slipping. "Good-bye, Tabby. Thank you for the ride." She leaped lithely from the sleigh, then turned and looked up at him in irritation. "And you might remember to call me *Mistress* Lorena. I'm not a baby that you should call me by my first name when you hardly know me!"

Tabby tried to look put out, but instead gave her a delighted look. What spirit she had! He'd bet that stripped down, she'd have a fine little figure too. But she was right, the vicar would haul him in by the scruff and demand he marry Lorena if he so much as pinched her bottom. He watched that fine little bottom now moving pertly down the street toward the vicarage.

Tabby sat and gazed after her until she disappeared through the vicarage gate. Then he wheeled his horse about and headed for the local inn, where he'd no doubt find his father drinking ale with some other good fellows with little else to do. But young Lorena would remain in the back of his mind. She was a wench worth waiting for!

Lorena swung lightheartedly into the vicarage. "I delivered the apples," she sang out.

"Did you?" said Flora with a smile.

Lorena nodded. "Oh, Aunt Flora, it was a wonderful day," she said blissfully. "The snow was so beautiful!"

Flora's eyes misted. She wanted Lorena to have wonderful days. There had been too few of them in the vicarage lately.

That evening after supper, when Lorena sat alone at the big dining room table reading three chapters of the Bible by candlelight, her Uncle Robbie came back from visiting a sick parishioner.

"I understand that you were out sleigh riding with young Tabby Aylesbury today," he said sternly. "You know you have been forbidden to ride alone with a boy!"

Lorena looked up from her reading with innocent eyes. "Whoever saw me must not have looked very close,

Uncle Robbie. I was sleigh riding with Tabby Aylesbury *and* with Alfie Wattle. You approve of Alfie, you said you did. And besides you didn't forbid me to ride with *people*, especially when the apples I was delivering for Aunt Flora were so heavy and I had so far to go! It was only partway!"

Flora looked up from her mending and gave Lorena a nervous look, but the vicar seemed mollified. He did indeed approve of Alfie Wattle, who appeared to him never to have had a lascivious thought—indeed, to be incapable of one. Lust—that was the enemy of the world!

"So long as you weren't riding with a boy alone," he said severely, lest Lorena think he had softened his stand.

Lorena told herself she would sink no deeper into hell for this half-truth about her afternoon adventures. With an innocent smile she returned to her Bible chapters, which were full of "begats." She wondered idly what Uncle Robbie would say if she turned her big eyes on him and asked him to explain what "begat" meant. She supposed he'd just sputter. Tabby Aylesbury, she guessed, did a lot of "begetting." He'd better be careful, or he'd have to marry one of them! Why that thought should make her heart lurch so painfully, she couldn't imagine.

But the memory of Tabby Aylesbury's strong arms, of his joyous impudent kiss, lingered to tingle in her memory, and after a while she looked up from the Bible and stared into the yellow candle flame, seeing radiant dreams of when she would be a woman grown, and a fit match for such as Tabby Aylesbury!

Northumberland

Chapter 13

Hardly less forbidding than Hadrian's Wall seemed the big gray stone farmhouse that loomed up before Lenore and her companions through the barren wastes of snow. Several outbuildings clustered near it, a barn and a stable, but somehow they all seemed forlorn, uncared for. Lenore told herself that it was just the effect of the snow, as she peered forward. All that whiteness made the windows seem dark. She would have been tempted indeed to believe they might be approaching an empty house save that a thin dark line of smoke issued from one of the tall chimneys, a darker smudge in a darkening sky. From but one of the chimneys, she noted wryly, knowing that that boded cold rooms and stamping one's feet in the morning to restore the circulation to them on the chilly boards. As they approached, lumbering over the landscape toward this barren destination, the wind whipped up again and became a shrieking gale. Such was the place that Lenore wished treacherously that Mistress Potts' half brother Amos would offer them shelter for a night and then turn them out, so that they might journey back to Durham or even more hospitable York.

"The house was built of stones quarried from the Wall," shouted Mistress Potts, waving a hand at the Great Wall and almost losing her balance. She sounded proud, but Lenore, who had been cursed by a sense of history, felt a little pang of loss that the Great Wall, built so long ago, should be chipped away through the centuries.

"They'll be surprised to see us," Mistress Potts said, beginning to stir about like some large cocoon as they neared the house.

"Surprised" was a mild word. "Shock" would better have described their reception. They came to a labored halt before the front door, and Elias would have lifted Lenore from the cart, but she nimbly gave her hand to his young helper, whose swarthy skin reddened as he helped her down. Frowning, Elias was forced to struggle with Mistress Potts' great girth as he conveyed her to the snowy ground. She squealed as her ankle connected with the snow, and with a sigh, Elias picked her up and carried her to the door, depositing her at the top of the front steps.

After what seemed to Lenore an interminable pounding on the heavy oaken panels with his knuckles—and finally Elias, losing his temper, added a couple of blows on the lower panels with his heavy boot—the door opened a crack, and they could see in the dimness a candle's gleam. As the wind whipped in through the crack, the candle flickered and almost went out.

"What d'ye want?" demanded a man's slurred voice from behind the crack.

" 'Tis me, Amos! Your sister, Abigail Potts! Let us in!" Mistress Potts' voice was almost lost in the now howling gale as she pushed forward against the door.

It opened grudgingly enough so that the man inside could command a good view of the little group shivering in the snowy purple twilight. Lenore saw in the dimness of the hall a tall emaciated form topped by an unkempt shock of straggly gunmetal hair. A pair of bloodshot eyes peered at them hazily, without recognition, trying to focus on Mistress Potts. The fellow wobbled slightly on his feet, and Lenore realized that he was very drunk and trying to collect his wits.

"Why, ye can't be Amos!" cried Mistress Potts, peering up at him. "Ye're too young by half! Ye must be one of Amos's nephews. Which one are ye, Caleb or Sedgewick?"

"I'm Sedgewick," came the hiccuping reply. "We—we thought ye were dead, Abigail. Ye never wrote."

"Well, I'm far from dead as ye can see," retorted Mistress Potts in a tart voice. "But I *am* near frozen from the journey, and so are my friends here, so stand back and let us in, Sedgewick, before we all turn to icicles out here."

Astonished that even a drunken man would keep them standing outside in such weather, Lenore watched Sedgewick lurch away from the door, and they trailed in, led by Mistress Potts, to stamp their half-frozen feet on the stone flooring that had once graced a Roman wall.

"Now go and tell Amos I'm here, Sedgewick," prodded Mistress Potts impatiently. "He'll be surprised, he will. It's been years!"

Sedgewick seemed to tilt over on his toes, and then precariously to regain his balance. Owlishly he leaned over and peered down at the short plump woman. "He's not here, Abigail. Amos is gone. Gone"—he hiccuped—"to York."

"Gone to York?" Mistress Potts' jaw dropped. "But *we* were in York, and *I* did not see him there!" She was so indignant that Lenore almost felt the need to remind her that York was a large city and they could have stayed there indefinitely without encountering a man Mistress Potts had not seen for more than thirty years. "Gone to York indeed!" Her voice rose stridently. "A fine thing! And in the wintertime too! When will he be back?"

"I'm sure I don't know," Sedgewick replied. "Amos never felt the need to inform *me* of his comings and goings. Ho, Caleb, we've visitors!"

From down the hall another door opened to show a crack of light, and a man's deep voice rumbled, "Who's there, Sedgewick?"

"'Tis Abigail Potts and three others, come to see Amos. I've just told her he's gone to York."

Tipsily Sedgewick led them down the hall where the door now swung fully open to silhouette a giant of a man with wide boots and a mustard velvet coat, who grunted a greeting and stepped back to let them through. They trouped past him into a large room which had once been handsomely furnished but was now quite shabby. It sported two armchairs, both with frayed coverings, on either side of the wide hearth, a couple of faded tapestries for wall hangings, and a great oaken board down the center of the room flanked by rude oak benches. But shabby as it was, bathed by the warm light of the blazing fire on the hearth, the room took on new luster and Mistress Potts paused to look around her with a wistful half smile. *She is remembering other times here long ago,* thought Lenore with a twinge.

"And how is it that Amos is in York at this time of year?" Mistress Potts demanded truculently of Caleb as they all moved toward the fire.

"All in good time, Abigail." Massive Caleb seemed to have taken control of the situation. He viewed her from beneath low-hanging heavy brows that shadowed his eyes. His thick unkempt mustache and flowing red beard hid any expression around his mouth. His feelings could not have been more cloaked if he had been wearing a mask. All that could be said of that face was that it was broad at the cheekbones and set upon a thick neck. Lenore noted that the coat he wore over his barrellike chest was gravy-stained and wondered that the servants did not attend to it. Come to think of it, no servants had appeared. Could the nephews be living with Amos in this great hall alone?

"First some hot buttered rum to warm ye," rumbled Caleb and waved negligently at Sedgewick.

With alacrity, Sedgewick stumbled toward a steaming pot at the hearth. He pushed back his straggly locks and grabbed three black leathern tankards from a shelf beside the hearth, dropping one with a clatter. Caleb bent to retrieve the "black jack" with a frown and Sedgewick, teetering on unsteady feet, promptly filled it, splashing a little of the hot liquid on Caleb's big spatulate hand as he did so.

Caleb seemed not to feel the hot brew that had contacted his skin. Without comment he turned and offered the rum to Mistress Potts, turning in Lenore's direction as he did so.

Lenore had a chance to study him then. She saw that he had a pinhead perched atop a gigantic body which gave him an ungainly look. In an apparent effort to make his small head appear larger, he had allowed his bushy red hair to grow to shoulder length and his beard to grow freely untrimmed. In his youth that might have served, but now that he was bald on top, the result of those frizzy flowing locks and all that uncombed red beard bushing out in all directions would have been comical had not the little piglike brown eyes that peered down from under heavy lowering reddish brows had a burning glitter. She would learn that Caleb's expression never seemed to change, no matter what the provocation. It was as if he had pulled a length of gauze over his features, masking the man he was. That bothered Lenore. So did his voice, which sounded as if it rumbled up out of a cavern, echoing, strange.

"Rum, Abigail?" he asked.

"Thank ye, no," Mistress Potts sneezed. She shivered as she waddled over to the fire and held out her hands to warm them. "My physician agrees with Mr. Thomas Garway's broadsheet on tea being good for dropsies—not rum."

Caleb grunted and Lenore remembered wryly that Mr. Thomas Garway's broadsheet, which he had published in 1660, had also claimed it would cure ague, fever, consumption, scurvy, kidney stones and bad dreams. She looked askance at her companion and hastily accepted the proffered black jack of steaming rum Sedgewick offered her. He did it with such an overdone display of gallantry, bending from the waist, that he nearly toppled over, and Lenore was about to to step back to get out of the way in case he fell. But he managed to right himself again and reeled to the hearth, to lean against the stones.

As he did so his bleary gaze passed over her in such a licentious way that she felt she might be back on the London stage with half the rakes in town trying to envisage from the pit how she would look stripped of her costume of silver gauze.

Lenore moved uneasily under that gaze, realizing that she had let herself be fooled by Sedgewick's prematurely gray hair and generally unkempt appearance. He was a young man with a narrow, dissipated face. Indeed, she might have met him in London . . .

She took a quick swallow of rum at the thought. The fiery liquid hit her with a shock, but it warmed her cold body and made it easier to stand without shivering, her backside freezing as her front was warmed by the roaring fire on the hearth.

Caleb rescued the other black jacks from Sedgewick and filled them, turning to Lenore as she quickly finished her rum. But she refused another, instead holding out her hands, stiff with cold, and beginning to peel off her gloves, pair by pair.

"This be Mistress Lenore Frankford with me." Belatedly Mistress Potts introduced Lenore. "And this be my driver, Elias Plum, and this be his helper." She nodded at the lad with him. "These be Amos's nephews, Lenore—Caleb Apperton and Sedgewick Robb. They be cousins, although they do not look like it, do they? But what is Amos doing in York at this season? Is he ill?" She looked alarmed.

The two nephews exchanged glances. Caleb ignored

the question, instead proffering a black jack of rum to Elias and another to his young helper. The helper seized his greedily, took a swallow and choked. Plainly he was not used to strong spirits. Elias took his in a red callused hand from which he had just peeled a heavy fur-lined glove. He swallowed the burning liquid almost at a gulp and solemnly passed it back to Caleb for more.

"A man gets dry on the road," he remarked innocently.

Caleb gave him a refill, but it was Sedgewick who leant perilously away from the fireplace and gave answer to Mistress Potts, whose head was thrust forward like a bird's as she listened. "Abigail." He gave his head a shake as if to clear it. "Uncle Amos is—is courting a young lady in York," he explained indistinctly, and Caleb's little head swung slowly toward him. "She's scarce more than a child," amplified Sedgewick in response to the wild look Mistress Potts threw at him, "but Uncle Amos does seem to fancy her. I doubt we'll see him this whole winter season."

"A young lady? Amos?" Mistress Potts' amazed outcry was interrupted by an explosive sneeze. "But he's near as old as I am!" It was the first time Lenore had ever heard Mistress Potts admit she was old.

"Old? Ye're not old, Abigail," came Sedgewick's slurred voice. He favored her with an ingratiating smile and darted a sly look at Lenore. That look made her feel as if a slippery hand had just been slid down into her bosom; she was instantly repelled. "We know not if the young lady fancies Amos, however," he added glibly, and now he seemed somehow a little less drunk. "Nor, more importantly, her father, who has the giving of her. We've not met her, but she's said to be pretty and there's a host of eager swains—" He stopped as he realized Caleb's little eyes were fixed on him, and unsteadily poured himself another black jack of rum.

With a tug, Lenore managed to remove her last glove. Her brow was furrowed. There was something indefinably wrong about the tone of this bizarre conversation. Some undercurrent. But one thing was now abundantly clear to her. Mistress Potts shouldn't stay and wait for Amos who might be gone "this whole winter season." Not in this isolated place with Amos's peculiar nephews. They should both accompany the cart back to York on the morrow and search for Amos there. And now that Mistress Potts' urge to see her old home had been satisfied, there would really be no reason to linger there; they should go all the way to London, if the weather let them. Before she could suggest this, Mistress Potts gave another sneeze that almost shook the room.

"Amos enamored of a young woman—at his age! Why, I can scarce credit it!" With a scandalized expression, the older woman collapsed onto one of the shabby chairs by the fire. "Well, I'll own I'm disappointed not to find him here to greet us, but Mistress Lenore and I will just stay until he returns—even if that be after the New Year!"

Again the two nephews exchanged glances. Caleb leaned over and busied himself with the rumpot, while Sedgewick pulled out the other chair by the hearth for Lenore with some ceremony, and then engaged Elias in conversation, telling him that someone called Tam would be in presently to help him with the horses and suggesting that he and his helper could sleep by the fire as he and Caleb were going to do, while the women could have the chamber just above which received some heat from the same flue. A skinny young fellow wearing a big woolen stocking cap poked his head in just then, was addressed as "Tam," and was told to build a fire in the room just above "for the ladies." He bobbed his head and departed.

"We'll see to the horses ourselves, Bob and me," decided Elias. "No need to wait for Tam there. And we'll bring the boxes into the hall."

"As ye like," Sedgewick agreed affably.

"I must speak to you in the morning before you go, Elias," Lenore called after the big driver. "I—I will want you to post a letter for me." She could hardly explain that she meant to persuade Mistress Potts to return with him. That announcement could come later.

The driver and his helper clomped out. There was a little silence while Sedgewick shifted his boots and Caleb studied them unblinkingly.

"I am surprised ye made it through, this time of year," Caleb rumbled.

"I owe it to Mistress Frankford," said Mistress Potts surprisingly. "She is most resourceful."

Both nephews turned to study Lenore. Sedgewick's hot gaze was speculative. Under that surveillance, she shifted her shoulders uneasily and was relieved when Tam came downstairs and announced the fire had been lit. Caleb sent him out to help Elias in the stable, and Sedgewick turned to Mistress Potts.

"Ye must be tired from your journey. Ye'd best to bed, Abigail," he said with what Lenore considered forced heartiness. "I'll bring up later whatever boxes ye require for overnight," he added insinuatingly.

So he did not expect them to wait for Amos either, thought Lenore with relief.

"The small chest with the tassels will do nicely for tonight," responded Mistress Potts in a tart voice. "Lenore knows which one it is." With deliberate emphasis she added, "The rest can be brought up tomorrow when Tam has the time."

She means to stay, thought Lenore grimly.

"It can be brought up later," agreed Sedgewick, sounding suddenly indifferent. "Abigail?" He gestured toward the hall door, and having warmed their bones with rum before the hearth, the two women now followed Sedgewick's wavering feet upstairs. He carried a single candle and its flickering light told Lenore that there were cobwebs about. She lifted her skirts and trod beside a puffing Abigail Potts up the dank, dusty stair. As they reached the landing, she saw through small frosted panes in the light of a new-risen moon that there were long icicles hanging.

"Ah, 'tis my old room, Sedgewick," sighed Mistress

Potts as Sedgewick opened with some difficulty a creaking door at the head of the stairs. "Never did I think to lay eyes on it again!" She swept forward into the center of a squarish room with big dormers and looked around her with the pride of possession in her old eyes. She was still puttering about, touching the big old bed with its four square posts with gentle fingers, swinging open the doors of the big press by the fireplace and emitting a cloud of dust as she did so, saying "Tch-tch!" as she touched the dusty surface of the white pitcher and washbowl that rested atop a low washstand, when Caleb set the candlestick on a low table beside the bed.

"I'll send Tam up with water and towels," he promised.

"And blankets," added Lenore.

Sedgewick leered at Lenore in a way that said if she'd come to his bed, he'd keep her warm. "And blankets," he echoed, and said good-night.

"Good night," said Mistress Potts absently.

Shivering, Lenore removed her clogs and flexed toes numbed by the cold in her thin slippers. Unhappily she envisioned what it was going to be like in the morning to step out upon that chill hardwood floor. "I'd best run down and get a couple of hot stones to wrap and put at our feet," she offered. "That bed will be freezing!"

"Thank ye, Lenore. 'Tis a good idea." Mistress Potts sank down upon the bed, still gazing about her, wonderstruck as a child. "I can't believe I'm really here," she murmured.

"*I* can believe it," said Lenore with irony. "I think I have frostbite to remind me!" She went downstairs and found the big room empty. Plainly Caleb and Sedgewick, as well as Tam, had gone out to see to the cart and the horses. She put one of the stones on the hearth into the long brass-handled warming pan and heated it over the fire, wrapped the stone carefully. And then another. Before she was finished, there was a great stomping of feet in the hall, and Sedgewick and Caleb and the others trouped back. The cart driver was carrying the little tasseled chest. Lenore took the little chest from Elias and set it down upon a wooden bench.

"I think we'll be accompanying you back tomorrow, Elias," she said and Elias gave her a broad grin. "That is," she added carefully, "I think Mistress Potts, when she thinks it over, will prefer not to wait indefinitely to see her brother Amos. She will probably wish to return to London."

She was unprepared for the look of sudden relief that passed fleetingly over Sedgewick's thin face. Caleb remained as unmoved as a statue.

"Not," she added in a rather tart voice, for she had formed an instant dislike for both of them, "that her brother Amos won't be heartbroken to hear he has missed her!" She snatched up the wrapped hot stones and went back up the stairs, stiff-backed, to join Mistress Potts, who was sneezing again.

Carefully Lenore put the hot wrapped stones between the sheets of the hastily made bed. She straightened up, feeling she might as well get this over with now. "Mistress Potts," she said sternly, "I don't think you should stay here."

"But of course I'm going to stay, Lenore. We both are."

Suddenly Lenore made up her mind. "Well, *you* may stay if you like. But *I* intend to go back with the cart. I'll get a job in Durham—or in York."

"But you can't!" Mistress Potts had been struggling with her pattens; now she looked up, aghast. "I'm counting on you, Lenore. I mean, suppose—suppose Amos doesn't welcome me?"

"Indeed he may not and you should think of that! What would it be like to be stuck out here, snowbound, cut off from the world, with a half brother who may not wish to have you here?"

"But—but he will, Lenore, once he sees you! Men always weaken when you look at them!" This ingenuous compliment opened Lenore's eyes a bit as to the older woman's reason for insisting she accompany her north.

"You forget, Amos already fancies a young woman," Lenore pointed out dryly, "and he may well return with her as his bride."

"Oh, let's hope not," said Mistress Potts so fervently that Lenore paused for a moment to study her. "You—you will stay?" she pleaded.

Lenore sighed. "I will think about it."

Then with a sneezing Mistress Potts safely tucked in the big bed, Lenore went back downstairs to bring up the little tasseled chest which she had forgotten.

Elias and his helper must have gone back to check on the horses once more because she found only Caleb and Sedgewick in the room. The nephews were deep in conversation, their heads close together and Sedgewick started at the sight of her.

"I forgot to take the little chest upstairs," she explained.

As she bent to pick it up, Sedgewick's voice stayed her. "Abigail looked very pale to me," he said, his voice sounding high-pitched and strained. "I realize she has got very stout—she was a comely young woman when she lived here, I've been told—but seeing her has made me wonder, what is the state of her health, that she would chance such a long and difficult journey in this inclement weather?"

With the little tasseled chest in her arms, Lenore hesitated. There could be no harm, she reasoned, in taking them into her confidence. Indeed, it might cause this cold pair to look more kindly upon Mistress Potts while they awaited Amos's return, for she was now certain Mistress Potts meant to stay.

"Mistress Potts saw a doctor before she left London," she told them frankly. "She told me she wanted to see her old home in Northumberland once more before she died."

There was a sudden stillness in the two men opposite

her. Then Sedgewick spoke, his voice sounding shrill and somehow false.

"We must do all we can for Abigail of course," he said, and Caleb rumbled, "Aye."

"I am betraying a confidence to have told you," Lenore added in a hesitant voice. "But I thought that under the circumstances you should know."

"You were right to tell us," Sedgewick said quickly. "And have no fear, Mistress Frankford. We will not let Abigail know that you have told us."

"What ails her?" shot out Caleb. The words seemed to issue from some deep cave.

"I believe it is dropsy," said Lenore. "Although I was not there during the diagnosis, and she does not like to talk about it."

He nodded morosely.

"At the moment," she frowned, "I am more afraid that she may have caught a cold from standing up in the cart looking out over the side with the icy wind whipping her face." Since neither nephew saw fit to respond to that, Lenore added grimly, "If she *has* caught a cold, at her age and in her condition, it might be better for her to wait here for her brother Amos's return rather than to accompany the cart and go searching for Amos in York."

That remark brought an immediate response.

"Abigail should stay here till she's mended," rumbled Caleb. "Amos would think badly of us if we sent her back to York to search for him in this weather," Sedgewick added hastily.

Lenore nodded. There was something puzzling in their reaction, but she could not quite put her finger on it. She went back upstairs to the big drafty room and set the little tasseled chest Mistress Potts had requested down beside the candle on the bedside table, moving it a bit so that one of the tassels would not be so near the candle's flickering flame.

Tassels . . . *Why, this wasn't the chest Mistress Potts always insisted on taking into the inns with her, the little leathern chest with the sharp corners that contained her valuables!*

"Mistress Potts," said Lenore sharply, "where is your little leathern chest?"

"Oh, I don't know." Mistress Potts made a vague gesture with her hand. "I left it in the cart, I suppose."

"But it contains your valuables!"

Mistress Potts gave her such a miserable look that understanding, like a bucket of cold water, washed over Lenore. "Mistress Potts," she whispered, "that's what's wrong, isn't it? You've run out of money!"

Tears welled into Mistress Potts' faded blue eyes. "I'd no idea how expensive the trip would be. I'd meant to have enough left to go away again in case Amos did refuse to receive me. But I had to pay extra for the sled runners, and then we had to stay over so long at inns along the way."

"You mean, we must wait while you send back to London for money?"

"No, I mean—well, I've been foolish about my expenses these last years, I realize that now. And I seem to have run out of money. All of it. I racked my brain where to go. None of my friends would have me, I'm sure—at least not for long. I was hopeful of my cousin at Cambridge, but she was dead when we got there. Amos was my last hope. I was so sure he'd take me in. . . ."

"Blood being thicker than water," murmured Lenore.

"No. Because he wouldn't let such a good chance pass to crow over me in triumph. He always said I'd end up without a farthing—and now I have."

So she'd come home to eat crow, sure she'd be welcomed—if only as an object of derision and scorn!

"Mistress Potts," sighed Lenore. *"Why* didn't you tell me?"

The older woman looked genuinely upset. "I know I should have," she admitted humbly. "But I kept thinking you wouldn't come along if I told you I was off to Northumberland to try to borrow money from my half brother. But I knew your kind heart wouldn't let a dying woman go alone to visit her old home for the last time!"

In spite of her chagrin, Lenore began to laugh. She laughed till tears ran down her cheeks. "Mistress Potts," she gasped when she could get her breath again, "you've missed your calling. 'Twas *you* that should have been on the London stage, not I!"

"You won't tell the nephews?" Mistress Potts leant forward anxiously. "I'm sure they must expect to inherit from Amos, having lived here with him so long—that is, unless he takes a bride and has children of his own. And if they knew I'd come back here as a pensioner, they might try to send me packing before Amos returns." She ended her remark with a great sneeze that shook her whole body.

"You can count on it, I won't tell them," Lenore said ruefully. "In fact, like a complete fool, I've just confided in them that you came home to die!"

"Well, that's good!" cried Mistress Potts with another sneeze. "You believed it, so 'twill have the ring of truth. Now they'll tell Amos and maybe soften his hard heart. He couldn't turn out a dying woman, could he, Lenore?" she asked anxiously.

Lenore shook her head. Mistress Potts' affairs were getting quite complicated, it seemed to her.

"You *must* help me do this, Lenore!" Mistress Potts reached out and seized Lenore's wrist in entreaty. "I'm afraid I can't manage it alone."

Lenore gazed into that tired worried face. How well she knew what it was like to have not a farthing! She was in the very same case at this moment!

"I'll help you," she promised more softly. "But now you'd best try to go to sleep and fight off this cold that's coming on, or you may indeed catch your death and die here! But I still don't think we should stay here at Wallham. I think we should go back with the driver to York and look for your brother Amos there. Perhaps he will be willing to pension you off so that you can go back to London."

"Aye, I'd like that!"

"For I really don't think you'd like living out your life in this out-of-the-way place."

"Do you think you could arrange that, Lenore?" The older woman's voice was wistful. "If the driver would be willing to take us back to York and wait for payment, I could look for Amos there. Sedgewick could give me the name of the inn where he's staying."

"I don't think the driver will deal in promises."

"Well, we have no coins to give him!"

"But you have handsome luggage and many fine garments that would bring a price. If you would be willing to sell some of them?"

Mistress Potts winced. She loved her rich broadcades, her embroidered gloves, her feather-plumed hats, her linens and ivory fans and laces. "If need be, I will part with them," she agreed gloomily.

"Maybe you won't have to," Lenore encouraged. "Maybe Amos will come forward and pay the driver." She didn't really have much hope of that because the look of this house was so shabby; large though it was, it didn't look like the abode of a wealthy man. Was it too ludicrous to imagine that Amos might be in York dangling after some heiress to mend his fortunes? "If he won't, maybe Elias will let me pay him back after I get a job, for our fare. He seems kind enough and maybe I can persuade him."

Mistress Potts closed her eyes. "All right," she said in a faint voice. "Tomorrow."

But on the morrow Mistress Potts awoke with a fever. Lenore knew she dared not make the trip with her in this condition. Nor did she fancy leaving her in this cold drafty house in the surly care of the nephews while she went back to York to seek out Amos on her behalf.

"Could the driver not stay over," she pleaded with Caleb as they stood by the hearth after breakfast, "until Mistress Potts is well enough to accompany him? She's not used to country life anymore, and it might be better if she saw her brother Amos in York before returning to London."

Caleb looked at her without speaking. She wondered if he had heard her. Then, just as she despaired of an answer, he rumbled, "I'll go up and see Abigail."

Lenore accompanied him upstairs, her step gossamer-light beside his heavy thumping boots. He opened the bedroom door and stared for a minute at Abigail Potts, her face flushed among the pillows. She greeted him with a large sneeze. Caleb closed the door. "Abigail should stay here," he told Lenore firmly. "Winter travel would be too much for her. The driver is welcome to stay over if he likes."

It was Elias himself who put up objections. "There be worse storms to come, Mistress Frankford, for winter is not yet rightly begun," he declared, his face flushed and earnest. "But if *you* ask it of me . . ."

"I do ask it, Elias," said Lenore, deliberately using his first name and looking at him steadily with her violet eyes. "Please stay over another day or two to let Mistress Potts get well—a week at the most."

Dazzled by the full power of that violet gaze, Elias promptly assented, and Lenore went back up to nurse Mistress Potts through her cold as speedily as possible. But the long hard trip and her age were telling on that lady's normally strong constitution. She remained weak and feverish, and by the end of the week was no better.

Ignored by Lenore, Elias had grown restless. Now he announced in a firm voice that he must leave on the morrow, "God and the weather willing."

Lenore sighed. She knew she could not keep him longer.

"Why do ye not go back with me yourself and leave the old lady here with her kinfolk?" he urged, following her out into the cold hallway where the stairs led up-ward.

"She's too ill," said Lenore sadly. "I think she well might die if I left her here."

"Well," ruminated Elias, "the old lady did pay me well. And if she'd be willing to part with some more coins, I might be persuaded."

Lenore moistened her lips and returned his gaze steadily. "I—we have no more money." She kept her voice down in case one of the nephews was listening from the room behind her, even though the door between was closed. "But Mistress Potts' luggage surely has some value, and she has many handsome garments that would bring a price if they were sold, say in York at the Christmas season. Could you stay and carry us to York on the promise we would pay you there from the proceeds?"

"Nay, I'd not do that." Elias shuffled his feet and avoided her eyes. "For if I took ye to York," he muttered, "the old lady would be sure to make an outcry and be sorry she'd promised to sell her things and I'd not have the heart to press her. But"— his voice deepened—"there's another coin ye could pay me in, Mistress."

Lenore had no doubt as to what that coin was. Elias Plum's meaning was all too clear. For emphasis he reached out and drew her to him. Her body went rigid as her breasts were pressed against the coarse material of his doublet.

She tensed and for a moment her senses swam. She could hear his strong hearbeat and smell the rum and tobacco that tainted his clothes. There was a rough tenderness in the way he held her that told her how badly he desired her. The thought teased her. She could buy her way out of this mess merely by sleeping with Elias Plum all the way to York. But she had never used this kind of coin to buy her way anywhere.

She would not begin now, with Elias Plum.

With a lithe gesture, she pulled free of him. "The luggage and clothing are the only coin in which I'm prepared to pay."

"Then I'll take my leave on the morrow," said Elias in a surly voice. "But," he added more kindly, "I'll carry along the letter you spoke of, Mistress, and post it where I can."

The letter! Lenore had forgotten all about the letter she had mentioned that first night. She went up and looked down gloomily at Mistress Potts, her face flushed as she lay sleeping, her breath making a rasping in her throat.

Mistress Potts was plainly in no condition to be moved.

That she could persuade Elias to take her back with him, gambling on possible recompense as she "got to know him better," she had no doubt. She could play him along, if she wished, all the way to York, ending with a promise to repay "when she could."

But Lenore was not a cheat, and besides that would mean leaving Mistress Potts to her fate. Memories flooded back to Lenore of how often Mistress Potts had helped her—when her money had run out in London, when she had been working the necessary "free" months to become an actress in the King's Company of Players.

She could not deliberately cheat Elias, nor could she desert her friend.

Gloomily she rummaged about in Mistress Potts' boxes until she found pen and paper. Then, seated at the little writing desk they had brought with them, she wrote a letter to Lorena. It was a lying letter, born of the bruising knowledge that she must stay in this desolate place nursing a sick woman, with no assurance of any secure future for either her or Lorena. A sob caught in her throat as she thought how she had prayed, had planned even, to have Lorena with her long before this. And now, who knew when she would ever see her daughter?

At least she could let Lorena believe that all was well, could give her a confident—even grand—view of the life her mother was leading!

I have left the stage temporarily, she wrote. *I am wintering in a great house in Northumberland with a friend whose home it is.* It *had* been Mistress Potts' girlhood home, she told herself with a twinge. Her pen rushed on, casually dropping the words *mansion* and *vast estate* and *gilded coach* and telling Lorena glibly that a great ball was planned. She refused to acknowledge even to herself that these all were lies and half-truths—this was the world as it *ought* to be! And for Lorena's young ears, would be! Recklessly she added that she would wear *my best black silk, which was made for me in France. All the gentry will attend,* she wrote, *and I will teach them all the new dances from London, for Northumberland is very merry now that the Christmas season approaches.* She cast a bleak glance through the window at the vast expanse of snow, the seemingly endless gray wall that leaped from crag to crag like a theatrical backdrop, and her lower lip caught in her teeth. Why should not Lorena imagine Northumberland to be bright and jolly?

After many admonitions to her daughter to be good and apply herself to her studies at the vicarage, after best wishes to Flora and the vicar, she started to pen her closing sentence. Her quill pen hovered above the parchment. She almost wrote, *When spring comes, I will come for you, Lorena, and we will be together again and get to know one another.* But—she could not do it. She could not hold out that false hope to her daughter, for she knew she would be hard pressed to feed herself when at last she left this place, let alone a growing girl!

With misty eyes she signed and sealed the letter, sat with it in her lap before taking it down to Elias to post for her.

In the distance through the window the gray wall seemed to waver like a snake along the high crags, reminding her how desolate was her situation.

In the dead of winter she was stranded in Northumberland with a sick woman, without money, and with no prospect of her life taking a turn for the better.

Claremont Court, Kent

Chapter 14

Bitterly cursing the first day he had laid eyes on Lenore, Geoffrey Wyndham blundered south from York through blowing drifts of snow. Gale-driven bits of ice slashed at his face as he told himself he hated her, that he was glad he had found her out for what she was. But his whole long body ached with the remembered sweetness of her surrender and he seemed to hear her voice, a sultry Circe-call on the wailing wind.

In Lincoln he was snowed in by a storm in which nothing moved for a week, and afterward it was slow going as the countryside dug out from under its heavy white blanket. He did not make it to Kent in time for Christmas. Instead he put up at the Star in London and devoted himself to drink. He propped his wide-topped boots on the hearth rail, glared into the fire, and ignored friend and foe alike as he drank himself insensible.

Yet he could not rid himself of the beautiful face that floated up accusingly—and so sadly—before him.

Wait, Geoffrey, let me explain!

What had she meant? What *could* she have meant, when her perfidy was all too clear?

But still that lovely face with the sad violet eyes would float up before him, no matter how hard he tried to drown it with wine.

At last he smashed his glass—and his last bottle— into the fireplace where it sputtered and flamed up; then he rose, jamming his hat down upon his head, and repaired himself to Kent.

There things were not much better.

"We did not see ye for Christmas, Geoffrey." Letiche had seen him come riding in and now she came rustling down the stairway to the great hall to intercept him. He noted wryly that, like a princess, she had assumed the royal "we" and her ice green gown looked no colder than her auburn eyes. "It was dull without you."

In point of fact, it had not been dull. Andre, her lover, had been down, along with the Marquis de Vignac and a host of other friends. They had swept Letiche into a round of country parties, but her heart had burned for parties at only one place—those at Whitehall where Louise de Keroualle and Barbara Villiers fought for supremacy.

"I am sorry, Letiche," he said wearily. At that moment he was. A little fortune hunter Letiche had been when she married him, but he was no better. And for a brief summertime in France he had believed that she had changed, that she loved him. There had been children born of those summer days, and although the children were gone, the tenderness had lingered, like cobwebs hard to brush away.

"Where were you, Geoffrey?" Her voice was as sharp as her eyes. She studied him, decided that his coat was not cut so well as de Vignac's, that his sword hilt was too—too serviceable, not at all like Andre's intricately worked hilt.

"In the north country—York."

"York?" She was startled for although Andre had laconically brought back word that Geoffrey had ridden

in, covered with snow, to the Star and locked himself in his room, that he was reportedly drowning himself with drink, she had not thought that he had traveled so far. "What did you seek in York?"

A shadow of pain flittered over his dark face, and Letiche was quick enough to see it. "Some business of the king's," he muttered.

That orange girl! she thought. He was out chasing after that damned orange girl! He has made me a laughingstock!

"Raoul was down," she said, hoping to twit him, for Geoffrey had sometimes crossed verbal swords with the marquis, believing him loyal to nothing. In that he was wrong; the Marquis de Vignac was passionately loyal to his class, to his way of life. He would have preferred death to dusty boots, a shabby suit, weathered-looking equipage. Men like de Vignac were the birds for whom the word "plumage" was created.

"And Malraux, I suppose, and all the rest of—" He had been about to say "those French hangers-on," but in deference to his wife's French blood he changed it to "that pack."

"I know you do not like Raoul and Andre, Geoffrey, but I wish you would not refer to them as *'that pack.'* They are not dogs!"

"Wolves," Geoffrey amended.

Letiche struck her white hands together angrily and her earbobs sparkled as she gave a jarring laugh. "And were your Yuletide entertainments so much more merry in York than they would have been in Kent?" she jibed at him.

"Did my gifts arrive?" he countered, for he had belatedly sent by messenger from London a hastily bought but elegant necklace and matching earbobs of amethysts and diamonds.

Letiche was taken aback. "They—were very nice, Geoffrey. I bought you a new saddle. In your absence it was taken out to the stable."

Geoffrey stood with his feet on the stone floor and

gazed up at his wife, leaning haughtily on the stair rail above, in some amusement. "Thank you. I will be glad to have it." He knew she was well aware how little he cared for a saddle's appearance so long as it was serviceable and fit the horse's back comfortably.

She sniffed. "I would hope you would use it instead of that dilapidated one you've been using. This one has gold stitching like Raoul's and silver fittings."

He was sure he would not like it. He had a distaste for fancy things about a horse. A good light saddle, strong light reins, and up and away! "I am sure it is in the latest fashion," he said ironically, "if it is the type de Vignac uses." He started up the stairs.

Letiche reddened at his veiled sarcasm. She was still smarting over his having been gone from her side during the holidays—her guests had remarked on it. It was one thing to be an unfaithful wife, enjoying secret trysts with her lover, and quite another to be an object of pity and amusement to one's friends because one's husband was forever absent!

"I am the most neglected wife in the kingdom!" she burst out.

"Not quite," he said, brushing by her ice green taffeta skirts.

"It is true, you are never home!" Those taffeta skirts rustled after him angrily.

From the landing above, Geoffrey paused and looked down at her. His face was tired, jaded, and his words fell on her bitterly. "Ask yourself, Letiche, if you really care? Would you not honestly prefer one reception at Whitehall to a whole year of my company?"

His jibe had struck home. Letiche fell back muttering and snapping her ivory fan open and shut. Her auburn gaze followed her tall husband's back dangerously. In France, during the apple orchard days with Raoul, no one had said her nay! Headstrong, spoilt, Letiche had grown up addicted to having her own way, and she had confidently expected it to be that way with Geoffrey.

In most things he had given in to her. This hand-some Tudor house, English to its foundations, had been furnished in the current French mode at her behest. Most of the servants were French. Letiche's gowns were of the finest materials, all imported from Paris. She chose them from little dolls sent over from France by couturiers, dolls dressed in garments that would be duplicated human-size for ladies of fashion.

She was mistress of Geoffrey's home, but she did not have his heart—had never had his heart. It infuriated her.

With anger to spur her usually leisurely pace, the ice green taffeta skirts swished imperiously up and down the long gallery built for exercise in inclement weather. But Letiche hardly noticed the sweeping expanse of parkland visible through the tall windows. Not even the gilt furnishings brought from France at such expense at-tracted her eye. She was flushed and irritable and—she had a problem.

By suppertime she had decided on her course of action.

She had chosen to adorn herself with a gown of silver tissue over gold-shot white brocade, her amethyst taffeta petticoats whispering as she swept into the long dining room. Her auburn hair was fetchingly arranged with lovelocks that danced about her ears, and Geoffrey's amethyst and diamond necklace and earbobs flashed con-spicuously from her throat and ears.

Geoffrey noted them in silence.

Letiche, aware that she would be wearing a deep décolletage tonight, had ordered the fire built high. Geoffrey, standing before it attired in boots, dove gray velvet coat and trousers and gray brocade doublet shot with gold, found the room unpleasantly hot. With a sigh he took off his coat.

"Must you do that, Geoffrey?" Letiche had meant to be placating, but now her voice crackled. "Must you appear like some lackey at your own dinner table?"

Cutting as it was meant to be, the remark amused

Geoffrey. "I'll be sure to tell the king your opinion of this doublet," he laughed. "His own tailor made it."

Letiche stamped her foot. "You know what I mean, Geoffrey. You know *very well* what I mean!"

Geoffrey gazed at her sardonically. "Indeed, I am well aware what you mean, Letiche. You never leave me in any doubt. When you are annoyed, you say everything twice. Will you not be seated and sup? Food has a way of mending tempers."

Flushed and biting her lips, Letiche flounced down into a gilt chair hastily pulled back by a green-liveried servant. She was seated at the far end of the long gleaming table when Geoffrey waved aside the French servant who dashed forward to pull back his chair and seated himself without ceremony at the head. Across the long board, with its great branched silver candlesticks, its enormous centerpiece of fruit surmounted by a pink marble cupid aiming his bow at the high-beamed ceiling above them, they regarded each other. Obsequious servants came and went, bringing numerous courses. Sallets, fricassees, meat courses—boiled, baked and cold; wild fowl, broths.

Before they had reached the Florentines and tarts, Letiche's high color had subsided. She gave her husband what was intended to be a melting look. "You did not note that I am wearing your Christmas gift, Geoffrey." She touched the jeweled necklace delicately with her fingers.

"I noted it." Geoffrey lifted a crystal goblet of wine in mocking tribute. "You are as handsomely got up as any duchess."

That remark stung her. She leaned forward and her voice became waspish, carrying to him down the long table. "A duchess? Indeed I *should* be a duchess! Why has not the king given you a title, Geoffrey? He has lavished titles on so many lesser men—why not you?"

"I did not want one. I told the king that I preferred something more tangible—a house and lands."

"You could have had both!"

"Perhaps." He shrugged.

Letiche fluttered her fan angrily and her breasts, half exposed in the handsome gown, rose and fell. That she should go untitled was a bone of contention between them. Only yesterday one of her French friends, an arrogant duchess, had twitted her about her lack of title!

"I would have thought this house, these furnishings, the fortune you spend on clothes would be enough for you, Letiche." Geoffrey took another sip of wine, eyeing her.

Down the table, across the great silver trenchers and chargers, his wife sniffed and her dark red curls quivered. "If you have no thought for me," she cried pettishly, "you should think of your children!"

Geoffrey started, at this reminder of their loss.

"I know!" She covered her face with her hands, watching him through her fingers, and gave a wrenching sob. "Our children died of a fever and I know you blame me for it!"

"Letiche, I have never said I blamed you."

"Oh, but you do, you do! They were so little, and you felt I should not have left them with that nurse. But how could I have known? How could I?" Her voice was piteous.

A spasm of pain went through Geoffrey's tall frame. He had loved his children, mourned them, missed them. But he had been away in Brussels at the time—who could say they would not have died of the fever anyway, even had Letiche hovered at their bedside? He felt a sudden compassion for the crumpled-up figure at the end of the table. Of course, she missed them too, blamed herself.

"Letiche." He got up and came around the table, and she clutched his hand convulsively, looked up into his eyes with tears sparkling on her lashes.

Her voice was husky. "There will be *other* children, Geoffrey."

He moved his shoulders irritably. It was true he had not come to her bed in a very long time. He could not bring himself to do it, feeling as he did about Lenore. Nor had he realized Letiche cared. He had thought her fully absorbed with hemlines and froufrou and the latest design in black patches.

Letiche gave him what she hoped was a fetching smile of enticement and fluttered her fan so that her musky perfume might waft up to his nostrils. She had reasons of her own for wanting Geoffrey in her bed—at least once. She had been careless lately with Andre—something could come of it. If she were to become with child, she had foresight enough to want the dangerous man she had married to feel certain that the child was *his*.

"I have neglected you," he admitted, giving her a troubled look.

"Yes, you have!" Letiche followed up her advantage. "You have become a scandal in London. Oh, do not think I have not heard about it. Women"—she did not want him to think it was Raoul who had brought her the news—"are quick to taunt other women about these things!"

So she had heard about his search for Lenore. Geoffrey disengaged his arm and began to pace up and down the floor. "Letiche, I should have told you myself. It is only fair that you should—"

"No, not another word, Geoffrey!" Letiche was alarmed by his demeanor. It might precede some declaration of his undying love for that—that orange girl! Any such declaration could only build a further barrier between them. "I do not want to hear about your women, Geoffrey."

His women. Geoffrey winced. *One woman only!* He supposed that from Letiche's point of view . . .

"It is *over*, Letiche." His voice carried weight.

Letiche looked at him in surprise. But then, she told herself, men always said that, didn't they? She peered with more interest at her husband. There *were* dark shadows under his eyes as if he had not slept well lately. She had assumed the tired look on his face to be the result of nights spent in whoring but—could he be losing sleep over that wench Raoul had spoken of?

Imperious, grasping Letiche could not believe that a mere orange girl had rejected the great manorial lord that Geoffrey Wyndham had become—even if he had no title. Could it be that he had somehow missed the slippery wench—again?

Her eyes sparkled for a moment with malice, and she dropped her gaze lest he see it.

Geoffrey's shoulders moved convulsively. Even now speaking of the loss of his children was painful to him, and the memory of Lenore was an open wound. "I must go back to London," he said. "I will start after supper. 'Tis a clear night; the roads are frozen over."

"But that's ridiculous. There are footpads on the road, highwaymen!"

That might be a good way to end it, he thought bitterly and almost hoped some "gentleman of the road" took careful aim at his heart and fired from ambush. "If I do not survive the perils of the road," he said evenly, "you will be well provided for, Letiche."

Her lashes flickered. He was leaving—again! And before he had served her purpose! "Ah, Geoffrey," she said in a soft voice, "how can you say that? When you know it is your welfare that worries me?"

He gave her a grim look. He had never been certain of this French jade, but at least he understood her tempers. Of this placating mood, he was wary.

"You give me no chance to be a wife to you," she wheedled. "You are always absent!"

That at least was mainly true, and the slight note of hysteria in Letiche's voice gave her words the ring of sincerity.

"What would you have me do, Letiche?" he asked soberly, reminding himself that this woman—whatever she was—bore his name, had once borne his children.

"Stay with me tonight, Geoffrey. Go to London tomorrow, that is time enough. Ah, please, Geoffrey!" She got up and came around the table toward him, her amethyst taffeta petticoats rustling. A green-liveried servant bustled by with his head down, careful not to look at them, and Geoffrey moved his shoulders uneasily. Letiche had no reserve; she never cared what she said before the servants, she treated them as if they were not there at all. It was a thing he could not get used to. Now she had reached his side and her musky perfume reached him. Her face was turned appealingly upward, her auburn eyes were anxious, her expensive earbobs sparkled. "You cannot ask me always to lie in a cold bed, Geoffrey," she pleaded, "while you are away in London, dancing to the king's tune in Whitehall."

His face hardened.

"I do not dance to the king's tune, Letiche. Need I remind you that all we have here—yes, even the clothes on your back—we owe to his majesty's favor?"

"Granted, granted," Letiche sighed. "But there was a time—oh, I know we got off to a bad start, and I hated you and even prayed for your death. But then you came back to France and you rescued me, Geoffrey, for I knew not where I would turn. And after the children were born, I thought—" Her voice faltered very convincingly. She was watching his face and saw a ripple of pain go through it. Quick to follow up her advantage, she put both her small hands beseechingly against his gray brocade doublet, picked delicately at the gold threads shot through it. "You *will* stay with me tonight, Geoffrey?"

The wistfulness in her tone cut at his heart. Letiche was not to blame that he did not love her! And he had long ago absolved her from any blame in the children's death. The nurse had been experienced, it had been only coincidence that Letiche had decided to stay the weekend at a nearby estate when they became so ill.

He looked down at her shining auburn hair, copper in the candlelight, and at her upturned face.

"I will stay."

Letiche took a deep breath. Her back straightened and her eyes glowed with triumph. She had him! "I will go upstairs now," she told him archly. "Do not—do not be long, Geoffrey."

He did not watch her leave the room. He had turned his gaze to the fire and looked remote.

Upstairs in her handsomely paneled boudoir Letiche hummed a wicked French ditty that was currently making the rounds as her maid, a young girl from Marseilles, undressed her. Geoffrey was a savage, of course—*all* Englishmen were savages in matters of love! Did not Raoul say so, Raoul who had taught her those enchanting byroads of sex that would not impair her virginity in that orchard so long ago? And Andre . . . ah, Andre! Letiche sighed and moved voluptuously as the maid's clever fingers undid the drawstring of her chemise. With a shrug of her white shoulders, Letiche let the chemise fall to the floor, stepped out of it and walked naked to the tall pier glass sent over from Paris just a month ago. She minced about before its marble base, considering her reflection. She turned about before the mirror, tossed her lovelocks so that they caressed her white shoulders, considered her small waist and softly rounded stomach, the gentle rise of her hips. Ah, she had kept her figure, had she not? Her breasts were as rounded, as enticing as when Raoul had first pinched them under that apple tree near Boulogne. The nipples had darkened from pink to rose, of course, but that was the price one must pay for motherhood. She frowned. She had never loved her children, never wanted them, never missed them—although she knew Geoffrey had. On learning of their death, she had screamed and fainted, but it was only in fear for herself, fear that Geoffrey would blame her for going off on a hunting party to a nearby chateau when the children's fever was so high. But she had brazened it out—just as she would brazen out tonight!

And one must admit that Geoffrey was all man! His frontal attack—for Geoffrey took all his objectives frontally—would be an interesting change from Andre's more subtle and more decadent ways of driving her to heights of passion. Ah, Andre *destroyed* her with his wicked lust!

Andre . . . she sighed. What was Andre doing to-night? Bedding some whore in London no doubt, for she had no doubt that he was unfaithful to her. *All* men were unfaithful as soon as they were out of sight. There was small comfort that Andre would be discreet—and he would put *her* first. Just as Geoffrey—her auburn eyes narrowed and she gave her naked thigh a soft slap—put that damned orange girl first!

She yearned to punish the orange girl.

Behind her the little maid coughed deprecatingly to tell her mistress she had heard a masculine boot on the stairs.

Letiche frowned. "You may go," she said haughtily. "No, first bring me some of that scent." She would not have it rubbed in all over her body tonight as she did on those occasions when she met Andre. No, a bit of scent on the shoulders and breasts and throat would be enough; that was where Geoffrey's head would lie.

The footsteps were coming closer now. Letiche dismissed her maid with an imperious wave of her arm, ran on bare feet to the big square bed whose embroidered satin coverlet had been thrown back, lightly climbed the ornate little two-step ladder that led up to it, and jumped in.

When Geoffrey opened the big double doors, Letiche was lying back against a pile of satin pillows, her arms behind her head. She had let down her auburn hair and it spilled carelessly over her arms and spread out around her. The light of a single bedside candle in a silver holder picked out a wicked sparkle in her auburn eyes and cast a golden glow to the rosy-tipped breasts that peeked from above the coverlet's edge.

Geoffrey strode across the room, blew out the candle. He cursed as he barked his shin against the little ornate bedside ladder and kicked it aside. His long legs needed no ladder to vault into the high thronelike bed.

Later, as he clasped Letiche's small resilient body in his arms, he tried to renew the feeling he had once had for her, so long ago in France. As she squirmed in his arms and seemed to melt against him, as she murmured words of love brokenly, his grip on her enticing body tightened, and he told herself firmly that he loved her still, that she was entitled to his protection, his trust.

Letiche was a skillful mistress of the art of love—having been taught by so many experts—and for a little while he lost himself to her charms, forgot that other redhead for whom his soul and body burned. When it was over, he fell into a deep sleep.

Had he stayed awake, he would have seen his narrow-eyed wife slip from her bed in the moonlight and steal into the next room and pen a letter to her lover.

We need not worry, Andre, she wrote to him in her beautiful fragile handwriting, her quill pen scratching happily over the paper. *Even though we were reckless last time*—a few curlicues here for emphasis—*I have enticed Geoffrey into my bed again—I told you I could. So if anything should happen, he will never suspect.* She left it unsigned.

She sealed the letter with sealing wax and looked thoughtfully at the door beyond which Geoffrey lay sleeping. With an impudent little shrug she penned another letter, this one to the Marquis de Vignac, in which she invited him down to Claremont Court to sup, adding at the end, *Please give the enclosed note to Andre.* She signed it *Letiche* and slipped the note to Andre inside, sealing it carefully with sealing wax.

Her auburn eyes were sparkling with malice and amusement as she stole back into her bedroom and into her connubial bed.

Tomorrow Geoffrey would wake refreshed and ride away to London—doubtless to seek that damned orange girl! But he would carry with him, all unknowing, enclosed in a letter to her old friend and distant kinsman, the Marquis de Vignac, a note to his wife's lover!

Wallham, Northumberland

Chapter 15

That winter was a terrible one for Lenore. It was a bad winter all over England, with great falls of snow and terrible blizzard winds that sent slivers of ice pelting against already frosted windowpanes. It was bitter cold clear down into Devon. Icicles dripped from church spires across the land, snow weighed down the yews and holly, and the icy roads were well nigh impassable. York was frozen in and all Northumberland was a white wasteland.

Winter had closed down on the Cotswolds too.

In Twainmere's vicarage, up in the high-peaked loft, Lorena lay wrapped in thick blankets of Cotswold wool on nights when frost made the moonlight seem but a whiter glow in a world asparkle with ice. But cold as it was, she could lie there with her feet pressed against a stone hot from the warming pan and smell the spicy scent of apples, for her bedroom doubled as a storage room, and Flora, knowing the vicar's penchant for putting Lorena on bread and water, had thoughtfully stored a barrel of apples up there. Lorena could lie there in bed and munch an apple and dream of her mother's glittering successes on the London stage. She had not yet received the letter Lenore had written from Northumberland, so she imagined her mother still to be in London, dressed in silver gauze and doubtless performing before the king himself. Dreamily Lorena imagined the thousands of candles burning in crystal chandeliers above the stage, the thumping applause from the pit, the boxes filled with great nobles dressed in silks and satins and eating little China oranges and taking snuff from jeweled snuff boxes. It was an elegant world she pictured for her mother—the world Lenore might indeed have had, had she seized her opportunities like Nell Gwyn.

Lorena "borrowed" a sheet of the vicar's finest vellum and wrote a letter to her mother, and daily she found reasons why there was as yet no answer: the roads were impassable, the mail could not move, her mother was too caught up in a round of gaiety to find time to reply—always a new reason.

She could not know that her mother was shivering in an even colder bedroom in Northumberland—for the fire seemed never to make the high-ceilinged drafty room really warm—as she sat anxiously beside an ill and coughing Mistress Potts. And as she bathed that fevered brow or tucked the covers in around that old neck, coming reluctantly to the realization that the older woman would never be able to leave Wallham until the spring.

That is, if her estranged half brother Amos did not return meanwhile from York and throw them both out.

The Twelve Days of Christmas were perhaps the worst days of the whole winter season for Lenore. For they brought back vivid memories, as she sat alone in the cold room listening to Mistress Potts' stertorous breathing, of another Christmas, in Oxford, when a tired Geoffrey had floundered home through the drifts to the house off Magpie Lane, a season of joy. How she had loved him! Her bruised heart—now that he had flung her aside—remembered things that brought tears to her lashes: their joined bodies clinging together in the big square bed while outside, snowy Oxford looked like a giant wedding cake. With her eyes closed, Lenore could hear Geoffrey murmur softly into her ear, could feel his light loving exploring touch on her naked body and tingle again with the rapture to which he drove her, while outside, Oxford's midnight bells were chiming. Geoffrey, Geoffrey . . . how could she face life without him?

The Twelve Days of Christmas had passed before Mistress Potts rallied and roused herself from her sick bed sufficiently to hobble downstairs to breakfast.

That was a memorable day at Wallham.

"It will not do to lower our standards," she told Lenore as she whitened her face with ceruse and added a large black patch on one cheek. When she finally tottered downstairs to make her dramatic entrance, she was such a marvel of wine taffeta furbelows, all overlaid with black lace and garnished with black velvet ribands asparkle with jet, that Sedgewick seemed genuinely awed.

"Abigail," he faltered. "Ye do look well this morning."

Mistress Potts acknowledged this tribute regally as she sat down at the shabby board. She gave skinny Tam, who doubled as cook, a disapproving glance. "Where are Amy and Nance?" She eyed her bowl of watery gruel in some alarm. "Surely Amos can't have let all the servants go?"

"Amos has had some reverses," Sedgewick told her quickly. "He had to sell the plate"—indicating the wooden bowls and cheap pewter cutlery and trenchers. "Amy died ten years ago, and Nance hurt her back and went off to live with her relations in Wales. If ye'd kept in touch, ye'd have known of it."

"Ye know perfectly well why I didn't keep in touch!" Mistress Potts' voice rose with indignation. "My father wanted me to stay single, to stay here and take care of my stepmother, who was no kin of mine. Like some hired servant! And Amos sided with him, of course. *That* was why we quarreled and *that* was why I did not write to Amos or visit him all the years I lived in Brighton and after!"

So Abigail Potts had quarreled with Amos. Lenore's heart sank, and she stared hopelessly at her gruel. Now she realized there was little hope that Amos would allow Abigail Potts to stay, once he returned to take over his household. Most likely he would send her packing immediately. It would be up to Lenore to find a way to keep them both out of the almshouse.

"They thought ye were too young to marry, Abigail," corrected Caleb heavily, and Lenore turned to look at him. With that pinhead atop his giant's body, he looked even grimmer than the winter landscape stretching forever away outside the icy panes. Beside him, Sedgewick seemed a reed. Caleb was the prime mover here, she realized, he was the *force*.

Beneath the ceruse whitening, Mistress Potts' cheeks flushed. "And did either of ye marry?" she asked tartly.

There was a little silence while heads bent over spoons. Then:

"Caleb did," said Sedgewick, looking up. "I didn't."

Caleb brought his clenched fist down upon the table with a force that rattled the trenchers and made Lenore seize her tankard of cider before it turned over. "My wife was a brazen women!" he roared. "I forbid you to mention her!" He surged to his feet, overturning his chair in the process. Everyone at the table sat paralyzed as Caleb glared at them from those little deep-set eyes. Then he threw down his napkin and stomped from the room. They heard the front door slam almost hard enough to break its heavy iron hinges.

"What—what was that about?" Mistress Potts whispered and Tam peered in from the kitchen door, looking scared.

Sedgewick too seemed shaken by the incident, for before answering he emptied his tankard which, Lenore guessed, contained something stronger than cider. His long face was pale when he set it back on the table.

"She left him, Abigail."

"She *did?*" Always gossip prone, Mistress Potts leaned forward. "Was it anyone I know, the woman Caleb married?"

"No. She was from London. Her name was Sylvie."

Looking around her at this shabby barren room where the cold crept in around her feet even though the fire blazed on the hearth, a place with no near neighbors, no one to talk to save the nephews and Tam—and Amos of course—Lenore marveled not that Sylvie had left, but that she had married Caleb in the first place.

"*She left him!*" Mistress Potts, her eyes alight, was still drinking that in. "Where did he meet this Sylvie?"

"Caleb often competes for prizes in strongman feats at the fairs," explained Sedgewick. "Wrestling, pitching the bar, throwing the sledge. 'Twas at Banbury Fair he met Sylvie and brought her home as his bride."

Lenore remembered the Banbury Fair: filled with hangers-on of all types—cutpurses, lewd women. She'd attended that Fair twice while she worked as an "advance man" for the strolling players. So big Caleb had married a London wench who had drifted up to the Fair.

"What was the trouble between them?" asked Mistress Potts avidly.

"Sylvie had a roving eye for men," Sedgewick said dryly. His mouth closed with a snap. He looked unhappy, as if he wished he hadn't said that. With unsteady hands he poured himself another tankard from a jug beside his chair, and Lenore felt a brief moment of sympathy for him. Caleb might easily pound Sedgewick to the consistency of a pudding if he knew Sedgewick was discussing his marital woes with Abigail.

But Mistress Potts was not one to leave so enticing an avenue untrodden. "Ye mean she took a *lover?*"

"Aye." Sedgewick downed the contents of his tankard.

Abigail leaned forward. *"Who was it?"*

For an agonized moment, Sedgewick stared at her over the rim of his empty tankard. " 'Twas not my business *who*," he muttered. " 'Twas Caleb's business." He jumped up and hurried out. Again they heard the front door bang.

"Imagine! A London girl. Marrying Caleb and cuckolding him!" Mistress Potts' eyes were round and shining. Lenore hadn't seen her so titillated since she claimed the stableboy had pinched her broad bottom in passing.

It snowed again that afternoon and Lenore, who had planned a long walk in the diamond-hard, diamond-cold weather, found her plans frustrated. The wind blustered around the eaves at supper, a wailing accompaniment to their voices.

"You should have a woman doing the cooking," Mistress Potts, who had struggled down in her finery to supper, told Caleb severely.

Caleb's lips drew back from his big teeth so that he gave the impression of having bared a set of yellow fangs. "Women," he snarled, "are the cause of all the trouble in this world. I'll not have one working here."

Down the table, Sedgewick gave him an uneasy look and Tam, the thin self-effacing servant, rattled the platters nervously.

" 'Twill be Amos's decision, not yours," retorted Mistress Potts.

"I told ye Amos has had reverses, Abigail," Sedgewick put in hastily. "First the sheep died, then there was a blight."

"That's no excuse for watery soup and undercooked game!"

Up at the head of the table, Lenore saw Caleb move abortively. Before an explosion could be provoked, she rose.

"*I'll* be glad to help Tam as long as I'm here," she announced. "Tomorrow I could check out the larder and see if we can have a meat pie and a pasty—something different."

"Good!" cried Sedgewick in relief. "We could all use a change of diet! Couldn't we?" Caleb nodded.

"I did not know ye could cook, Lenore," marveled

Mistress Potts. "Living in inns as ye did. Lenore was on the London stage," she told them proudly. "She's an actress, she is. The king himself noticed her."

Caleb turned his lowering gaze upon Lenore, and she sensed a lightninglike hostility stab from those mean little eyes. Plainly he disapproved of the stage and all who walked upon it. Not so Sedgewick.

"An actress, by God!" He brought down his tankard with a clatter. "What d'ye mean the king 'noticed' her, Abigail?"

Lenore had sunk back into her chair at this unwelcome announcement and now she gave Mistress Potts' ample foot a kick under the table, but that irrepressible lady was not to be stopped. "Wanted to make her his mistress, he did! But she refused," she added regretfully.

"*Refused?*" Amazement spread over Sedgewick's sallow face. "Surely ye jest, Abigail?" He turned to Lenore. "Come now, Mistress Frankford, are we to believe that ye turned down the king?"

Lenore bit her lips but her friend spoke for her.

"Aye, that she did." Mistress Potts bobbed her head vehemently. "He sent for her to come to Whitehall, and she went and fought with his mistress there, that Lady Castlemaine. But he gave Lenore a Royal Pardon all the same."

"A Royal Pardon!" cried Sedgewick. "What was her crime?"

"Mistress Potts!" exclaimed Lenore, vexed beyond endurance at this interchange.

"Murder," supplied Mistress Potts camly. She took another bite of cold wildfowl. "But the king pardoned her."

Lenore had the full attention of both nephews now. Feeling uncomfortable under their intent gaze, she burst out, "I was innocent. 'Twas all a mistake. A—a traveling companion of mine was murdered, yes. But not by me."

"Of course, of course," agreed Sedgewick hastily,

and fell to eating again. But the look he gave Lenore was thoughtful.

Caleb's unblinking gaze continued to rest on her. There was no expression in that face—but then there never was. She could not tell what he was thinking.

Lenore was flushed with embarrassment at these unwelcome revelations. At that moment she could cheerfully have wrung Mistress Potts' plump neck. It was the sheerest folly to parade her lurid past before these two men, one of whom considered all women in a malignant light, and the other a drunkard whose lascivious gaze stripped her every time he looked in her direction!

The next day it was still snowing. While the wind howled around the house and piled up great white drifts that crept up the windowpanes, Lenore checked the larder. Considering the indifferent meals they had been eating, it was surprisingly well stocked. Venison and salted fish and pork and mutton and bins of apples and barrels of wheaten flour and crocks of lard and butter and preserves met her eye. There were even some spices and herbs. But the condition of the pots and pans and other kitchen implements was pitiful, for overworked Tam gave everything a lick and a promise.

Tam followed her around during her inspection. He looked glum, and she guessed he expected to be scolded. Her encouraging smile soon disabused him of that and brightening, he began to show her things she'd missed. Lenore got Tam to bring her some big empty crocks and pots and pans and scrub them clean. She found him a cheerful worker, who whistled out of tune as he worked. Soon she was up to her elbows in flour as she rolled out dough for meat pies and a great tart.

Lenore was only a passable cook, but the meal she prepared, and which Tam served with glee, was obviously the best Sedgewick and Caleb had eaten for some time. After his second bite of venison pie, Caleb rumbled, " 'Tis plain ye're a better hand with pastry than Tam here, Mistress Frankford."

"Tam has too much to do," Lenore protested. " 'Tis unreasonable to expect him to take care of the stables and do the housework too."

Tam, serving the fluffy rolls Lenore had made, gave her a grateful look and she smiled at him. She felt sorry for young Tam, who must be lonesome stuck up here with the dour nephews in this lonely place.

"I remember when my mother entertained visiting friends from Lincoln here," said Mistress Potts pensively. "The table fairly groaned! We had green sallets and a shield of brawn prepared with mustard, a chine of beef and boiled capon, roast fowl of three kinds including black swan, a venison haunch as well as a pasty, olive pie and capons and dowsets—I can't remember all of it. But I do remember how good it was and she called it just a simple dinner! Did you know that this table will hold twenty-two dishes, Lenore?"

Lenore felt that her simple rolls, venison pie, and great tart were completely eclipsed by this recital, but Caleb snorted, " 'Twas entertaining like that near ruined your father!"

"A ruin from which his second marriage rescued him," muttered Sedgewick.

Mistress Potts gave him a withering look. "D'ye think you could make some Florentines, Lenore?"

Lenore shook her head. "We've the eggs and sugar, but not the kidneys and currants and cinnamon." She looked up to see Caleb studying her.

"We'll go out hunting tomorrow," rumbled the giant in what was his only note of appreciation of a good meal, "and shoot some fresh game for ye to prepare."

Lenore hoped her slight skill would be equal to the task. She rose to help Tam clear the table.

Sedgewick too rose tipsily. "So ye were on the stage . . ." He leant over, the better to peer down her dress.

Lenore, who had just picked up a charger of rolls, took a step backward. "I was, Mister Robb," she admitted shortly.

"Sedgewick. Call me Sedgewick."

"Sedgewick." Lenore had already started for the kitchen when Sedgewick's mocking voice reached her.

"Abigail remembers better days at Wallham. With our newfound penury, we must not be so free with sugar and salt and spices."

There was an angry squawk from Abigail, but Lenore felt that that was true, for sugar and salt and spices were expensive "bought" items, not like the eggs laid by the hens in the barn, or the milk from the brindle cow.

She turned and gave Sedgewick a level look. "I will try to be more frugal in the kitchen." She hurried into the kitchen and hastily dished out a huge trencher for underweight Tam.

Sedgewick caught up with her in the empty bakehouse, still fragrant with the smell of freshly baked bread.

"Ah, that smells good," he remarked, looking about him at the dim interior. "Not like the hardtack we had before you came to us. 'Twould fair break a tooth, the loaves Tam used to serve us."

"He's but a lad," defended Lenore, wishing Sedgewick would not stand so close. "And with but little knowledge of cooking. Whilst I once worked in a bakeshop."

She moved about, straightening up, and Sedgewick followed her. She gave him an unhappy look as she edged away from him. Lenore's back was brought up abruptly against the stone wall, but Sedgewick kept advancing. Suddenly he reached out a finger and touched her bosom. Lenore stiffened.

"Sedgewick," she said. "I think we must come to an understanding. I was an actress—not a whore." She stepped back and he dropped his hand.

"I did not think that of ye," he said eagerly.

"But you hoped it."

He looked discomfited. " 'Tis dull living out here beneath the shadow of that great wall with none but Caleb and Tam for company," he complained.

"You should have married," said Lenore recklessly, "as your cousin Caleb did."

"Caleb married a whore," he said thickly. "A little tart from the Fair. But you—you're different, Lenore. You could run a great house, receive guests, move about in society."

Lenore was tempted to ask ironically if Sedgewick had a great house to offer her, when he suddenly seized her in a powerful grip and crushed his mouth down upon hers. Lenore struggled but she was held firm. Sedgewick's alcohol-laden breath poured down her throat, nearly choking her, and his tongue was thrust passionately forward. In fury she heard the material of her bodice rip and felt his eager hand plunge down her smooth bosom seeking to cradle her breasts. As he found and grasped his objective, a groan rose up in him and suddenly his loins were pressing her struggling body back against the rough stone wall, flattening her buttocks against its hard surface.

With an abortive effort, Lenore managed to wrest an arm free. She struck Sedgewick a blow in the temple with her balled fist.

It was not such a hard blow, but it sobered him. He released her and stepped back, breathing heavily.

"Ye're as hot for me as I am for you," he accused.

"No, I am not!" Free of him at last, Lenore moved warily away. She pulled her torn sleeve back up over her shoulder and tried to hold her torn bodice together, for he was gazing fixedly at her bare skin. "Whatever you are offering me, I decline it."

He stared at her. "As ye declined the king, no doubt?"

"Yes," said Lenore evenly. *"As I declined the king. Only he did not tear my dress."*

Even in the dimness she could see Sedgewick's sallow face darken. Lest he reach for her again, she brushed by him and fled back to the dining room, now occupied only by Abigail Potts.

"Why, what's happened to ye, Lenore?" The older woman was startled by Lenore's flushed face and torn dress.

"Nothing."

"Nothing?" she gasped indignantly. "It seems ye do need a chaperon here!"

But Abigail's chaperonage was short-lived, for the next day she suffered a relapse and went back to her bed. As the gray days of winter passed, Lenore found herself wishing for Amos's return—but he apparently preferred to remain comfortably in York drinking toasts to his lady's eyebrows. At Wallham, one snowy featureless day followed another, and laboring in kitchen and bakehouse and caring for Mistress Potts, Lenore began to understand how boredom might have driven Sedgewick to drink. She even came to look forward to those times when she would trudge out on high pattens, wearing a borrowed shawl and three pairs of gloves, to lean against the howling wind and beat her way to the barn or stable to gather eggs. In the stable she would sometimes fling herself down in the hay, for the heat of the animals' bodies made the stable an island of warmth in an icy world, and she would then remember nights when she was fleeing with Geoffrey across England and they had slept in haystacks or on piles of straw in remote barns.

Out of sheer boredom, she tried pumping Tam about matters at Wallham. But though she had completely won him by her kindness, Tam seemed to shrivel up whenever she asked him anything regarding the nephews, replying in monosyllables. She gathered that Tam was afraid to talk about his employers for fear of losing his place in the household. And this was borne out one day when she stepped out of the bakehouse to shake her apron and Tam ran up to tell her about a great flight of black-capped terns he had seen winging over the snow-covered fields early that morning. Caleb, stomping by, stopped to glower at them.

"Mind ye've milked the cow and fed the stock, Tam," he rumbled. "Or I'll be takin' a whip to ye."

Tam blanched and whirled as Sedgewick, coming up behind, chimed in, "Ye spend too much time gabbing with Mistress Frankford, Tam. Don't talk, lad—work."

Lenore blinked at this uncalled-for attack on hardworking Tam. "Tam does the work of three lads!" she declared stoutly. Deliberately she shook her floury apron so that a cloud of white dust rose and caught Sedgewick full in the face. He sneezed and backed off.

But Tam worked too closely with Lenore for them not to communicate. It was Tam who turned the meat on the spit, Tam who rocked the big butter churn, Tam who carried in the smoked meat from the smokehouse under Lenore's direction, Tam who took out the table scraps to the chickens. Sometimes she saw him watching her shyly. She guessed he had a childish crush on her and was gentle with him, knowing "puppy love" could be painful. And one day, as she plunged her floury arms elbow-deep into a bowl of soft dough she asked him what Sylvie had been like.

"She were a very devil!" Tam burst out hoarsely. "She used to tell Caleb lies about me so's he'd beat me. She run Nance off, said she stole something, and Amos threw Nance out without giving her her year's wages."

Startled, Lenore turned to see Tam's thin face working with rage, his fists balled in memory. "But I thought Sedgewick said Nance injured her back and went to live with her relations in Wales."

"*Sylvie* hurt Nance's back. She took a broom to Nance as she left, and Nance run away holding her back. And crying. Sylvie sang all day."

So the London tart had hated people. "What did Sylvie love, Tam? Her horse?"

"She didn't love nothin'!" he cried scornfully. "She didn't care nothin' about her horse. She near killed him one day with her whip because he threw a shoe!"

Lenore wondered how anyone could love this woman. "Was she so beautiful, Tam?"

"Some people thought so, but not me! She had long

black hair, like a witch. And big black eyes you couldn't help but look at. They looked holes through you. She were narrow and not so tall and her clothes were all fancy and red, and when she walked she—" He groped for a word.

"Swaggered," supplied Lenore softly, and turned back to her dough.

But speaking of Sylvie seemed to have unloosed a floodgate of grievances in Tam. "Sylvie kept a whip in her room, and if her breakfast wasn't right or her tea wasn't hot enough, she'd give her maid a lash or two."

"Her *maid?*" Lenore thought incredulously of this ruinous house. "I'm surprised Caleb could afford a maid."

"He couldn't. Amos got her the maid 'cause Sylvie was always askin' the servants to do things for her and they complained. There was lots of servants here then, and sheepherders to mind the stock, and extra help at lambing time."

"What happened to them all, Tam?"

"They was all let go."

"When?"

She'd expected him to say "When Amos had reverses," but he surprised her by saying "After *she* left."

"Who? You mean Sylvie?"

"Aye." Tam rose restively. "I've got to go feed the stock."

Lenore was left to think about black-haired Sylvie who loved to inflict pain.

On an impulse, after she had finished making the bread, Lenore left the dough to rise and hurried upstairs. With the nephews out hunting, Tam in the stable and Mistress Potts napping, she had the house to herself. Now she was determined to explore the upstairs.

She knew she was prying as she walked down the dusky hall trying each door. None were locked, and she opened each and peered within.

The first was square and rather small and littered

with empty bottles—that would be Sedgewick's room, at least the room he occupied in summer when he and Caleb did not huddle downstairs by the fire.

The second was large and characterless. Big pieces of oaken furniture stood there unpolished and dusty, and a man's clothing hung in the big press—in plain sight since the press door was open. But there were no little things lying about, except an inkwell in which the ink had long since dried, and an assortment of dusty quill pens on a little writing table. Beside them was a shabby candle-holder and sealing wax. Except for some crumpled parchment carelessly thrown on the floor, the room was rather spartan and neat. She guessed this must be Amos's room, because the clothing that hung there would fit neither Caleb nor Sedgewick; it had been made for a smaller man than Caleb, a stouter man than Sedgewick—a man who favored brocades and rich dark colors.

Lenore approached the fourth and last bedchamber eagerly, for this must have been the room Caleb had occupied with Sylvie. The door swung open with a loud protesting creak and she stepped into the most charming room in the house, medium-sized and sunny, with a southern exposure. The furniture was of fruitwood and the andirons and fender were of brass. On the floor lay a red Turkish carpet.

But the room looked as if it had been struck by a tornado.

The hangings had been torn from the windows and their ripped pieces trailed across a large square bed that tipped crazily as if a maniac had shaken it. One of its four posts was snapped off. Above the once-handsome washstand, the mirror was splintered into a thousand fragments, and broken shards of what had been a delicate blue and white washbowl and pitcher lay about the floor. No attempt had been made to sweep them up. The brass andirons were speckled with bits of plaster from the walls. They now lay at either end of the room and Lenore could see where the walls had been gouged. The delicate brass fender that matched the andirons had been crumpled by a blow from one of the andirons or perhaps crushed by a big boot. Even the Turkish carpet was rent—slashed with a sword or perhaps a butcher knife, and the floor beneath it was scarred. The door to the big press hung crazily on one hinge as if it had been wrested open with force enough to break it, and the clothes there were slashed to ribbons. Most of the mutilated fabric was red. Lenore identified rich vermilion brocades and scarlet satins and ruby velvets, along with fine lawns and torn bits of black and silver lace and bits and fragments of what must once have been red silk petticoats. Shoes with their red heels ripped off, broken combs, crushed lacquered fans littered the floor.

It was as if a large angry bear had been locked in this room and tried to smash his way out. Failing that, he had clawed and crushed and battered everything in sight to smithereens.

Lenore closed the door carefully and leant upon it, closing her eyes.

Caleb had done this in the first flush of anger when Sylvie had left him. Lenore felt it in her bones. This was the evidence of Caleb's hatred of women.

Quickly she hurried back downstairs, knowing it would not be wise to cross him, ever.

BOOK III:
Lorena—
Too Unwise

Twainmere, The Cotswolds

Chapter 16

It was on a Friday that Lorena fell in love. Painfully, irrevocably, forever.

With Tabby Aylesbury.

Market day had dawned bright and sunny and Flora, busy with the churning, had sent Lorena to buy some fresh eggs. In the crisp air Lorena swung along in her woolen cloak, its hood thrown back. She leaned down to smile at a squirrel, digging under the snow at the base of a gnarled oak for nuts, and her bright hair glimmered like spun gold in the sun.

The little market in the center of town was crowded, for the good weather had brought everyone out. Lorena had no difficulty filling her basket with eggs, for on a day like today the market was filled with country produce. She spoke to people she knew, lingering there in the sparkling weather, like everyone else, loath to go. But she must get back, it was a busy day at the vicarage. The vicar had not given up on making a match between

Mistress Plimpton and old Mister Oakes, so Flora was having them both to supper again. She turned to go and was confronted by a large farmer who surged forward carrying two live geese. To avoid colliding with him, Lorena stepped back quickly, bumping into Goody Kettle, the village gossip. Lorena had inadvertently stepped on the woman's foot, and Goody Kettle gave a howl. In a strident voice she began to berate Lorena.

Everyone nearby turned to look, and Lorena shrank back, muttering apologies.

Among those who had turned to look was her half sister, Kate Tilson. That morning Kate had quarreled with her mother over "going too far," and had quarreled with her boyfriend the night before over "not going far enough" and driving him wild. She was in a vengeful mood.

Kate had seen what nobody else seemed to have noticed: that Goody Kettle, who was now jumping up and down in a passion of spite shrilling against "charging girls who'd run a body down in broad daylight!" had managed to dislodge her most prized possession, a small gold locket which she always wore suspended on a narrow gold chain around her neck. In her excitement as she waved her arms at Lorena, the chain had caught in the handle of the new broom she had just bought, and broken. Locket and chain had slipped unnoticed to the ground.

A wicked gleam appeared in Kate's blue eyes. Here was her chance to avenge herself on Lorena!

She slipped forward unobtrusively through the crowd, bent and picked up the locket from the churned-up muddy earth, eased behind the embarrassed Lorena and managed to drop it into Lorena's basket of eggs, where it slithered to the bottom, sliding in among the eggs. She was unnoticed, even by scarlet-faced Lorena, for all eyes at that moment were riveted on Goody Kettle, who was screaming that Lorena was not content merely with kissing boys in the hedges, she was now trying to lame her elders!

"I didn't mean to hurt you!" Lorena gasped, humiliated by the attention paid Goody Kettle's energetic performance.

"Well, I should hope not, Lorena Frankford!"

Lorena turned away and would have fled from the market except for Goody Kettle's sudden shriek behind her. "My locket! It's gone! Somebody's stole my locket!"

"Look in Lorena Frankford's basket," called a clear carrying voice, for Kate was now some distance away. "See if you don't find it there!"

Lorena whirled to meet Kate's mocking gaze. "I don't have her locket!"

"Oh, no? Then give me that basket, Mistress, and we'll soon find out!" cried Goody Kettle, surging forward toward Lorena.

Sure that she would be instantly vindicated of any wrongdoing, Lorena readily surrendered the basket. But her face whitened when Goody Kettle's thin hand, thrusting down among the eggs, came up with the muddy locket and chain dangling from her fingers.

"Thief!" she shrilled. "Thief!"

A shudder went through Lorena's slight frame. The punishment for theft was swift and terrible. Last year a thief had been branded on the face and lashed out of the village tied to the tail of a cart.

"I didn't take the locket!" she cried.

"Aye, that she didn't, for I saw it all," a calm voice called, and everyone turned to see Tabby Aylesbury standing tall behind the crowd, a frown upon his usually smiling face. He had caught Kate by the wrist and was holding her. "No, don't run away, Kate. A joke's a joke, but this one's gone too far. I saw ye slip up and pick the locket up from the mud—and see?" He held up her hand for all to see. "The mud's still here."

Frowning faces now turned toward Kate, and she shrank back, scared. Visions of the stocks—or worse yet the pillory, with her ears nailed to the wood and village boys throwing rocks at her eyes—rose up before her.

"Go on with you, Kate," said Tabby more kindly,

giving her bottom a swat. "We all know 'twas but a prank. Own up to it now! Ye'd never have let Lorena be taken up for a thief when 'twas your own doing."

Kate wasn't so sure. She gave Tabby an anguished look. "I meant no harm," she mumbled. "I thought 'twould be fun—"

"Fun!" Indignantly, Goody Kettle took after Kate with her new broom. Tabby chuckled as Kate gathered up her bronze skirts and ran away.

The crowd watched as the two running figures disappeared behind a hedge, from whence issued several shrieks as Goody Kettle cornered Kate and began beating her with the broom. Then they all turned back to whatever they were doing before all this happened.

But Lorena stood still and gazed at Tabby lounging there, all her heart in her grateful blue eyes. He had come to her aid when she thought no one would—again. For the vicar's daughter had never had anyone to champion her—until Tabby. He smiled back at her, that easy smile that made the girls' hearts flutter. A lock of his russet hair fell down over his eyes and he pushed it back with a careless gesture.

It was at that moment Lorena fell in love with him: a wonderful, indescribable sensation that seemed to rise dizzily from her toes to the top of her head. All at once she knew a great yearning to be held in the arms of this tall fellow who smiled down at her so steadily, a deep affection for his kind heart and quick wit, and a humble wish to measure up to what Tabby's sleepy gray eyes told her he thought of her. With a sudden rush of blood to her face, she knew she wanted to grow up fast and marry Tabby and bear his children—all boys, all to look exactly like him!

All the jostling, chattering crowd seemed to melt away, as if they were standing there alone in the sunshine. Her whole being focused on Tabby, Tabby alone. After a long time she turned away, smiling shyly, and walked home—not on slushy mud, but on air, all the way.

She loved him, she loved him! It sang like a refrain in her secret, dancing heart.

Lorena did not see Tabby for some time after that. She learned that he had gone to a nearby town for a fortnight to visit an ailing aunt.

But her heart skipped a beat when Flora told her to take a message to Aylesbury's Mill on the outskirts of Twainmere. She was to tell Lyle Aylesbury, the miller, that the vicarage needed another barrel of wheaten flour.

That would mean she would see Tabby! She knew he was back, for she'd seen him ride by the vicarage on his light sleigh only this morning!

Lorena dressed very carefully in her best gray dress and pulled up over her slim ankles the stockings Aunt Flora had given her for Christmas. She studied her plain square-toed shoes and wished desperately she had a pair with red or yellow heels, but these would have to do. She took especial care with her shining fair hair, peered anxiously into the piece of polished metal which served her as a mirror, and hurried away to the mill.

Her heart was beating like a drum as she crossed the footbridge above the frozen millrace and studied the big stone mill that rose up like a giant in the snow.

But Tabby was not there.

Cloaking her disappointment, Lorena smiled up at the miller and delivered Flora's message.

"Aye," said Lyle Aylesbury, looking down from his great height at sparkling-eyed Lorena and thinking her the prettiest little girl he had ever seen. "I'll send the flour by Tabby. 'Twill be there today for certain, Mistress Lorena."

Lorena sighed and used a ruse. "Will Tabby be back soon?" she asked plaintively. "For I turned my ankle on the way here, and I'd like to ride back with him in the sleigh if it wouldn't be too much trouble?"

"No trouble at all." The tall miller dusted off his arms, for he'd been weighing grain and some of the wheat and chaff had stuck to them. "Have ye ever seen the inside of a mill, Mistress Lorena?"

Lorena admitted she had not.

"Just rest your hand upon my arm to take the weight off your ankle and I'll show ye round." Gallantly, he proffered a muscular arm, and Lorena's small white hand rested on it as lightly, he thought, as the wings of the swallows that nested up under the eaves. He found her charming company as he showed her through the great dusty mill, exhibited the heavy weights that were used in weighing out the flour and grain, and explained the workings of the big mill wheel, now frozen solid in the icy millstream.

Lorena chattered gaily. She liked Tabby's father—but it was Tabby she'd come to see.

At last Tabby returned, and his gray eyes lost their sleepy look and widened at the sight of Lorena, there in the mill on easy terms with his father. His father and Lorena kept up a running conversation while he loaded the barrel of flour onto the sleigh, and Tabby watched while his father gallantly lifted Lorena up into it, for her ankle, he insisted, would scarce bear her weight.

"See she gets there safe," the miller admonished his son sternly. Tabby, who had a knowing hand with horses and had never in his life overturned the sleigh, gave him back a look of astonishment.

Lorena turned proudly to Tabby. See, she thought silently, your father likes me!

But Tabby, who had never seen his rather silent father talk so much to any girl—or woman either for that matter, since Tabby's mother died—frowned as he drove the sleigh down toward the old stone bridge that crossed the millstream some distance below the race and the footbridge. He knew his father for a determined man. Only yesterday Lyle had commented on his son's wild ways and said sternly it was time that Tabby settled down and took a wife. Tabby had shrugged it off. But now he wondered. Could it be, he asked himself uneasily, that his father had decided to take matters into his own hands and choose a wife for Tabby? Had the vicar sent Lorena over that Lyle Aylesbury might talk to her and judge her qualifications as a future daughter-in-law?

For it was a day when "arranged" marriages were the usual thing for sons of men of property. Tabby's father, the miller, considered himself a man of property.

The thought galled Tabby. Lorena was growing up to be a beauty, and indeed he might ask her to marry him one day, but he wanted to decide on his own bride, without interference and in his own good time.

He frowned at Lorena. "When did ye hurt your ankle?"

Lorena jumped guiltily. "Oh, it isn't bad—I turned it a little. I tripped over a root under that big beech tree just before I got to the footbridge."

"Ye should not have attempted the footbridge with a hurt ankle," Tabby told her severely. " 'Tis not a proper footbridge, but only planks stretched across with no railing. The millrace lies below it. Suppose your ankle had given way and ye had plunged to the ice and broken through it? Ye'd have been swept away downstream under the ice!"

Lorena gave him an unhappy look. She could hardly say she had lied to his father to have an excuse to stay and wait for him. "I didn't think of that, Tabby," she sighed.

"Well, ye should have," Tabby growled, turning the light sleigh up onto the bridge.

Lorena sat back, crushed. Here she was, riding through Twainmere in Tabby's sleigh through a white world of big old rough-barked trees, their heavy branches weighted down with snow, passing snow forts built by children—deserted now for the children were at supper. Candles glimmered through frosted panes in the snowy dusk, making the cottage windows rectangles of soft, golden light. In this romantic setting she was alone with the lover she had chosen—and she could find nothing to say to him. Shyness had trapped her tongue and she, who had found it so easy to talk to his father, now that she was alone with Tabby, found herself tongue-tied.

For Lorena it was a new experience.

Tabby, hard pressed with his own thoughts, also had the barrel of flour to think about. It rode precariously on the back of the light sleigh and he must needs pay attention to the icy ruts to keep it from turning over. So he did not notice this unwonted silence on Lorena's part as he might have on some other occasion.

To Lorena's chagrin, he pulled up before the vicarage, helped her down—for she had to keep up the fiction of an injured ankle—and hoisted down the barrel of flour, without their having exchanged more than a few words the whole way.

"D'ye want it in the kitchen? I could take it around back."

"No, use the front door," insisted Lorena, limping ahead to swing it open for him. "It's closer and besides you might slip on the ice if you go around back, and drop it."

Flora, working at the kitchen table in an apron, looked up in surprise at the sight of Tabby lugging a barrel of flour from the front hall into her kitchen.

"Ye're late, Lorena," she said as Tabby carefully lowered the heavy barrel to the clean stone floor. "Robbie's been asking where ye were."

Robbie's been asking . . . Then the vicar hadn't sent Lorena to the mill to be "considered" for a wife! 'Twas only flour she'd wanted!

Tabby straightened up, his face clearing. "Lorena hurt her ankle on the way to the mill," he explained with a smile at Lorena that struck fire to her young heart. "And my father made her wait until I came home and could take her back in the sleigh along with the flour."

"Well, sit down and rest your ankle, Lorena." Flora couldn't help noting how easily Lorena had stepped out of the way of the flour barrel as Tabby set it down. "Won't ye stay to supper, Tabby?"

Tabby hesitated. He'd promised to have supper over

at the Meadows'. Harve Meadows had promised to teach him to play chess. At the moment he wished he hadn't promised Harve, for Lorena looked very enticing. It was strange how much more beautiful she'd grown, now that he realized she wasn't being forced on him!

"I'd like to stay," he told Flora. "And 'tis kind of ye to ask me, but I'm expected elsewhere for supper and I'm already late."

"Another time then," Flora said kindly.

Lorena, remembering to limp, accompanied Tabby to the door and watched him go regretfully. It was strange he hadn't mentioned being late for supper somewhere on the way over. A sudden suspicion flared in her mind. He was off to meet Tess, no doubt, and eager to get away!

She closed the front door harder than was necessary and stomped back to the kitchen. Oh, she hoped Tess's Pomeranian bit him!

"I see your ankle's improved of a sudden," observed Flora, handing her a crock. "Here, stir this batter for me. That Tabby is a nice lad."

Lorena took the crock and gave Flora a stormy look. "I think Lyle Aylesbury is *far* nicer than his son!" she cried in such a ringing tone that even the vicar heard it in his study. She began beating the batter with such energy that some of it spilled from the crock.

Flora watched her. "I think ye've beaten it enough," she said at last. "Ye can go in and set the table now, Lorena."

She watched the child's straight-backed exit—for "child" Flora still thought her. She had not yet realized that Lorena, for better or worse, was becoming a woman—and dreaming a woman's dreams.

It was the wedding of pert little Lillie Austin in late February that brought Flora squarely to a consideration of Lorena's future. For chestnut-haired Lillie was barely two years older than Lorena, and now she'd jumped over the stile with old Sam Brown and gone off to live in a shepherd's hut.

A shepherd's hut wasn't what Flora wanted for

beautiful Lorena. She had watched Lorena, the prettiest bridesmaid of them all, walking proudly in the wedding procession, and thought about that. And when two weeks later Lorena came home bursting with excitement and told her the miller, widower Lyle Aylesbury, had stopped his cart in the street and asked her if she could do some work about the house in the afternoons, Flora gave her a thoughtful look. She knew how Lorena felt about Tabby.

And she'd noted that twice Lyle Aylesbury had found occasion to call at the vicarage lately—something he'd certainly never done before. Tabby, she thought. Lyle wants to throw Tabby and Lorena together—and make a match of it, so Tabby will stay home and mind the mill and not go running off to sea—for it was no secret in Twainmere that Tabby Aylesbury was always asking what the American Colonies were like and sometimes talked of going to sea.

Well, Flora wasn't averse to a match between Tabby and Lorena. Tabby, with his sleepy gray eyes and flashing smile, was a favorite of Flora's. One day he'd inherit the mill. It would be a good match for a young girl with no prospects.

"Since Mr. Aylesbury's wife died last year, he and Tabby haven't had anybody helping out," Lorena was explaining earnestly. "They've just been 'batching.' I told him"—she reached up to push back a lock of fair hair that kept falling down into her eyes—"that I wasn't a very good cook, but he said he and Tabby weren't critical, they'd eat all my mistakes and never know the difference."

"He should have spoken to Robbie first."

"He's going to this afternoon. But first he wanted to be sure I would want to do it, before he asked Uncle Robbie. He said he didn't want any 'unwilling workers' straightening up or getting supper for him and Tabby."

"He's a kind man," murmured Flora. "And 'twould give you incentive to learn to be a good housewife, for being on your own would put you on your mettle. Still—I know not what Robbie will say."

"Aunt Flora." Lorena's voice was wistful. "It would give me money of my own to buy gifts for you at Christmas and—and you know I've always wanted a pair of yellow shoes with red heels and a yellow dress."

"Red heels? Robbie would never stand for that."

"Yellow heels then. Oh, you *will* talk to Uncle Robbie about it, won't you, Aunt Flora? So he won't say no when Mr. Aylesbury asks him?"

"Of course, child," said Flora gruffly.

But the hours passed and still Lyle Aylesbury did not come. In her impatience, Flora sent Lorena out on an errand and knocked on the study door. She was carrying the straw broom she used to sweep the house, and her jaw was set.

"Robbie," she began, "I know ye're busy writing your Sunday sermon, but there's a matter about which we must speak."

The vicar knew that tone. He put down his quill pen, got up from his slanted writing desk and went to stand at the window with his back to her. "Go on," he said in the controlled tone of a man who has much to bear.

Flora looked at his straight back impatiently. "Robbie, I've spoke to ye before about this, but now we must come to grips with it. We must think of Lorena's future. The child's changes have come upon her so early that already she's filling out and becoming a woman! 'Twas Lillie Austin's wedding brought it home to me, for all the young lads' eyes were upon Lorena and not the bride!"

The slight jerk of the vicar's shoulders was not lost upon Flora, but she was at a loss to account for it. Why was it that any mention of Lorena these days set off such reactions, as if Robbie were a wound-up top and the very mention of the child's name sent him whirling!

Flora waited and when he said nothing, she began again. "Lyle Aylesbury is coming over to see you."

Still he did not turn. "What about?"

"He wants Lorena to help out in the house afternoons.'Twould be good experience for her, Robbie, for one day she'll have a house of her own to manage—perhaps that very house, for young Tabb Aylesbury is a likely lad with good expectations, and I doubt not Lyle thought of his son when he asked Lorena to help out."

The narrow shoulders seemed to be widening, but having begun, Flora now plunged on. "In any case, Lorena is eager to make some money of her own to buy us gifts for next Christmas and perchance some yellow dress material and a pair of yellow shoes—"

"*Yellow shoes!*" The vicar spun around. "I'll not have Lorena parading through the streets in brazen yellow shoes. No, nor in a yellow dress either!"

Flora sighed, recalling the red-heeled shoes with which Lenore had paraded through the village. Aye, and she had notched those heels, 'twas said, for every conquest she made! She remembered the apple green dress in which Lenore had ridden away to snatch Jamie from the Battle of Worcester.

"Very well, a gray dress. But the child would still like to earn some money, and I think 'twould be a good thing for her to be out on her own a bit." Away from the vicarage with its stern rules which were going to cause Lorena to rebel, she thought.

Jerkily, as if his muscles would not obey him, Robbie drummed his fingers on his thigh. Each tap hit his ragged nerve ends like a blow. "Young Aylesbury?" he burst out. "How could you suggest him, Flora? The lad has eyes for every wench."

"Aye," agreed Flora dryly. "And they've all got eyes for him as well. But she'd come to no mischief in the house, for Lyle Aylesbury's an upright man—"

"Aye, but young Tabb isn't!"

"You don't know that!" Flora challenged. She was growing angry. "Tabby Aylesbury spent two hours fixing the wheel on Mistress Fowler's carriage when it broke down in the street—and charged her *nothing* for his trouble."

"No, but he pinched Mistress Fowler's daughter on the bottom! I saw him do it."

Flora sniffed. "Jennie Fowler's the kind who would egg on anything in breeches, we all know that."

"I do not know it!" The vicar's voice was growing shrill. "Ye've only to look into that hot young face of his to know him for what he is. Exactly like—" He stopped at Flora's wooden expression.

"Exactly like my brother Jamie. Why don't you say it?"

"I do not wish to provoke a quarrel with ye, Flora. But all know Jamie's and Lenore's was not a proper marriage. They were—"

"Living in sin, I grant ye that. I've never held with handfasting."

"*And* she'd have been off to another man before the year was out!"

"How can ye say that, Robbie?" Flora looked at his flushed face in amazement. "How do you know what she'd have done or not done? You *liked* Lenore when she came back to us with the baby, and you were good to her and kept down the gossip while she stayed with us. What's come over you, Robbie?"

The vicar passed a hand over his brow. The hand shook slightly and came away damp, for he was perspiring even though it was cold in the study. "Naught has come over me," he said hoarsely, "save that the girl is like her mother."

"Then best she be thinking of marriage soon," cried Flora. "And lucky we are that Lyle Aylesbury wants her to work there. Ye'll be well advised to allow it!"

"Unchaperoned? Alone in a house with two men? Never!"

They glared at each other and then Flora banged down her broom and went out, slamming the door.

The vicar stared unseeingly at the solid oak panels of that door. He was seeing instead a head of long thick shining hair, white as hemp, that shook out like silk around a lovely appealing young face, and a child's body that was rapidly becoming a woman's. Those clear blue eyes challenged him as a man, but he would not admit that even to himself. The devil had constructed a temptress in Lorena—just as the devil had constructed a temptress in Lenore. Lenore had driven men to distraction and so would Lorena.

He sat down heavily and mopped his brow with a clean white kerchief and told himself angrily that he would not be sending the child into the miller's house to consort with a young rake such as Tabb Aylesbury. The lad was as bad as Jamie had been, lusting after every skirt! Why could Flora not see it? In every other way, she was a saint!

Too saintly for a licentious man such as himself to touch.

For Robbie had always judged himself harshly. He had pored over every impulse of his, assessed them. Did he see a woman walking to market and notice her fine figure and swaying walk? That was evil—see, it was the devil at work in him! Did he note the carefree laughter of a young girl, her childish gaiety? Ah, that was frivolous of him and not to be borne.

In his heart of hearts Robbie considered that he was the vilest of human beings and fast being overtaken by the devil.

For every time he looked at Lorena, licentious thoughts leaped into his mind. Her cool smooth skin cried out to be touched. Her blue eyes seemed to hold a challenge directed at him alone. Her light step beat like a hammer across his heart. Sometimes at supper when Lorena served him and inadvertently touched his sleeve, his heart pounded so loudly in his chest that he was sure Flora must hear it.

His secret desire for the girl was driving him mad.

And here was Flora suggesting she be driven into the arms of the town's most notorious young rake, Tabby Aylesbury!

And yet, Robbie knew his sainted Flora was right: Lorena must prepare for her future—a future in which he could have no part. He would doubtless—his lips curled bitterly—be called upon to perform the ceremony that would unite Lorena with some worthless lad, no better than her father had been.

God in heaven, what was he to do?

He wanted his foster daughter with a carnal passion that jangled his nerves and drove him out of the vicarage at times lest his passions betray him, and he demonstrate his desire for her in some manner.

That desire had driven him very far indeed.

Almost at the breaking point, the vicar bent his head upon his clenched hands and wept.

Robert Medlow had never told Flora, but both his father and grandfather had been notorious rakehells who roared with laughter when Robbie had timidly suggested his desire to enter the ministry. When he had come into his portion, he had done it anyway, leaving Dorset and all his shuddering memories behind him. It was a past he never talked about. His grandfather had died at ninety, from falling off a horse dead drunk. His father, who could not match the old fellow, though he tried valiantly, had died raving mad of the "gallant disease," caught from one of the numerous whores he patronized when he went up to London for long spells of dissipation and drink.

Robbie's mother, long suffering, kind and basically stupid, had borne it all without a murmur. On Robbie, her only child, she had lavished all her affection, and, out of her protective love for him, had warned him constantly against "wanton wenches that lift their skirts to any man" and "giggling girls who lead a man to hell." She had meant the *wrong sort* of woman, but her son had taken her quite literally.

To the young Robbie, *all* women were sinful— Unless they resembled his sainted mother.

Flora looked like his mother. It was what had first attracted him to Flora—and what kept him from going to bed with her. His mother had been a saint. Flora resembled her, therefore Flora too was a saint. One did not bed a saint.

That Flora was far from saintly, that she was a good, kind, hot-tempered woman whose passions were kept hidden behind a wall of Scottish reserve, had never even occurred to Robbie. Humbly he thanked his deity for sending Flora his way.

Behind his placid decorous ministerial facade, he let his anguished glance wander over every piquant breast or pouting lower lip or slender ankle that came his way. The sizzling blood of his grandfather, diluted in his father, had not quite sputtered out. Robbie lusted for women—but he did so secretly and was deeply shamed by his wholly natural desires.

That Flora sometimes seemed to long for him to come to her bed, he brushed aside as an unworthy thought in himself. He had imagined it, he was mistaken. So his life stumbled and dragged along until beautiful Lenore walked into his household, carrying her baby in her arms.

Lenore had never given Robbie a second look— although he, to his shame, had memorized every curve of her lissome young figure, every gesture, every shrug. But he recognized trouble when he saw it. He was wary of Lenore and backed away from coming too close to the fiery beauty.

Lorena was a different matter altogether. An innocent babe, she had been given into his keeping. He grew to love the child as if she were his own, patiently helping her to learn to read and write and cipher. In his way Robbie loved Lorena as much as Flora did.

But now that she was growing up, he could already see in her the reckless fervor that had lit up her young mother. Already he could see the wide well-paved road to eternal damnation opening up before the glorious creature who was his ward.

Sometimes he would pause in carving a roast and gaze uneasily down the table at her, thinking he saw devil-lights sparkling in her blue eyes. She was so beautiful—and as yet, so pure. She was growing up, but he could not abide the idea that any man would touch her, have her, use her—in *that* way. The thought of a marriage bed for Lorena spurred in him a kind of madness. That Robbie was in love with her, he would not admit even to himself; it was too shocking.

Yet whenever Lorena ran lightly through the house, her bright hair flying and her sweet young body outlined against the sunlight that struck through the tiny panes, he ran his tongue over his lips and felt perspiration break out on his forehead and an ache begin in his groin.

For he wanted his foster daughter as a man wants a woman: in his bed.

Then on a cold day last fall, when the trees were losing their leaves and the bite of snow was in the air, Robbie had been returning to his vicarage from a discussion with the sexton about the purchase of a new rope for the church bell, the last one having succumbed to excessive use over the years. In the course of this discussion he had climbed briskly up to the bell tower. Dressed lightly against the biting wind, he had hurried through the vicarage gate and had just reached the front door when the pain had struck him, struck him in a sharp agonizing burst that seemed to explode just over his heart.

With a gasp, his face gone gray, he collapsed against the vicarage door, clawing at its oaken surface, for now the pains were radiating out through his chest and down his left arm.

I am dying, he thought, and opened his mouth to call Flora when suddenly the paroxysm ceased. Feeling came back to his left arm and behind him he heard Lorena's cry of alarm as she came through the gate. "Is something the matter, Uncle Robbie? You look so pale!"

Back in the land of the living, Robbie had flexed his now usable left arm. " 'Twas nothing," he declared hoarsely. "I tripped on the step and caught myself against the door."

Lorena had given him a doubtful look, but when he went on inside as if nothing had happened, she forgot all about it.

Robbie did not.

He knew the attack for what it was: Death had come looking for him—and found him unready.

Certain now that he was going to die—die, he realized with a jolt, without ever having lived, without ever having held a woman carnally in his arms, without ever having known love beyond the spiritual—Robbie began to change. He wanted to live before he died! Plagued by an agony of the spirit—for Robbie was a secret fellow who took no one into his confidence in important matters—that change began to show. Flora noticed it. Lorena noticed it. He was often angry now, and hard on Lorena where before he had been gentle with her. Fiercely he chastised her for infractions with a willow switch. Each time the beatings became harder as Robbie sought, before he was called to his Maker, to render her forever chaste and pure and innocent.

It was an impossible task, but he refused to believe it. And when switching seemed not enough, he added confinement to her room on a diet of bread and water.

Hurt and bewildered by this treatment, Lorena had begun to hate him.

Flora was bewildered too, and being of a combative nature, began to quarrel violently with him. To Lorena's dismay, their arguments rent the air, sometimes day and night. But Flora was never any less saintly in Robbie's eyes for arguing. Indeed, his sainted mother had argued with him too on occasion, and he blamed his own ineptness for not presenting matters to Flora in a way that she could immediately accept.

He was a setup for Lola Hepworth, the young woman who had married Martin Hepworth. Whenever he went over to pray with her husband, he found those bright devouring eyes on him, making his hand falter as he accepted oat cakes proffered on a pewter tray.

The poor vicar had never met anyone like her.

Lola Hepworth—she had been Lola Metters before she married Martin Hepworth—should have been a courtesan. She had the feel for it, almost the looks for it. She was a slightly overripe beauty with passionate amber eyes and peachy skin and luxuriant coarse red hair, almost ruby red. Fate, which should have made her a courtesan, had made her a dairymaid, and an indifferent one at that. She had bestowed her favors too early and too liberally to marry well in Chipping Campden. And she found it difficult to hold a job, for the wives of diarymen kept a sharp eye on the dairymaids, and Lola was at heart lazy and restless, desiring to be kept by men—in the plural.

When Martin Hepworth, newly widowed, passable looking and possessed of a farm of his own outside Twainmere, had come along, Lola had considered him a godsend. Within a week of their marriage, she considered him a bore. When he fell from the loft and injured his back, her brilliant amber eyes began to rove over what was offered in the neighborhood.

Into her lair wandered the vicar, to pray with her for her husband's speedy recovery.

Lola always prayed with him upstairs in her husband's bedroom, kneeling by the big oaken bed—and afterward, quietly let him out. But one memorable Sunday afternoon she modestly requested, as she led him downstairs again, that he join her in a small prayer in the living room. Robbie assented.

The living room was square and low-ceilinged. Its two low windows faced the road not far distant, and its floor had no carpeting, but was covered in country fashion with rushes.

Kneeling on the rushes, Robbie bowed his head in prayer, murmuring devoutly. But Lola kept one wary eye open, and the moment the vicar had said "Amen," she sighed and appeared to collapse in a dead faint.

"Mistress Hepworth!" Anxiously Robbie bent over her. "Mistress Hepworth!" He fanned her distractedly with his palm, and tried to tear his fascinated eyes from her ripe body. For he could not help but notice that she had fallen most delightfully, in disarray. Her skirts had somehow ridden up above her knees. Air, she needed air! With nervous fingers he loosened the top of Lola's bodice, fumbling ineptly with the hooks.

As the hooks were unloosed, Lola Hepworth gave a great sigh.

Ah, thought Robbie, almost faint with relief as he knelt beside her in the rushes, she was alive!

With her eyes still closed, Lola reached out and twined both arms around his neck.

"Mistress Hepworth!" protested Robbie, feeling his head bent perforce before his words were suddenly cut off by Lola's warm demanding mouth.

With surprising strength, she drew his body to her, down, down, down against her soft upthrust breasts and wide responsive hips.

When their bodies met, a strange thing happened: Robbie forgot he was a vicar, forgot he had a wife, forgot his ever-present, all-demanding God. With a strangled cry he seized Lola, pulling her ample body so close that he almost squeezed the breath from her lungs.

If Lola was surprised by this sudden demonstration of passion, she gave no sign of it. After all, she had never had a vicar before. Perhaps this was their way! Wrapped tightly in his fevered embrace, she frowned suddenly. The vicar was gnawing passionately on her earlobe, gasping her name between nips, but he did not seem to know quite what to do with the other parts of her anatomy.

For a moment this worried Lola. Then with a barely perceptible shrug—Robbie, chewing that peachy ear, never noticed—she reached out a competent hand and guided her inexperienced lover to his mark. Robbie stiffened and his eyes widened in shock. *This* was the carnal knowledge he had so often preached ringing sermons against!

He had never experienced anything like it. Drums seemed to be beating in his temples and his groin was afire. As his passions built he was actually sobbing, and when at last he achieved his goal, it was as if great kettledrums and cymbals clashed, and the very heavens opened, bathing his sweating body in radiance.

He slid away from her, collapsed panting onto the rushes, and closed his eyes, every nerve atingle.

"Now wasn't that nice?" Lola cooed complacently. She sat up and began to push her tumbled dark red hair back in place. She did not bother to rearrange her skirts. They still rode up around her hips displaying her heavy but shapely white thighs.

At the sound of her voice, Robbie came back to himself. His eyes flew open in purest horror.

There before him were those inviting naked thighs between which moments before he had been straining! What could have possessed him? He sat up, almost groveling.

"Mistress Hepworth," he cried in a hoarse distracted voice, "I most humbly beg your pardon."

Lola Hepworth stopped patting back her hair and turned to look at Robbie rather fixedly. So this was how vicars did it—an impassioned plummet and a quick apology. An odd lot, vicars! "No need for that," she said easily.

"Then I will go and beg your husband's pardon," announced Robbie. Head sunk abjectly, he rose on trembling legs to do the thing, when suddenly a determined and detaining arm curved around his right knee, effectively pinning him.

"There's no need to do that either," purred Lola, who actually was rather frightened by the thought that the vicar might actually burst into her husband's bedroom unannounced with such a story. She was suddenly mindful of the musket her husband kept over the mantel.

"Ye—ye think not?" Robbie's attention was jerked back to his knee, and now his thigh, up which Lola's other hand was creeping.

"Robbie—I may call ye Robbie, may I not?"

"Aye," said the vicar after a moment's hesitation. "Although not in church, nor in the village. It might cause some talk." He gave a little nervous jump as Lola gave his private parts a roguish squeeze. "Ye may call me Robbie!"

"Well, sit down a moment beside me, Robbie, and let's talk, for 'tis very lonely for a woman—and a stranger

261

to these parts at that—to be stuck out here in the country."

She pouted prettily and Robbie sank down beside her. In another moment he was flat on his back, gasping, with a giggling Lola atop him, riding him like a rocking horse.

Amused by both his inexperience and his starry-eyed delight, Lola ran him through all her paces. By afternoon's end, Robbie had been thoroughly seduced.

When at last he staggered away, Lola gave him a basket of oat cakes "for his wife, back at the vicarage," and murmured "Next Sunday afternoon?"

The vicar nodded dizzily and stumbled home.

Sunday afternoon at the Hepworths became his custom. All week he looked forward to it, with an ache of expectancy in his groin. And Lola, who found others to amuse her on weekdays, sometimes giggled to a chance-met lover over her Sundays with the vicar. Word got around. People began to give Robbie sideways speculative glances.

And this was the woman whose name Kate Tilson had taunted Lorena with that day on the ice. Lola Hepworth, with her violent red hair and smoothly swiveling hips. Kate was but quoting local gossip.

Robbie of course did not know he was the subject of whispered conversations. He thought—as men in his position so often do—that his secret was well kept, known only to him and the woman and to a frowning God.

Now he sat at his desk in the vicarage with the quill pen raised, his face ashen. He was torn between the wife he *would not* touch, the foster daughter he *could not* touch, and the seductive woman who belonged to another man.

Now the quill pen was lowered and the vicar fell forward on his desk with his anguished head cradled in his arms. And wept.

Upset, Flora marched out of the vicarage and strode up the snowy street. It was a cold day but her anger kept her so warm she did not need her shawl.

Suddenly she came up short. Lyle Aylesbury, astride a big chestnut stallion, was riding her way.

Flora hailed him, and he gave her a flashing smile that showed his strong white teeth. How like Tabby's his face was, she noted absently. He could be Tabby ... twenty years from now.

"I guess ye know I'm headed for the vicarage," said Lyle, dismounting, his big boots crushing down the snow.

"Aye." Flora took a deep breath. "I was wondering why ye'd picked Lorena to work for ye, when there are so many young girls in the village who are better cooks than she?"

Lyle Aylesbury shifted his broad shoulders a bit and cleared his throat before that level gaze. "As ye know, I'm a widower," he told her bluntly. "I'd thought to marry again. I thought if Lorena got to know—"

"You thought to settle Tabby's future before you settled your own?" interrupted Flora, her late anger making her speak more swiftly than was her wont.

"Why no!" Surprise washed the solemn expression from Lyle's face. "I thought to marry the girl myself when she's of marrying age."

Flora felt her breath leave her. Not Tabby—*Lyle!* "I see," she said, careful not to offend him. "Well, I'm glad I caught ye before ye came to the vicarage, Mister Aylesbury, because Robbie won't hear of Lorena working for ye. He doesn't want her alone in a house with two men and no woman about to chaperone her."

"But I'd see she got into no mischief!" Lyle looked honestly aggrieved.

"I'm sure of that," sighed Flora. "But Lorena's too young yet to think of marriage, so 'tis best ye forget about it."

The jaw that was so like Tabby's jutted a bit more as his gray eyes studied Flora. "I'll be speaking to the vicar when the wench is of marriageable age."

"As ye like," said Flora indifferently. " 'Tis too soon to be putting ideas of marriage into the child's head."

She watched him ride away, back toward the mill.

There was no doubt Lyle would be a good provider, and there was no more difference between his age and Lorena's than there was between Sam Brown and little Lillie Austin who had so recently jumped over the stile together.

Her jaws closed with a determined snap. 'Twas Tabby—not his father—young Lorena had her heart set on. Suddenly cold, Flora went shivering back to the vicarage and opened the door of the study unceremoniously.

She found the vicar still studying his great Bible. He looked like he'd been crying.

"Ye were right," she told him gruffly. "It wouldn't have been a good thing at all for Lorena to go to work for Lyle Aylesbury. Why, he said he was going to ask for her when she's of marriageable age."

Robbie seemed to shrink within himself. He thought of Lorena—and the big miller. It was a lash on his raw emotions. Yet, Lorena must marry someday. Better it be Lyle Aylesbury, who could at least take care of her, then Lyle's rakehell of a son.

His adam's apple worked. "I'll speak to Lyle about it," he said hoarsely. "When Lorena is older, they can be married."

"You can't mean it!" cried Flora. "Lyle's too old for her."

"Better a man than a green boy," mumbled the vicar, heaping self-punishment on himself with every word. Somewhere in the back of his mind he was imagining Lorena on her wedding night, Lorena disrobing, Lorena—The suffering gaze from his sunken eyes was fixed on Flora. " 'Tis a good match, Flora."

She could not dispute it, but she went away muttering. After a while she came back and found him still sunk in thought about the Bible. His head was bent. She thought he might be praying.

"Robbie," she began haltingly, for once feeling that God was not her ally. He looked up, his face haggard.

'Do not tell Lorena. Wait a while. Let her be a child for a time yet—no need for her to know she is betrothed."

Looking up into his wife's pleading eyes, the vicar nodded in dumb misery. Flora saw how troubled he was and believed he was bent upon saving Lorena from her wild course. Gently she closed the door of the study, but she walked away with dragging feet. All of her arguments, she felt, would not avail with Robbie. Flora's face grew bleak.

For it was a man's world, and between Robbie and Lyle—the church and commerce, both of them powers in this little town—they would be able to enforce Lorena's obedience, to bend her to their will.

Summer, Flora knew in her bones, would see Lorena married to the miller.

Wallham, Northumberland

Chapter 17

It was Mistress Potts who brought the first glimmerings of a grave new doubt to Lenore.

The last week in January Mistress Potts began to improve. By late February she was up and about, criticizing everything and fretting that they had run out of her favorite sweet wine, tawny bastard Malmsey.

"You've a fondness for sugar," laughed Lenore, glad that her crochety patient was up and around and sitting by the hearth downstairs at last.

"Aye. Lenore, why don't you make tansies for supper? Ye've the eggs to scramble and the cream."

"Have you forgotten that tansies also require violet leaves and strawberry leaves and walnut tree buds?"

"Well, perhaps you could leave those out. After all, you have the sugar and salt and grated bread and nutmeg."

"And what about the wheat blade juice and cinnamon and spinach?"

Mistress Potts gave a deep sigh. "I keep thinking of

that wonderful marrowbone pie I ate at the George—all those tasty layers of potatoes and sugar-spiced marrow. My stomach rumbles every time I think about it."

"Before you suggest we have marrowbone pie for dinner, tell me where we'll get the tasty layers of dates and currants and artichokes and candied eringo roots? Mistress Potts, I do not have the ingredients and I doubt I am a good enough cook to make such a complicated dish. If you aren't willing to eat plain food, you must go to Newcastle—or Durham or York."

Mistress Potts jumped up, her multiple chins wobbling with new-found energy. "That's it!" she cried. "I'll write to Amos in York. I'll tell him that when he comes he must not fail to bring with him a variety of spices and a good supply of dates and currants. I will make a list. Lenore, you must stop what you're doing and help me make it."

Lenore, who had brought a bowl in from the kitchen and was beating eggs by the hearth with a wooden spoon, in order to be company for Mistress Potts, cast her eyes to the heavens. But Mistress Potts bustled away to get inkwell and parchment. She lit a candle at the long board and soon was scratching away with a goose quill pen.

"There! Now I need Amos's address in York." Mistress Potts sealed the letter with wax. "Will you get it for me, Lenore, when the men come back? I want to go up and change my gown for supper."

Still beating the eggs, Lenore nodded. Through the window she could see Caleb and Sedgewick returning from hunting, trudging through the crusted snow with their guns over their shoulders. She peered through the long shadows that reached dusty blue across the snow to see if they had caught anything. Yes, a pair of rabbits. That meant rabbit stew for supper.

Tam came running up and took the rabbits. Caleb headed toward the stable and Sedgewick came in, seated himself by the hearth and began to struggle out of his wet boots.

"Mistress Potts has written a letter to her brother

Amos in York," Lenore told him. "Do you know the name of the inn where he's staying?"

"Amos"—Sedgewick gave a great wrench and came out of his right boot—"always stays at the Ox and Crown." He looked up at Lenore and for a moment she saw something in his face besides his usual lechery; he looked uneasy.

"But you don't think he's staying there now?" she challenged.

Sedgewick gave up for the moment the struggle with his left boot. "Why d'ye say that?"

"Because 'tis plain from your face that you think he's staying at the house of his young lady and I gather you don't want Mistress Potts to write him there." Head on one side, she studied him. "I realize 'tis not my affair, but is there some mystery about Amos's relationship with this young woman?"

"No, no mystery," Sedgewick panted, coming free of the other boot. He stuck his feet into dark blue velvet house slippers. He did not meet Lenore's steady gaze.

"Some scandal perhaps that you don't want Mistress Potts to know about because she's so garrulous?" she guessed with a shrewd look at Sedgewick.

"Yes . . ." Relief flooded Sedgewick's voice. "I said he was *courting* her but in point of fact he's *bedding* her. She's left her husband, and they're staying together at her sister's, I think. We've begged him not to bring her here, for her husband—who's away in France just now—is a notorious firebrand, and he may well kill both his wife and Amos when he returns!"

"What are you telling Mistress Frankford, Sedgewick?" Caleb's stern voice chimed in with Sedgewick's last words, and both their heads swung round to see Caleb standing in the doorway in his mustard velvet coat. His giant form seemed to fill the doorway. He so overpowered the room, it threw off one's sense of scale, Lenore thought absently.

"I will tell you later," Sedgewick said. "In the meantime, there's a matter outside I would see you about,

Caleb." Sedgewick hurried over and grasped Caleb's enormous arm, made to push him from the room. Lenore could hear Sedgewick's still booted feet clomping down the hall. She heard the front door open and close.

The two men came back in a few moments later, and Mistress Potts entered almost simultaneously, asking what was for supper? So it was not till that evening in their bedroom that Lenore had a chance to speak to Mistress Potts alone.

"I don't think Caleb and Sedgewick want you to know where Amos is staying," she told her friend bluntly.

"Nonsense," said Mistress Potts airily. "Whilst you were helping Tam carry out the dishes, Sedgewick told me that Amos is staying at the Ox and Crown in York, and I gave him my letter to post for me."

So Sedgewick had not told her about Amos's affair. Perhaps it was just as well. Lenore kept silent about it too.

In the days that followed Mistress Potts wrote yet another letter to Amos, giving him an additional list of foodstuffs he should bring. And then another.

All the letters were given to Sedgewick to post.

"Mistress Potts," sighed Lenore. "Amos would need two wagons to bring all you've asked for—and you aren't even *sure* he wants you here!"

"Nonsense!" Mistress Potts had recovered her ebullience. "I've changed my mind about Amos. If he can pursue a young woman at his age, there's juice in him yet. He's not some old stalk who wouldn't greet a half sister kindly! I tell you, Lenore, there's naught to worry about except whether Amos brings what's on the list I've sent him. Did I remember to put currants on it, Lenore?"

"You've put them on twice," Lenore groaned. "Poor Amos may come home riding atop a wagonload of fruit!"

But Amos did not return, with a wagon or without one, not even when spring burst all at once upon the countryside. Lenore considered it a minor miracle, this northern spring. One day it was winter, cold and slushy and wet, and the next day icy water was gurgling in little brooks, red campion was springing up among the bracken, and chaffinches were filling the air with song.

"If Amos doesn't return from York in *this* weather," Mistress Potts announced cheerily at breakfast, "I may just ride down to York myself and bring him back with me!"

A sudden silence greeted this remark. Lenore, looking at the stout lady beside her, doubted Mistress Potts' ability to ride at all and wished impatiently she would stop acting as if she had plenty of money when actually she hadn't a farthing.

In her irritation, Lenore determined to get away from the house for a while.

"I'm going out," she announced after breakfast. "I've been cooped up all winter and I need exercise. There is cold ham and cheese and bread and cider for your lunch, and Tam can get supper if I'm not back in time."

"But Lenore!" Mistress Potts' aggrieved voice followed her. "Tam just isn't up to cooking a real meal!"

"Then try *your* hand at it," Lenore called over her shoulder as she found her cloak and walked back toward the kitchen, for she meant to be out all day.

Taking an apple and some bread and cheese for lunch, she set off for the high wall that laced the crags together. It was a long walk, hard and steep, and her shoes were soon soaked in the soft damp earth, where snow had so recently lain and through which tender green blades of grass were pushing. But it was invigorating, the air smelled fresh and new. Lenore felt she had come suddenly out into another and better world as she made her way through the bright spring sunshine all the way to the Great Wall the Romans had built.

When she had reached her destination, she stretched and sank down in contentment on a sun-warmed stone at the base of the Wall and bit into her apple. Beside her one of the old stones bore a scar she guessed might have come from some long-ago Roman sharpening his sword when the Wall was new. It was a relief to think about something besides preparing meals and listening to Mistress Potts describe other dinners long gone, and watching Caleb brood with his pinhead sunk into his thick neck and great shoulders, and trying to avoid Sedgewick's lascivious gaze even while trying to respond to his empty—and usually drunken—chatter.

Lenore felt a real affection for Mistress Potts but after months cooped up in the house with her, she felt she would be glad to hand her over to Amos. She would be glad to see the last of Wallham, and hear the last of Sedgewick's sly innuendoes and constant references to her life as an actress, as if she had been walking the streets instead of the boards. It had indeed been a long winter!

But now the warm spring sunlight soothed all these irritations away. The wind ruffled her red-gold hair and she opened the top hooks of her bodice to let that warm wind caress her smooth white throat and bosom as well. She leaned back and studied the Wall, seeing that there were many gaps and holes where stones had been quarried to build the stone farmhouses and barns of the district, just as Wallham had been built. But far off in the distance in either direction, she could see, silhouetted against the clear blue sky, the mile-castles that dotted the length of this great man-made barrier that stretched across England from coast to coast. Those mile-castles gave a look of mystery, as if the Wall were some strange, continuous town reaching back into antiquity.

Below her was open treeless country, punctuated by huge, ancient stones. Winter frosts had broken some of them up into ungainly piles where grasses had grown right up to their mossy sides. In the distance the stone buildings of Wallham seemed like dollhouses in the crystal air.

There was a somnolence in the air, a promise of a rich summer to come, when the hum of bees would rise above waving grasses and banks of brilliant wild flowers. Lenore stretched out and took a nap.

She woke with a start: something had roused her.

She sat up and saw that a flock of starlings had winged up and veered off to her left to land in a clump of thick grass below. To her left a pair of larks soared, and as she rose, a swift-winged kestrel swooped down over her head and seemed to dive straight down into a sea of air toward Wallham in the valley below. Lenore guessed the birds had been perched atop the Wall and something had disturbed them. Her senses were alert now because there might be some prowling wild beast about. She would not wish to meet a wolf out here!

Lenore heard a rumbling sound, and saw that one of the big rocks at the top of the Wall, perhaps cracked by the winter's ice, had loosened and was tumbling toward her. With a scream she dove to the right and the heavy stone shot past her, making its way, leaping and bounding, into the valley far below.

Lenore scrambled to her feet, shaken by her near approach to death. For the heavy stone would have swept her away with it and sent her broken body tumbling down that long incline. Now that the rock had fallen, everything was very still, a kind of waiting stillness.

To Lenore, this quiet place had lost its charm. She snatched up the linen napkin in which she had brought her lunch and hurried back down the long way she had come. The light was fading now and she did not want darkness to catch her in the shadow of that Wall. As she hurried along, the long slanted rays of golden sunlight made a play of light and shadow among the broken field of rocks. She wondered if they had all arrived in the field as that last boulder had, fallen away from the wall. Men should have come in wagons and carted at least the smaller ones away, giving more room for growing things, she thought. But it was obvious that Wallham had been left to ruin.

Soon wild flowers would be blooming here, even though on the shady side of some of the bigger piles of stone the drifted snows of winter had not all melted. But the snow there was no longer pristine white, and in the dimness of this slanted light it looked gray and dirty.

Except *that* patch there . . . Lenore had got a pebble in her shoe and as she stood on one foot, pulled off her shoe and shook it, trying to get the pebble out, her gaze remained fixed on the patch of whiteness in the dirty gray.

And froze, wide-eyed.

That . . . patch of white . . . was not . . . snow. Lenore dropped her shoe and her stockinged foot came down on the cold damp ground.

She did not even feel it.

With a sharp exclamation she ran toward that streak of whiter white in the dirty snow.

From among the rocks a bony, fleshless hand stuck out as if beseeching her. Propelled by horror, Lenore approached the spot, bent down. She could not move the great stone that wedged the bones of what must be a wrist and arm, but her foot bumped against something round and moved the object an inch or two out of the melting snow. She jerked her foot back.

It was a skull.

As she stared at it, she realized that it could have been the skull of a child or of a small woman. Rocks had apparently been heaped upon the skeleton, but rodents and insects and perhaps birds had eaten away the flesh, and the skull—that crushed skull which must have stuck out from among the pile of rocks—had broken off and rolled down here, and the contour of the earth had so positioned it that the bony hand seemed to be pointing in macabre fashion to the skull. A tattered bit of red cloth remained nearby. Speared on a thorny branch, it had survived the winter and fluttered gaily, like a flower.

Lenore shrank away from it.

Whatever had happened here was not accidental: it was murder.

And Sylvie had loved red.

Twainmere, The Cotswolds

Chapter 18

Elias Plum, the driver who brought Lenore and Mistress Potts to Wallham, took Lenore's letter with him when he left, stuck conveniently into his boot. His intentions to post it were honorable enough, despite the slight grievance he felt against Lenore for failing to succumb to his masculine charms. Since the letter carried an address deep in the Cotswold Hills, Elias decided to take it back to York with him and post it there. Several times he curiously studied the red ceiling wax that sealed it, and he might have opened it and read it save that he had never learned to read.

But in Durham on his return journey Elias met with misfortune. He slipped on the icy cobbles outside a butcher's shop and fell heavily, crashing through the shop door and cutting his leg on a meat cleaver that the butcher dropped as he leaped aside to get out of the way of Elias's big body. The wound seemed superficial and Elias chose to ignore it. But in Darlington it festered and he ended up passing most of the winter there, forgetting all about the letter he had promised to post. He might not have lingered quite so long in Darlington but that one of the local tavern maids, a girl named Pris, found him irresistible, and Elias spent a sultry winter despite the cold, locked in her round, white arms.

With a sigh Elias left Pris in the spring and he was in York again before he remembered the letter he had promised so faithfully at Wallham to mail. Thus it was late spring before Lorena received her mother's letter from Northumberland and by then much had happened in Lenore's turbulent life.

Lorena did not recognize the letter for what it was—a desperate cry wrung from a woman's soul, for beneath the embroidery of glittering lies was woven a proud woman's anguished desire for a better life. The whole letter rang with a passionate appeal to her daughter to forgive her for all the years apart and to think of her with tenderness.

But Lorena's brilliant blue eyes fastened instead on the words *vast estate* and *great ball* and *black silk and lace*. Her sunny face turned ecstatic as she devoured the exciting words, reading over and over again until she had memorized them. Then even though she knew its contents word-for-word, she continued to reread Lenore's letter until it became dog-eared.

Watching her, Flora sighed. She wondered briefly where Lenore really was and what she was doing, for the tinsel prattle of the letter had not fooled her one bit. She knew shrewdly—and with a pang in her heart—that the bravehearted woman from Twainmere would have come back for her daughter if things were as the letter said. It was not some great ball that was holding her there in the north country. Something else was holding her.

The ill-matched nephews were holding her as if she were in some isolated prison, but Flora could not know that.

"*I am a guest at Wallham, which is a great mansion on a vast estate,*" Lorena read from her mother's familiar scrawl. "*It does belong to a brother of my dear friend*

Mistress Potts, with whom I traveled here by gilded coach. She spends her days planning a great ball to be held in the spring and urges me to wear my best black silk and lace, although the ball may never come off as she herself is ailing and never leaves the manor house to walk about the grounds."

As she read that, Lorena's breath expelled in a long, rapturous sigh. A manor house! Surely her mother would send for her now, and she too would dance at great balls with belted earls and wear black silk and lace.

With dreaming eyes and the precious letter tucked into the waist band of her kirtle, Lorena walked under drifting clouds that cast moving shadows on the beeches and the flowering fruit trees. Beneath her feet were the golden cups of the butterflowers and about her drifted the pervading scent of the whitethorn blossoms. Rooks flew overhead, and once when she bent to inspect a burst of yellow daffodils, she overturned a heap of moss and saw a little quilled hedgehog sleeping. Her light touch had not disturbed the little fellow, who was only about twice the length of a sparrow, and as she leaned closer she could hear the rhythmic sound of his snoring. She pressed the moss back gently, not to wake him, for hedgehogs ate not only insects but poisonous adders. Quickly she looked up, alerted by a sudden flash of white. High up a pure white swan winged across the sky. Perhaps, she thought wistfully, it sought the River Avon—that swan river where whole brigades of swans floated majestically. Maude's mother, who hailed from Stratford, had told her of them.

Now Lorena approached the Cardwell cottage with a springy step, eager to tell Maude about the letter. From the front door a small boy darted. He was pursued promptly by Maude, who ran him down and held him firmly—though he was kicking and gasping—beneath a big flowering pear tree.

Lorena hurried up. "What's the matter?" she cried.

"Oh, 'tis you, Lorena." Maude looked up from dragging her young brother along toward the house. His face was screwed up and he seemed to be fighting for breath.

"Naught's the matter. Little Alfie here suffers from hay fever—and he doesn't like his medicine." She laughed. "He saw Ma make it—woodlice steeped in wine—and he refuses to swallow a mouthful."

Lorena shuddered. When Mistress Piper had been sick with yellow jaundice in the village, her deaf sister had roasted a peck of large snails, beaten them up with earthworms, mixed them with ale and herbs and white wine and fed them to her. Lorena silently thanked God that she was healthy.

"Come *along* now!" Maude gave her brother's worn breeches a swat as she propelled him back into the cottage. "Ye need medicine. 'Twill help ye to breathe." He staggered forward through the door, wheezing, and Maude turned and gave Lorena a sharp look. "Have ye been to the mill lately?" she asked in a careless voice.

Lorena missed a step. Maude knew how she felt about Tabby and was always giving her advice. *Faint at his feet, make him carry you home in his arms. Just holding you will heat up his blood and you'll be in his bed in no time!* Lorena always blushed at Maude's bluff, salty advice; she couldn't bring herself to follow it.

"I was at the mill yesterday." Lorena tried to sound casual. "Aunt Flora thought she'd been cheated on the weight of some cheeses and I rode over and weighed them for her on the mill scales."

"Good. That's twice this week you've been there. Last time you ran out of flour."

"How—how do you know that?" faltered Lorena.

"Goody Kettle saw you when she rode by the mill and she told Mistress Markham and *she* told—"

"Oh, you can stop," Lorena said crossly. "I suppose they think I'm running after Tabby?"

Maude nodded and grinned. "Any luck this time?"

Lorena blushed and looked away, digging her square-toed shoe into the sod in embarrassment. Tabby had smiled at her and joked with her a bit, but that was all.

"Your aunt used to keep you so close to the vicarage. Can't understand what's made this change in her that she lets you go out."

Lorena turned and gazed soberly at Maude. Her aunt was much freer lately. And although she ascribed it to the fact that she was growing up fast, that was not the reason.

*   *   *

. The vicar's decision to betroth Lorena to the miller—even though it was agreed they'd keep it secret from Lorena for a time—had marked a change in Flora. Now that spring was sighing through the Cotswolds, now that the larks and jays were singing among the apple blossoms and the world seemed made for lovers, she felt unloved.

Never a demonstrative woman and too inarticulate to say what was in her heart, Flora had been deeply hurt when she realized that hers was to be a marriage in name only. But her pain had not found direct expression—which might have solved her problem. Instead she had busied herself fiercely about the house. Sometimes the lid blew off over some small difference and she was catapulted into brief, explosive arguments with her husband—*always* over unimportant problems and never about the one problem that kept them apart.

In a way, she had learned to live with it.

But now of nights when the wind sighed against the windowpanes and the vicar busied himself with other matters, never coming to her bed, sleeping instead on a cot in the study, Flora found herself dreaming of the Highlands of Scotland, the land of her birth. She fell to remembering, as she had not for years, the blithe young husband who had frozen to death while out hunting.

Ah, Robbie, her second husband, was a world of difference from her Kenneth—*he* had been her lover as well as her husband, while the tense, dedicated vicar was only the latter. Now Robbie had changed so and seemed to be venting his spite on Lorena.

Poor child—his beatings were growing harder; sometimes she had to bite her lips to keep from crying out. Flora could do nothing. Her entreaties elicited no response. Beads of sweat would form on his brow and a vast rage seemed to gather that must sometime burst forth. Indeed he seemed to take a righteous, evangelical zeal in "reforming" Lorena, and Flora noticed that he was always at his worst on Sunday afternoons after returning from the Hepworths.

Staring from her empty bed into the darkness where a single white star blinked through the windowpane, Flora grimaced as she remembered last Sunday. Surely Lorena's turning her head in church had not rated such a savage switching. The girl had emerged near tears and exhausted. She had staggered against the wall and nearly fallen off the ladder as she made her way on wounded, trembling legs up to the shelter of her loft.

Later Flora had looked in on Lorena. She had found her lying across the bed asleep, still fully clothed, with a look of exhaustion on her tearstained young face. Flora guessed she had cried herself to sleep. Back downstairs she had remonstrated with Robbie, but had found him unrepentant.

Maybe, she told herself with a sigh, it would be best for Lorena to marry—and soon. At least it would get her away from Robbie's constant punishments, and the kindly miller would never be cruel to her.

Abruptly, Flora began to allow Lorena more privileges. The moment the vicar cleared the door on some visit to a parishioner, Flora would find an excuse to let Lorena wander out abroad. That she was trying to give Lorena the chance to make her own way in life, to give her time to win a lover and perhaps to run away with him, Flora did not admit even to herself.

Lorena, whose ebullient good spirits were hard to crush, even by the vicar's wickedly wielded switch, made good use of this new freedom. Delighted with her sudden release from the confines of the vicarage, Lorena now wandered about the village—and her wanderings often took her across the wooden footbridge that spanned the millrace to Aylesbury's mill. Once there, she always pretended a great interest in the milling of grain.

Lyle Aylesbury, the miller, was flattered. Enchanted by Lorena, he took the girl's interest in the workings of the mill as a desire to be near him.

His son Tabby, who—like Lorena—had been kept in ignorance of his father's secret betrothal, took a different view.

"Hello, Lorena," he said one day as he came round the corner of the mill carrying an empty barrel and saw Lorena just stepping daintily off of the footbridge onto the sod.

"Hello, Tabby." Lorena tried to keep the bright color from rising in her cheeks at sight of him—and failed. "Your father said I could watch the making of flour today," she announced in a shy voice.

"Aye, and help with it too, if ye've a mind." Tabby was amused. Young girls had made their way to the mill before, seeking him . . . and found him willing. His gaze narrowed as he considered the rosy-cheeked girl before him. She really got prettier every day.

Lorena squirmed under that gaze. "I'll just go inside," she said in a muffled voice.

His arms still locked about the empty barrel, Tabby watched her disappear into the dusty dimness of the mill. Indecision gnawed at him. Instinct told him Lorena was his, a ripe plum for the taking, and yet—she was so very young. It would be on his conscience if he took her and . . . anything happened as a result of it.

Frowning, he set the barrel down with a thump, and stood and listened to his father's bluff voice greeting Lorena. As he worked with the barrels outside, Tabby could hear the murmur of their voices from within and her girlish laughter, and the thought of her there, young, lovely and so very *touchable,* wore on his mind.

He was tired from wrestling with himself when he heard her call a lighthearted good-bye to his father and run across the footbridge, snubbing him by never even looking his way.

Tabby gave a deep sigh and leaned his broad shoulders against the stone wall of the mill and brooded. And that night found he could not sleep for thrashing about and thinking of her.

But on waking, he decided he would wait for Lorena to grow up. He would *make* himself wait.

Oddly enough, it was Snowfire that brought them together.

Now that spring had come to the Cotswolds, Lorena frequently rode out on Snowfire, wandering down muddy country lanes, across flower-strewn fields, wherever fancy and the white horse took her.

But one day as she rode past the mill and peered back over her shoulder—for she had seen Tabby moving about outside the mill—Snowfire was distracted by a rabbit breaking through the low roadside brush and jumped aside. It was a bad step. His right forefoot slipped on a rock and he went down awkwardly, throwing Lorena over his head. The girl was up in an instant, for she was resilient and had not been riding fast.

But in the dust of the road Snowfire was floundering. Lorena knelt beside him and with a gasp, realized his leg was broken.

"Tabby!" she screamed. "Tabby!"

Hearing Lorena scream, Tabby was almost instantly beside her. He came to a stop, grimly looking down at the suffering white horse.

"His leg's broken, Lorena," he said slowly.

"I can see that. Oh, Tabby!" The face she turned to him was chalky white. "What am I to do?" she whispered. "I can't let him die, I can't!"

From the mill, Lyle Aylesbury too had heard her scream, and now he came running up to them. He too came to a halt, staring down at the anguished horse. "I'll get my musket," he muttered.

"No!" cried Lorena. "You'll not kill him while I draw breath!"

Father and son faced each other unhappily. Though neither knew of the depth of the other's affection, both of them loved this girl. And both of them knew in what regard she held the horse.

"We've a block and tackle," Tabby said, speaking rapidly to his father. "Could we not hoist him up in a stall and hang weights on the leg to set it?"

The miller nodded soberly. "Aye—but 'twould be a fair job to get him there. Even then, the leg might heal crooked."

"Crooked or not," sobbed Lorena. "Just so he lives."

Tabby gave her a worried look. "Could we but get him onto a sledge?"

Lyle Aylesbury looked at Lorena, seated on the road with the horse's big white head cradled in her lap. Her tears were falling on his white mane as she stroked him, murmuring gently to him. "Well, we've a sledge," he muttered. " 'Tis worth a try, I suppose."

The two men walked rapidly toward the mill, and Lorena was left in the spring sunshine beneath a sky of brilliant blue. But for her the world had gone dark. "Oh, Snowfire," she whispered into the silky mane that cascaded over her gray skirt. " 'Twas my fault. I was looking over my shoulder at Tabby, else I had seen the rabbit and could have jerked your head up and perhaps saved you."

The suffering horse gave a low whinny as if to comfort her.

Soon Tabby and his father were back, bringing with them a long heavy wooden sled used for hauling timber. Drawing it were four strong plough horses.

"We'll never get him up onto it," the miller said, worried. "The sledge is too high."

Tabby took another look at Lorena, sobbing quietly with her arms about the horse's neck.

"If the sledge is too high, we'll lower the road."

Lorena lifted her head and looked at him, thrilling to his determined words, even through her grief. The look in her blue eyes was compensation enough. Tabby turned away from her and swallowed. "We can do it with picks and shovels," he announced.

His father sighed, but he swung his pick as mightily as Tabby when his son brought out the picks and shovels. They were both strong men and before long they had scooped out a shallow incline beside Snowfire into which the unwieldy sledge could be lowered.

By now several passersby—two on foot and one on horseback—had stopped to watch this unusual proceeding. All were voluble in their advice, and assured the straining miller and his son that it would never work; even could they get the suffering horse to the miller's stable, the leg would never heal right—best to shoot him now.

Lorena cried out a protest at that and Tabby, panting from his work with pick and shovel, gave his advisers a black look and wondered aloud if his critics might not help him a bit with his folly. They were willing enough and soon the heavy sledge was lowered into the shoveled-out depression. Its top was just slightly lower than the roadside.

"We can slide these horse blankets under the horse, if Lorena here can keep him quiet," said Tabby gravely.

Lorena gave him a look of absolute trust and gratitude that nearly blinded him. "I'll keep him quiet," she promised. "Snowfire, 'tis all right, 'tis all right." Her soft soothing voice kept pouring gentle words into the horse's ear and gradually the blankets were eased under his trembling body.

"Now if we can pull him onto the sledge," worried Tabby. "Lorena, ye'll have to get out of the way."

"Snowfire needs me to encourage him," she returned. "I'll edge along just ahead of you."

Tabby frowned, knowing she might be crushed, but Lorena beat back all their protests. Her cheek was brushing that snowy mane as, straining and gasping, the men managed to slide the white horse onto the sledge.

"And now ye must keep him there, Lorena," said

Tabby grimly. "For though 'tis no distance to the stable, 'twill frighten him when the sledge starts moving, and he may try to scramble up."

"We'll make it, Snowfire and I," Lorena declared staunchly.

Watching her, Tabby saw that her manner was determined, almost serene. *What a girl she is!* he thought.

"We'll strap him to the sledge," said the miller gruffly.

Overriding Lorena's protests that the straps might hurt Snowfire, they passed a couple of straps across the horse's body. Then slowly, slowly, walking the plough horses, they eased the sledge over the ground, both father and son thankful that the way was not too uneven. At first when the sledge moved, Snowfire's great head went up, and he strained against the straps in a bid to flounder off of it. But Lorena's slender arms were wrapped firmly around his neck, and her soothing voice calmed him.

Tabby, looking back, tossed the russet hair back from his eyes and felt his forehead breaking out with sweat. For he knew that if the horse panicked he could well break the straps and roll over and crush the girl. His father was leading the other plough horse, and now they exchanged uneasy looks.

But somehow they made it to the stable and there prepared the block and tackle. Heavy canvas was slipped under the horse's stomach and he was heaved upward, suspended with his legs off the floor and supported by heavy chains draped over one of the stable's enormous oaken beams. Lorena watched tensely while weights from the mill scales were affixed, wincing as Snowfire gave a very human scream of pain.

" 'Tis necessary, Lorena," panted Tabby, struggling with the weights, "if the leg is to set straight."

Lorena's face was white, and she was trembling as badly as the horse by the time they had straightened out the broken leg and wrapped it with splints.

Snowfire seemed to understand what they were doing. At first frightened and pawing, he was calm now and drank some water and ate some hay and grain that Lorena proffered him.

"Ye're in worse shape than the horse," said Tabby gruffly, seeing her sag against the stable wall.

"Come along, I'll make ye a hot posset," said the miller.

"Thank you, but—I'd rather stay here with Snowfire," said Lorena in a tremulous voice.

"The horse needs rest," Lyle Aylesbury told her bluntly. "And so do ye, by the look of ye. Come along now."

She nodded, too exhausted to protest further, as he propelled her toward the house. Inside the Aylesbury's pleasant living room, Lorena sank down onto a wooden bench and waited in silent exhaustion for the hot posset.

"Will Snowfire really be all right?" she roused herself to ask Tabby.

"He'll be fine," Tabby told her recklessly, and was rewarded by that wonderful glowing look that set his heart racing.

"I can't thank you both enough," she told the miller humbly as she held out her hand to accept the hot posset.

Lyle Aylesbury smiled down at her. Seeing her in this room where soon she'd come wearing her bridal wreath was an exhilarating experience for him. He looked down at the girl's pale, delicately shaped face, so innocent in its loveliness, at her dainty arms and legs and delicious torso, and imagined her bustling about here, moving the benches about, sweeping and arranging the cups—and smiling up at him, her fortunate husband.

It was a glorious vision. He almost told her then that there was no need to thank him, that they'd be jumping over the stile together soon enough, and she and the white horse would both be his to cherish and care for. But he held his silence, he respected his promise to Flora to "let her be a child yet and carefree."

"I'll come over every day and feed Snowfire and water and curry him," Lorena promised. Her voice was stronger now that the hot posset had brought the color back to her cheeks.

"And welcome ye'll be, though we can take care of him well enough."

"I think you were both wonderful to do this," said Lorena shyly. "I'll never forget it. Never."

Both masculine faces broke into smiles, and there was a slight swagger in two pairs of brawny shoulders. Father and son were tired. They'd done the unheard of. They had a big horse suspended on chains in their stable, his body resting on strips of canvas, and no doubt they'd have half the county coming in to gawk the next day, as if at some freak at a fair. But the girl's flushed cheeks, the glory in her tired blue eyes as she thanked them, was tribute enough.

"And now, I must go." Lorena got to her feet and shook out her light gray skirt. "Aunt Flora will wonder what has happened to me."

"She's probably heard by now," said the miller dryly. All of Twainmere would have heard the story by now!

"I'll take you home, Lorena," offered Tabby. " 'Twill take but a minute to hitch up the horse."

" 'Tis not far and you've not had your supper," she said. "And besides I—I want to say good-bye to Snowfire first." She ran from the room, turning to wave at them.

After she'd gone, the two men looked at each other.

"She loves that horse," sighed the miller. "I hope he mends, for 'twill break her heart if he doesn't."

"He'll mend," murmured Tabby, watching the door through which Lorena had darted.

"I don't know," mused the miller. "But 'twas smart of ye, Tabby, to think of this way of doing it. At least, now he'll have a chance."

But at the moment his tall son's thoughts were not on the horse's chances, but on his own.

The vicar seemed dazed when he heard about Snowfire's injury and what had been done about it, but Flora's enthusiasm bloomed. "That Tabby!" she cried, hearing

Lorena's story. "Wouldn't you know he'd think of something like that?"

Yes, thought Lorena. Good for him. If she hadn't loved him before, she'd have loved him now. *Tabby* . . . The name sounded in her ears caressingly. A soft sound, a lovely name . . .

After the first shock, the vicar lost interest in Snowfire's plight and bizarre deliverance. Things were coming to a head at the Hepworths. He was over there three afternoons a week now and was hard put not to make it five—or seven. Always he mumbled to Flora that Martin Hepworth was "worse today." Flora, now caught up in Lorena's affairs as her secret nuptial date approached, paid scant attention; the vicar was always off to somewhere. Her heart ached for the young girl, so soon to be forced into marriage with a man so much her senior, and she let Lorena go every day to the mill to feed and stroke and encourage Snowfire. Though she never quite admitted it to herself, she hoped that Tabby would scoop up Lorena and carry her away—perhaps to the Highlands of Flora's youth.

Snowfire's leg mended slowly, and Lorena, with her bright fresh ways and smiling face, was carving a deep hold into two men's hearts: the miller and his tall son.

Usually Lorena left the mill before dark, but if darkness fell while she was still in the stable talking to the horse and petting him, Tabby hooked up the bay horse and took her home in a light cart.

Lorena was very flirtatious during these rides. She sensed his response and enjoyed baiting him. For Tabby it was a kind of delicious agony. He felt the muscles in his groin tense and harden whenever her laughing face came so close to his that he could feel her fresh breath on his cheek and smell the faint lemony scent of her shining fair hair. Inwardly he groaned at the strong pull of her nearness and he was hard put not to respond to the lure of her seductive lips and body, the challenge he read in her blue eyes. Although he had kissed her lightheartedly on his sled in the winter, Lorena had woven a spell about him now, and he did not trust himself any longer to stop with a kiss on the lips. Once she was in his arms, his hot blood warned him, he might not stop until he made her his completely.

"I think you're afraid of me, Tabby," she taunted him one day as, perched beside him, they rode through Twainmere toward the vicarage in the dusk.

From his height above her, Tabby gave her a quelling look. "Why, are ye then so fierce?" he scoffed.

"I might be." Impudently she let her fingernails trace a light trail along his forearm and his flesh shuddered at her touch and leaped to fire. "Don't you like me, Tabby?" She leant around and peered pertly into his face.

Tabby restrained himself with an effort. His voice sounded labored to his own ears, but somehow he kept it steady. "Of course I like you, Lorena."

They had reached the vicarage now, and Lorena didn't wait for him to help her, but vaulted down, skirts flying. She turned to look up at him wickedly, her eyes shining in the dusk.

"Don't wait too long," she warned in a deliberately provocative voice. "Else I may jump over the stile with someone else, and *then* you'll have lost your chance!"

Tabby swallowed and clung to the reins with a numbing grip. He watched her pick up her skirts—a shade higher than was necessary—and run to the vicarage door, where she turned to wave a laughing good-bye.

But for of all her flaunting, her deliberate teasing of him, it was the millrace that finally catapulted Lorena into Tabby's arms.

It happened on a sunny afternoon, when the jays and finches sang in the branches and the boughs of the fruit trees were alight with flowers. Lorena, taking her usual shortcut, sang lightly as she strolled beneath the great beeches that led to the mill. In her straw basket she carried not only some wheaten cakes wrapped in a linen napkin that Flora was sending to the miller, but a chunk of loaf sugar for Snowfire and a big handful of the sweet grasses he loved. She was still singing as she set her foot upon the narrow planks of the footbridge that led across the millrace to the mill. From outside the mill, where he was sweeping up grain that had fallen out of an over-turned barrel, Tabby heard her light voice singing "Greensleeves," that love song said to have been written by old King Henry as a young man. He turned from his work to watch her coming across the footbridge, swishing her light skirts as she walked.

Midway across, a hawk in pursuit of a sparrow swooped low over her head, and dodging with a cry, she teetered for a moment with her basket waving wildly, then plummeted from the footbridge into the millrace.

Before the rushing waters closed over her head, Tabby had flung aside his broom and begun to run. He leaped into the millrace without even taking off his heavy boots. He had entered the water below where she had fallen and now, bearing down on him through the rapid running waters of the race he could see Lorena's white face, her blue eyes looking scared as she fought the water.

"Here!" shouted Tabby, striking out for her with bold sure strokes.

She saw him and tried to swim toward him, but the irresistible current turned her aside. Then with a sudden capricious toss it drove her toward him. Her body collid-ed with Tabby's, and she would have been wrenched away, to ricochet downstream into the jaws of the turning mill wheel, save that he reached out and caught her by her long wet hair as she went by. But the current, Lorena's thrashing weight, and his heavy boots were too much for Tabby and along with the girl in his grasp, he too was swept away.

Below loomed the great mill wheel, inexorably turning—and the fast current was sweeping them down toward it.

Over the millrace, just before the mill wheel, the

bough of an old oak leaned down, almost touching the water. In desperation Tabby reached up and seized that low-hanging bough as they were swept under it.

Her mad course downstream thus suddenly arrested, Lorena gave a cry of pain as her long hair was nearly wrenched from her scalp by Tabby's powerful grip. But Tabby's muscular arm was wrapped firmly around the bough's rough bark now. Lorena sputtered and choked as he pulled her in to shore by her hair. Then he got a leg up, reached down, and grasping her arms, dragged her, limp and dripping, onto the bank.

As she fought for breath, gulping in air, Lorena's gaze swung in horror to the mill wheel.

"It would have ground us up!" she gasped.

"Aye," agreed Tabby grimly, his breast heaving from the exertion. "I've told ye before the footbridge is dangerous." He tossed back a lock of wet auburn hair. "Suppose I'd not been there?"

"Ah, but you were." Lorena's ebullient spirits rose as she shook out her long fair hair and tried to wring the water out of her skirts. "You've saved my life, Tabby, so"—she gave him a roguish look—"now I belong to you!"

Tabby grinned, leaning back on one arm. "So that's the way a wench is won, is it?" he murmured.

"Of course." Lorena leaned back on the grassy bank and smiled up into his face. "Poor Snowfire," she murmured. "I was bringing him some loaf sugar, and he loves it so much. Now 'tis gone, like the wheaten cakes I was bringing to your father, down the millrace to feed the fish downstream."

"Better the cakes feed the fishes than ourselves!" In the shade of the leafy enveloping bough, Tabby leant over her. Wet or dry, Lorena was the loveliest thing he had ever seen. Her sweet challenging face looking up at him was tempting . . . too tempting. Urged on by an instinct he could not resist, Tabby bent and pressed his warm lips on hers.

The result was electrifying. As their lips touched, a wave of feeling seemed to leap between them. It sent the blood racing through Tabby's veins, and Lorena started violently. With an abrupt gesture, he gathered Lorena to him, felt her pliant body at first stiffen, then yield; felt her lips move softly, luxuriously, finally parting under the insistent pressure of his probing tongue; felt her defenses melt away as with a little moan she strained toward him.

As suddenly as he had seized her, he let her go, drew back. Every nerve in his body burned, but he kept himself under iron control.

"It shouldn't happen like this," he said huskily. "I'll not take ye like any light wench in the hay, Lorena."

But Lorena had felt the urgency of his lips, the tension in his taut body, and now she recognized in his husky voice the clear undertone of desire. She knew she had reached him. She sat up, flexing for the first time the strength of her young allure, recognizing it for what it was—a force that could move men and reshape her world.

"What makes you think I'd *let* you take me, Tabby?" she murmured in a lazy voice. She reached out with unsteady fingers and broke off a grass stem, studied it. When she looked up, it was to give him a slanted look through her lashes. "Maybe . . . I'm only playing with you. How can you be sure?"

Tabby's shoulder muscles jerked, but he made no reply to her taunt. Instead he rose, asking curtly, "D'ye want to see Snowfire or would ye rather I take ye home so ye can change into some dry clothes?"

She had meant to tease him, to inflame him by her arch remark, but it had not had the desired effect. She would have to practice this baiting game if she was to be good at it. For she could not have been wrong—a moment ago Tabby had wanted her. Desperately. With all his heart and being.

Just as she wanted him.

"I think I'll go see Snowfire. He won't mind if my clothes are wet! That is, if you can mange to find me a bit of loaf sugar?"

Tabby nodded and strode ahead of her toward the mill. With mock meekness, Lorena followed along behind. In her wet clinging garments, she waited outside the cottage while Tabby found her some loaf sugar for the horse.

Inside the miller's house, after Lorena had gone dripping to the stable, Tabby was changing his wet clothes when his father strode in. "What's this? Ye're all wet!" he exclaimed.

"I've been swimming in the millrace," said his son wryly, "Lorena fell in. I had to jump in and pull her out."

To Tabby's astonishment, the miller's face went white.

"Lorena? In the millrace? My God, she could have been killed."

"Aye," agreed Tabby.

"But ye saved her." Lyle Aylesbury's voice softened. He laid a big affectionate hand on his son's muscular shoulder. "And I thank ye for that, Tabby, for I love that little wench."

Tabby was about to respond ruefully that he loved Lorena too, but something rich and deep in his father's voice made his head swing round in surprise. The way Lyle Aylesbury had said "love" was not fatherly, nor brotherly—it had been spoken like a lover.

Lyle Aylesbury caught his son's puzzled look. "Aye, Tabby," he admitted sheepishly. "I should have told ye before. Lorena and I are betrothed. Flora wished it kept a secret, and that's why I've not told ye. But we'll be wed when Lorena's of an age to marry."

Married! His father and Lorena? His mind awhirl, Tabby peered down at his wet boots lest his father see the consternation on his face.

"She's young," he muttered.

"She'll age," countered the miller. "All girls do.

Your mother was but thirteen when I took her to wife. 'Tis a good thing altogether for a girl to marry young. Ah, Tabby, ye'll see how much better it is living here with a woman about, laughing and talking and straightening up."

Tabby wasn't listening. His dazed eyes were still fixed on the tops of his wide boots, which he tugged at viciously. But another voice rang in his ears—Lorena's voice, saying, *Don't wait too long, else I may jump over the stile with someone else.* She'd meant his father! She'd been playing him for a fool all along! Or else—he straightened up and gave his father a haggard look which was interpreted by Lyle merely as surprise. Else young as she was, Lorena was playing a dirty game and intended to have them both!

He flung out past the miller.

That evening a puzzled Lorena went home alone.

Wallham, Northumberland

Chapter 19

"Dear God," whispered Lenore. "This is Sylvie's skull, Sylvie's hand. Sylvie did not run away. She is lying here crushed somewhere beneath these rocks."

A picture of that room at the end of the hall where everything was broken, bent, torn, flashed back to her. That destroyed room was not the only violence giant Caleb had done to the woman who had betrayed him.

Lenore sat back on her heels, a light film of perspiration gleaming on her forehead. Whatever she had expected, it was not *this!* Caleb was mad—had to be to have done this thing. No wonder Sedgewick was so watchful of him! No wonder Tam feared him so!

All her instincts warned her not to return, to start walking away from Wallham and to keep on until she reached a dwelling, a village, there to pour out her story and ask for shelter.

But she could not leave Mistress Potts at Wallham unprotected. Several times she had angered Caleb. Suppose—?

Lenore's scalp prickled. If only she and the older woman could reach York and inform Amos of her discovery.

Her mind came to a full stop.

Did Amos know about it already? Was that the real reason he had not returned, because he knew his nephew to be a murderer and could not bear the sight of him—yet could not bring himself to turn him in to the law because blood was, as Mistress Potts **was** fond of saying, "thicker than malmsey"?

Even if Amos did know, they must find him. For herself, Lenore knew she could find a job, could make her own way. But Mistress Potts was too heavy a load for her to carry. Amos must be made to help out! And if he had covered up for Caleb thus far through family feeling, he would certainly assist Mistress Potts, however reluctantly, once he was made aware that she knew about the murder.

Lenore regained her feet and turned her footsteps reluctantly toward the house that loomed gray in the distance. Once there she must manage to conceal this frightening new knowledge. She must brazen it out until she could get Mistress Potts away from Wallham.

Where before her mind had been filled with the beauty of the wild landscape stretching about her, Lenore now strode along without even seeing the rabbits and grouse that scurried away at her approach, or noting the soft cries of sleepy birds calling to their mates.

Walking fast over the damp spring sod, she found herself abruptly back in the yard. Above her the gray house walls seemed to loom like a prison. Looking up at those sightless windows, Lenore restrained a shudder. It was all she could do to force herself to enter the gray forbidding building.

As she closed the front door behind her, she saw Sedgewick's narrow form silhouetted against a wedge of light at the end of the long dim hall. She guessed he had been watching for her. At least it was not Caleb waiting there! Lenore moved forward briskly.

She would have brushed by his knife-thin figure, but

he leaned down to look squarely into her face. "What is it, Mistress Frankford?" he wondered. "Ye're pale. Have ye had a fright?"

Inwardly cursing her pallor, Lenore squared her shoulders and reminded herself grimly that she was an actress—this was but another part and she would play it!

"I *have* had a fright," she admitted frankly, walking past him into the large candle-lit room where plates had now been laid for supper. "I climbed up to the Wall and ate my lunch. And I think a wolf or some other large animal must have been lurking atop the Wall—at least a large stone rolled off. It missed me by a breath!"

Lenore hoped she had carried it off. She thought Sedgewick believed her, for he shook his head. "Ye should not take long walks alone around here," he cautioned. "For there are wolves out there. In spite of all we do, a wolf does carry off a sheep now and then."

Lenore, who was from sheep country, had seen no shepherds from the Wall. Nor any woolly flocks in the distance. She turned away to hide her skepticism and Mistress Potts' round face peered out at her from behind a chairback. Lenore saw that she was clutching a quilled pen. "I'm writing Amos to be sure to bring me some pins and a length of riband for my chemise, Lenore. Is there anything you want him to bring you?"

Lenore shook her head. "I'd hardly charge a stranger with buying me ribands and pins!"

"*I* would be glad to buy your ribands, Mistress Frankford," interposed Sedgewick with an ingratiating smile. "The next time I am in Newcastle." He moved a step closer.

Newcastle! That could be their chance to escape. Lenore smiled at Sedgewick. "Thank you, but I'm sure both Mistress Potts and I would rather go along to Newcastle with you and select our own ribands."

Sedgewick lookd uncomfortable. "I have not yet decided when I will go," he said vaguely, and Lenore was left to hide her disappointment with an offhand, "When you do go, let us know."

Supper was an ordeal. Lenore could hardly bear to look at Caleb's massive form when he lumbered into the dining room, but she forced herself to nod pleasantly. The sight of him carving a bird at the head of the table, knife cutting through flesh, was almost too much for her. Vividly the sight recalled those pleading bony fingers. Shaken, she looked rapidly down at her trencher.

"Lenore, ye're not eating," chided Mistress Potts. "Ye are but toying with your food—and after being out all day too!"

Lenore gave her friend an unhappy look. She wished Mistress Potts hadn't said that, for it alerted Caleb that she had been gone long enough to have discovered Sylvie's bones. "I'm not very hungry," she mumbled.

Sedgewick, already half drunk on wine, leaned forward from down the table. "Mistress Frankford had a fright today, Abigail. She walked to the Wall and a stone fell off above her, as they often do in spring." He turned to Lenore. "The ice in winter breaks them up and they come tumbling down into the valley below," he explained. "Next time you go out walking, Mistress Frankford," he said thickly, "ye'll have me for a chaperon. To save ye from being affrighted."

Sedgewick's lecherous company was the last thing Lenore wanted. "I'm over my fright now," she stated coolly and met Caleb's suspicious gaze with a calm stare before she quickly began to eat the badly cooked food on her plate.

That night Lenore fought back the urge to blurt out to Abigail Potts all that she had seen. Caution kept her silent. Mistress Potts had never been any good at dissembling; whatever she felt was apparent on her kind round face. If she were to learn the truth, her shock and horror would be reflected in her blue eyes whenever she looked at Caleb—and that would bring them both down.

Studying Abigail's stout form as she prepared for

bed, Lenore decided not to tell her until the very moment when Caleb and Sedgewick cleared the door the next time they walked out to shoot game. She would tell her then, all in a rush, and they could stuff whatever would fit into saddlebags and be off on the horses from Wallham's stables. Next day hopefully.

But the weather foiled Lenore's plans, for the next day it rained. Lenore, who had scarce slept all night, dozed off just before dawn and awoke to the patter of rain on the slates of the roof. She ran to the window and peered out: the sky was a sodden gray and water ran in rivulets down the windowpanes. This damp murky weather was ushering in the season of flowers, she realized, but it meant that the men of the house would not go hunting.

The weather being damp and cool, after breakfast Caleb and Sedgewick both lolled about the fire, their boots propped up comfortably on the big iron fender. Lenore, tense and keyed up, found herself nervously dropping things in the kitchen. She broke a crock half filled with cream and Tam gave her a puzzled look, for she was usually so deft—it was *he* who broke things!

All day the rain continued and by evening Lenore's nerves were so frayed that when Mistress Potts uttered a complaint about the sauce she snapped at her. She was instantly sorry for the older woman looked stricken.

That night as they undressed for bed, she asked Mistress Potts if she had any friends in Newcastle, for a plan was forming in her mind.

"Aye. Abby Charlesford and Abby MacDonald. 'The three Abbys' we used to call ourselves, for we were all great friends. But Lenore, if ye are thinking that I'll call on either of them when Sedgewick takes us into New-castle to buy ribands, ye're mistaken. I've no desire for my old friends to see me with my fortunes brought so low! 'Tis why I did not write to them that I was coming back home to Wallham. Why, they'd have expected to see me come driving up in my own coach with a footman to hand me down from it!"

Lenore gave her an impatient look. "But they still live in Newcastle; you've corresponded fairly recently?"

"Oh, yes." Mistress Potts nodded her curls vigorously. "I heard from Abby Charlesford shortly before I left London and she said she'd dined the day before with Abby MacDonald and they spoke about me."

Well, that was a relief! At least she would have someone to hand Mistress Potts over to, if she could manage to get her to Newcastle. Friends, who would see she reached Amos.

All that week it rained. Water cascaded over the roof slates, poured down the windowpanes, sat in glittering puddles on the sodden ground. The nephews hardly left the house, spending their time dozing by the fire, drinking, and playing an occasional game of whist.

Lenore fretted. If only people came to the house, someone with a cart that they could find an excuse to ride away in. But no one ever came to Wallham. Apparently Caleb and Sedgewick had no friends, or else had alienated them all, and Amos's friends obviously knew he was in York.

The perpetual downpour jangled Lenore's taut nerves. Inside the house the air was damp and the walls were sweating.

She became so used to rain that she could hardly believe it when she woke one morning to see the sun shining, although a little water still dripped from the eaves. Outside the landscape had turned a vivid green and songbirds flashed by the windows singing their hearts out.

Today, she told herself, was the day.

"We could use some fresh game for our supper," she suggested at breakfast. "We're down to salt herring and smoked meat."

The nephews promptly took the bait. The air outside was warming, and they did not mind slogging through the mud if they could bring down a bird or two for their dinner.

Lenore watched from a downstairs window as their

forms, one so massive and one so thin, disappeared from view. Then she turned to go upstairs and tell Mistress Potts they must pack, they were leaving. Mistress Potts had gone back to her room after breakfast, and this suited Lenore perfectly because that lady was sure to exclaim loudly at what she had to tell her, and she did not want Tam in the kitchen to hear. Tam—he might be a problem. She would send him off on some errand, but first she must get Mistress Potts started on her packing.

But just as she went from the dining room into the hall, moving fast, she heard a scream from the upstairs landing and Mistress Potts's ample form catapulted down the steps toward her. Her fat little hands clutched at the railing, unable to rise. "Someone must carry me upstairs," she was moaning.

If Mistress Potts couldn't make it up the stairs, she'd certainly never make it to Newcastle. That much was self-evident. They'd be staying at Wallham until the ankle healed enough to bear her weight. Between them, struggling, Lenore and Tam managed somehow to get her great bulk upstairs.

A week later when the men were out hunting and Tam and Lenore were in the bakehouse, companionably munching some hot bread she had just baked, Tam said with his mouth full, "The old lady must be better. I heard her walking upstairs this morning."

Tam had sharp ears, thought Lenore. But it was true. Mistress Potts could now hobble to the chamber pot without assistance.

"Tam." She shot a speculative look at him. "What really happened to Sylvie?"

Tam didn't quite meet her eyes. "She run away," he mumbled. And then, lower still, "Lots of bad things has happened here."

She waited but he continued to munch in silence.

Tam's attitude preyed on her mind. As if the very rooms themselves would somehow tell her what had happened, that afternoon she prowled the upstairs, opening the bedroom doors one by one.

All but Sylvie's room with its slashed fabrics and destroyed furniture. That room made her shudder and she kept away from it.

With some hesitation she ventured into the sparsely furnished room she believed to have been Amos's and searched the little slanted writing desk. Nothing there but some old receipts. She looked up at a sound and through the streaked panes saw a thrush singing from an oak branch. Behind him the sky was blue with fleecy white clouds, piled up like white goose down waiting to be stuffed into a feather mattress.

Lenore abandoned the desk and looked around her restlessly. This must once have been a pleasant room. Feeling an urge to make it look less unlived in, she bent down and picked up one of the crumpled pieces of parchment from the floor, automatically smoothing it out.

As she peered down at it, she felt her scalp prickle.

The name "Amos Barrow" was written over and over. And at the bottom a jab as if a quill pen had been thrust through the parchment in anger.

A terrible thought occurred to Lenore. Frowning, she gathered up all the crumpled pieces of parchment from the floor and smoothed them out. They were all the same, covered with the name "Amos Barrow."

A sane man, Lenore reasoned, would hardly sit and laboriously inscribe his own name over and over on expensive parchment, and then litter the floor with the result.

It hadn't been Amos! Someone had sat here at this writing desk and painstakingly practiced Amos's signature. Who? Sylvie?

Lenore flew downstairs and went looking for Tam.

He was not in the big, spicy-smelling kitchen where the red coals of the breakfast fire still glowed. She ran outside, over the newly appearing spring grass-blades toward the high-peaked stone stable. Dodging heaped up piles of manure, she burst through the big double doors to see Tam busily pitchforking hay for the horses to eat.

He looked startled when she seized him by the shoulders. "Tam!" Goaded by fear, she began to shake him. "You've got to tell me! What happened to Sylvie? And to Amos?"

Suddenly a long sigh escaped the boy. The rigid shoulders into which her fingers were digging, relaxed. He let his pitchfork fall into a pile of hay and she dropped her hands and stepped back. His gaze focused on some long cobwebs, hanging dustily down from a heavy beam and the story poured out of him, almost with relief. Listening, Lenore felt that Tam had wanted to tell someone about it for a very long time.

"Sylvie and Amos was plannin' to run away together."

His words hit Lenore like a solid blow. Young Sylvie—and Amos! It was something that hadn't occurred to her.

Tam sank down upon the hay, studying his thin callused hands, and Lenore sank down beside him, absorbed in what he had to say.

"Sylvie had her eye on Amos from the first. When Caleb brought her home from the Banbury Fair, there were a great to-do over it. Amos said it was his house and Caleb had no right to bring a wife here without his permission and he'd a mind to turn them both out. And Caleb said he'd worked long and hard for Amos without pay, just for his keep because he was Amos's nephew and Amos had no wife or sons of his own. He said he had every right to bring his wife here, and Amos should take them both in and be glad he had another unpaid hand to help him."

Lenore was inclined to agree with Caleb on that point. "And did he?" she asked.

"He grumbled some, but then he said they could stay here temporary until they found other quarters—and after Caleb took Sylvie upstairs I heard Amos mutter to Sedgewick that Caleb had brought home a young whore.

But 'tweren't a month before he'd changed his mind about Sylvie and began to spoil her. Everything she wanted, she *got*. First pretty clothes, and then a maid."

Tam was deep in his brooding excursion into the past. "Pretty soon Sylvie began to boss everyone, and one day I followed her and found out she were meetin' Amos in the stable and lyin' in the hay with him."

Lenore grimaced. Sylvie, the clever London whore.

"Did you tell anyone about it, Tam?"

He shook his head vehemently. "I were afraid to mention it, but that day, the day I heard 'em plannin' to run off together, I were asleep in the hay and their voices must have woken me. I heard Sylvie say, 'What do you think Caleb will *do* when he learns tomorrow night that we've gone?' And Amos said, 'Nothing he can do. He's got no money to follow us with and once we're safe in London I'll arrange from there to sell the property. Ye'll be safe from him, Sylvie.' And she laughed, kind of nervous like. I was afeard to move. There they was rollin' in the hay not ten feet from me, and I was afeard to move. I got a cramp in my left leg from lyin' so still. And then Sylvie must have got up because I could hear her movin' around, and she said, 'I'm afraid one of the servants will tell Caleb—you know they all hate me.' And Amos said nobody was goin' to tell Caleb, on account of he was goin' to send Caleb and Sedgewick off on different errands next morning and he'd already told all the servants they could spend tomorrow at the fair. The house would be deserted. I didn't tell no one what I'd heard.

"Next day there wasn't no room for me in the cart that was going to the fair and Amos told me to take a load of wagon wheels out to be fixed. But the horse threw a shoe and I had to come back. The place looked deserted when I got here—and then I saw the two horses saddled and tethered by the house and I knew Amos and Sylvie hadn't left yet. I didn't want them to see me, so I drove the horse and wagon into the stable. And then I saw Caleb come over the rise and make for the house. He was walkin' real purposeful like he knew somethin' was afoot and he came up close to the house and stood behind that big oak tree and waited until they came out. And then he stepped out from behind the tree."

Lenore found her fingers clenching with suspense as she waited for the boy to continue.

"Sylvie lost her head and screamed when she saw him. And Amos tried to jump on his horse and ride away, but Caleb pulled him off the horse and dragged him to the ground and began to stomp him with his boots. Sylvie, she stopped screaming and her face was white and she backed away from them through the front door and run back into the house. And Caleb just kept stomping and stomping Amos till there weren't much left of Amos but blood and clothes."

Amos was never coming back. Caleb had killed him.

"Then Caleb went into the house and he must've busted Sylvie's door down because I heard a crash and more screaming. I could hear her screaming at him to let her go, and sobbing, and hear things breaking."

Lenore could envision the nightmarish scene. Sylvie in her red dress, crouched in the middle of the room while Caleb crashed about, smashing everything in the room. She could imagine Sylvie leaping up and trying to dart away—and being tossed inexorably back to the bed. Could picture Sylvie's tearstained face as she pleaded with Caleb when her dresses were attacked, moaning 'Oh, no, not my clothes,' while Caleb slashed them viciously to ribbons.

She found that her lips were dry, but her voice was remarkably calm. "And did he kill her there, Tam?"

"No, he dragged her downstairs, screeching all the way. He took her outside and dragged her along that way." He nodded morosely in the direction of the great Wall, along the route where Lenore had found the whitened skull. "And then he let go and told her to run. She looked at him dazed for a minute and then she scrambled up and took off. Caleb let her run a little ways and then he picked up a big rock and heaved it at her and dropped her as she ran."

Lenore shuddered. Giant Caleb, who hurled the sledge at fairs . . .

"It must've broken her leg, 'cause she couldn't walk after that, but she kept trying to drag herself away. Caleb was shouting at her that she was an adulteress and he'd give her the punishment they gave adulteresses in Bible days—he'd stone her to death. And he did. He just kept walking around her in a circle and hurling more stones at her until he'd piled up a big pile and only her arm and one foot stuck out."

That crushed skull, the bony fingers of that beseeching hand that stuck out from beneath a great pile of rocks—Lenore felt physically ill.

"Caleb were still out there cursing and finding more rocks to pile on Sylvie when Sedgewick came home. He saw Sylvie's hand sticking out of that rock pile and he jumped off his horse and said, 'My God, Caleb, what have you done?' And Caleb wouldn't answer him. He just kept piling up rocks on Sylvie. He did it all day long and then he fell down in the field and slept there all night. It were Sedgewick who took Amos's body away somewheres and buried him."

"Where, Tam? Where did he bury him?"

"I dunno. I hid in the stable till next day when the rest of the servants come back, and mingled in with them. Neither Caleb nor Sedgewick seemed to notice I hadn't come in with the rest. But Sedgewick, he come out of the house and gave everybody the sack, accused them of working together to steal the liquor and the meat from the smokehouse. He said Amos had told him to pay them off. They was mad too at being accused like that, and they packed up and left in a huff. I stayed behind."

"Oh, *why,* Tam?" burst out Lenore. "You should have gone too!"

He gave her a sad jaded look. "They's starvin' at home," he muttered. "So I stayed and when Sedgewick asked me why I didn't go with the rest, I told him I never stole nothin' and I had nowheres to go. And Sedgewick, he thought about it and then he said in a kind of different voice, 'All right, you can stay, Tam. Sylvie has left Caleb so we won't ever mention her name again. And Amos was upset about it and he's ridden away to York. We don't know when he'll be back.' "

"I guess he kept you so you'd tell people that—if anyone asked," murmured Lenore.

Tam nodded soberly. "And after that, Caleb and Sedgewick began to sell off the flock, one or two sheep at a time. And the horses. All that's left are the horses the four of them rode. I guess they thought it'd look conspicuous like if they sold Sylvie's gray mare or Amos's big roan."

So the nephews had been cautiously dismantling these holdings ever since Amos's death. But the looting had been systematic. And next they had doubtless planned to sell the property, but had failed at copying Amos's signature, as the crumpled parchment upstairs proved.

"I think they plan to kill the old lady," Tam volunteered in a gloomy voice.

Lenore felt fear gush through her like a hot tide. In the white heat of these revelations she had forgotten that Mistress Potts was Amos's next of kin. Even if the nephews could make it appear that Amos had staggered off somewhere drunk and been killed beneath an avalanche-like fall of rocks, they could not inherit, for Abigail Potts' ample form barred the way.

"They'll kill *us* too, Tam, because we could testify against them."

"Oh, no, we don't need to worry," Tam informed her earnestly. "They don't think I know nothing, and anyway they don't plan to kill *you*. I heard them talking. Sedgewick's decided to marry you. Because a wife can't testify against her husband."

Twainmere, The Cotswolds

Chapter 20

The news of Lorena's betrothal to his father had an instant and violent effect on Tabby.

He went wild. His whole nature seemed to change and worsen. Any evening now you could find him steadily consuming ale in the local tavern or brawling in the streets.

When Lorena came to feed Snowfire, he was always absent. Once he brushed by her on horseback as she approached the mill by the long way, for she now carefully avoided the treacherous footbridge over the race.

"Hello, Tabby," she said eagerly, her face brightening. For she could not understand the change in him and only half believed the stories that were circulating about him.

Tabby looked down irritably from his horse. His eyes, she thought, were quite bloodshot. "Sorry I can't stay to talk, Lorena," he told her in a clear brutal voice. "Can't keep Tess waiting."

Lorena stiffened as if he had struck her. With her

back held straight, she turned and marched away from him, down to the stable. And shed wounded tears against Snowfire's lustrous white mane. The big horse, who was mending now, looked down at her with sad understanding eyes.

"What did I do wrong?" she mourned. "Oh, Snowfire, I was only teasing him when I told him I was only playing with him. I didn't mean it—didn't he know that?"

The miller had given himself another explanation for his son's erratic behavior. Lyle Aylesbury thought Tabby was busy sowing his wild oats now before there was a woman in the household to criticize his comings and goings. Best the lad sow those oats now, he told himself comfortably when he heard that Tabby was bedding Floss, the tavern wench—she was bragging about it. And mayhap 'twill end well, for he's going with Tess too. 'Tis probably Tess saying no to Tabby that has driven him to Floss's arms, Lyle told himself with a chuckle. Could be we'll have two weddings in the family this summer!

But Tess had not said no; she had not been asked. Tess pouted and showed her jealousy of Floss, and finally in a pettish mood betrothed herself one fine spring day to a likely lad from the next town—and all in the hope that Tabby would realize he was losing her and straighten up and propose marrige.

But Tabby continued to drown himself in ale.

He was openly rude to Lorena sometimes, for by now the wound she had dealt him had festered and he saw her as a teenage Jezebel, bent on destroying his father as well as himself. But his strong young body ached for her. It was painful to hear her light step, hear her soft-voiced greeting—more formal now than heretofore, for Lorena felt wounded too. And there were long terrible nights when the creaking sound of the mill wheel endlessly turning became for Tabby the creaking of a bed as he envisioned Lorena, slender and naked and totally desirable, enfolded in the arms of his father, laughing and gasping and—!

At times like these he would bring his fist down in a

numbing blow upon the hard wooden planks of the floor and groan aloud.

Lorena and his father—it was too much to bear.

The pressure in his skull was like an iron clamp around his head these days. It could be relieved only by ale—or action.

Inevitably he clashed with the law, and was sentenced to a day in the stocks for drunkeness.

Lorena was shocked and saddened when she learned through Flora, who had had it from Mercy Meadows, that Tabby must spend a day in the stocks. Tom Prattle, her dissolute uncle—yes, for Tom staggered down the street unsteady from gin even in the morning. But Tabby—never! Her young heart grieved for him.

That was the day that Flora had promised Mercy Meadows she would go to the next town with her, for both of them were fascinated by a new type of butter churn they had been told about, one that would do the job in far less time with less work, and a cousin of Mercy's had had one sent out from London and was eager to display it.

Seeing Lorena's despondent face, Flora almost decided to stay, since there would not be room for Lorena in the Meadows' small cart, not with all the goods Mercy was taking to her wealthy cousin! But the lure of the butter churn was great, the spring day beautiful.

"A day in the stocks is not forever," Flora consoled Lorena. "And perhaps 'twill teach Tabby something."

"I care not if he spends a week in the stocks!" declared Lorena with a toss of her fair head.

Flora reached over and impulsively gave Lorena's hand a compassionate squeeze. She too had once been young and had lied about her feelings for a young man.

"I—I don't care about him at all," muttered Lorena defiantly.

Flora sighed. "When ye finish making the butter, Lorena, and your other chores, ye can go and spend the rest of the day with Snowfire. I'll be back before nightfall. There, I hear Mercy calling me now." She hurried down the hall, stopping by the study to call, "Good-bye, Robbie."

Lorena heard the front door close and turned back to the churning. She was very conscious of the vicar at work in his study. At any time he might come out and give her one of those long suspicious looks with which he had been favoring her lately and perhaps insist on some long Bible reading that would prevent her from visiting the injured horse. She stopped rocking the churn abruptly as she heard the study door open and saw the vicar, tall and looking very authoritative today, emerge.

"I must go and pray with Martin Hepworth today," he announced in an austere voice.

"You were there yesterday," said Lorena, looking at him in surprise across the wooden churn. "Is he worse then?"

"I had thought him to be mending a bit, but he's taken a bad turn again," said the vicar testily, angered that he should be expected to explain to the chit. Actually Lola had been baiting him. Bored with her ailing husband and her relative inactivity, she had taken to taunting the poor vicar, taking amusement from his pallor and faltering responses. Last Sunday she had told him she thought she was pregnant—with his child. It was untrue, but it had stirred up such a furor in Robbie's chest that he had felt a sudden blast of the old angina pains over his heart. He had managed to conceal the attack from Lola, who had thought his contorted face and the sudden alteration of his breathing were from shock at her announcement, and he had managed to drag himself away. Yesterday, when he had gone again to the Hepworth's house "to pray," and Lola had sobbed pitiably about her "plight," watching him with bright eyes through her fingers, he had felt the pains strike lightninglike again. They were quickly gone, but the pressure within him remained.

Now he walked out of the house in sedate fashion—although he would have liked to run all the way, for he could spend unexpected stolen hours with Lola now that Flora would be gone all day. In his sober brown homespun, dull dark stockings and prosaic hat, his expression rather prim, no man could have looked less like a lover on his way to a tryst with his mistress.

Lorena never suspected it of him.

But his going meant to her a blessed release, could she but finish all her chores, the main one being the butter-making, for she could then dash down to the mill and spend the day with Snowfire. The vicar never followed her to the mill. Impatiently she tried to hurry, but butter took its own time.

She was almost ready to go when old Evan Moresby beat on the vicarage door and burst in to tell her with wringing hands that his wife was took bad, doctor said she wouldn't last the afternoon maybe, and where was the vicar? For she wanted the vicar to pray with her for her soul.

"Uncle Robbie's at the Hepworths'," she told him. Seeing how winded he was, she said, "You go back home and I'll run to the Hepworths' and tell him he's needed."

With his quavering thanks still ringing in her ears, Lorena took a shortcut behind the stone cottages, ran across the forbidden footbridge that crossed the millstream, fled past the mill without stopping and, still taking the shortest route, reached the rear of the Hepworth property which lay past the Whitleigh's place, just outside town.

She approached the house from the rear, rounded the corner and headed in her square-toed shoes for the front door.

Normally Lorena did not stare into the windows she passed. But as she ran soundlessly over the soft grass, some sound from within the cottage must have arrested her. For a moment she paused and shot an uncertain look toward the small panes.

What she saw within froze her in her tracks and caused her jaw to drop open.

On a pallet on the living room floor—a pallet that had been used by the injured Martin Hepworth before he retired permanently upstairs—the vicar and Lola Hepworth were writhing. She could see the vicar's contorted face and Lola's white legs thrashing from her purple petticoats as he took her.

So stunned at the sight that she was for the moment unable to move, Lorena stood and took in the scene.

So *this* was what Uncle Robbie did when he came to the Hepworths "to pray"!

Lorena forgot her mission. She drew back from the window stiffly, as if she were some jointed doll whose arms and legs would not obey her. That pair inside must not know she had seen them!

Numbed in mind and body, she had stumbled halfway back to Twainmere, this time going by the long route that would lead her down the main street and past the village square, before she remembered the message she had come to bring. Her square-toed shoes came to a halt as she hesitated. No, she could not go back. She did not think she would ever be able to look at the Hepworths' cottage again.

A passing farm cart gave her the answer. Lorena knew the farmer who nodded laconically as he passed.

"Wait!" she cried. "Are you going by the Hepworths'?"

"Aye." The farmer looked down at her curiously.

"Then would you mind stopping and giving the vicar a message? Evan Moresby's wife is dying, and she wants him to come and pray with her."

"Aye, I'll give him the message."

The cart lumbered on, and Lorena's halting footsteps continued to carry her back toward Twainmere.

What she had seen now seemed like a bad dream. Watching them there on the floor through wide horrified eyes, she had almost not believed the scene was real. The righteous vicar and moist-eyed seductive Lola Hepworth—and she with a crippled husband right upstairs!

Ah, now Lorena felt she understood. As she ran from that place, understanding had crowded in on her: Uncle Robbie's zeal in punishing her, with every week the blows growing fiercer. Why, he was not even thinking of her as a person; he was punishing himself by proxy! Boy kings had whipping boys who took their whippings for them when the young kings misbehaved. *She was Uncle Robbie's whipping boy!* She guessed that he hated himself for his weakness, hated himself for stooping to a liaison with a coarse woman, hated himself for his unfaith to his "sainted" Flora. By striking at Lorena for every small infraction he was doing penance. Doing it the easy way!

Tomorrow Robbie would sin again, and tomorrow. And these sins would be scars upon his consciousness which he would try to erase through abusing *her!*

Such thoughts of a man she had thought almost holy made Lorena feel sick and for a moment nauseous. Dizzy now, she paused and leant her pliant young body against the rough bark of a tree until the world steadied. As she moved away, her fair hair caught in the bark and pulled painfully.

It reminded her of the last time she had been "bad" (her crime was laughing too loudly on the Sabbath and, Uncle Robbie had also insisted, brazenly displaying her trim ankles as she skipped over a mud puddle to keep her new shoes clean). "Daughter!" he had said in that stern voice that always preceded punishment, for he never called her "daughter" except when he was angry. And then abruptly he had seized her by the hair and pulled her across the room.

Lorena had shrieked at this unexpected assault, and Flora had come running from the kitchen still holding a long-handled spoon. "In God's name," she had cried, dropping the spoon and seizing her husband's arm. "What are ye about, Robbie?"

"I'm going to teach this young whore decorum," he had cried in a shaking vocie. "Lorena, you will bring me a willow switch."

"I'll bring you *three* willow switches!" cried Lorena defiantly. "One for each of us! For I have done nothing—nothing!"

She ran from the room, still feeling the pain at the roots of her hair where Uncle Robbie had pulled it so cruelly and sped outside toward the willow tree. Behind her she could hear Flora's bewildered voice crying, "But what has the child done now, Robbie? Tell me! What?"

In a towering rage, Lorena had torn off three switches, brought them in, and out of pain and indignation and humiliation—and a stiff-necked pride that she had inherited from her wild young mother—she had flung the switches into the vicar's face so that he flinched back. "There!" she shouted. "What do you imagine about me now? What excuse have you trumped up so that you can beat me again?"

"Ye'll not take that tone with *me,* wench!" Robbie had leaped forward, arm upraised, and knocked her down. Lorena felt his hand crash against her cheekbone. She fell and struck her head against the wainscoating and passed out. When she came to, lying on the floor, the vicar was methodically switching her legs, and she moaned as she came up out of the darkness, moving her legs and trying to elude the bright pains that ran along her calves and thighs.

"Robbie!" Flora was beseeching. "Enough, Robbie!" She seized the switch from him, and they wrestled for a moment as the girl on the floor watched dazedly. Lorena could see that the vicar's eyes were wild and held a fanatical gleam. "Dear Lord in heaven," gasped Flora. "Whatever the child has done, ye must not assault her so fiercely, Robbie!"

Breathing hard and swaying slightly on his feet, the vicar had stared down white-faced at Lorena. She looked up at him hopelessly. Her head had begun to ache and she felt that her face was swelling.

"Do not interfere again, Flora," the vicar warned in a choked voice. He turned on his heel and went into his study, slamming the door behind him.

"Lorena, child." Flora was bending over her, concerned. "Your head, you struck your head." She stroked back Lorena's hair and the girl winced. " 'Tis a bad bruise," she pronounced severely, "though your face is none so bad—a bit swollen maybe. Best ye get some rest, but first we'll sponge your face and wash away those marks that switch made and apply unguents."

Lorena had choked back her sobs. "What did I do?" she demanded, bewildered. "It seems to me that every Sunday evening Uncle Robbie comes home in a frenzy and attacks me. What did I do this time?"

It was only later that she learned he had heard her laughing too loudly as she waved good-bye to the Pearson children, to whose home she had been sent on an errand by Flora. She had not seen the vicar going by at the time, but he had seen *her,* and followed her progress malevolently as she lightheartedly leaped over a mud puddle to save her precious new shoes, thereby displaying her trim ankles.

"Aunt Flora," she said, when she heard. "I can't live like this."

"I know." Flora did not look up from her mending. "I know, Lorena."

"Sometimes I think Uncle Robbie hates me."

"No." Flora's needle paused thoughtfully. "Robbie *couldn't* hate you, Lorena, for you've done nothing to deserve his hatred. Ye've brought light and laughter into our lives, and for that he should be grateful—as I am."

"Well, he isn't," muttered Lorena.

"No," admitted Flora, for she was, above all, honest. "He isn't." She sighed and plunged the needle back into the cotton stocking she was mending.

They were both silent for a long time, with Lorena staring unhappily out at the rose bushes and the low garden wall. Suddenly Flora put away her mending and went over and put her arms around Lorena and gave her a reassuring hug. Never a demonstrative woman, it was for Flora an unusual gesture. Lorena was touched by it.

But it had not solved the problem.

Neither of them had found any solution. They had stated the problem but they did not know how to meet it.

And now—this!

Lorena's step was steadier now as she passed the

low stone walls and pleasant stone cottages that lined the street leading to the village square. Her face was thoughtful, sad, disillusioned. *How terrible, how terrible all this was for Flora, who didn't know about it, of course—else how could she have gone blithely off to look at a new butter churn?*

On she walked, her mind occupied with brutal imaginings: someone would tell Flora and erase all her happiness. Worse yet, *Uncle Robbie might run away with that Hepworth woman!* Were all men like that? If one couldn't even trust Uncle Robbie, who was always bleating loftily about proper conduct, who could one trust? Flashing like sheet lightning in the back of her brain was the shocking memory of the vicar and Lola locked together in the sweating frenzy of a fiery embrace.

She had reached the village square now and was brought up short at the sight of Tabby, locked in the stocks. His wrists and ankles were both encased firmly in wood, leaving only his head and body able to move.

Tabby—buffeted by the shock waves of Uncle Robbie's behavior, she had forgotten Tabby was spending the day in the stocks.

Now across the empty square—for even the loiterers had gone home to lunch—she studied that big loved head of russet hair, shining in the sunlight, the strong hard body in homespun garb now held immobilized in the grip of the stocks.

Tabby, sitting glumly in the stocks with the sun beating mercilessly down on his head from which the brimmed hat had long since been knocked, did not see her. All morning with a steady gaze he had faced his tormentors: the women who passed him, drawing aside their skirts and giving him distasteful glances, the young girls who giggled and pointed and whispered, and worst of all the mocking ring of children who circled him, calling out taunts. He had cursed under his breath and ducked when three of them had begun to throw rocks at him, before the town constable wandering by had driven them off. One of the rocks had drawn blood from a small gash below his right eye—a little higher and he'd have been blinded. Grimly Tabby promised himself that tomorrow he'd go seeking the lad who'd thrown it and warm his breeches so he'd stand up to eat his supper for a week!

All morning he had held his head up proudly, but now all those who wished him ill had gone home to eat, and he let his head sink down dejectedly on his chest.

It was thus Lorena saw him—and felt a sudden rush of pity.

She started across the trampled grass toward him and he looked up and saw her.

His heart gave a lurch. His arms and legs were numb from being held motionless in the stocks so long and his whole body ached from his cramped position, but it was as nothing compared to the pain that went through him at sight of the girl, moving toward him beneath the branches of the gnarled giant oaks, gazing at him with such witchery. Her beauty struck him forcibly like a slap, and he felt its sting with more force than he had felt the rock which had nearly cost him his eye. Ah, she was so light-footed she seemed scarce to touch the ground, he thought. And now the dappled sunlight knifing down through the big trees alternately struck gold in her hair or left it pale and shining.

Instantly his face, which had looked so vulnerable before, hardened. A kind of dull hatred grew in his gray eyes, leaving them cold and murky, like dirty ice. Even *she* had come to mock him.

Before that hard gaze Lorena's step faltered. Why should he look at her like that? What had she ever done to him? And then anger washed over her, drowning out any pity she had felt before. Who was Tabby to criticize anyone? Wenching with anyone who'd have him these days, was the gossip about Tabby. He'd ruined Tess, and who knew how many others? Tess had married too quickly, rumor had it.

Lorena's fair head lifted and her blue gaze grew malicious. Here was Tabby, a captive audience at last. She would tempt him, tantalize him—one last time. And then reject him! She did not realize she was going to make him pay for the sins of the vicar, for all her newfound anger against men. At that moment she was a beautiful predator—as her mother had been when *she* was growing up in Twainmere—and Tabby was her chosen victim.

Arms akimbo, eyes gleaming, she moved toward Tabby with a hip-swaying walk.

Watching her approach was pure torture for him.

Two steps away she noticed the little trickle of blood that had dried beneath his right eye.

"Someone has hurt you!" she cried, stricken.

"Not half so much as I'll hurt *him* once I'm out of here," growled Tabby. *She-devil,* he thought. Turning her witchery on him, and now pretending to care for his hurt!

His cold manner stiffened Lorena's spine. Her lower lip curled, and she gave him a contemptuous look.

"So they've locked you up?" she said lightly.

"In wood, as ye see," growled Tabby.

"Strange. . . ." She bent down, broke off a grass stem, bit down upon it with her small white teeth. "You seem not half so fierce now, Tabby."

He gave a short laugh, watching her narrowly. He wished she had not bent down so that the tops of her white breasts were revealed to his aching gaze.

Hips swaying seductively, Lorena came closer. "And what would you do if I were to kiss you now, Tabby?" she murmured, fixing him with her blue gaze. "Would you flex those big muscles and shatter the wood that holds you?"

Tabby tensed. She was very close now, he could smell the fresh light feminine scent of her, like wood violets sparkling with dew in the morning mist.

Suddenly she bent and pressed her warm lips against his. For a moment her slender arms were twined round his neck, her soft breasts crushed against his heaving chest.

Tabby drank deep of that kiss, reveled in it. He could not help himself. She was like wine to his blood, this girl, and he savored her lips, the pressure of her young sweet body, with longing.

Lorena *felt* that longing. It passed between them like a lover's sigh, telling her that this tall lad—no matter how he glared at her—still wanted her. Desperately.

Filled with exultation she drew back, laughing wickedly. "You could have had *me*," she taunted him. "And you took Tess and that tavern wench instead!"

Her laughter burst like a bomb through Tabby's head. *You could have had me* . . . and she betrothed to his father all the time! Lorena was still only a breath away, teasing him with her delicious nearness, and now he suddenly dipped his head and his strong teeth caught in her bodice and the light chemise beneath. Lorena, feeling his teeth graze her naked breasts, understandably jerked away and Tabby had gained his purpose. With a loud rip the material of both bodice and chemise tore away, leaving her round young breasts exposed to his tormented gaze.

Lorena looked down with a cry, snatching at her torn bodice and chemise. She was dizzy with shame and hurt—that he should humiliate her so!

"You're a beast," she gasped. "No, you're not even that. You're—you're nothing!"

She lifted her slender arm and struck him across the face. Tabby took the blow calmly, watching her with hard unblinking eyes. Only his shoulder muscles beneath the homespun seemed to bunch and grow.

"I don't understand you!" Her wild voice broke into a sob.

"Nay, but I understand you!" The vicar's accusing voice thundered in her ears, and Lorena was suddenly caught from behind in a fierce grip. "Hellcat!" he cried. "Whore of Babylon!"

She twisted in his grasp. In their rapt concentration

319

on each other, neither she nor Tabby had heard him come up.

"Come away with me now!" He gave her a rough jerk that caused her to lose her balance. She lost her grip on her torn bodice too, as she stumbled to her knees. The vicar gave her no chance to regain her feet. " 'Tis a lucky thing none but myself and this young buck have seen ye like this. Ah, there'll be trouble if Lyle Aylesbury hears of it!" He was dragging her along urgently over the ground as he spoke.

Seeing her being forcibly hauled away, Tabby found his voice. "She was not to blame," he called hoarsely. "She taunted me and I lost my head. She was not to blame."

But the vicar and his ward were already some distance away, and making too much noise themselves to hear him. With a groan that he could not go to her, Tabby tore his gaze away—and saw across the green from him, Kate Tilson. She stood silently beneath a tree, watching the scene with avid eyes. As he watched, she turned and and sped away from him, running in the direction of the mill.

Tabby strained against the solid wood that held him fast and groaned. Now his father would hear about this— from Kate, who hated Lorena and would trump up some terrible story, no doubt. His anger and torment had left him exhausted and his head sank down on his chest.

The afternoon passed for him like a bad dream. He heard taunts, but could not have told the words. He felt a rock strike his head and ducked automatically; felt warm blood gush in his hair, but did not identify whoever had thrown it. He was living with an inner hell, and it was a worse punishment than anything the stocks could afford.

At last, as darkness fell, he was released from the stocks to stumble home on numbed limbs. He came free and stood up, rubbing his wrists and ankles, stamping his feet to restore the feeling to them.

All his bones ached as he made his weary way home

to the mill—to find his father standing in the doorway of their cottage, his big body silhouetted against the candle-light within.

"I heard what ye did to Lorena," Lyle greeted him curtly. "Shaming her before all the village."

Tabby was almost shaking with fatigue. "She taunted me," he mumbled. "And anyway there was none to see."

"Save the vicar—and Kate."

"Yes, they were there." He moved wearily to enter.

The miller's big body seemed to swell. He barred his son's entrance.

"Ye knew how I felt about the girl," he said sternly. "Ye knew that we were betrothed. And yet—"

"I lost my head."

"Ye lost your—!" With a sudden howl of rage the miller's clenched fist swung out and caught a surprised Tabby squarely on the jaw, sent him measuring his long length across the grass.

For a moment Lyle Aylesbury stood there looking down at his son as he rubbed his skinned knuckles.

"Ye're lucky I don't take a whip to ye," he growled. "Get out of my sight, I don't want to look at ye!" He went in and the cottage door slammed behind him.

Hardly believing, Tabby struggled up from the ground and wandered out aimlessly to the millstream. There he washed his face in the cold water and then was violently sick. When he got to his feet, he had made up his mind. He could not live in the same house with his father and Lorena.

He waited until his father had gone to bed, then he let himself into the house through an unlocked window. Moving stealthily, he put coarse brown bread and cheese and a leg of mutton into a bag and then, with some hesitation, he took a few coins from his father's strong-box, hidden beneath some sacks of grain. After all, he reasoned, even an apprentice received something for his work, and these coins would get him to London.

. For Tabby was about to do what he had always threatened to do, without half meaning it. He trudged away from the mill in the slanted moonlight, heading east toward London. As the mill disappeared behind him, his broad shoulders squared and his step became more determined.

Tabby Aylesbury, the miller's gray-eyed son, had run away to sea.

*   *   *

Meanwhile, Lorena had had the humiliating experience of being dragged home by the vicar. Her clothes were further torn and covered with dirt and grass stains by the time they reached the low stone wall outside. Mercifully, their progress had not been observed, for everyone was home eating. But Lorena was sobbing with rage, and the vicar had not relaxed his punishing grip. He was still muttering all the evil things that lay in store for such as she, as they burst through the vicarage door.

"Aunt Flora!" cried Lorena, struggling to get away from him.

But Flora was not home yet. She was still about the business of the butter churn with Mercy Meadows.

Through the dusky hallway he dragged her, and into his study. He slammed the door behind him with his boot and flung her against the wall. Her shoulder came up painfully against the wainscoating, and she managed to right herself, stood massaging her hurt shoulder. In the light from the windows she could see the gleam of sweat on his forehead. Well, he should be tired, she thought grimly, considering how he had spent his afternoon! The face turned to her was like granite, and the eyes held a fanatic evangelical gleam.

"Ye'll bring me a pair of willow switches, daughter," he ordered curtly. "I see ye must be twice beaten for the good of your soul."

She might have quailed before him, but blistering memories boiled up in her, and she swung round on him like a tigress. "I am not your daughter—and I thank God for it." She almost spat the words.

The vicar had been catching his breath by leaning heavily upon his knuckles on his writing desk. Now he straightened up and his eyes took on a vengeful gleam. "So? Ye're evil of tongue today, is that it? Mayhap I should take a whip to your rebellious flesh instead of a willow switch!"

"Neither whip nor switch!" Lorena cried. With a lightning plunge she leaped past him and ran from the study, leaped like a cat to the ladder that led upward to her loftlike bedroom. "And you'll never punish me again," she panted. *"Never*. NEVER!"

"Vixen!" Overcome with rage now, the vicar pursued her, tried to snatch at the hem of her gray skirt as she pelted up the ladder. She kicked at his hand and heard him pant, "By all that's holy, I'll humble you this day!"

"You will not!" Lorena screamed at him from above. "You will never touch me again!" She skittered out upon the loft floor and turned at bay just as the vicar's head appeared through the open trapdoor in the floor.

"Will I not?" he roared. "Dare ye say I will not?"

"You'll not touch me because I saw you today—I saw you with *her*. I saw everything!"

The vicar was arrested in his upward path. He stayed where he was, clinging to the ladder, staring at her.

"What are you saying, girl?" he demanded hoarsely.

"I was at the Hepworths' today. I saw you rolling on the floor with Lola Hepworth. And if you ever lay a hand on me again I'll scream it to the whole village!" She was sobbing now, sobbing with pent-up rage, with resentment and sorrow for Aunt Flora and—yes, she was sobbing with grief for Uncle Robbie too. For although she'd learned to fear his heavy hand of late and at times had even hated him, she had respected him as a good and honest man. She had thought him pure and cold, not of this world, better than others in some towering way, a man whose standards were impossible to live up to.

But now her idol had fallen. Uncle Robbie had turned out no better than the rest—worse even, for he was also a hypocrite.

From the trapdoor, as her words sank in, she saw his face whiten, saw his mouth open in a snarl. His eyes were staring. She thought he was trying to speak, to denounce her, but had choked on the words. His pale face was still working and his breath rasped as he suddenly clutched at his chest. With a weird half-human cry of pain and fear and rage, he slithered down the ladder, spun away from it and lurched against the door jamb of his study, righted himself and tottered down the hall to the front door.

It was an attack of sharp violence, and he knew instinctively that it would be his last. The pains were terrible now—and increasing.

He came out of the vicarage moaning and threw himself upon his horse, who had followed along forlornly as the man of God dragged along a daughter of the world, back to the vicarage, there to extinguish whatever flame of passion burned in her.

The horse knew the way by now. Without urging, the patient animal carried the vicar back to the Hepworths' where Lola Hepworth gasped at the sight of him and came running out the door with her purple skirts caught up in her hand. He almost fell from the saddle into her plump white arms. She could not get him inside, but she bore him gently to the grass, collapsed there with him.

The vicar, when he felt Death stealing over him, had made one last abortive dash back toward Life. For Life to him, he now admitted for the first time, was the tempting passionate woman who had made him feel at last that he was a man.

With the last of his strength he had won through to her. His arrival, plummeting down into her arms, ashen-faced, was for him like the entry of Adam into the

Garden of Eden. Lola for once was merciful. She saw how stricken he was, and cradled his head in her purple skirts, and told him over and over, in a burst of guilty tears, that she loved him.

The vicar looked up at her gratefully.

And died in the arms of his profane love.

Wallham, Northumberland

Chapter 21

Sedgewick intended to marry her! Lenore sat back, stunned.

" 'Twon't be so bad, I guess," mused Tam. "You could have Sylvie's room—if you could get it fixed up. Caleb wrecked it real bad."

Lenore stared at Tam. She felt she was trying to hang onto her sanity in a crazy world. "Even if Sedgewick forced me to marry him—and I don't see how he could do that—a wife can *choose* to testify against her husband, Tam."

"They say you *won't*," Tam replied laconically.

"Not testify? Why not?"

Tam's young face was solemn. "Because 'tis the law that a man can beat his wife with a stick as large as his thumb, and Sedgewick's got big hands. Big thumbs. If you even thought to try it, he'd beat you till you couldn't stand. They talked about it."

So they'd talked about it, had they? They meant to

murder poor Mistress Potts and force her into silence through fear—and bed her to boot!

Lenore rose, trembling. "Tam," she said tensely, "we've got to get away, all of us. Today. Mistress Potts has friends in Newcastle. You must take her there—to a Mistress Abby Charlesford or a Mistress Abby MacDonald. Mistress Potts can direct you to their homes, she's known them all her life. When she tells them what's happened, they will take you both in."

Tam was looking at her, round-eyed. "And what about you, Mistress?"

"I'll lead the pursuit away from you."

"They'll catch you!" he declared hoarsely.

"No, they won't. I'll ride that big roan with the white forelock—the one that belonged to Amos. They'll never catch me, Tam. Now I'll tell you how we'll do it." Swiftly she outlined her plan.

Within the hour they got a limping, protesting Abigail Potts out of the house. "My things!" she wailed. "All my clothes—what will happen to them?"

"You can come back for them," promised Lenore. She gave her old friend a long hug. "I must lead the pursuit away from you," she said soberly. "So it may be that we won't meet again for I'll be far from Newcastle."

Too choked up to answer, Abigail nodded and, through brimming tears, watched Lenore go.

Lenore's own saddlebags were packed and in the stable. Now she must watch for the nephews' return. It seemed an eternity but just as she finished getting supper ready she saw them, striding over the slight rise that lay in the direction of Newcastle. Lenore felt her scalp prickle. Had she sent Mistress Potts and Tam off earlier, they must surely have run into Caleb and Sedgewick—armed and dangerous.

Lenore waited until the men were well in the house and then, from the kitchen, gave a great rending scream that could be heard all the way to the stable. Simultaneously she knocked over several large crocks.

That scream was the signal. While both men rushed to the kitchen to extricate a wailing Lenore from a sticky jumble of broken crockery and spilled marmalade and cream, Tam and fat Mistress Potts rode unnoticed out of the stable and headed away from Wallham toward Newcastle-on-Tyne. By the time Lenore had stopped requiring the nephews' attention they were over the low rise and out of sight.

While the discovery of the skull had left Lenore shaken, now that she knew the worst, that Caleb was a double murderer and that he and Sedgewick planned yet more cold-blooded killings, she found herself strangely calm. She felt she had engineered the scene in the kitchen masterfully and now she went through her paces in the dining room airily, saying that poor Mistress Potts wouldn't be down to sup, she was coming down with another cold—it could well be her death this time! She thought she saw a gleam of hope in Sedgewick's eyes as she said that, and reminded herself that Sedgewick had not killed anyone—he had just helped cover it up.

She fussed over Mistress Potts' tray, determinedly humming a little tune as she did so, and went lightfootedly up the stairs, called loudly, "All right, Mistress Potts, I'll tell him," as she came back downstairs and into the dining room where the nephews were.

"Tell him what?" wondered Sedgewick curiously. His feet were propped up and he was consuming a tankard of wine.

"Oh, she wants to make a list of riband colors for you to buy for her in Newcastle," said Lenore indifferently. She began to clear away the dishes.

"Let Tam do that," said Sedgewick. "Where is Tam? I haven't seen him about."

Lenore went cold. "Tam's sneezing and coughing worse than Mistress Potts. He helped me get supper and then I sent him off to bed before we all catch it. 'Tis the damp spring weather."

"It's been a bad day all around," grumbled Sedgewick, looking vindictively down into his wine. "Abigail hurt, Tam taken sick, you falling and breaking half the crocks in the kitchen, and Caleb and me frightening off all the birds. Every time we thought to shoot one on a branch, up it flew and we missed!"

Lenore had always thought it unsporting that birds should be slaughtered as they perched in trees, even though it was the custom of the day. She gave Sedgewick a cold look. "Yes," she echoed feelingly, "it's been a bad day all round." She carried her laden tray into the kitchen.

For a brief time during supper it had seemed a kind of game, like a part she might play on a stage, but now in the dim kitchen as she cleaned up, she realized again how deadly was her danger. Any tiny thing could bring on disaster—even something so small as a fox frightening the hens in the stable and one of the men going out to investigate, finding two of the horses gone . . .

She fought back an urge to run out of the back door and flee into the night. She knew she had to give Tam and Mistress Potts a long head start, for anything might happen—the unsteady old lady might even fall off her horse and Tam might have a dreadful time getting her back on. But if they could reach Newcastle, they'd be safe.

Tense and sleepless that night, Lenore was taut as a coiled spring when she went downstairs the next morning. Her hands seemed all thumbs as she prepared breakfast, she had to force herself to eat and it was a relief when she could rise to clear the dishes.

"Ye're a fool to do Tam's work for him," Sedgewick told her testily. "Tam!" he roared. "Get yourself in here, lad!"

Lenore's heart fluttered. If Tam should be discovered missing—! "His cold is probably worse," she muttered. "I'll take a bite out to him in the stable and get him started."

"What, before ye take a tray to Abigail?" he mocked. "It seems ye're fond of taking care of everybody's needs in this house but mine!"

Lenore gave him a level look. "She can wait for once."

"Well, since ye're going to the stable, ye can tell Tam to saddle my horse. I'm riding into Newcastle today."

Lenore's heart gave another lurch. "I'll tell him," she said coolly. If Sedgewick should decide to deliver his own message and beat her to the stable, he would find his horse gone for Tam was riding Sedgewick's horse! She felt like breaking into a run, but she forced herself to saunter out to the kitchen with her armload of dirty dishes. Once there, she tossed a couple of rolls into a large linen napkin and went out the back door. With an attempt at jauntiness that cost her dear she strolled to the stable.

Once in the great dim stable she was able to breathe again. Quickly she saddled the roan with the white forelock—he had been Amos's horse—and tossed onto his broad back the packed saddlebags she had secreted yesterday in the hay. She affixed a short length of rope to the gray mare's bridle as a lead—for she dared not leave behind a horse that could be used in pursuit—sprang to the saddle, and was just wheeling the roan around to ride him out the stable door when a voice arrested her. "Going somewhere?"

Lenore jerked around to see Sedgewick blocking the open stable door.

"I saddled your horse for you," she said coolly. "Tam was too sick to do it."

He eyed the big roan narrowly. "That's Amos's horse."

Lenore shrugged. "Why should you not ride him?"

He cast a look about him. "I don't see my horse. Or Caleb's."

Lenore's throat was dry. "Tam took them out behind the stable to graze."

She thought he accepted that explanation, for his next remark was, "Ye think I need to ride two horses to Newcastle?"

She lifted her chin. "I'm going with you."

He laughed. "With saddlebags. Ye're a liar, Lenore."

Lenore did not wait. She dug her heels into the roan and rode straight at Sedgewick. Expert horsewoman that she was, she lifted a foot and kicked him squarely in the jaw just as he jumped aside with a shout to keep from being run down. The shock of the contact nearly unseated her. Her toes felt numb but Sedgewick was knocked sprawling.

Ducking, she was out of the stable door and both the roan and the gray mare, excited by this unusual action, were heading away from Wallham at a dead run. She turned the roan's head south. The mare perforce accompanied on her lead. Looking back over her shoulder, Lenore saw Sedgewick racing for the house, shouting at Caleb. As she urged the horses on, he disappeared inside.

When he came out again, Caleb accompanied him.

And they had their guns with them.

Lenore felt a flash of fear. She wished she had dared to make off with the guns, but both men cleaned their guns at night and since they slept in the room with their guns she had had no chance at them.

As the first shot rang out, Lenore crouched down. Bending low over the horse's neck, she rode a zigzag trail. That first shot had gone wild but looking back, she could see Sedgewick sprinting after her and now he stopped and was sighting along the barrel of his musket.

Sedgewick was a better shot than Caleb.

She veered the roan suddenly to the right, almost colliding with the gray, and felt rather than heard the shot go past her, the ball almost grazing her shoulder.

She looked back. Sedgewick was running again, loading as he ran. She turned and studied the way ahead of her. This was open country which made her an easy target but if she could but reach that grove of trees up ahead, she would be safe from Sedgewick's marksmanship. For by the time her pursuers reached that grove on foot she'd be well away!

The second shot cut the bark from an oak tree just as the roan carried her behind it. Lenore drew a long shaky breath and slackened the horses' breakneck pace.

For the moment at least she was safe.

Gradually the shouting and musketry died away and the soft rustling silence of the woods took over. Lenore patted the horses' heads, hoping they'd be able to keep going. All that day she rode, first on one horse and then the other, staying mostly aboard the big roan who was stronger than Sylvie's dainty gray mare. It occurred to Lenore that Mistress Potts might have had a smoother ride if Tam had put her up aboard the gray mare instead of leaving Sylvie's mount for Lenore. She supposed the lad had wanted no reminder of Sylvie who had made life so uncomfortable for him at Wallham.

That night Lenore slept in the open, shivering a little for she had forgotten to bring the cloak she had carefully secreted in the stable. Her saddlebags contained only food and the black satin slippers and black gloves with which she had left London. Not that she intended to wear such finery. It had been her intention to travel light, but they might be useful to barter for lodgings or hay for the horses.

The next evening found her approaching an inn. She had covered considerable territory and although she was in strange country, she considered it safe enough to stop here and try to sell her black slippers and gloves. They might bring a better price out here in the country than in a city. And there was no way there could be an alarm out for her here, for she had left the nephews far behind.

She stopped in the deserted innyard, lit only by fitful moonlight and the long yellow glow of light from the small candlelit windows. Throwing her horses' reins over the hitching post, she dismounted, stretching to ease the weariness of her long ride.

Behind her now she heard a horse approaching and was instantly alert. And as instantly scolded herself inwardly, for she realized that it was only the tension of her situation that had finally gotten to her—now that she was really safe, she was beginning to get an attack of nerves.

Nevertheless she paused and studied the approaching rider and saw with relief that he was no one she knew, but a rather soberly clad gentleman in a dark cloak and a broad-brimmed black hat with a modest gray plume.

With a shrug, Lenore lifted off her saddlebags and went into the common room. It was not very large as such rooms went, and sparsely furnished, but its floor was clean scoured and the long-handled copper pots that dangled from the big stone fireplace gleamed in the candlelight. She was glad to find it almost unoccupied—a single gentleman wearing a cloak and sleeping on his arms in a far dim corner of the room was the only occupant. Her gaze passed rapidly over the sleeping figure and focused on the landlord—for he could be none other, such was his proprietary air—bustling into the room to welcome her.

"And what can I do for you, Mistress?" he cried heartily. "Lodgings? A good meal? We've both to offer."

"I need hay and stabling for my horses and lodging for the night," said Lenore. "But I lost my way and rode through some heavy brush and somewhere as I fought the branches I seem to have lost my purse with all my money in it."

She had reached the center of the room as she spoke and could no longer see the man sprawled on his arms on the table, but his head went up and he turned to gaze curiously at her.

The landlord's face lost its smile of greeting, the heartiness chilled from his voice. "We run no almshouse here, Mistress."

"Nor do I expect you to. But I have here some items of value." She held up the saddlebags. "A pair of fine gloves and a pair of black satin slippers of the latest style. From London. Would they pay for my lodgings and food for my horses?"

"Well, let's see." The landlord, who had stiffened on

hearing she had no money, unbent again. That he approved her looks, even in her travel-stained condition, she could see plainly. He had eyes more for her bodice than for the contents of her saddlebags—for *those* wares he'd obviously give her a good price! Lenore turned her shoulder to him, which put the gentleman in the corner at her back.

"Spread out your wares, Mistress," said the landlord in a voice gone oily. "And I'll call my wife and see if anything catches her fancy." He turned and called sharply, "Martha, come here."

As Lenore silently spread out the black gloves and satin slippers on the wood of the table top, worn smooth by many arms, she was reminded sharply of Geoffrey. She'd been wearing these when he'd rescued her from Lord Wilsingame's house on London Bridge. It seemed an eternity ago.

She looked up as the door opened. The man in the dark cloak she'd seen riding up a few moments before and who'd seen her dismount, was just coming into the room.

Now the innkeeper's short wife, wiping her floury hands on her linen apron, bustled forward. Her eyes shone greedily as she looked down at the dainty gloves and slippers. "Why, they're beautiful!" she cried. "They look like they've come fresh from London!"

"From London maybe," said a scathing voice, "but certainly by way of Wallham."

Lenore's back stiffened as she turned to stare at the stranger. His eyes gleamed beneath his broad-brimmed hat and his broad body blocked the door.

"I don't know what you mean, sir," she said coldly.

"I think ye do. That pair of horses ye have out there—the roan with the white forelock belongs to Amos Barrow. I'd know him anywhere by the scar on his fetlock—I was there when he got it. And the gray mare is one I sold to Amos myself more than a year ago."

Lenore's streak of bad luck had held. It had followed her all the way to this remote place.

"And that goods on the table that ye're considering buying is most likely stolen too," continued the stranger in a menacing tone. "I'd not touch it, were I you, innkeeper." He turned to the innkeeper's wife, who was unhappily studying the beautiful things spread out on the table. "Bring me some rope that I may bind this woman and take her back whence she came!"

Twainmere, The Cotswolds

Chapter 22

The village was both shocked and titillated by the news of the vicar's death. That he should die at Lola Hepworth's house! What had the doctor said—that he'd found the vicar lying on the ground dead with his head cradled in Mistress Hepworth's arms when he got there? Of course, she had quickly explained how it all happened: the vicar had returned for another prayer with her ailing husband and suffered a stroke at the front door—but what she said made no difference. Lola Hepworth could blandly deny everything, the village knew!

Flora, as everyone knew she would, took it very well. Dressed in black, she stood tall and erect and grim at the funeral, refused to cry, accepted condolences with a nod or a word, and went her own way.

But for Lorena it was a time of agony, for she felt she had killed Uncle Robbie. Now she remembered with horror the time that he had lurched ashen-faced against the vicarage door. She should have realized then how ill he was. Anyway, what right had she to judge him? she flayed herself. She had been wrong to taunt Tabby in the stocks—and the vicar had seen her and been about to justly punish her for it. She'd been wrong to defy him so openly, to drive him into a heart attack! For now that Uncle Robbie was gone, the memory of him panting in Lola Hepworth's arms was fast fading, and all the fierce switchings she had endured, the bread and water, the endless punishments fled from her mind and she remembered him as he had been when she was little, all those years when he had been her beloved "Uncle Robbie." Tears streamed down the face of the slender figure in black, who stood beside Flora at the funeral. But Lorena was grieving for *that* dear Uncle Robbie, the kindly father figure of her childhood, not the changed tormented man who had been snatched dead from his mistress's arms.

The widow and her ward came home to an empty vicarage and for a moment Lorena didn't want to go in because every wall would accuse her, remind her. But Flora flung open the door and strode inside.

"We'll have to clear out of this house, of course," she said matter-of-factly, opening her mouth to speak for the first time since they'd left the graveside.

Lorena started. She hadn't thought of that, but of course the village would have a new vicar. New people would move into the vicarage. She and Flora could not stay here.

"We'll move back to the cottage behind the smithy," decided Flora. "Though 'tis hardly livable now after having been deserted all these years. Lorena." She turned to the girl and spoke more gently; there was a suspicion of moisture in her fierce blue eyes. "Why don't you take a walk? You might go by the smithy and see what you think needs to be done to the cottage. I—I want to sit alone in the study for a bit."

With her head bent, Flora went into the study. Lorena, fighting back her own tears, saw her spare frame at Robbie's little slanted writing desk, where he had composed all his sermons, those sermons he had delivered in such ringing tones to the sinners of Twainmere.

Blindly, Lorena left the house.

But it was not to the smithy her steps took her. Instead, pulled by a desire that was stronger than remorse, stronger than self-preservation, she found herself taking the shortcut that led by footbridge over the dangerous millrace to the mill.

She didn't know what she would say to Tabby, but somehow she meant to make it up with him, to ask him directly what was wrong between them and—yes, to apologize for taunting him and then striking him when his arms were held fast in the stocks.

Her generous nature chose to forget how Tabby's strong white teeth had contemptuously ripped away her bodice, to forget how cold his gray eyes had been, and to remember only his swift fiery response to her impudent kiss, and the message of desire that had flashed to her from his taut body.

She would find Tabby, she would make things right between them and find solace for her bruised spirit in his arms.

She walked beneath the spreading branches of the trees and the miller's cottage came into view. Seated on the front step she could see the miller. He was holding a scrap of paper slackly in his fingers, staring at nothing. But his bleak expression changed at sight of her. His eyes brightened and he watched her fondly as she approached, tripping lightly over the footbridge. Ah, what a sweet maid she was! What he had done, he had done for *her*. Tabby had deserved the blow that felled him, for the lad could not be allowed to show disrespect for his father's future bride. Aye, he had needed to be humbled but . . . he had not meant to turn the lad out, he had not thought a cuff and a harsh word would drive the lad from his home. Lord, how he would miss Tabby! Still, he comforted himself, as he studied the graceful lines of the girl who now was hurrying to him over the grass, there would be other sons born of his loins, sons borne by this lovely young creature who for so long now had filled his waking thoughts.

Abruptly Lyle realized that Lorena was dressed in black. Mourning . . . Immersed in his own grief over Tabby's departure in the night, Lyle had forgotten to attend the funeral, had even forgotten that the vicar was dead. In fact, he had not even shaved today. His weathered face, usually so clean-shaven, had grown stubbly.

Lyle rose heavily at Lorena's approach, opened his mouth to offer condolences, but before he could speak, she said in a tense voice, "Hello, Mister Aylesbury. Where's Tabby?"

Lyle Aylesbury winced as if she had flicked a raw wound. "Tabby did not mean to hurt ye yesterday, Lorena," he declared huskily.

Intent on her need to see, to touch the man she loved, Lorena impatiently brushed that aside. "I know that, Mister Aylesbury. Where is he?"

"He's gone."

All of Lorena's attention was focused on him now. Fearfully. "Gone? What do you mean, gone?"

Lyle's voice was heavy. "He's run away to sea. Left me a note." He waved the paper vaguely.

Before him, her young face seemed to break up. "Oh, Mister Aylesbury, how could Tabby run away?" she cried brokenly. "I loved him so."

If her hands had not flown to cover her face at that moment, she would have seen the big miller stiffen incredulously. *I loved him so.* Gradually the shock of that sank in. *I loved him so.* So it was not himself, as he had thought in his pride, that had drawn Lorena day after day to the mill to laugh and talk with him—*it was Tabby!*

He felt sick, as if a horse had kicked him in the stomach. The betrothal between them was over; he had lost a wife—for he knew he'd never press the girl to wed him when her heart wasn't in it—and he'd lost a son into the bargain. Yet surely it was not for him to blame her. She was young and Tabby was a fine strong lad. He'd have stepped aside, had he known.

Before him Lorena was swaying, as if a strong wind had buffeted her, and he reached out a quick hand to steady her. She gave him a look of wild entreaty and ran back the way she had come, pelting across the footbridge with her hands clutched to her mouth, as if to keep herself from screaming.

The miller sank back down on the step and watched her go. Out of his life. His heart seemed to turn and crunch painfully inside his chest. All his dreams were crashing about him like hailstones and he felt suddenly old and tired—and a failure. In the surge of his desire for this bewitching child-woman he had cost himself everything. Now at last he understood poor Tabby, who had wanted her too and yet could not bring himself to wrest her from his father and destroy his father's happiness. Tears stung the miller's eyes. No wonder Tabby had run away!

That night found Lyle Aylesbury drowning his sorrows as Tabby had—in the local tavern. And the late hours found him, as they had Tabby, locked in the arms of Floss, the exultant barmaid, who the next day bragged to all who would listen that she had tried them both, father and son, and of the two the miller was the better lover.

Loud guffaws greeted this assessment.

But for Lorena, scurrying home in her newly fashioned black dress, her face in white contrast against her somber clothes—and never guessing she had left the miller brokenhearted behind her—Tabby's going was a crushing loss.

Tabby was gone, she told herself wildly, gone forever, gone to be swallowed up by the sea that lured so many strong English lads away and never returned them to the women who loved them.

Clenching her hands and swallowing to keep from crying, she hurried back to the vicarage.

And found Flora down on her knees, scrubbing the study floor. She looked up as Lorena entered. "I wouldna want the new tenants, whoever they be, to find the place looking less than Robbie would ha' wanted," she said, her

340

Scots brogue thickening as she spoke. Then she seemed really to see Lorena standing there, her whole body shaking. "Did you go by the smithy, child?"

"Oh, Aunt Flora, Tabby's gone, he's run away to sea, he's never coming back!" It was a cry of despair.

Flora pushed aside the scrub bucket and gave Lorena a look of compassion. Young love was hard to bear.

"He'll come back, you'll see," she encouraged Lorena. Tomorrow she would call upon Lyle Aylesbury and tell him the betrothal was off. Lorena would not have to marry the miller after all.

She did call upon Lyle the next day, tall and somber in her black dress. She found him standing in the door of the mill, bleary-eyed, hungover. He answered her "Good morning" with a grunt, listened silently as Flora explained that she had never agreed with this betrothal, that she considered Lorena too young to marry.

He heard her out and when she had finished, he gave her a look she could not fathom. "The horse is ready to be taken home," was all he said. "Lorena can come and get him any time now. His leg has healed."

"We thank you for all you did for the horse," said Flora, feeling awkward. "And I want you to know—"

"I wouldn't ride him for a bit yet," interrupted the miller. "His leg will still be weak." There was a finality in his tone.

Doggedly, Flora kept on. "I—I'm sorry about Tabby."

Lyle Aylesbury nodded and turned away, busying himself with picking up some weights for weighing grain. Abruptly he swung about, his voice hot with accusation. " 'Twas not me the girl wanted, 'twas my son. Why did someone not tell me?" His face was bleak. "I'd have stepped aside."

He'd have stepped aside. Why indeed, Flora asked herself, had they not told him? Feeling helpless, as if she were tossed about on some great sea with no land in sight, Flora left. Everyone had lost, she thought sadly as she trudged home. Tabby, Lorena—even the kindly miller. The world took a toll of you. Ah, it was not the kind of world she'd have created, had she had the ordering of the universe!

When she returned to the vicarage, Flora found Lorena, dressed in black, bringing her few things carefully down the ladder from the loft.

"Should I throw these away, Aunt Flora?" the girl asked wistfully, holding up the two thin gray linen dresses she wore for every day. "I mean, we'll be wearing mourning for such a long time . . ."

The brisk walk home had made Flora foursquare with her world again, brisk, competent. The funeral was yesterday; today's crises had to be met. But the word "mourning" gave her a pang.

Like a knife thrust, a sharp memory of yesterday's funeral came back to her: of Lola Hepworth, her predatory face unaccustomedly sad, her lush body swathed in black as she swung along . . . and of people leaning together and whispering, bright-eyed, behind their hands, when they saw her. *Lola . . . mourning Robbie.*

Flora was no fool. She told herself she had not seen because she had not wanted to see. But now a wave of bitterness swept over the tall Scotswoman. Good wife she had been to Robbie all these years! Patiently—too patiently, she now realized—she had waited for him to come to her bed and claim her and become a real instead of a counterfeit husband. But Robbie had taken the love that was in him and laid it at that worthless Hepworth woman's feet.

Now Flora turned fiercely to Lorena. "We'll not be wearing mourning, either of us. What mourning we do will be inside our hearts. When we leave this vicarage, we will leave our black clothes behind us. Yes, throw both those dresses away, Lorena, for you are young and they are too sober for you. You should be wearing blue and green and yellow, as your mother did. We will get rid of all the things Robbie chose for you—for they were his doing, not mine. And you will live your young life and not be driven into marriage with some man old enough to be your grandfather!"

Her voice broke and she turned and fled into the kitchen. Lorena, still holding the worn gray dresses in her arms, stared after her, startled, for *everyone* wore mourning for a lost husband—it was an obligation. Suddenly her eyes widened in comprehension. Somehow Aunt Flora had found out—perhaps by simple deduction. *Aunt Flora knew about Robbie and Lola Hepworth.* Lorena kept on with her packing, scrupulously avoiding the kitchen. She had the feeling that she and Aunt Flora would never speak of the vicar again.

A replacement for the vicar was readily found and Flora and Lorena promptly removed to the tiny cottage behind the smithy. Although they had known all along about the vicar's affair with Lola Hepworth, the villagers were shocked when Flora and her niece put away their mourning garb. Scandalized eyes rolled when Lorena appeared in a new linen dress of lemon yellow, tucked up to display a frothy white lawn petticoat.

"That girl's wearing shoes with red heels," muttered Mercy Meadows, watching Lorena fill her basket with fresh eggs at the market.

"Like her mother before her," agreed Goody Kettle with a frown. She turned to Mercy. "D'ye think she'll notch her heels like Lenore did?"

"Like as not." Mercy gave her head a bewildered shake. "It shows what Flora's come to, now that she's not got the vicar to steady her!"

"Not that *he* was such a pillar of piety!" said Goody Kettle, and they both laughed.

Neither had noticed the lost sad look in Lorena's blue eyes.

Finding release in work, Flora and Lorena had scrubbed the little cottage behind the old forge until it shone, they had repaired the broken shutters, and had the roof fixed where it leaked, they had cut down the weeds that rose waist-high, and Flora was even trying to reclaim the jungle that had once been her herb garden.

But this humble hut was a far cry from the vicarage, stateliest home in the village.

Lorena did not care. Grief and her conscience weighed heavily on her these days. Even the new clothes Aunt Flora made for her did not help. She was not only bereaved by Tabby's departure, she felt herself a murderess as well.

"You don't pay any attention to the lads now that Tabby's gone," Maude told her bluntly, when they met one day at the market and she noticed how pointedly Lorena ignored every hot interested look that came her way.

Lorena shrugged. "They don't interest me, Maude."

"Suppose Tabby don't come back?"

"I don't expect him to," sighed Lorena. How could she explain to lusty Maude, who never cared very long for one man, that her young heart was broken? That her love for Tabby had been no mere childish crush, but deep and real, founded on trust and faith and—yes, on a firm belief that deep inside him he returned her regard.

"Ye could wind up an old maid," warned Maude, who had carelessly refused three offers already.

"I don't care if I do." Lorena turned her attention to some live ducks being offered for sale.

Maude sighed. Lorena, she felt, was taking Tabby's departure too hard. After all, if Tabby cared no more for her than to leave without saying so much as a good-bye, why should she weep for him?

But nothing could alter the wound in Lorena's heart.

It came as a shock to the village when one night Lyle Aylesbury, who had taken to reeling home singing drunken songs every night, slipped on the treacherous footbridge over the millrace and was caught in the mill wheel and drowned.

Flora almost blurted out to Lorena then that she had

been, briefly, betrothed to the well-liked miller, but she bit back the words. The child was saddened enough by Tabby's going, no need to make things worse.

And of course, there would be other suitors.

Northumberland

Chapter 23

There in the inn's common room, for a moment Lenore stood motionless, stunned by the threat that they would take her back and deliver her to Caleb's vengeance. Convulsively she struck out at the accusing face that was thrust into her own and tried to dart past him, running between the landlord and his wife—but they were too quick for her.

"Hold, she's getting away!" cried the soberly dressed stranger and together the two men fell upon her, pinioning her with two pairs of hands, so that all her struggles were for naught. " 'Tis plain admission of her guilt!" he crowed triumphantly. White-faced, Lenore cursed herself for her sudden action. Seldom in her life had panic seized her, but she had been drenched in horror at the thought of being returned to the pinheaded giant with the huge spatulate hands. Now horror washed over her again and she struggled so fiercely that the perspiring stranger gasped, "Get rope, woman!" to the innkeeper's wife.

When the innkeeper's wife hurried back with a length of rope, they bound Lenore's wrists and ankles with it and pushed her into a chair. When she protested, they stuffed a gag into her mouth so that she sat there helpless, unable even to speak up in her own defense, as she listened to them argue about what to do with her.

"I could keep her here while you alert the law, sir," suggested the landlord.

"The law's to the north of us, and I'm bound west," said the soberly dressed fellow irritably.

"I'll not keep her here while my husband goes for the law!" squeaked the innkeeper's wife. "Why, I'd be blamed if she escaped!"

"Perhaps I could help you gentlemen," chimed in a new voice. From a table in a dark corner of the room where he had appeared to Lenore to be asleep with his head in his arms, leaning upon the table, the only other occupant of the common room now sat up and stretched. He yawned delicately and rose, sauntering toward them with an easy grace. "Allow me to introduce myself, sir," he said to the man who had accused Lenore. "My name is Dorn. I am the son of the Sheriff of Nottingham and I'll be glad to relieve you of this culprit."

Christopher Dorn! His gaze flicked over her and Lenore stared back at him in shock. She saw that his Van Dyke beard was just as golden as it had been in York but the crystal eyes that considered her held no pity.

"I'm traveling north," he said, "and would gladly deliver this woman—indeed any offender—into the hands of the law, and that speedily."

The innkeeper hesitated momentarily. This culprit was a woman and the speaker was a stranger to him, a gentleman who had chanced into the inn but an hour ago. It was hardly seemly to deliver a lone woman into the hands of a passing stranger.

But the soberly dressed accuser carried the day. "Good," he said with a contemptuous look at Lenore. "If the woman lingers here, there's indeed more chance for her to escape. Off she goes with you, my good fellow."

At the familiarity of his tone, Christopher Dorn's affable manner vanished. His back stiffened and the crystal eyes he turned on Lenore's accuser seemed made of ice. "Do I know you, sir?" he demanded stiffly. "That ye call me your good fellow?"

"I'm a minister of the gospel," responded the other in surprise. "And as such, know all men."

"Ah, I see," murmured Dorn with some irony. "We are all a fellowship under God and bound to do good as we see it?"

The minister frowned, annoyed by the arrogance of the tall fellow before him. "I must be on," he said in a frosty voice. "I am late already and would not have stopped had I not recognized the horse."

"Off to a christening or a hanging, I wonder," murmured Dorn, but his remarks went unheard in the creaky closing of the inn door.

"It don't seem fitting to send a woman off in company of a man alone in the night," grumbled the innkeeper, weakening in his resolve now that the forceful minister had left. "There's the smell of rain in the air. Why d'ye not stay the night and take her away with ye in the morning?"

"Besides," chimed in his wife, her greedy eyes still fixed on the shoes and gloves that lay on the table, "ye'll have to untie her ankles so that she can ride, and in the dark she may escape you."

" 'Twill be no problem," announced Dorn, "for I've no intention at all of untying her." He pulled out some coins to pay for his dinner. Then he bent down and scooped up Lenore, tossed her lightly over his shoulder, proving he was stronger than she had thought from his drunken encounter with Geoffrey in York. "We'll need these for evidence," he added with a sunny smile at the innkeeper's wife, and gathered up the handsome shoes and gloves.

The landlord and his wife followed them out to the post where Lenore had hitched the horses. "I dare say the owner will be glad to get his beasts back," remarked

Dorn, tossing Lenore over the saddle as indifferently as if she were a sack of flour. She reposed thus uncomfortably with her head hanging down one side of the horse and her feet dangling from the other.

"To ride far like that will make the poor thing sick," remonstrated the innkeeper's wife, scandalized by such treatment.

"Pah! She'll hardly notice it," shrugged Christopher. But he tossed her the shoes. "These gloves will be enough to prove she pilfers shops as well as steals horses. Although," he added laughingly, "their owner may come to claim them if ye brag too much about the taking of this thieving wench!"

"We'll say naught about it," declared the innkeeper's wife hastily. "Won't we, John?" She gave her husband a sharp dig in the ribs.

The innkeeper winced and agreed. But his gaze was still doubtful as Christopher Dorn walked the horses away, moving out leisurely into the night.

"I dunno that we did the right thing," he muttered as he followed his wife back into the inn.

"Of course we did," she said absently. She held up the black satin slippers that she might better admire them. "We'll just forget the woman was ever here."

Jolting along in the darkness in her awkward position, Lenore could feel every step the horse took reverberate through her stomach. When the inn had disappeared in the distance, Christopher Dorn reached down and removed the suffocating gag from her mouth. Lenore took a thankful, gasping breath. "Chris, they can't see us now. Untie me and let me down."

The man beside her did not slacken his mount's pace. If anything, he increased it a little. "Why?" he asked coolly.

"Because," she sputtered, "riding in this position is killing me!"

"And all this to a man ye left struck down and unconscious on the floor of a stranger's room in York," he murmured with real wonderment in his tone. "Faith, I wonder that ye deign to speak to me at all, since ye left York without a word before I was fit to rise the next morning."

"You were drunk," stated Lenore, feeling strength return to her voice. "And I *did* ask the serving wench about you and she said you were alive."

"Ah . . . alive. Well, I'll return the compliment. As I look over there at ye, ye appear to me to be alive also. Certainly more alive than I was when ye departed York."

"But 'twas not my fault that—"

"Ye hoodwinked me in York, Lenore," he accused hotly. "Leading me on and getting my head bashed in by your tall fellow—and then telling the chambermaid to say ye'd left with him."

Lenore winced. "Yes, I *did* lead you on, Christopher. And I did tell the chambermaid to say that. But as to getting your head bashed in, I'd no part of that. I thought Geoffrey was still in London."

"And ye leave all your men behind," he mocked. "Geoffrey. Me."

"*Chris*topher!" she wailed.

He moved closer. His horse's flanks nearly brushed her.

"Please untie my hands," she pleaded, choking as some dust from the road, kicked up by the horse's hooves, clouded up in her face. "It's a lonely road," she pleaded. "No one will happen along now!"

"Ah, ye're right enough about that." There was an undertone of amusement in his voice. "We're all alone at last."

Now what did that mean? Lenore tried vainly to swivel her head to look up at him but all she could manage to see was his wide-topped boot. Angrily she struggled to free her hands. How dare he jolt her along across this saddle like some piece of luggage being packed in?

They continued to jolt along.

A pebble from the road flew up and struck her temple.

A sob escaped Lenore.

Instantly the horses were brought to a halt. Christopher Dorn dismounted and cut her bonds with his knife. Lenore gave a deep gasp of relief as her hands were unshackled, and began to rub her half-numbed wrists.

Off to the west sheet lightning flashed. It illuminated the long shimmering strands of her hair that hung down toward the road from her upended head. It illuminated the road below, and reflected off the horses' hooves.

Strong hands hauled her off the horse and stood her on her unsteady feet, held her just a moment too long there in the dark beneath the roadside trees. She could feel a tremor go through those hands that held her.

Lenore took heart from that tremor. For a moment there she had actually thought Christopher Dorn was going to deliver her to the law.

"That was clever of you," she said, "pretending to be the son of the Sheriff of Nottingham."

She was looking into his face as she said it and caught a glint from the crystal eyes. His voice held a touch of frost. "I *am* the son of the Sheriff of Nottingham. All know his name is Dorn."

Lenore's eyes widened and she felt her body stiffen. "You're his *son?*" she whispered.

"Aye."

To the west sheet lightning flashed again and there was a grumble of thunder. It illuminated the tall form towering above her. A smile she could not quite fathom lit up his face.

"Have you eaten?" he demanded.

She shook her head wanly. "Not for a long time."

"Even the condemned are fed," he said with faint irony. "I've a bit of bread and cheese in my saddlebags. Ye can munch on that as we ride."

Lightly he lifted her, set her back on the big roan. She looked down at him, troubled. There was that in his expression when the lightning had flashed that made her now consider nudging the roan with her knee and trying to outdistance him.

"Ah, I wouldn't try that, my lady," he said softly, following her thought. "Ye know not this countryside like I do. And if they're hunting ye—as I suspect they are—ye'd lose yourself and they'd be on ye in a trice."

"I wasn't considering running away," retorted Lenore with a toss of her red-gold hair. Even to herself the words had a guilty ring.

"Yet somehow prudence tells me not to turn my back on you," he grinned. Before she knew what he was doing, he had lifted her from the horse again. For a long moment he held her to him and as her taut body lingered in his arms, she could feel the strong beat of his heart against her breast. Abruptly he let her go. "The bread and cheese are in the saddlebag on this side," he instructed. "Take what you like."

"But I don't want to go north, Christopher," she protested plaintively as she rummaged for the food.

His voice came to her over her shoulder. "And who says I'm riding north?"

She turned sharply. "You did. At the inn."

"Then I must have lied," he laughed, "for at the crossroads up ahead I'm turning south."

"Good," she sighed, reaching back to close the saddlebag. "So am I."

Distant thunder followed them to the crossroad, became louder as they turned south. Lenore ate hungrily, riding beside him in silence.

His head swung toward her. "Did you really steal those two horses, Lenore?"

"Yes, but not from Amos Barrow. From the man who murdered him and to whom our friend of the cloth would have returned me. And now the horses belong by rights, I suppose, to my friend Mistress Potts, whom he planned to kill also—and she'd be glad to give them both to me, for I saved her life by riding away with them and confusing the pursuit. That is, she'd give them to me if I was successful and she's still alive."

"Ye lead an adventurous life," he chuckled.

"By accident, Chris," she sighed. "Not by design."

"Have it as ye will. I take it ye're not in funds?"

Lenore shook her head sadly. "I left with no money at all. Indeed I was lucky to escape with a whole skin."

"I too am down to my last few coins," he declared in a gloomy voice. "I'd hoped you were in better case."

"Are you bound for Nottingham then, to seek money from your father?"

He gave a short laugh. "My father's not spoken to me since the day I sold my commission. He was set on an army career for his son, you see." He was silent for a while. Then, "Ah, well, the horses should bring a fair price where we're going."

She gave him a curious look. "And where is that, Chris?"

"York."

She nodded, satisfied.

He was thoughtful for a while. At last he said, "The shoes and gloves were most certainly yours. I remember them from York." He continued to study her. "I heard about the manner of your leaving York."

"Good. Then we won't have to talk about it." Her tone was more brusque than she had intended.

But Christopher was not to be put off so easily. "There was an old gentleman who sat late that night in the common room of the inn, by name Sir Torrence Dane. He announced the next day that he had recognized the tall gentleman with the hard hands who took you from me—and whom you pursued past him to the courtyard in the snow. He alleged him to be Geoffrey Wyndham, close as court plaster to the king."

Lenore felt herself shrinking. "Sir Torrence was right on both counts."

"Sir Torrence also dredged up from his memory where he had seen you before. On the London stage where it seems you were known far and wide as the Iron Virgin."

Lenore felt stifled. "On second thought," she said unhappily, "I think I will not go to York with you after all."

"Why?" he probed. "Because you would not care to meet Sir Torrence again? But he left as soon as the roads improved and is doubtless back in London by now."

And telling everyone how the orange girl rushed past him half-naked in pursuit of Geoffrey Wyndham! thought Lenore, wincing.

"I thought that might give you cause to reconsider York," Christopher said coolly. "Considering your notoriety there, what say we make for Leeds, avoiding all the large towns on the way?"

She gave him a grateful look. "Christopher," she said softly, " 'tis very kind of you to do all this for me, a wanted woman."

"Pah, 'tis no bother at all," he countered cheerfully. "For at the moment I'm a wanted man."

"You? A sheriff's son?" She gazed at him in surprise and her laughter bubbled up. "What was your crime, Chris?"

"Cheating at dice, they say. In Newcastle."

"And did you? Cheat at dice?"

In the lightning's flash he gave her an enigmatic look. "Luck is a practical lady. She beds with the resourceful."

Lenore grimaced. "And do you also cheat at cards?" she wondered.

"I have been known to win at cards. A bit too frequently, 'tis rumored."

"Is that how you make your living, Chris? Dicing? Gambling?"

"Only sometimes. I take my opportunities where I find them." His smile reminded her that he had seized the opportunity she had given him in York.

Lenore fell silent. So she was riding down the north country lanes with a cardsharp and a gambler, a man doubtless pursued from town to town.

"Why Leeds?" she asked him curiously.

"Because there's a fair there next week."

A fair. The giant Caleb went to fairs to compete in feats of strength like throwing the sledge. She thought it only fair to warn Christopher of the chance he was taking in bringing her along. In terse sentences she told him of Wallham, adding, "Caleb well might pick up my trail. He's vengeful, a great mountain of a man. He could easily break us both in half."

Something about that remark irritated Christopher. His voice had a hint of ice in it. "I'd be forewarned this time that those who pursue you, my lady, have hard fists—and I'd do something about it aforetimes." He patted his sword hilt meaningfully.

That would not have availed you against Geoffrey, she thought suddenly. For he's a fabled blade. But against Caleb—who could tell?

She guessed Christopher felt she was impugning his manhood, implying that he could not protect her, and hastened to make amends.

"I have not thanked you yet," she said, "for saving my life. For certainly Caleb would have killed me, had they taken me back."

"I'll give you the opportunity to thank me properly," he said with a grin. "We'll make camp just head in that grove of trees. They're pines. The needles will provide a mattress."

A mattress... Lenore's pulse quickened and she gave him a long steady look, unsure how she felt about him. In York she had been rebellious, fighting against the invisible bonds that held her to Geoffrey. Now ...

Christopher Dorn did not wait for any comments from her upon the subject. Already he had increased his pace and now he beckoned to her and she followed him off the road into a thick stand of pines. More than once Lenore had to duck lest she be swept off her mount by the low-hanging pine branches, but she could tell from the steady pace Christopher maintained up ahead of her that he knew where he was going.

He halted in a tiny clearing, hardly as large as a room. A tall pine tree had once stood there, but the woodcutters had long since taken it away and now there was a gap in the trees where starlight shafted down upon a thick carpet of pine needles. Over to their right a tiny wet-weather spring glimmered in the darkness.

The thunder grumbled again as they dismounted. Thirsty, they made their way to the rushing spring, knelt, and drank together. Around them the trees closed in like high walls and the air was heady with the clean, sweet resin scent of the pines. Lenore was aware of Christopher's arm lightly brushing hers as they rose in unison from the spring, causing her arm to tingle and warm her. He appeared not to notice, moving competently to unsaddle the horses and water them.

He brushed aside her offers of help. "There's a bit of pasture just beyond these trees where they can graze till morning." He was leading the horses away as he spoke, and Lenore stood restively looking about her at those high green walls. She had led Christopher on shamelessly in York; he was right to think she would fall easy prey to his charms. She must explain—

Her thoughts bit off as he emerged silently from the darkness into the clearing.

Lenore tensed. "I'm very tired," she said in a defensive voice.

"Aye, ye've ridden a long way," he agreed carelessly. He stood there, making no move to approach her. Somewhere off to their right came the wild cry of a loon.

"Well, then . . ." With an odd, half-disappointed sense of relief that he was keeping his distance, she went over and sank down beside the bole of a big pine on the edge of the clearing.

"Ye'll like this spot better. The pine needles are thicker here." She saw that he was testing their depth with his boot, making a soft crunching sound. In a sudden flare of sheet lightning she saw him spreading his cloak upon the ground with a lazy gesture.

Leaning on one elbow, Lenore watched him in alarm. She'd been lulled at first by the apparent waning of his interest in her, but now all her senses had come alert.

Something in his movements, a kind of swagger to his broad shoulders.

"My lady." He turned to her with a sweeping bow and indicated the bed he had prepared.

So she was to sleep upon his cloak?

"I'm well enough here," she said uneasily.

"Ah, I think not." He strode over and swooped down and seized her by her right wrist, swung her lightly to her feet. His voice was vibrant.

"We began something in York that we've yet to finish!"

Her senses thrilled.

Of a sudden she was swept into his arms, held there in a hard embrace. She felt his lean body tauten against her pliant form pressed so close against him. Before she could protest, his mouth had closed over hers—arrogantly. The pressure of his lips was demanding, almost punishing. And then those lips grew gentler as a tremor went through her body, that treacherous woman's body, responding against her will. As she gasped she felt his tongue break through her suddenly parted lips and probe impudently beyond. Held fast, Lenore felt something wild and young and lighthearted soar up in her, like a bird released from a cage, and was conscious of a wild tumultuous clamor in her head.

A bolt of crimson lightning split the night.

Satisfied with the impression he had made, Christopher released Lenore and stepped back from her. In the lightning's flash she saw that his crystal eyes held a steely light.

"When ye kissed me in York, Lenore, 'twas another man ye kissed."

Telltale color flooded Lenore's face. Even in the concealing darkness she felt Christopher could see it. She was shamed that he should know, but she could not deny it. In York Christopher had been for her only a surrogate Geoffrey—it had been Geoffrey her heart had kissed.

"But tonight 'twill be Christopher Dorn and no other

that ye kiss," he said with cold deliberation, and pulled her back to him with a suddenness that left her breathless against his beating chest. "There'll be no room in our bed tonight for another man!"

"Christopher, no!" She tried to hammer at his chest, to tell him this was not the way to begin, that she was no fort to be besieged, taken by storm.

But she had no chance. Even as she tried to marshal her confused thoughts, to gain time, his lips were on hers, his hot breath seared her throat, and already his expert hands were unfastening the hooks of her dress.

The blood beat in her temples as, weakly, with the last of her reserves, she tried to stay him. But like the onrushing storm from the west, Christopher was in a hurry. And like a soft meadowland parched for rain, Lenore's woman's body was ready for him.

She lay on her back on Christopher's cloak, cushioned on a soft bed of pine needles, and felt her senses shimmer and fuse at his swift wild lovemaking. His strong body moved expertly above her own as he taunted and tempted her with hands and lips into a burst of passion.

She could feel her clothes slipping away, urged by his impatient fingers, could feel those fingers tinglingly warm and searching on her too-responsive skin, felt a mad shiver of delight as his hand slid insidiously down under her armpit to her incurving waist and lightly caressed the soft outward thrust of her hip and thighs, and the silky area between.

A soft sob rose in Lenore's throat at his delicate yet demanding touch, at the authority with which he held her, at the grace of his masculine movements as he led her on and upward through showers of inward sparks until her legs seemed to melt beneath him and all her fiery flesh cried out to him that she was his, his for the taking.

Now with parted lips and eyes wide open, she looked up at the wild night sky through the pine branches overhead. The wind sighed through the pines, drenching her with tangy resin perfume. Like her pulsing senses, the trees seemed to bend and waver and regroup. Convulsively she clutched Christopher to her.

A jagged bolt of pink lightning rent the night sky as he entered her and Lenore's eyes fluttered shut as if her world had turned too blindingly bright to gaze upon. And with the great jarring crash of thunder that followed hard upon the bolt, the invisible bonds that had bound her to Geoffrey were burst asunder.

Vividly now she felt each mounting thrust within her as her wild new lover roved and explored her secret places, opening long-locked doors, causing long-banked fires to flare up again, burn bright. Amid crashing thunder and bolts of lightning he led her with him in a mad sweet rush toward fulfillment, until all at once the floodgates of passion burst, sending out a torrent of joy, of blazing release that burst white-hot through her senses and made her forget the world.

For now there was only Christopher.

Beside them the tiny brooklet fed by the wet-weather spring gurgled beneath the pines. Away in the darkness a loon called to its mate, a wild cry beneath a darkling sky. And the storm, as if in wonder at their ecstacy, sheered off to the north, seeming to tiptoe around their tiny glade, and retreated into rosy sheet lightning in the distance.

Spent, the lovers slept.

Lenore woke once in the night and for a wild moment wondered where she was, and how a man's arm came to be flung lightly over her naked breasts.

Then she remembered, and settled more closely against him, with her soft hip touching his hard stomach and his manhood brushing her silken thigh like a promise. Through the pine branches overhead she could see the last weak flash that lit up far away scudding clouds.

Pink lightning and a bold new lover . . .

Claremont Court, Kent

Chapter 24

By spring Geoffrey Wyndham, prowling restlessly about his big house in Kent, was wild with anxiety about Lenore. Bitterly he blamed himself for leaving her there in York at the mercy of that golden-bearded rogue. What Lenore had been trying to tell him by her wild "Let me explain!" was plain to him now. She was saying she had been tempted but that the golden-bearded rogue was not her lover, she had not yet catapulted over the brink.

Doubtless, he told himself, *he* had been the catalyst that sent her at last into that other fellow's arms. A groan broke from Geoffrey at the thought and he smote his knuckles so hard against the wooden top of his writing table that its legs nearly collapsed.

Now he felt he had been wrong about Lenore in York—just as he had been wrong about her so long ago in Oxford. He was sure of it now. Jealousy had made him believe her a liar then, just as jealousy had made him believe her a liar in York.

Lenore was true to him! He would ride north and prove it!

He remembered now that the groom at the George in London had told him the ladies had been put off a coach bound for Durham. It had been only happenstance and a fast horse that had brought about that wild encounter in York.

But, he asked himself, frowning, had Durham really been their destination? Why not some other town along the way between York and Durham? On this point, the groom at the George had been no help.

It was with no wrench at all that Geoffrey tore himself away from Claremont Court. Letiche, her skin as usual whitened with ceruse, her cheeks rouged, her auburn hair pomaded, and wearing a new orchid brocade creation from France, had shown no interest in him at all since that night when she had lured him to her bed.

This sudden about-face he put down to her whimsical nature. What Letiche desired ardently one moment, she recoiled from the next moment. It was almost with relief that he had stayed away from his wife's bed, for he could not forget Lenore. This woman who had a hold on him—had always held him fast with her thirst for life and yes, her love for him. God, how sweetly had she fitted into his arms that night in York. And he, fool that he was, had thrust her back from him into the snow!

During breaks in the weather that winter, guests from France had braved the snows of Kent and come down to Claremont Court in tinkling sleighs. Some of them had a clandestine air about them; they had closeted themselves with Letiche and whispered in French. Watching, Geoffrey had sighed. Letiche, he knew by now, could not resist intrigue; it was in her nature, in her very blood. That her intrigues were political, he was well aware, but he doubted anything would come of them. After so many years in exile, England's king sat firmly on his throne and Geoffrey Wyndham, who had accompanied his monarch in those days of exile, still basked in the royal favor. It was doubtless the French throne Letiche intrigued against—for Geoffrey was shrewd enough to guess the thrust of de Vignac's frequent visits. But he reasoned that King Charles would care little about their powder-puff intrigues against the throne of France, and put the whole bunch of them from his mind. In the main he hardly noticed these intruders who invaded his house in Kent and spent most of his time at the Hart in London.

Heavy spring rains kept Geoffrey in London, impatiently tapping his boot on the hearth rail of the Hart's common room, for the roads were too mired to journey north. Indeed they were barely passable when he set out astride a powerful chestnut stallion whose last owner swore the beast could wade all day in mire and remain daisy-fresh. It was in fine spring weather that Geoffrey pounded north to York and swung at last into the innyard of the Fox and Bow.

The Fox and Bow's landlord remembered Geoffrey. Unpleasantly. He recalled him as the tall gentleman, who, on being taken to a shared room upstairs, had flung one of the inn's guests across the hall into another room where, fortunately, the occupants were so much the worse for wine they did not hear of his untimely entrance until the following morning. And then this same tall gentleman had locked the door and threatened to blow out the landlord's brains if he intervened. God knew what he had done to the woman, but after a time he had come charging out again, down the stairs and out of the inn with her pursuing him, half-dressed; such was the chambermaid's report.

His inn's reputation had suffered because of this tall determined fellow who now came seeking word of the woman with the red-gold hair!

Warily, the landlord greeted Geoffrey. Silently he heard him out. In his heart he preferred such dangerous fellows at this one to stay at some other inn. But malice prompted him to respond with a half-truth: the ladies had indeed left the following morning. The golden-bearded man had remained for another week. As to where the ladies had gone, he smiled genially and lied. The ladies had gone to—Whitby, wasn't it? Yes, Whitby, he was almost certain that was where they were bound.

On to Whitby, that port on the North Sea where ships were constructed for commerce, Geoffrey slogged impatiently. Past jet mines and alum manufactories he rode, arriving on a Saturday—market day—in this ancient town that had been destroyed by the Danes in the ninth century, and then become a Danish colony. At all the inns and taverns he asked about Lenore. No one remembered a lady of that description arriving in Whitby before the last Yuletide season—and Lenore was memorable. Geoffrey glanced uneasily at a sailmaker's establishment, and then at the white sails bobbing in the harbor. She *could* have taken ship . . . No, not across the North Sea in the dead of winter. The landlord must have been mistaken. Or perhaps Lenore had told the landlord she was going to Whitby to cloak her trail lest Geoffrey follow her.

A pain went through him as that thought occurred to him. She had reason enough to hate him, he told himself humbly, had his spirited lady.

As he mulled it over, he became convinced the landlord at the Fox and Bow had lied to him—doubtless in retribution for the trouble he had caused that snowy night at the inn. He cursed himself roundly for not having double-checked the landlord's information with the grooms and serving wenches. Swiftly he rode back to York—and to the stables of the Fox and Bow. There he found a groom who remembered the high-sided cart driven by big Elias Plum, who had said as he left that he was taking the ladies to Newcastle, weather permitting.

In a blinding rage, Geoffrey again invaded the Fox and Bow. This time he charged in and struck the landlord a blow that stretched him out on the floor, then charged out again and was gone with a clatter of hooves up the crooked streets before the addled landlord could collect his wits enough to howl for the constable. But the detour to Whitby had cost Geoffrey dear. Had he gone directly to Durham and thence to Newcastle and Wallham, he might have found Lenore and helped her to make her escape. As it was, she was already gone from Wallham before Geoffrey rode into Durham.

At Newcastle he would not have known where to turn but that the answer was furnished providentially. The whole town was agog with the story of the murders and the hanging. It seemed that one Mistress Potts, who had spent her youth in a big house near the great Roman Wall, had returned to find her half brother and his nephew's beautiful young wife murdered. She had escaped to Newcastle with the help of a serving lad and told old friends her story. They had interceded and the law had taken its course, hanging one of the culprits, a fellow named Sedgewick Robb, who had confessed all from the gibbet. The other murderer, a giant named Caleb Apperton, had escaped, but a reward had been offered and all were certain he too would be brought speedily to justice. Mistress Potts! Geoffrey recognized the name.

He sought out Mistress Potts and found her at the home of her old friend, Abby MacDonald. She had gained a few pounds since the hanging and was in the best of spirits, thoroughly enjoying being a heroine. Everyone she had ever known in Newcastle—and many strangers besides—and flocked to her side to listen avidly to her story.

And now Geoffrey Wyndham, Lenore's lover!

With interested eyes, Mistress Potts studied the tall travel-stained gentleman in the MacDonalds' front parlor.

"I know not what happened to Lenore," she admitted frankly. "Except that she got away, I'm sure of that, for I went to the jail and pressed Sedgewick on her whereabouts and he said he did not know, that she had eluded them."

"D'ye know where she might have gone?"

"Nay." Mistress Potts was thoughtful. "Lenore did not know the north country. 'Twas in London I knew her; we were the best of friends and shared lodgings at the

George from time to time, when she was low in funds. I had money then," she added wistfully. "But now I've spent it all and must be a care upon my friends and such as will take me in. For Wallham was heavy with debt and I'll inherit only enough to keep me for a season." She peered at Geoffrey with regret "I've often heard Lenore speak of you. Why did ye not come sooner? She loved you so."

A shadow of pain crossed Geoffrey's dark face and for a moment Mistress Potts saw the strong gauntlet-gloved hands clench.

"If ye see her," he said huskily, "tell her I wronged her. I know now that she was not untrue to me."

"She was never untrue to you," said Mistress Potts severely. "Not in all the long years that I knew her."

"And tell her"—that proud mouth twisted—"tell her that I love her."

To be the bearer of such a message! Mistress Potts' romantic nature flared up—and then dimmed. "But," she mourned, "I'm not likely to see Lenore, for I doubt not she's returned to London by now."

Geoffrey sighed. Lenore knew her way about London too well—he had lost her trail there before.

Although he scoured the countryside roundabout, Geoffrey's search ended effectively at Wallham. No one seemed to have seen Lenore.

Once again she had vanished into thin air.

Thoughtful now, Geoffrey returned to Newcastle and put to Mistress Potts a proposition.

"Would ye consider going back to London to live?" he asked her bluntly.

"Aye," responded Mistress Potts in surprise. "But I've no money for the journey nor funds to keep me once I'm there!"

"I will have ye sent by stage to London and make arrangements for your keep at the George. Where are your boxes?"

"I—I have disposed of most of them," gasped Mistress Potts. "To keep me in pin money and to buy little gifts for my friends. Some of my luggage was stolen at Wallham by vandals who broke into the house after it was empty. But why should you—?"

Geoffrey gave her a grim smile. "D'ye think if ye were in London, Lenore might return to you?"

"I think she might—if she knew I was there."

"Good. Then I will ask of you only two things: that ye walk or ride about London every day, so that ye are visible, and that ye ask after her of all who know her. And if ye should learn her whereabouts, report to me at once. The innkeeper at the Hart will send a man on a fast horse to my home in Kent if I am not in London. Do this, and I will arrange with my London solicitor that ye shall have a pension for life."

" 'Tis a bargain!" cried Mistress Potts, enraptured. "Oh, and I do thank ye, Mister Wyndham, and hope that Lenore be restored to ye soon."

"So do I, Mistress Potts," Geoffrey murmured. "So do I."

Balked in finding Lenore, Geoffrey drove his chestnut horse harder than he would have on the return journey to London—and so missed Lenore and Christopher Dorn by one day at an inn on the North Yorkshire Moors.

Had he lingered but a day more he would have met them there—and that meeting would have changed the course of all their lives.

As it was, Geoffrey returned to London alone and sober-faced, through a land that sang of spring, with birds everywhere on the wing and wild flowers splashing the landscape with color—and found himself once again the talk of the town.

The old gentleman who had broken his clay pipe in York when Lenore rushed by him pursuing Geoffrey as he flung out of the Fox and Bow was indeed Sir Torrence Dane. He had a passing acquaintance with Geoffrey Wyndham although that night at the Fox and Bow had been his first sight of Lenore. Addicted to gossip, Sir Torrence came back to London with a rare tale about a beautiful redhead in a black silk dress. Sir Torrence had a meticulous eye for detail in women's clothes and Lord Wilsingame, hearing the story in London, squirmed, for he recognized the dress Sir Torrence described as the one he had forced on Lenore at the aborted orgy at his house on London Bridge; she'd been wearing that dress when she escaped him!

This redhead, reported Sir Torrence, had fomented a near duel at the Fox and Bow which was stopped by some golden-bearded fellow. Sir Torrence recounted how the golden-bearded fellow and the lustrous wench had gone swaying upstairs together, how Geoffrey Wyndham had come in from the snowy courtyard a little later, given him, Sir Torrence, but a curt nod of greeting and himself repaired upstairs. Heated words from above stairs, the sound of blows, the landlord rushing up, and rushing down again as Geoffrey roared in a voice that could be heard throughout the inn that he was teaching his lady a lesson—and then a silence long enough to encompass seduction—or rape! Then Geoffrey had hurtled back down the stairs again and out into the snow. A moment later the wench, with the torn remnants of her black silk dress clutched around her half-naked body, had followed Geoffrey precipitously out into the courtyard. At this point, realizing how enthralled his listeners were, Sir Torrence always embroidered on the truth a bit. He had peered out the window of the inn, he said, and seen Geoffrey riding away with the wench clinging desperately to his boot until he had kicked her away into the snowy innyard. Geoffrey had disappeared into the blowing snow and no more had been seen of him. In London a short time later, he had put up at the Star and stayed so drunk that his friends could not converse with him! As for the wench, she had trailed back into the inn weeping and the next day had departed with the elderly lady who accompanied her, some said for Durham. The golden-bearded fellow had come unsteadily downstairs about noon with a jaw twice the usual size and his head bandaged, looking exceedingly glum. Sir Torrence had struck up an acquaintance and learned that he was Christopher Dorn, son of the Sheriff of Nottingham. But Christopher had been reluctant to talk about the incident and a week later had departed for parts unknown.

Soon the story was all over London. Geoffrey and his orange girl! A feast for wagging tongues.

And now that spring had come, it was reported that Geoffrey had gone north searching for her fruitlessly once again and returned alone in a grim mood. The wags at Whitehall had a merry time with that.

And all of it was reported by Andre Malraux and the Marquis de Vignac to Letiche, who roamed Geoffrey's great manor house in Kent, fuming.

She charged him with it when he came home.

"Do you know what the wags at Whitehall are saying about you, Geoffrey?" she demanded shrilly. When she had seen his great chestnut horse coming up the drive, she gathered up her saffron taffeta skirts and ran downstairs to meet him.

Geoffrey gazed at his wife's pointed face, flushed now beneath its coating of whitener, with distaste.

"No, but I've no doubt ye'll tell me."

Hands on her taffeta hips, Letiche barred his way.

"They're saying that King Charles commiserates with you—between guffaws—about having been turned down by the same orange girl who turned *him* down! They've even composed a verse about you that some fool is to recite to you in the king's name the next time you appear in Whitehall! Don't you want to know how it goes?"

"Not particularly," Geoffrey said coldly. He moved to pass her.

Letiche stood her ground firmly in her satin slippers. Her face was red with anger as she chanted:

"I'd offer ye a dukedom
If 'twould help in your pursuit!

368

> But she wouldn't have a king,
> So what hope she'd have a duke?"

"Nice of Charles," he said in a scoffing voice. "And he's right, it wouldn't help. Move aside, Letiche. I'm dusty and yearn for a bath."

But for all his careful lightness, the words had knifed through his heart. *She wouldn't have a king* ... Ah, that was his Lenore. She was never one to be bought with gold or glory. All she had ever asked of him was that he love her—which, God knew, he had—and that she wear his name, a gift he could never give her, though he would have laid it at her feet gladly if he could.

"You have made yourself a laughingstock, and now you are making me one!" shrilled Letiche, stamping her foot. "People titter at me behind their fans!"

Geoffrey brushed by her. He was tired and his boots were caked with mud. He had even considered not coming down here, but there were pressing estate matters that demanded his attention.

"Enough, Letiche," he said wearily. "Hold your foolish tongue and ignore what people say. 'Tis only your pride that's been pricked, not your heart."

He went up the stairs two at a time, his spurs jingling. Below him Letiche slammed the door with all her might. The noise did not even make him break stride, but he determined that he would stay even less at Claremont Court in the future.

BOOK IV:
Lorena–
Too Impetuous

Twainmere, The Cotswolds

Chapter 25

That summer a sober Lorena kept dismal counsel with herself. She stayed away from people—both those who shunned her for not wearing mourning and those others who now pressed forward eagerly, believing her a hot wench and easily bedded. Avoiding even Maude's pleasant company, she roamed the countryside alone and restless on a recovered Snowfire. She had found it helped to cool her searing thoughts if she could feel the wind blow fresh and free on her hot face. Sometimes she would find a woodland glade and fling herself down on the soft grasses beside some small brook as she rested the affectionate white horse.

All summer she was restless, riding almost daily, for Flora understood her rebellious mood and did not bid her stay. Instinctively she felt that Lorena must work out her own problems, must come to terms with her own wild nature.

Sometimes Lorena's rides took her far afield, for Snowfire was as eager as she for these outings. One day she rode farther than she intended and found herself in strange country. It was a sultry day in late August and flights of swallows were swooping down into the meadows to gobble up the jumping insects that hid in the tall meadow grasses. Birds sang sleepily and there was the scent of wild flowers in the air.

Lorena paused to let Snowfire cadge a few bites of the succulent grasses and looked around her. Over the humming of the bees the cool sound of water pouring over rocks attracted her attention and she turned sharply. The sound was faint and distant, off to her right beyond the trees that edged this little clearing.

"Come on, Snowfire. I know you're thirsty and I could use a swim." She nudged the white horse with her knee and they were off, thundering across a meadow strewn with yellow wild flowers. Lorena's flying pale hair was turned into a golden halo as she rode. Her fair skin had been toasted to pale honey by the summer sun, while her flushed cheeks added a bright touch of pink. Today, with her thin white bodice sticking to her lovely developing figure and her green kirtle riding up around her white-stockinged legs, she was a sight to tempt a man.

Together horse and rider plunged through the trees and into a shadowed copse where the tinkling stream that sang as it wandered down through the hills widened out into a clear sparkling pool.

The place was silent and desolate, dozing in the summer heat. How inviting the water looked! Quickly Lorena disrobed, tossing aside bodice and kirtle, easing out of her chemise, kicking off her shoes and pulling the cotton stockings from her dainty legs. For a moment she stood and stretched, letting the air cool her damp naked body, and smiled at the old horse who drank contentedly from the sparkling water she was about to enter. Then she plunged in and swam about, a naked nymph, her fair hair at first spilling out around her white shoulders in a pale fluffy torrent, then as the water took it, streaming down like a mermaid's.

Lorena relaxed, frolicking like a young otter, bringing a white leg or a white arm up from the water now and again, and laughing as a rain of bright drops flew high in the air. Playfully, she splashed a handful of water at Snowfire's soft muzzle, laughed as he jumped back with a low reproving snort.

Through the branches an avid pair of brown eyes set in a square heavy-jowled face watched her. They were the eyes of a big man of middle age with the powerful shoulders and heavy shanks of a man used to handling livestock. His clothing marked him as a well-to-do farmer, for although his garments were of leather, his boots were handsome and the hat that lay beside him beneath the concealing branches was of a fashionable shape with a long feather. His face would have been remarked anywhere for a broad "V" was gashed in his forehead, the white mark of an old scar where a ram had kicked him as a child. Aside from that it was an unremarkable face, browned by the weather, and at the moment bearing the look of the hunter for the hunted.

Unaware that she was being observed, Lorena swam a bit and then splashed languidly about in the clear pool. In a shallow place she rose in the waist-deep water and splashed the cold liquid upon her firm round young breasts until the shell pink nipples hardened to quivering firmness.

Still as death now, her watcher drew a deep shivering breath and felt a familiar stirring in his groin. His tense gaze focused on the girl ever more fixedly, roving down her torso and into the water that circled her waist to probe toward the soft out-thrusting hips.

Something brushed her knee—perhaps a flashing silver fish, for this was a trout stream; indeed it was the fishing that had attracted him this day- -and Lorena reacted by taking two swift steps that brought her hips dripping from the pool and left the cold water lapping about her white thighs. She turned restlessly to brush away a dragonfly.

Her back was to the observer now, and her fair hair hung down heavy and wet, touching the pool's surface as she bent forward, looking down at a little school of tiny darting minnows.

He passed a red tongue over his lips as a single drop of water made its way down the back of her neck, sparkled a path down her spine and lost itself in the damp cleft between her pearly buttocks. Thoroughly aroused by now, he noted with regret that the girl was across the pool from him now and wondered whether he could plunge in and flounder across before she could clamber up the bank and scamper away,

He decided uneasily that he could not.

As he pondered, his problem was solved by the white horse.

Snowfire, noting the richer grasses on the pool's farther side, had walked a little way up where the stream narrowed and picked his own dainty way across, his hooves ringing on the wet rocks. Now he walked down to the edge of the pool and stood munching contentedly on the opposite bank from Lorena's little pile of clothes.

The girl frowned. Tired of paddling about, she did not want to get out and dress and then flounder back across the slippery rocks of the stream to mount her horse. Shivering a little, for even though it was August the mountain water was cold, she knifed back into the water, cutting it cleanly. Her hair streamed out behind her as she sought the shore where Snowfire's muzzle was lost in the soft green grasses.

Behind the branches he tensed. This was better than the watcher had hoped, for the girl was climbing out of the water almost into his arms!

As Lorena came out, he made his move. Too excited now to time the thing correctly, he burst through the branches and plunged toward her. At the abrupt and violent parting of the branches, the crunch of twigs beneath heavy boots, Snowfire neighed and reared up, pawing the air. Lorena, for a moment bewildered, spun to the side, her white body eluding her attacker like some silvery darting fish.

Carried forward by his own momentum, his boots skidding on the wet grass Lorena had splashed as she emerged, the big man slipped sidewise into the pool.

The splash of his entry into the water sent a shower of drops over both horse and girl.

But he was fast. In an instant he had righted himself.

Lorena took one horrified look at him, rising up with water pouring off of his leather jerkin and coursing down his broad shoulders over his heavily muscled arms. A very demon he looked to her, with that white V etched into his forehead, his face set in a wolfish snarl. Water streamed from his clipped chestnut beard as he whirled and plunged for shore. Maddened with desire, the pupils of his eyes were so dilated that to the girl they appeared black. With a half-human howl he lunged for her—but Lorena was already up on Snowfire's back and away.

She did not even stop for her clothes.

Behind her, the big man in his wet leathern garments staggered up the bank and plunged after her, his big body crashing through the underbrush.

Lorena, flashing through the trees on Snowfire, heard him and prayed to God that he might not have a horse.

She was lucky. He did not. He had arrived at the trout stream afoot, a circumstance that caused him to curse roundly as he came to a winded halt, staring after the flying horse and naked rider disappearing across the flower-strewn meadow. He watched them go with a mixture of agony and chagrin. Slip of a girl though she was, the very sight of the wench had coursed fire through his entrails. He had burned to hold her. Bilked of his design, he now smote the rough bark of a nearby tree hard enough to bring blood springing to his hurt knuckles.

With an angry grunt at the sudden pain in his hand, he flexed his wounded knuckles gingerly and stared at the spot in the trees ahead where the white horse with its naked rider had disappeared. And now a crafty look spread over his lustful weathered face.

He'd find out who the wench was, and he'd have her yet, by God!

* * *

Fleeing in naked panic, her white body flashing through the trees, the words Uncle Robbie had so often spoken knifed through Lorena's mind: *God punishes the wicked.* It was one of his favorite sayings. Another was *God's vengeance is swift.* In her case God had indeed swiftly punished her for dashing away for a ride and a swim instead of staying to sedately pluck dandelion greens for their supper.

Her body still trembled with shock and her breath was sobbing in her throat as she streaked for home. Out of nowhere that man had come, leaping for her -and she had escaped him by only a breath. His face came up before her now, with that terrible white V etched into the forehead. She felt she would never forget that face, would see it in nightmares for the rest of her life.

At last she pulled Snowfire to a halt and cast a worried look behind her. In the panic of the moment she had given no thought at all to leaving her clothes behind, but now she dared not go back for them lest her attacker be hiding nearby waiting to leap out at her. Yet she could not ride into the village stark naked!

Biting her lips and letting Snowfire dance a bit—for he too was still nervous from the encounter—she pondered her problem.

She could wend through sheltering trees until she was almost to the village. But what then?

Undecided, she rode along with the sun through the branches dappling her white skin. Far in the distance a haymaker caught a glimpse of her, blinked, and the apparition was gone. He rubbed a hand over his eyes and stared, awed, at the empty strip of woodland where for a moment he had seen a beautiful naked maiden on a white horse, then muttering he turned back to work.

Unknowing—for she had not glimpsed the silent farmer agog in the meadow off to her left—the girl rode on.

As time passed, she grew more anxious. She was tempted to turn Snowfire around and ride back—to chance it, in the hope of recovering her clothes.

It would have been a mistake, for the man still lounged by the pool, hidden by the branches, waiting alert for her return. Sometimes he reached out a rough hand and touched the soft fabric of the girl's chemise and felt a thrill go through him at the thought that this soft cloth had caressed her fair young body.

But Lorena did not turn back. She had had an idea.

The Demming's croft lay almost in her path—and today was market day in nearby Wapping. John Demming had a sister in Wapping and made a practice of taking his whole family there every market day.

That meant the croft would be deserted.

Lorena's heart beat a little faster. The cottage would be locked but she could slip into the barn and make off with a horse blanket which she could easily return by carrying it to Maude's, for John Demming's wife was related to Maude's mother and called once a fortnight. It was unlikely the blanket would be missed and it would amuse Maude to be part of a plot to replace it.

Lorena felt a moment's distaste at the thought of riding the back ways to Twainmere wrapped in the prickly thing. The rough wool would be cruelly rough to her tender bare flesh—but at least she would be decently covered and could mumble some story about having run into a skunk and abandoned her clothing, if she were unlucky enough to run into somebody.

Looking anxiously about to make sure she was unobserved, Lorena turned Snowfire into the Demming's little meadow, at the far end of which lay the barn. It was out of sight of their tiny cottage which lay over a little rise. It was just as well that Lorena could not see over that rise, for the Demming's door was open. Their younger son had come down with a cold and the Demmings had decided to forego their usual trek to Wapping. At the moment both father and mother were occupied with spooning down their younger son's throat a homemade concoction that Mercy Meadows had recommended. It tasted terrible and smelled worse and John Demming was hard put to hold the lad while his wife spooned the sticky black mess down his throat.

Since three spoonfuls was considered the required dose and the lad was both muscular and rebellious and had already spat out two despite having his ears boxed, Lorena would have plenty of time.

Warily she rode toward the barn, sighing with relief when she saw that the big doors yawned open. She had feared they might be locked!

At those doors she dismounted, peering hesitantly into the dim interior. She jumped when Snowfire neighed a low greeting which was returned from inside the darkened barn—and then sternly calmed herself, for she knew the Demmings had no stable and kept their horses in the barn.

But Snowfire's neighing had alerted someone else too.

Watt Demming, the crofter's nineteen-year-old elder son, had been hiding in the barn to avoid his chores. Although his father supposed him to be making hay at a neighbor's—for the Demmings, like the other crofters, traded work with each other—Watt was lazing on a pile of hay, resting from a hard night spent in the loft above with the milkmaid.

At the sound of hooves, Watt had leaped up and slid behind a wagon. And winced as he heard Snowfire's whinny, for his father would take a strap to him if he found him there! After a moment, when he did not hear the stranger's halloo or his father's stomping boots entering the barn, he peeked out from behind the wagon.

The sight that met his eyes was a dazzling one.

With her pale shimmering hair streaming down over her naked back, young Lorena, completely nude, was peering cautiously out of the sunlight into the dark barn.

"Lorena!" Watt came out from behind the wagon, his black eyes round with amazement.

Lorena gave Watt a horrified look. Watt was one of the lads who often whistled at her as she swung along with her market basket. How awful that he should see her thus!

Her whole cringing body was suffused with a soft glowing pink as the blood rose up to her skin in embarrassment. In panic she stumbled backward into the sunlight and again leaped to Snowfire's back, careening off to the right and thundering away in the direction of home.

"Wait! Come back!" Watt called after her, but Snowfire was clearing the meadow at full gallop and horse and naked rider were about to plunge into the woods. Watt was still running after her, his usually dull eyes alight. Lord, she was a beauty, wasn't she? And she must have had *some* reason to seek out their barn—wait till Tom and Andy and Dick heard about this!

With his mind on the winsome Lorena, Watt failed to focus on the hog wallow that lay just ahead. Suddenly he slipped and went down, to stretch the length of him out in the mud. He struggled up, spitting muddy water and cursing even as he choked. Lorena was for the moment forgotten as a barely recognizable Watt, covered with dark slime from head to foot, took himself back to the cottage and the ministrations of his astonished mother.

Sobbing with embarrassment, Lorena bent low over the horse's back, trying to make her slender body as inconspicuous as possible. Ducking through the trees she made her way, fortunately unobserved, to the smithy on the edge of Twainmere where they now lived. The forge beneath the spreading chestnut tree was cold for the smithy was no longer in use—only the cottage behind it.

Quickly Lorena stabled Snowfire and snatched up a horse blanket, wrapped it around her, not minding that the rough wool prickled her skin.

She peered out. Aunt Flora was busy in her herb garden, which she was trying to bring to life again. She did not look up from her marjoram and rosemary, but called, "Is that you, Lorena?"

"Yes, I'm back," said Lorena. With her eye fixed on that bent head, she made it through the back door and leaned against it in relief.

Tomorrow she would go back for her things. Aunt Flora need never know.

But Lorena had not reckoned on Watt Demming, for by the next day the titillating story was all over Twainmere.

The last shreds of Lorena's reputation—if, as wild Lenore Frankford's daughter, she had ever had one—were irretrievably lost.

Like mother like daughter, chuckled the gossips of Twainmere. For hadn't Lenore ridden naked on a white horse into the Battle of Worcester? They shook their heads happily and all agreed that Lenore's precocious daughter would come to a bad end too.

London

Chapter 26

Late summer found Mistress Potts bouncing about London in a sedan chair carried by two stout puffing lads. After the gloom and fright of Wallham, and her sudden notoriety in Newcastle, she was at last her old self again, bridling at every strange man who met her gaze (for she was secretly sure that half the men in London meant to waylay and rape her if she did not watch out). She thought often and affectionately of Lenore, and adhered scrupulously to the bargain she had made in Newcastle with Geoffrey Wyndham. Every day, except in the severest weather, Abigail Potts went abroad in chair or hackney coach, asking at inns and alehouses, scanning the streets and alleys with a bright interested gaze for a glimpse of Lenore.

She could not know that Lenore was half across England, riding nonchalantly beside a golden-bearded gambler with a flashing smile, sharing his wine and his laughter—and eventually his love.

She did know that Geoffrey Wyndham came round to the George whenever he was in London for news of her. Always there was the glint of hope in his gray eyes when he marched in, his spurs jingling across the stone floor of the common room as he strode forward eagerly to inquire about the wheareabouts of his lady. Always that dark hawklike face seemed to lose something, to deaden, when he learned there was no word.

Mistress Potts, kindhearted soul that she was, hated to be giving him sad tidings all that summer and fall. Toward Christmas he seemed to her more restive, and she wondered if he could be having trouble at home for on her scouting expeditions she had often seen Letiche Wyndham sailing haughtily by in a gilded coach, with jewels sparkling in the enormous plumes of her hat. Once or twice she had seen that coach pull up before rather impecunious lodgings on an out-of-the-way street and watched Letiche peek out furtively and peer up and down that street before she hurried inside.

Mistress Potts had guessed Letiche's secret: Letiche Wyndham had a lover.

But although she loved gossip, it never occurred to Abigail Potts to voice to Geoffrey her suspicions of his wife's behavior. A man so fierce—why, he might strike her down at the mere suggestion of dishonor to his house!

The Christmas season came and with it snow. Snow to decorate the chimneys and rooftops of London, snow to cover the dirty cobbled streets with a clean white carpet. Big flakes drifted down as lazily as eiderdown when Mistress Potts sat down to a Christmas dinner of roast goose stuffed with apples and onions, juicy capon garnished with savory pignolias and an enormous helping of minced pie. Her gown of russet taffeta over its Italian silk petticoat rustled as she ate and she wiggled her toes in her new slippers. For Mistress Potts had made good use of the generous allowance Geoffrey's London solicitors doled out to her every month and was fast replacing her lost wardrobe. She had been astonished to learn that her stipend was to go on for life, and felt very easy about her circumstances now.

She did not see Geoffrey Wyndham that Christmas or for days thereafter and assumed he was celebrating Christmas in Kent with his wife.

Twelfth Night found Mistress Potts warming her plump hands before the hearth in the George's common room before retiring to her own much colder room upstairs. She had spent a wholly satisfying day. In the morning before she went out she had peeked into the bakehouse of the George where the Twelfth-cake was being baked. It would have a bean in it and whoever found that bean in his slice of cake would, by ancient custom, lord it over the other revelers for the rest of the evening.

It was the sight of that Twelfth-Night cake that had decided Mistress Potts to dine at the George on a collar of brawn, although she had fully intended to sup at the Cock and Crown, which had advertised that they would "roast a goodly surloyn of beefe." Now it was growing late but she hated to leave the revelers and go upstairs. But she was alone, not part of any of the jolly groups. . . . For a moment she felt that loneliness go through her old bones like an ache. Then she reminded herself how lucky she was to be in London again, a London with the Puritan reign a thing of the past and Christmas—which the stern Puritans had banned—being celebrated again with roast goose and plums in pottage pots all over the city. And music too. Everywhere there was music, for the organs—removed from the churches in Cromwell's time—had been brought back by merry King Charles and Christmas carols filled the air.

Now she heard the inn door open and one of those carols was loudly borne into the common room, for outside the George's lighted windows a group of tipsy gentlemen were roaring out "God Rest Ye Merry Gentlemen."

Behind her a pleasant masculine voice spoke.

"I wish ye merry, Mistress Potts. Any word yet of my lady?"

Plump Mistress Potts turned her fire-flushed face toward the voice and, as always, caught her breath at the sight of Geoffrey Wyndham. For in spite of the melancholy that rode his dark hawklike countenance of late, he was a sight to make feminine hearts skip a beat.

On this evening he was clad in a silver-shot doublet of dove gray with velvet breeches of the same shade and wore a short cloak of black velvet lined with red satin. The lace that foamed about his throat and frothed over his strong wrists was as white as the snow that fell outside upon the twisted candlelit streets. His wet boots—for he had just come in out of that snow—were dark and gleaming and their wide tops supported frosty white linen boothose trimmed in lace point. A heavy gold chain rested upon his chest and a ruby of price gleamed from his index finger as it rested lightly upon the hilt of his chased basket-hilted dress sword.

But the steady gray eyes beneath the broad-brimmed hat with its sweeping gray plumes were sad and Mistress Potts' heart, full to bursting this Christmas season, went out to him. For hadn't she seen his wife—"that French trollop" as she secretly called Letiche—stop her coach in the Strand only yesterday, look furtively about, and let in a foreign looking dandy who had hailed her?

"Nay, Mister Wyndham," she cried unhappily. "There's no word of Lenore. And I've been out every day, like I promised, looking for her. No one has seen her."

He had been expecting that, of course. Why should the words ring so gloomily upon his ears? Because it heralded yet another lonely night without her.

"I do miss her so." Tears welled up in Mistress Potts' faded blue eyes. "For we did spend Christmas together whenever we could—and hearty dinners we ate too!" She dabbed at her face with a kerchief.

Geoffrey, who had been about to head for Whitehall and the festivities there, was brought up short. Here before him was the woman who had befriended Lenore in the years when he had been in France. A lonely woman . . .

"Mistress Potts," he said gravely. "There is some Twelfth-Night revelry at Whitehall tonight. Even now a masked ball is in progress. I am expected and I have no lady. Would you do me the honor to accompany me?"

Mistress Potts gasped. She could not believe she had heard him aright. It was one thing for the great courtier Geoffrey Wyndham to pay for her keep, but quite another for him to offer to take her to the royal palace!

"Will—will not your wife object?" she blurted.

It occurred to Geoffrey that if Letiche knew he was taking an old woman of low degree to Whitehall, she would sneer and say that he had found fitting company.

"My wife spends her Christmas season this year in Surrey," he explained courteously. "With friends. Her friends are not my friends. Indeed," he added humorously, "I am in sad need of a lady for this night's gala. Will you not take pity on me and accompany me?"

Mistress Potts, who knew that Letiche Wyndham had not been in Surrey yesterday afternoon, straightened up and her face took on a cherubic glow. "I'd be honored—honored, sir."

"Then make you ready straightaway."

Old Mistress Potts' fat legs had never taken the stairs so lightly.

Ever after she would remember that evening, for it seemed to her a dream of summer madness that had come upon her in the midst of an English winter in the winter of her life.

She wore her finest gown—a rich concoction of gold lace over purple velvet. Her feet were encased in slippers of purple satin—and thrust hastily into high pattens for the snow outside was getting deep. She whitened her face with ceruse to a fashionable deathly pallor and then dabbed at her cheeks with "Spanish paper" to rouge them. When she stood up and looked critically into the mirror, she told her sparkling-eyed reflection that she looked young and handsome enough to attend a ball with a court gallant! Throwing a plum velvet cloak over her finery, she hurried downstairs and Geoffrey's sweeping bow from below quite took her breath away.

"Ye look very splendid, Mistress Potts. Come, we must hurry. Our coach is waiting."

Voices were hushed in the common room and all eyes followed their progress to the door. Basking in all this attention, Mistress Potts tried to trip across the floor as daintily as any actress treading the boards at Drury Lane.

As Geoffrey handed her into the coach, a servant girl brushed by, homeward bound. She was carrying a big basket of Twelfth-Night gifts and humming the "Coventry Carol." Her light voice was drowned out by a jostling group of soldiers, much the worse for drink, squalling "Our Joyful'st Feast." The coach door closed as they drunkenly reached the line, "The wenches with their wassail bowls . . . about the streets are sing-ing!"

Mistress Potts, who usually scorned drunkenness, gave the singers a tolerant smile. *She* was going to Whitehall!

A Twelfth-Night masque had just ended when they arrived and the dancing had begun. Geoffrey swept Mistress Potts out upon the marble floor, his dexterity and grace making up for her awkwardness. Looking down into her bedazzled face, he wished that he had thought of this before. Lenore would have been pleased.

The end of the dance brought them near his majesty and Geoffrey presented Mistress Potts to her monarch, straight-faced, as "Countess Abigail Potts." Startled speechless, Mistress Potts sank into a curtsy so deep she nearly had to be helped up. Over her head King Charles' amused black eyes twinkled into Geoffrey's as his gaze flicked from Mistress Potts' astonishing girth to Geoffrey's impassive face. What was Wyndham up to?

But Geoffrey whirled Mistress Potts away before anything cuttingly mirthful could be said by the group around the king and swept her toward the refreshments. These, glittering beneath crystal chandeliers, entirely eclipsed anything that lady had ever seen, even in her youth when Wallham set a groaning board. She could not count the dishes, but she gorged herself on plover and stewed larks, roe knuckles and bitterns, partridges, herons, cranes, snipe, woodcock and—she gasped—great swans and peacocks who rode the huge trenchers in full feather. There were gilt sugar decorations amid a forest of silver, any piece of which looked too heavy for one man to carry, steaming wassail bowls, a great boar's head, a mammoth plum pudding that had to be wheeled in, blazing with blue flame, upon a cart. Any everything spiced and sauced and curried, golden with saffron, filled with plump raisins and currants and nuts and oysters. Mistress Potts gave thanks inwardly that Geoffrey had presented her to the king *before* this repast, for had it been after, when she curtsied she would surely have broken her stays!

And when at last Geoffrey—seeing the party was fast reaching its later and wilder stage—prudently brought her back to the George and gravely removed her cloak and shook the snow from it and escorted her to the hearth that she might warm her cold gloved hands, she looked up at him, her old eyes abrim with tears.

"I'll never forget this night," she whispered. "Not *ever.*"

But Geoffrey, holding the cloak before the hearth to dry it, was not looking at her. His gaze was on the fire where the orange flames burned no brighter than the shimmering remembered hair of his lost Lenore.

"I hope somewhere my lady fares as well," he murmured, and Mistress Potts' tears spilled over.

"Oh, sir," she quavered. "I do hope so too. Oh, I mustn't spoil your evening by crying!" She snatched her cloak from him and made for the stairs. There was a faint crunching sound as she moved, for she had filched a number of cookies which she would bring out later and munch to prove to herself that she had really been to Whitehall and danced in company with the king. Halfway up the stairs she turned and said in a muffled voice, made shaky by emotion, "I'll keep looking for Lenore, Mister Wyndham. Ye can depend upon Abigail Potts!"

"I know ye will," he said absently. "I know ye will."

Still, long after she had gone, he stood with one boot propped on the low brass railing around the hearth in the deserted common room and stared into the flames that leaped about the heavy Yule log.

Where was she tonight, his beautiful Lenore? Whose arms enfolded her? It was a thought to grind the soul. Geoffrey's gauntleted hands clenched and he turned abruptly from the fire, in which he saw too many visions. With a haggard face, he made his way back to the debaucheries of Whitehall.

And upstairs, Mistress Potts, still agog over what she would forever after call her "evening with the king," wondered too where Lenore was tonight.

And being of an endlessly romantic nature, she imagined the beautiful "orange girl," as the wits of London insisted on calling Lenore, as having found shelter in some great country house—a turreted castle with reflecting moat was not too much to hope for—where she was surrounded by attentive liveried servants and every evening by candlelight a belted earl sank upon his aristocratic beribboned knees and hopelessly begged her to wed him.

A far cry indeed from the truth.

The Rovers

Chapter 27

"Lenore," Christopher studied her narrowly. "In all the time we have been together, you have never once asked, 'Do you love me, Christopher?' "

Reclining with her head resting on her outstretched arm, Lenore gave him a lazy smile. Eve might have smiled like that, he thought.

"You don't answer me, Lenore. Yet 'tis a question women always ask. *Do you love me?*"

They were lying together, naked, stretched out upon the greensward in a grove of oaks outside Wells. A whole year had passed since Christopher had stepped forward in that inn in Northumberland to save her. A year in which they had traveled together, slept together, waged their private war upon the world together.

This week a fair was being held in Wells. They had arrived last night and elected not to go into the town until today because the spring night was warm and their passions even warmer. They had made love till their bodies glowed with it and, sunk deep in ecstasy, had fallen asleep in each other's arms.

Now at his insistent question, Lenore laughed. "And would you lie to me, Christopher? Would you say promptly 'Of course I love you, Lenore.'"

Christopher Dorn frowned and gave his beautiful relaxed companion an uneasy look. Like quicksilver, he felt he had never really held her. Her body, yes. But where was her heart? It was not love that looked back at him so steadily out of those reckless violet eyes. Yet their joinings were tumultous, like great bursting storms that rose out of tall thunderheads on summer afternoons, joinings that wracked the senses and staggggered the mind ... and worked havoc with his emotions.

She intrigued him, she fascinated him. When he took her it was wonderful—but never enough.

He had never known a woman like her.

Was she mocking him? he wondered uneasily.

"You are not like other women, Lenore," he muttered.

"I am *exactly* like other women," Lenore told him composedly. "Perhaps a trifle less lucky at times."

She rose and stretched her slender white arms while he lay there on the grass and admired her lithe naked beauty. Fondly his eyes, with their strange crystal clarity, traced the swanlike line of her throat as she stretched, the round rosy-tipped breasts that drew taut as her fingers stretched upward to the sky. He admired the waist that narrowed to nothing, the flattened stomach the soft outthrust of her hips and the pale gold of the silky triangle between them. Long graceful legs– clean-limbed, neat— and dainty ankles, slender bare feet that took her gracefully across the grass to her little pile of clothes.

He watched her don her chemise pull on her stockings. He hated to move, hated to let this moment end. Her back to him, she dressed rapidly and stood combing out her long shimmering red-gold hair with a silver comb he had bought her.

Yes, he admitted to his heart, he loved her, this

lustrous woman who asked for no declarations of love, but only to ride beside him and share his days and nights.

He loved her—but he did not understand her.

Christopher Dorn had had more than his share of women. He had pursued them ardently, but they had never meant much to him. It was the chase that counted; once the quarry was snared a man must look forward to some other quarry, even more difficult.

He was not entirely sure he would ever catch this one.

She slept in his arms by night, her body trembled beneath the wild heady assaults of his lovemaking, her lips sobbed occasional endearments into his ears—the stuff of dreams, of moonbeams.

But now he wondered, with a twang of jealousy, where was her heart? With him, or with that tall fellow back in York?

He dared not ask.

Yet he was guiltily aware that he had brought her back to Wells as a reminder that it was in Wells he had first seen her, that it was here he had tossed her the whip that saved her life. He supposed it was because, not content with what he had, he wanted some declaration from her, some assurance that he—and only he—held her heart in keeping.

Perhaps it was too much to ask of such a woman.

Now he too rose to his feet. He cut a masterful figure as he stretched. Long muscles rippled under his pale skin. Lenore, turning with her comb still running through her long hair, thought he had the build of a fencer: narrow, strong, flexible.

He was a remarkable lover.

And she liked Chris, felt sympathy for him—and gratitude that he had saved her from being dragged back to Wallham and almost certain death. But she knew he wanted her to look straight into his eyes and say, *I love you, Christopher*.

She could not do it.

Walls as tall as castles had been built up around her heart by Geoffrey's defection. She was not sure she could ever love anyone again. Not even someone as kind, as loving, as Christopher Dorn.

He was dressed now and stood booted before her in his silver-shot doublet of olive damask. His pinkish gray trousers had a silvery sheen and were gartered with rosettes of olive ribands. He had donned fresh white linen boothose, which flared out, edged with lace points, resting on his wide-topped boots. The Mechlin at his throat was a gift from her, for they had been lucky of late, and his carefully cropped golden Van Dyke beard brushed the expensive lace with an air, she thought. His crystal eyes roved over her with a last yearning look and then he seized his orange-plumed hat and abruptly his mood changed. Lightheartedly he beckoned her. "On to Wells," he cried. "On to the fair!"

They came out of their sheltered little grove of oaks—and saw that indeed it had been none too sheltered, for a farm cart was lumbering across an oat field nearby.

"It was good we dressed when we did," Lenore murmured, laughing. "We'd certainly have shocked that farmer if he'd seen us!"

Christopher brushed her ear with a kiss as he swung her up onto her gray horse, then lightly leaped astride his own mount. He hoped there'd be money in Leeds today, travelers with handfuls of it and in a mood to gamble. He jingled the dice in his pocket. Ah, they had never failed him.

For he wanted to buy Lenore things. Perversely, since she asked for nothing, he was the more determined to drape her in gold chains shot with rubies, to buy the finest of fabrics to caress her silken skin, he wanted to hang ropes of pearls around her white neck and see her ears drip diamonds.

Now as he rode beside her, he laughed ruefully to himself. Never before had he felt this way about a woman.

In time, he promised himself confidently, she would come to love him.

On the main road, they joined the jostling motley crowd heading for the fair, and as they rode into the lovely old cathedral town, Lenore thought whimsically how much better dressed she was than when last she entered it. Then she had arrived wearing a worn dress of apple green over a yellow petticoat—a dress in which she'd fled all across England—and she'd left the town by night, wrapped in a filthy woolen shawl filched from a stable with ashes smeared over her face to simulate bruises. Now her gaze roved down to her dress: it was handsomely cut, a gown of lime green China silk that hugged her lovely torso and billowed out over an emerald silk petticoat, whose material matched the lining of her big slashed sleeves. She had left Wells before in worn-out shoes, and now she returned in slippers of emerald kid with brilliant yellow heels.

Christopher had bought her the dress and shoes in the last town, where his luck had been exceptionally good.

As they jostled their way through the crowd at the city gates, Lenore looked around her cynically. Once she'd considered these people, these eager fair-goers, just innocent ignorant men and women bent on having a good time, on laughing and dancing and eating sweetmeats and applauding acrobats and tumblers—the simple pleasures.

Now she knew them better.

In this crowd through which they carefully picked their way were thieves and pickpockets, bawds from all the seacoast towns and as far away as London, confidence men—and gamblers like Christopher Dorn, and striking women like herself who accompanied such men, attracting attention by their beauty and thereby giving their companions a chance to meet those, whom they would later fleece.

Lenore had no illusions about herself or her life. She worked with Christopher, luring strangers with her beauty, her challenging attitude, into making ever more reckless wagers against Christopher's loaded dice.

She knew with pain that seared her heart that it was a world into which she could not bring Lorena.

She had thought to send for her daughter—oh, she had thought to, after that first fiery night with Christopher in Northumberland. She had waked at dawn and almost at once had begun to weave plans, lovely shining plans, in which Christopher was magically reformed and reunited with his father, in which she was magically reunited with Lorena and they all lived happily ever after.

But the day they had ridden into that first fair at Leeds she had seen how it was going to be.

Christopher had given her instructions and she had obeyed them. She had stood just out of earshot, watching the three men with whom he gambled. Stout local farmers, two of them, the third a dissipated rake, probably some younger son of county gentry.

As the stakes grew higher, she had sidled nearer in curiosity and Christopher had looked up at her and frowned. He had told her to stay near the horses and if he leaped up and ran toward her, to mount up and ride without question wherever he led, for he knew the country around Leeds.

Still she lingered in defiance of that frowning look, drawn there by something that puzzled her in the eyes of these men as they looked toward her, the naked desire she could see unmasked on their three faces. Not desire for gold—and there was plenty of that on the ground before the squatting figures as they hoarsely exhorted luck to aid them in throwing out the dice—no, it was desire for a woman. For *her*.

That they should display that desire so openly puzzled Lenore.

Now she heard one of the farmers say thickly, "This throw will win me the wench. See if it don't!"

Lenore stiffened.

They were dicing for *her!* No wonder Christopher

wanted her to stand near the horses. They might have to run for it any minute now!

Alert now, she edged back toward the horses.

Now Christopher was getting up, dusting off his knees. He was laughing, commiserating the losers. Three sullen pairs of eyes gave Lenore a last look of chagrin as they skulked away, disappointed of their goal.

But in case the losers should have second thoughts about the honesty of the game and come back to question the dice, she was prompt to comply when Christopher muttered, "Mount up. We're leaving Leeds."

"You were dicing for *me*, weren't you?" she asked tightly as they rode away from the fair. "*I* was the stake? Don't lie, I heard that man say it."

Christopher shrugged and turned to give her his easy smile. He was always easy and relaxed when he won. "The ground was uneven and my dice rolled wrong. I was out of coins. You were the only thing I had left to dice with."

"There were the horses," she reminded him bitterly.

"Oh, I'd already lost them." His voice was casual. "And my doublet and sword as well. But no matter, I won them all back at one stroke. They'd have bet anything for a chance at *you*."

Lenore gave him a startled look, understanding fully at last what it would mean to ride with Christopher. She would always be at risk.

It meant she could never have Lorena with her.

Still, what else was offered?

Always adaptable, Lenore swiftly grew used to their roving life. By fall she was an accomplished ally of Christopher's whom he regarded with admiration for her good sense and daring as well as her beauty. She told herself philosophically that perhaps this was the sort of life she was cut out for. For hadn't she proved an admirable partner for Christopher, leading men on with a smile that seemed to promise everything?

All that fall they were lucky, and in December, when

the icy weather drove them south, they wintered in the south of England, in Torquay, in a house set amid a row of terraced cottages flung helter-skelter up a steep incline, its small walled garden overgrown with roses that filled the air with their heady perfume.

For Lenore it was a season of drifting, rootless, without memories. Always she found Christopher amusing company, and by night a competent lover, stirring her as she had not thought any man but Geoffrey could ever stir her.

But sometimes, looking up at the stars as they flickered like tiny diamonds above the English Channel, stretching out through the scented darkness to Europe and beyond to the broad Atlantic, sometimes she asked herself what she was doing here—here in another man's arms when Geoffrey's arms should be holding her. At those times, although she scolded herself for being ridiculous, she felt inescapably like an unfaithful wife.

But with the spring their money ran out and the soft winds of Devon blew them north and east.

And now they were riding into Wells.

"There, up ahead," Christopher muttered as he leaned toward her. "That well-dressed fellow with an air about him."

Lenore gave the fellow a cynical look. A court dandy, he looked to be. Pomaded, perfumed, dressed in mauve taffetas with faultlessly white lace cuffs. He could have been one of the men who had cheered her from the pit when she was a London actress—and pinched her when she was a orange girl. What was such as he doing at a simple country fair?

She turned from her observation and gave Christopher an imperceptible nod.

They were agreed, this dandy was to be their target for today.

Now she urged her gray horse forward until she was just ahead of the man in mauve taffetas, and then dropped her kerchief with a little cry.

The cry attracted the dandy's notice. The wide dark-lashed violet eyes in which he seemed to lose himself atttracted him even more. Gallantly he whipped out his dress sword and swept the lace kerchief up on the point, removed it with a hand that flashed rings and proffered the kerchief to her with a bow.

Lenore gave him her best smile. The result was dazzling and he was plainly staggered by it. "Thank you, sir," she murmured, accepting the kerchief. "You are most kind."

"Surely a lady like yourself is not riding alone?" he murmured, looking about for a maidservant.

"Oh, no, I am bound for the fair, with my brother." Her nod indicated Christopher Dorn, riding a length or two behind her. He cut a striking figure in his silver-shot doublet and his hat with waving orange plumes. She saw the mauve-taffeted gentleman's dark eyes widen and felt a moment's pride in Christopher. He too had an air about him. Indeed anyone would have mistaken the pair of them for what they seemed to be: young aristocrats pausing to take in a local fair.

"And why does the fair attract you?" he wondered.

"Oh, it does not," Lenore hastened to assure him, with just the right amount of amused scorn in her voice. "We are for London to join our father, but my brother loves gaming and hopes to find some game of chance at the fair to interest him." She shrugged indifferently.

"Indeed?" A crafty light lit up the dandy's dark eyes. "I too seek such a game. Perhaps we can find it together." He slowed his horse until Christopher, who had been lagging behind deliberately, caught up, and introduced himself. He was Simon Arbuthnot of Bath and he was dawdling on his way to Southampton to visit his sister. The sister was pregnant with her fifth child and since she had drawn the line at four, could be counted upon to have the vapors—thus the detour to the fair. He was very voluble, but his dark eyes followed Lenore lasciviously as he talked.

She returned him a challenging look, then rode on, keeping a length or two ahead of them. She would have preferred to fall back and listen to the conversation, but Christopher had insisted that at these moments it was best that he fan the flame of lust for gold with his words, while she, riding before them like a picture, fanned the flame of desire for her lovely body—for she kept always in sight and her straight back in the saddle and graceful gestures were a joy to see.

In this manner they proceeded to the fair.

There they left their horses with a boy to watch them and strolled about, the three of them, visiting the stalls. They shared some hot cross buns bought from a vendor. Lenore had her fortune told—she was promised a brilliant marriage and a sea voyage—and they tossed coins to some jugglers and acrobats they had paused to watch.

Then the men got down to the serious business of the afternoon—gambling.

They found several others of like mind, but these others soon found the game too rich for their blood and stood back, watching the two richly clad men as they diced. Arbuthnot was a clever gambler and after each successful toss—he was using his own dice—he would look up and give Lenore a bright unfathomable look. Standing nearby, Lenore saw that Christopher was losing and began to watch the dice. Somehow she did not like the way they fell.

Christopher had lost the horses now to Arbuthnot, and the watchers, attracted by a pair of scantily clad female wrestlers, had wandered away.

Now Christopher, having lost all his gold, was playing for his handsome doublet and sword.

Lenore tensed as he lost.

They were still playing with Arbuthnot's dice. Christopher had so far had no chance to palm off his own, for Arbuthnot had had an amazing run of luck.

She felt a shiver go through her as Christopher

laughingly said, "I've naught left to wager save my sister!"

Arbuthnot, who had been about to rise with his winnings, turned sharply to Christopher. "And would ye wager her?" he wondered.

"I'd wager London if I owned it, or my grandmother's coffin were it handy!" Christopher looked so lightheartedly rueful as he said that, that even Lenore believed him.

She opened her mouth to protest but Arbuthnot was speaking. "Ye mean ye'd leave the lady in my keeping and ride away to London alone?" he asked bluntly.

Christopher had the grace to hesitate. Then, "Aye," he sighed reluctantly. "I would."

Arbuthnot turned to Lenore who was looking delightfully confused. " 'Tis ridiculous," she protested. "You cannot wager me, Chris!"

"Still we cannot ride on to London without our horses," pointed out Christopher reasonably. "Nor without money. And since no one here knows us, who's to advance us any?"

"But—but—to *wager* me to this gentleman! I can hardly credit—"

"Should I win, I'll return your horses," Arbuthnot told Christopher. His color was rising and Lenore saw that he was trying to keep his gaze from her delectable body.

"But I—sir, you cannot mean—?" Lenore faltered, playing her part to perfection. She even managed a blush.

"I ask only that ye accompany me on my journey to Southampton," Arbuthnot said smoothly, "for my sister is most uncommonly dull at any season, and now that she's about to give birth to her fifth—!" He rolled his eyes. "But after a short stay in Southampton, I'll send ye by coach to London. Ye have the word of Simon Arbuthnot on it!" His voice rang.

"Come now, Lenore," Christopher urged. "Our friend here is a gentleman and will do you no hurt. He but wishes pleasant company for his journey. Ye'll be staying at his sister's. And I would hasten on to London and be back for ye speedily!"

"Well, I—" Lenore gave Christopher a helpless look. "I suppose there's little choice."

"'Tis no problem anyway," Christopher declared grandly, making an energetic bid to sweep up the dice. "For after such a long run of bad luck, I'm sure to win this toss."

"Not so fast there." Arbuthnot was too quick for him and his wiry fingers secured the dice first. "These dice have been lucky for me thus far, I'll stay with them."

Christopher gave Lenore an uneasy look as Arbuthnot threw out the dice.

An eight.

If he made this point—and he had been steadily successful thus far—she wondered how far out of town they would get before she was fighting for her virtue.

Now she leant over, watching tensely, as Arbuthnot threw the dice out again. She was studying his hands. They were the supple hands of a gambler. This was no simpering dandy but one of the gamblers who, like Christopher, haunted the fairs.

She and Christopher had been tricked.

And she might well pay for it!

Hardly breathing, they all stared down at the dice as they rolled to rest on the hard-packed earth.

It was an eight.

Arbuthnot had won.

He laughed as he reached forward to scoop up the dice but Lenore's yellow heel crunched down on his hand so hard the laugh turned into a cry of pain.

"Break the dice," she ordered Christopher tensely. "Break them!"

Christopher seized Arbuthnot by the arm before the man could wrench his hand from beneath Lenore's foot.

"Ho!" roared Arbuthnot. "This pair are cheating me at dice!"

Instantly they were surrounded by a curious crowd.

Lenore felt cold. Arbuthnot might well bluster it out—and then the crowd would turn on *them*.

From out of her skirts she suddenly produced a large pistol, aimed it at Arbuthnot's head. "This man has induced my foolish brother to play at dice with him," she told the crowd. "And now he has robbed us of everything. I say, break the dice!"

"Aye," called a big man. "Break the dice!" His cry was echoed by others from the crowd.

Crouched, held by Christopher's vicelike grip and with Lenore's hard heel crunching down on the back of his hand, Arbuthnot screwed his head around at the crowd. What he saw made him uneasy. These country crowds could be rough with a cheat, this brother and sister whom he'd thought so soft were tougher than he'd thought, and he had no doubt he'd be pummeled black and blue if the dice were broken. They might even break his bones.

"The dice are a gift from my father," he panted, still struggling in Christopher's iron grip. "They've always been lucky for me and I treasure them as a keepsake. I'll give back what I won from this lady and gentleman and keep the rest." He meant he'd keep what he had won from the yokels who'd been run out of the game so handily and long since vanished.

Lenore's violet eyes gleamed. Her instinct had been correct—and now she had him!

"Break the dice!" she commanded, crunching down harder on Arbuthnot's hand and feeling him wince.

Someone produced a hammer. The dice were broken, the weights discovered.

An angry growl went up from the crowd. Arbuthnot's face was as white as the lace at his cuffs. In a moment they'd be on him like a pack of dogs.

Lenore drew a deep breath, for she and Christopher were gamblers too, and she had compassion for her kind. "This man wagered everything against my accompanying him to Southampton," she told the crowd. "And my foolish brother was weak enough to accept the wager.

You'll not harm him for I want no violence done on my behalf." She brandished the pistol at the crowd to get their attention. "But he *should* be humiliated. I want him set on his horse backwards and my brother and I will ourselves see him through the city gates!"

There was a roar of laughter from the big fellow who had first echoed her "Break the dice!" "A good punishment, my lady!" he cried. "That will humble the fellow. Come on, lads!"

Caught up in his infectious laughter, a tense moment was dispelled in mirth and Arbuthnot was rushed along beside them to where the horses waited.

"Up, Arbuthnot!" Lenore mocked, as a dozen willing hands hoisted the man in mauve taffetas upward. "Up on your horse—backward!" She vaulted without help upon the gray mare's back and gave the crowd a light-hearted salute as Christopher seized Arbuthnot's bridle and wheeled his horse around, placing that unfortunate between them.

"We'll see he leaves the fair!" Christopher shouted above the mirthful catcalls.

"I think I recognize that woman," rose the voice of a tall farmer, who jostled forward, squinting at Lenore.

"Aye, you might," laughed Lenore, giving her horse a nudge with her knee, "for I raced here once." She turned and called over her shoulder as she rode away, "They called me the Angel of Worcester then!"

A murmur of excitement swept the crowd, for that race and Lenore's pell-mell escape with Geoffrey after it was over had become a legend in Wells.

Arbuthnot, riding wedged between them and facing backward, muttered, "I've a ruby of price hidden in my cuff. 'Tis yours if you ride away and leave me."

"Nay, we'll see ye through the gates," said Christopher equably. "Lest ye manage some lies to the authorities that set a search party after us—which might land us all in the same jail!"

"You see," Lenore told Arbuthnot demurely, "we're in the same line of work."

Arbuthnot's jaw dropped as he gazed from one to the other. "I'd never have known it," he declared honestly. "For to me ye seem like an aristocratic brother and sister, passing through the town and stopping to look in at the fair."

"And *you*," smiled Lenore, returning the compliment, "seem like a court dandy from my London days."

"Ye'll—ye'll not keep all the winnings?" Arbuthnot wheedled. His eyes had grown crafty again. "Ye'll share a bit with me, seeing as we're in the same line of work?"

Christopher laughed aloud. "Why should he not join us, Lenore?"

Lenore felt she wouldn't sleep nights if the dark-eyed man accompanied them. She'd always expect to wake up and see that a knife had been slipped between Christopher's ribs and find Arbuthnot's too-clever hands ripping off her chemise.

"I think not," she said sweetly. "We'll part company outside the city gates. And we'll keep our winnings. Let this be a lesson to you, Arbuthnot, to trust no one!"

They left him muttering ruefully, and rode light-heartedly away to the east with gold jingling in their pockets. Onward their chancy life led them, always onward to yet another town.

And then one day, Lenore looked up and her careless gaze fell upon the familiar spires of Oxford rising up out of the Salisbury Plain.

She caught her breath. How long had she ridden without caring which way they went? She could not return to Oxford, that city of spires and commerce, where the River Cherwell joined the Thames and flowed eastward toward London; that city where she had loved—and lost—Geoffrey so long ago. Where her daughter Lorena had been born. Where all her bright hopes had been quenched.

She took a grip on herself and lifted a rebellious chin. She *would* go into Oxford! She would ride in proudly beside Christopher, forget the past and the golden chains of bittersweet memories that bound her to it.

"There's always a bit of easy money in Oxford," Christopher was saying as they crossed the bridge—that same bridge over which she had ridden with Geoffrey so long ago. "Tradesmen, wealthy students, travelers—all eager for a game of dice, a town fattening off the gown."

"Yes," she said without interest.

At her tone he turned and gave her a sharp look. "You're looking pale," he observed critically.

"A slight headache—nothing really."

But that night, after they had made love in their room at a decent inn and Christopher was snoring into his pillow, Lenore rose and stood for a long time at the window. Outside the moonlight poured down over the tall university spires and the Great Tom Bell was sonorously tolling.

How that brought it all back to her! The Great Tom Bell had tolled when Lorena was born. Unbidden, tears coursed down her cheeks. She started as a hand touched her shoulder. It was Chris.

"You can't sleep?" he asked, and turned her gently about to face him. She turned her head away but he did not miss the tears that sparkled on her cheeks in the moonlight. "What's this?" he asked softly. "Am I so inept a lover that ye must cry about it?"

"You're not—inept," she choked. "The fault is mine. Oh, Chris, I used to live in Oxford. With Geoffrey. We went by the name of Daunt."

He drew a deep breath. "Ah, the tall fellow with the hard fist," he murmured. "Isn't it time you told me about him?"

And so she did. All of it. "My daughter was born here," she told him huskily. "In a house off Magpie Lane owned by a Mistress Watts. She is being brought up in the Cotswolds by a woman who believes her brother to be the father, but she is wrong—the child is Geoffrey's."

"Ye mean the tall fellow who knocked me down in York never acknowledged her?"

"That's right. He knew I'd been handfasted to a blue-eyed fair-haired Scot, and when Lorena was born she had the Scot's coloring. Geoffrey left me then ... It was all so long ago, Chris, but at the time I thought I'd die of grief."

Christopher was silent for a long time. When he spoke, it was almost as if he were talking to himself. "I did not realize how it was with you. You love him still."

" 'Tis a curse!" she burst out. "I cannot rid myself of him, no matter how I try. He—he *follows* me!"

"No, you take him with you, I fear. In your heart." He sighed. "So I have found myself a lady whose heart is otherwise engaged. Ah, well, 'tis not the first time for me."

She gave him a questioning look.

"There was a girl in Coventry with long black hair and a winsome smile," he said half humorously. "Though I tried my best to please her, I could not rid her mind of a certain yokel in large muddy boots. In the end she left me for him."

"I will not leave you, Chris."

He laughed. "That's as may be, my lady. Times change and so do lovers—even such as you and I. But come, we've done too much confessing already. Let's have us a sip of brandy"—he was pouring out from a smuggled bottle of French brandy as he spoke—"and get us back to bed where I'll hold ye safe and warm against your memories."

Grateful that he did not reproach her for feeling as she did, she took a sip of brandy. "And tomorrow we'll leave Oxford?" she asked hopefully.

"I'm afraid not, for we're out of funds," he admitted ruefully. "But another two weeks and we'll be gone, Lenore."

For Lenore those were terrible weeks. Unable to resist, she visited all her old haunts: the house on Magpie Lane where Mistress Watts had been so good to her. Mistress Watts was gone now and her white cat with her, but another cat, white save for a pair of golden paws and a waving golden tail, perhaps a grandkitten of the first, purred on the stairs. Lenore remembered how the white cat had leaped at a mouse and tripped her and brought on her labor.

Through the familiar streets she walked and remembered other days and other voices: Michael's, Lally's, Ned's. But the rich tones that overrode them all were Geoffrey's. His long shadow had come like a wedge between her and Christopher.

In an attempt to understand her better, Christopher too visited the house on Magpie Lane. Alone. He viewed the meager rooms Lenore and Geoffrey had occupied and shrewdly envisioned the life of privation they must have lived there.

Well, he would give her more! He would give her all the world had to offer, and he would do it with a pair of loaded dice! He squared his shoulders and found a dissolute don who had won all his friends' money—and relieved him of it.

That night began a lucky streak for Christopher. It seemed he could not lose. "Yet another day," he would tell a drooping Lenore. "The money here is easy."

But on the night he won a coach-and-six—and sold it for double its worth—he returned to the inn and swept her up in his arms.

"Start packing," he told her gaily. "We're for London!"

Lenore gave him a surprised look. It was on her lips to refuse to go back to London, but she steeled herself. Someday she was bound to run across Geoffrey again.

It might as well be now.

Dover's Hill, The Cotswolds

Chapter 28

"Lady" Bennett, that celebrated London bawd, adjusted her vizard mask, settled her wide turquoise taffeta skirts about her plump body more comfortably, and cast a speculative look about her.

The sight that met her shrewd brown eyes was a remarkable one, for she was seated atop a high flat plain known as "Dover's Hill", looking down into a natural amphitheatre where several men fought desperately with cudgels. Here every Whit week since around the turn of the century—save for a break during the Civil Wars—the famous Cotswold "Olimpick Games" had been held. But "Lady" Bennett's gaze passed over the contestants with bored indifference and sought instead the motley group of onlookers who thronged the hill. A great crowd had assembled here for the contestants had come from all over England to compete in feats of strength and every type was in evidence.

A roar rose from the crowd as one burly contestant was felled.

"See that?" cried the man beside her.

"Lady" Bennett nodded and wafted her fan delicately as her gaze passed over the crowd. The delicacy had been learnt in later years, for like Nell Gwyn, "Lady" Bennett had been the daughter of a bawd and brought up in a London whorehouse.

The "lady" in the turquoise skirts had not come to the Cotswold Olimpick Games" to admire a lot of lusty brawling men with huge muscles, but on a matter of business. Last year her chief competitor, that other famous London madam, "Mother" Moseley, had wheedled away from the crowd at these very Games a pair of most promising virgins. Spirited away to London by an offer of domestic employment from this apparently motherly soul, the two wenches had earned "Mother" Moseley a pretty penny, thought "Lady" Bennett enviously. So this year she had herself journeyed to the Games on the same kind of scouting expedition. Her need was great for she numbered among her principal clients the Duke of Faltrop, founder of the infamous Hellfire Club, whose demand for virgins was insatiable. Indeed, she had not been able to supply enough virgins for their orgies, even though in desperation she had tried to fill the gap with "manufactured" virgins she recruited from among the young whores of the London streets.

Behind her fan, "Lady" Bennett had just been bragging to the hard-faced fellow who had accompanied her here in a jolting coach, how one "manufactured" a virgin.

"First the girl must not practice her profession for several days. Two weeks would be best, although they do grumble at being off the streets for that long," she muttered with her famous lisp. "Then she must be coached in shy ways. She must be taught not to meet a man's eyes with a bold stare but to hang her head submissively when spoken to—are ye listening, John?"

Her companion, John, who had a patch over one eye—gouged out by a ladies' maid he'd kidnapped three years ago from the London docks where she was about to board ship for America—grunted. His one good eye was fixed firmly upon the combatants below, where the downed fellow was up and flailing again at his opponent, but he was mindful that his employer expected him to show interest. "D'ye drug them then?" he asked, for he himself was expert at doping drinks and slipping drugs into wine or even pasties—a talent "Lady" Bennett found useful in her establishment.

"Of course not," "Lady" Bennett lisped indignantly. "These be bright wenches as knows what they're doing, not country dolts who don't know a hackney coach from the backside of a cow! But after the wench has practiced mewling around a bit, *then* I give my client a chance to see her, sitting in my parlor looking downcast."

The man with the patch turned and gave her a blank incurious look. Few of the wenches at "Lady" Bennett's London establishment—even stolen ones—dared look downcast, for punishment for disobedience or listlessness was swift and terrible. He knew, for he meted it out himself. He glanced down at his gnarled hands with some approval; those hands had broken the spirit of many a defiant, screaming wench.

"I tell the client about the girl's background, how well brought up she is, how *pure*." "Lady" Bennett fanned herself more energetically. The fitful breeze did not penetrate her heavy black wig and she was half suffocating in this early unseasonable heat, but she had no mind to remove her wig and show the straggly graying hair beneath.

Black Patch wished she'd get on with it. She was growing garrulous these days—and fat. "But how do ye fool him that she's a virgin once he's in bed with her?" he demanded.

"Keep your voice down, John." "Lady" Bennett's famous lisp deepened in annoyance. It came from two missing front teeth which, although it certainly marred her fading beauty when she smiled, had not stood in her way in a day of only rudimentary dentistry when even duchesses might have broken, blackened or missing teeth.

She'd lost those teeth in her younger days in a wild battle with a Birmingham prostitute over the purse of a young dandy who's fallen to the street in his drunkenness; "Lady" Bennett had triumphed and the lisp and the missing teeth had become her trademark. "The wench must protest when he mounts her, of course—and cry out frequently as if in pain and declare she cannot bear it."

Her companion's lifted eyebrow said much. All the virgins he had bedded had been swiftly deflowered with a brutality that left them numb with pain and too terrified to protest.

"Ye do not understand the gentry, John," reproved his employer. " 'Tis the *chase* they enjoy as much as the fulfillment!"

John snorted. "No matter how the wench babbled, I'd know whether I was spearin' a virgin or a bawd."

"Lady" Bennett sighed, and brushed away an insect from her turquoise skirts with a swish of her ivory fan. "Of course the wench is also given a little vial of watered sheep's blood, which she must skillfully use to best advantage after the deed is done, John!"

"Look there!" cried John, forgetting all about virgins and leaning forward eagerly to watch the combatants. "The big one's down again. I think he's killed him this time!"

"Forget the Games, John. Remember we're here on business. The Duke of Faltrop will pay well for these fresh country wenches if they be comely. Look——there to your right down the hill, John. I think I'll just stroll down that way for *there* is the kind of girl I am looking for."

She was looking straight at Lorena as she spoke, for Lorena had come to the Games with Maude to compete in the country dancing. The sun was shimmering on Lorena's hemp-pale hair; she was wearing a new linen dress of robin's egg blue, and she was laughing. Even a hardened bully like John felt a brief stirring at the sight of her.

It had taken a deal of persuading for Flora to let Lorena accompany Maude to the Games, for the Games had fallen into disrepute since the death of Robert Dover, the lawyer whose patron, being Groom of the Bedchamber to James I, had secured not only the king's approval for the holding of these "Olimpick Games" on Thursday and Friday each Whit Week, but even some of the king's old clothes to add a royal touch to the gathering.

Dover had taken the Games seriously and had managed them with style and grace during his lifetime. He had caused a twin-towered wooden castle to be erected whose guns would boom out on Whitsun Thursday when Dover, dressed in the king's elegant castoffs, complete with plumed hat, rode into the great natural amptitheatre to announce the opening of the Games. A great and varied menu was provided—everything from backsword play, quintain, wrestling and leaping, headstands, coursing of greyhounds, horse racing, throwing the bar and hammer, jumping in bags—on and on. And for the women, dancing to bagpipes. The prizes were generous, admission was free and everybody came—even Will Shakespeare from nearby Stratford-on-Avon, it was said, for he mentioned the Games in his famous play *The Merry Wives of Windsor*.

But since Robert Dover's death in 1652 the Games had sadly degenerated and were now frequented by the worst sort. Pimps and madams from the brothels of London, cutpurses and thieves from all over England.

But Lorena had seemed so sad since Tabby's going that Flora hated to quench her now that she had shown an interest in something at last. She had agreed to Lorena's accompanying Maude only when she had learned that Maude's mother, Jane Cardwell, planned to take her whole brood along to enjoy this free event; her husband Jonas would be driving the cart.

Flora would not have been so complacent had she known that when Lorena arrived at the Cardwell's croft, Jonas Cardwell had just fallen from a rickety ladder in the barn and wrenched his back. His wife elected to stay and minister to her complaining spouse, and keep the younger children with her. So it was only Maude and

Lorena—Snowfire having been left at the smithy with Flora since the girls had expected to travel to Chipping Campden in a cart—who unhitched the cart and mounted the Cardwell's two indifferent horses for the ride to Dover's Hill that day.

The trip to Chipping Campden had been uneventful, but the narrow lane that wound up the ascending mile from Chipping Campden to Dover's Hill had been full of travelers bound for the Games, some of whom called out bawdy greetings to the blushing girls.

"One of us'll win the country dancing, I know we will," predicted Maude, abrim with confidence. "For haven't we been practicing all year?"

Looking about her at all the lithe, laughing country girls riding the hay carts, Lorena had her doubts. "What do you think the prize will be?" she wondered.

"Gold, I hope," said Maude fervently. "But Ma would be pleased if we won so much as a live turkey."

"What'll you do if it's gold and you win?"

"Why, then I'll have me a dowry! And I'll marry Joe Turner. Pa wouldn't stop me then even though he won't hear of it now because he says Joe can't take care of me."

Lorena gave Maude an affectionate look. With characteristic energy, Maude had spoke of little else ever since last fall when Joe Turner had wandered into Twainmere selling pins and needles from a pack on his back, and stayed to help out the local cobbler, for Joe was versatile even though impecunious. Joe and Maude had taken one look at each other and it had been love at first sight, but Joe made barely enough to keep himself and, as Maude's father so frequently pointed out, Maude was a strapping girl of good appetite.

Once they arrived atop the ridge northwest of Chipping Campden where the Games were being held, the two girls watered their horses at a public trough provided for the travelers and fed them the hay they had packed in, in large bags behind them, to the merriment of the people in the carts they passed. Then, carrying their lunch in a big linen square, they mingled with the crowd.

"I'm glad we rode in bareback," muttered Maude as they passed a group of furtive-looking men whose darting eyes unclothed them. "I think our saddles might have been stolen."

"I think we'll be lucky if the horses aren't stolen," said Lorena uneasily, looking around her and sizing up the crowd.

"D'ye think so?" Maude looked alarmed. "Ah, but they wouldn't do that the first day, would they? The Games go on another day, but the dancing contest's today and we'll be going home tonight. Look out!" She grasped Lorena's arm and jerked her aside as they walked uphill past a broken stump. "There's a beehive there at the base of that stump! You'd think someone would have cleared it away with all this crowd coming, wouldn't you?" She sounded indignant.

Lorena looked down nervously at the gray beehive she had almost blundered into. From it there issued a steady buzzing. Had she stepped on that hive, she'd not have been dancing today! She ducked as a bee, annoyed that strangers should venture so close to the home hive, flew at her face.

"We might as well eat our lunch now," said Maude, "for there'll be no safe place to leave it, and we can see the horses from here."

Lorena nodded and the two girls sat down to enjoy their lunch. Maude observed that the pair of women wrestlers who now stepped forward to the delight of the crowd, looked more like cows than women and Lorena laughed, showing her even white teeth.

It was while she was laughing at Maude's remark that "Lady" Bennett caught sight of her.

"Look," cried Maude in amazement. "I think the big blonde is going to tear the red-haired woman's head off!"

Lorena looked on in distaste, and wondered if she'd get grass stains on her new dress. She blinked into the sunlight and saw that the large blonde woman, who styled herself "Soho Sal" and had breasts as large as coconuts, did indeed have both her huge arms wrapped around her red-haired opponent and appeared to be breaking her neck. But as they watched, fascinated, the red head, "Bristol Bess," kneed her tormentor in the stomach and the blonde let go her hold and staggered backward.

"Awful sight, isn't it, girls?" lisped a friendly voice behind them. Maude and Lorena turned to meet the broad smile of a handsome woman of medium height and florid complexion, her face above its ingratiating smile hidden by a vizard mask, her ample figure squeezed into a gown of turquoise taffeta garnished at the bodice with seed pearls and gold thread.

Maude gasped at the sight of so rich a gown, but Lorena said in her clear sweet voice, "Indeed it is! I hope they don't kill each other."

"Oh, they won't. I've seen them fight before," laughed the woman, languidly waving her ivory fan. The fair-haired girl who'd answered had an educated lilt to her voice, she noted. And a beauty too. Faltrop would pay a price for her, all right! "I'm from London," she explained, "and I've seen Soho Sal fight at the Bear Garden. And Bristol Bess too."

"You're from London?" Lorena was instantly interested. She moved over to make room for the newcomer on the grass.

"Why, yes. I'm Lady Bennett." This with a slightly haughty intonation that was spoilt as she sank down awkwardly in her tight clothes.

Both young girls looked respectful at the thought that they were addressing a titled lady—exactly the effect "Lady" Bennett had intended to achieve.

"This is Lorena and I'm Maude," Maude said instantly. "Won't you have some lunch?"

"Lady" Bennett, who generally lunched on gin, blinked a refusal and the girls finished their lunch watching the wrestlers. When Bristol Bess disposed of Soho Sal, the sound of bagpipes struck up over the din and Maude roused herself. "We came to compete in the dancing contest," she told "Lady" Bennett. "D'ye think it could be about to start?"

"Oh, no, that's not for another hour yet, my dear." "Lady" Bennett was an authority on the time of the dance contest. It was the one event of the afternoon in which she was interested as it would show her a cavorting selection of young country girls, many of whom might be tempted by an offer of a job in London. Even as these two might.

"Do you work around here, Lorena?"

"No, I live at home. In Twainmere, like Maude."

"A village, I take it? Ah, then I suppose you two like the rural life and wouldn't be interested in coming to London?"

Maude was silent but Lorena said eagerly, "Oh, no, I've always wanted to go to London! Sometimes somebody comes by and brings us the London gossip." Her voice had a wistful note that "Lady" Bennett was quick to catch.

"Do they now? Well, when I left, all London was laughing because Nell Gwyn—she's the king's mistress, you know—had bought her drunken old mother a nice house with a little stream running through the yard out back. And the old lady got so drunk on gin she fell into the stream and drowned—in that little bit of water! All London's laughing over a woman who could drink whole jugs of gin—yet drowned in a cupful of water!"

Maude's ready laugh rang out but Lorena frowned. What was there to laugh about in some unfortunate old woman drowning?

Astutely, "Lady" Bennett caught that look. "But I see ye're softhearted, my dear!" she cried in a solicitous voice. "Yes, wasn't it terrible that they should laugh over that? And all because the poor thing started out as Nellie Gwyn did—as a bawd?" She gave her fan an irritable tap. She too had started out as a bawd and often she drank

417

too much gin and some day she'd grow old too—and perhaps drown in a cupful of water with no one about to save her.

"I suppose some people will laugh at anything," muttered Lorena, and Maude looked affronted. "I didn't mean you, Maude," she added hastily. "I meant—London."

Gently reared, guessed "Lady" Bennett. Good manners, tenderhearted. Ah, this got better and better! She had a feeling this was going to be her lucky day. She kept talking brightly to both girls about London until it was time for the dance contest. Then Maude and Lorena joined a number of other bright-eyed country girls who danced and stamped to the wild music of the bagpipes.

Although they were both light-footed and graceful, neither Lorena nor Maude had had the advantage of practicing to music and both could have used more practice. So even though they stamped and whirled and smiled, neither won a prize, and they returned panting and disappointed to flop down beside "Lady" Bennett.

"The judges did notice ye," consoled "Lady" Bennett, who had already singled out three or four likely lasses among the dancers, "until their attention was attracted by those girls who were tossing their skirts so high. But they noticed ye till then."

But Lorena had been noticed by someone besides the judges. From the crowd a man with a V-shaped scar on his forehead had eyed her avidly as she danced while recognition dawned on him. Slippery little wench! He'd combed the countryside for her in vain after she had darted out of that trout pool last summer and ridden away. *Now* he'd find out who she was.

But he hesitated to approach Lorena while she sat beside that richly dressed woman in turquoise, for he believed her to be some relative. If the girl recognized him, she well might make some accusation and that woman looked more than capable of handing him over to the magistrate. Not that he'd actually *done* anything; it was what he had *intended* to do that gave him this feeling of guilt. So he held back, intending to seek out the girl later—perhaps when darkness had fallen and most of the onlookers had drifted back to Chipping Campden and those who had pitched their tents hereabouts were strolling through the summer darkness or lounging by their campfires. He hoped she was staying overnight here on Dover's Hill, but judging by the rich garments of the lady in the vizard mask they well might have rooms at the best inn in Chipping Campden! Now he eased near them, intending to keep an eye on her, lest she leave the Games early.

Fortunately for her peace of mind, Lorena was serenely unaware of the scarred man's steady scrutiny—just as she had been that day at the trout pool.

"Ah, now here's a boring event," sighed "Lady" Bennett, fanning herself. "Throwing the sledge." Her brown eyes were fixed in distaste on the contestants, giant men who had come up and were standing almost uncomfortably close to the three seated on the grass. "They do say that huge man yonder, the 'Newcastle Wonder,' will win it," she added, nodding indifferently at a huge fellow whose pinhead rode a giant frame and who was now flexing the spatulate fingers of his enormous hamlike hands.

Had Lorena but known it, this "Newcastle Wonder" was Caleb, from whom Lenore had fled so precipitately at Wallham.

When the law had closed in and Sedgewick was taken, Caleb had fled Wallham to the west, believing the main pursuit would tend toward York or Newcastle, or north to the Scottish border. For a time he had hidden in the wild hills, hiding in the bracken whenever he saw a horse and rider, taking a rabbit or a bird now and again for sustenance. Then when he reasoned the chase had cooled, he had ventured to Carlisle and remained there in a small cozy inn brooding over his downfall. It was all caused, to his way of thinking, by women—first by his unfaithful wife and now, by another woman: Lenore Frankford. Sometimes during those days, wrapped in a nondescript cloak and with a wide-brimmed hat pulled down to hide his features, he had walked out and stared at the great Roman wall that lay to the north of the town and stretched away to Wallsend in the west and past Wallham, seat of his downfall, in the east.

It was then that he would shake his fist at the Wall and curse all those runaway couples who dashed nine miles away across the Scottish Border to Gretna Green to be married by a smith at his forge, with an anvil for an altar. *Fools,* he would snarl to himself. Damn fool men, being made fools of by women—even as he himself had been.

At those times a red mist would spread over his piglike eyes and he would flex his great spatulate hands yearningly and remember Sylvie, beautiful teasing evil Sylvie—and wish he could kill her again. Sometimes Sylvie's image became confused in his mind and Sylvie would take on Lenore's features, and the image of Lenore Frankford pulsed and shimmered through his mind, borne by that red tide. Had it not been for the Frankford woman he'd be a rich man today instead of wondering when the landlord would ask him for the money he did not have—and wondering what to do next!

His hatred for Lenore grew and grew until finally in his mind she merged with Sylvie and they became one. Some days he could not be sure which he had killed, but then he would sit down and in his madness, slowly, methodically get them straight. Sylvie had been his wife, Lenore had stolen his horse. That was all that separated them in his deranged mind.

But when the innkeeper in Carlisle began to look at him in a lowering way, Caleb became afraid the law would be brought in to press payment of the debt—and then they'd discover that he was on the run from the authorities in Newcastle for murder plus a variety of other crimes.

So when spring came again, it had found him— through desperation, not design—on his old circuit once more, going from fair to fair. He shunned the north of England, hewed to the south, and would not even have ventured so far north as the Cotswold Hills had not the "Olimpick Games" drawn him like a magnet.

Now he stood flexing his great muscles and pondering whether the burly man from Lancaster on his right or the lanky giant from Southampton on his left would be the man to beat, never dreaming that the daughter of the woman on whom he had pinned his hatred was seated but a few feet from him on Dover's Hill.

"Dull, dull," muttered "Lady" Bennett, fidgeting in her tight dress. "Give me the theater any day—not these rough country games."

"Oh, do you know the theater?" Lorena had been waiting for an appropriate opening, for "Lady" Bennett had given both girls her London address and explained languidly that she was in dire need of upstairs maids in her London house and hoped they might be interested. She had looked brightly at Lorena and Lorena's color had risen a little higher. It had galled her to be considered "upstairs maid" material when her mother probably attended the same London parties as did this grand lady. So the remark about the theater was doubly welcome.

"Aye, that I do," affirmed "Lady" Bennett, and there was the ring of truth in her voice. "Nell Gwyn, and all the other actresses—I know them all."

"Then you must know my mother." Lorena's voice rose proudly. "Lenore Frankford?"

Behind her vizard mask, "Lady" Bennett's eyes widened in amazement. The Iron Virgin of the London stage had a daughter? "*You*," she cried in a loud carrying voice. "*You* are Lenore Frankford's daughter?"

About to swing the heavy sledge, the giant Caleb's huge bulk swung around in time to see Lorena toss her head in a gesture so like Lenore's, and say defiantly, "Yes, I am Lorena Frankford—Lenore Frankford's daughter. My mother is an actress on the London stage."

All his pent-up anger at Lenore boiled up in Caleb

at once at the sight of this chit of a girl who calmly claimed to be Lenore's flesh and blood, boiled up and exploded.

"Ho there!" he bellowed. "You, the Frankford girl. *Your mother stole my horse!*"

He came at her in a rush and Lorena, bewildered, but seeing this awesome colossus bearing down on her, roaring, scrambled to her feet and darted away.

His boots pounding, Caleb pursued her and the crowd parted prudently to let this furious giant pass— even as they would have parted to let through a charging bull.

In his mind, burning red with hatred of the woman he felt had caused his downfall at Wallham and near cost him his life at the end of a rope in Newcastle, Caleb confused the running girl ahead of him with Lenore, or perhaps he wanted to vent his rage on the flesh of her flesh. In any event, he did not pause, but continued to charge after her. Behind him the other contestants stood open-mouthed, gawking at this giant gone berserk.

Lorena was fleet, but she knew with terror that the monster who thundered behind her had staying power— and no one in that stunned crowd had thought to trip him or try to drive him off. Now her mind worked furiously.

Ahead and to her left she saw the broken tree stump where Maude had jerked her back from the beehive on the ground as they proceeded up the hill. Now as she ran, a desperate plan was forming in her mind. She bore to the right so that Caleb must pass the tree on that side, and then darted left just past it so that Caleb's big feet pounded over the sod toward the stump.

She had taken a long chance for Caleb, the "Newcastle Wonder," was closing the gap.

Lorena took a quick glance back and saw his big foot come squarely down upon the gray hive.

The bees—some of which Caleb's boot had crushed —reacted violently to this unwarranted attack upon their home. The leaders buzzed upward toward Caleb's face. Now a wave of bees was swarming out and pursuing their attacker in a cloud. From behind him a shout of warning went up from the watching crowd, but it was too late. Already the angry bees were zooming around his ears, now they were darting in, in a suicidal attack, to drive their stingers into his face. Before their onslaught the giant flinched and staggered to one side. As half a dozen of the leaders stung him in unison he let out an anguished howl and forgot all about Lorena, intent only upon escape as he ran frenziedly hither and thither, bellowing, stumbling and beating at his face, trying to rid himself of the pursuing bees.

The crowd, stunned at first, had now broken ranks and was spilling down the hill, attracted by what seemed a new kind of game. But farther down Lorena had a head start and kept on going. She had had enough of the Games and of the half-drunken raucous crowd. Being pursued by a madman had been too much—she was going home!

"Lorena!" shouted Maude. At first as stunned as the rest, she had broken free ahead of the crowd and was running downhill, giving a wide berth to the crushed beehive. Out of the corner of her eye she could see the "Newcastle Wonder" who was now charging like a wounded bull across the great natural ampitheatre pursued by a long dark streamer of bees. Maude ducked automatically as a bee zoomed by her and plunged downhill after her friend.

From the crowd, Lorena's scarred attacker of the trout pool had watched in open-mouthed astonishment as big Caleb turned and charged at the girl. He could only imagine that she had called out same taunt, for he had been too far away to hear what was said. He had fought his way through the milling throng and now he could see that Lorena was heading for a pair of horses that were tethered to a tree at the base of the hill. She was about to mount up, he would lose her! Pushing aside several people who stood restlessly gawking, he now joined those who were sprinting downhill after Maude and Lorena and the "Newcastle Wonder." But halfway down, the toe of his boot caught in a tree root and sent him headlong.

When he sat up, groaning, he found he could not rise. His ankle had been painfully twisted by the fall, and he had been trod upon by one or two behind who could not dodge his fallen form in their path.

Cursing, he managed to gain his footing with the assistance of a passerby and stood leaning on a stout stick someone handed him. But the space where the horses had been tethered was empty now and Lorena was nowhere in sight. He looked upon the spot where she had disappeared and the taste of regret was bitter in his mouth. He had meant at least to find his own mount and ride after her but his ankle was too painful even for that. He must needs be taken home ignominiously in a cart.

He looked about for a cart driver to carry him there—and he was lucky. From the crowd, with his rolling gait, came the heavyset figure of Tom Prattle of Twainmere. Bleary-eyed but otherwise in health, Tom had come to Dover's Hill not to watch the Games but in hopes of making enough coins to keep him in gin for a week by hauling away the injured—for there were always injured bystanders to be hauled away from the Games since brawling and fighting usually broke out in the crowd before the first day was over. As for the "Newcastle Wonder's" sudden pursuit of Lorena, Tom had seen the whole thing. It had irritated him to see so much attention called to Lenore's brat and he was still glowering over it as the cart jolted along toward Chipping Campden. When the injured man lying on a pile of smelly blankets in the cart behind him asked if he knew who the girl was who'd been pursued down the hill by the giant, Tom replied in a surly voice, "She be my niece by marriage, Lorena Frankford, though I'm not proud of her." He had then launched into a vicious tirade against Lorena's mother, whom he had once pursued to the smithy in Twainmere—and look what came of it!

By showing interest and letting Tom talk, the man with the V-shaped scar soon knew all about Lorena, who now lived in the cottage behind the abandoned smithy with the vicar's widow.

"The wench will soon be wed, you'll see," Tom pronounced gloomily. "Have to, no doubt!" There was a sneer in his voice and behind him, the passenger's horse which was following on a lead behind the cart gave a sudden whinny, as if in derision.

The passenger pricked up his ears. His eyes beneath the V-shaped scar narrowed. "*That* kind of girl, is she?"

Tom shrugged. "Not if Flora can help it. She'll try to keep Lorena pure till she can wed her to some young buck. But the wench has wild blood. Last summer she rode into the Demming's barn stark naked. Watt Demming stepped out to ask her what she was doing there and she jumped back on her horse and rode away like a wild thing. Watt told the whole town about it!"

His passenger's eyes glinted. Well indeed did he remember that day last summer, and the young girl whose lovely white body had been silvered by the water in that sylvan setting. Remembering her now, his blood felt fevered, and he could still feel the silky wet feel of her smooth back as he tried to grasp her and fell instead into the trout pool.

The man with the V-shaped scar was a bachelor. Well-off and selfish in his pursuits, uninterested in producing offspring, it had not occurred to him to marry. He had a housekeeper who was an indifferent cook, and a scullery maid—the post was frequently vacant and had to be refilled—whose bed he frequented until the wench became either pregnant or sulky at this double duty, at which point he tossed her out to fend for herself and found another for the post.

Not until he had snatched at—and lost—the naked girl in the pool last summer had he considered marriage, what it would be like to have such a lovely young creature serving his meals, accompanying him to market and to church while people murmured and nudged each other and envied him, what it would be like to have her lissome body in his bed every night.

That the vicar's widow was bent on keeping Lorena "pure" was indeed good news, for the thought of marriage with the young beauty had taken possession of his mind and seeing her again had only inflamed his desire.

"So ye think the vicar's widow might be ripe for a marriage offer for the girl if the man be responsible and well-to-do?" he shouted at the driver's stolid back.

"Flora?" Tom Prattle turned around, his red-nosed face looking surprised. "I don't think 'responsible' or 'well-to-do' got much to do with it. Talk was that the vicar had betrothed the girl to the miller, but Flora thought he was too old for her and after the vicar died, nothing came of it." In point of fact, Tom had gotten that story from Lola Hepworth when he cut some wood at her house one day, for Tom was down now to doing any sort of job. Drink had been the ruin of him; he was close to losing his cottage and had taken to doing odd jobs where he could. He had admired the handsome Lola, swaggering about, and she, unable to resist flattery from men, no matter how menial their position, had preened herself in the glow of that admiration. She had sat down on a log before the sweating Tom as he chopped up kindling and told him all the things the vicar had told her about Lorena. "Now the miller's dead so can't nothing come of it," Tom added with some satisfaction.

His paying passenger, reclining in the bouncing cart while the heavyset driver yelled all this information back at him, had been listening contentedly until he heard that last. But now his scarred brow furrowed.

"Wants a young man for her, does she?" he murmured in a voice Tom Prattle, cursing as the cartwheel hit a stone and nearly overturned, could not hear. Well off he certainly was, with a good farmhouse over Cirencester way, but young he wasn't. Still, seeing the girl again, swaying and laughing in her country dance with her robin's-egg blue skirts blowing in the breeze, had made him want her with such an aching violence that he was more than willing to marry her—he was even willing to pay a handsome price to the vicar's widow for the privilege. And now this bulky, bleary-eyed relative of the girl's up there ahead of him driving the cart, was telling him that he wouldn't qualify, that Flora was set on having a young man for Lorena.

"Flora oughta get married herself and forget about Lorena," Tom howled back over his shoulder. "Good cook and housekeeper like her! Any man'd be lucky to get her if he didn't have to take that young hellion into the bargain!"

His passenger had been chewing on his lip as the cart jolted along the road to Chipping Campden. Now he gave Tom Prattle's broad back a look of astonishment, as if he had discovered human intelligence in a crossroads marker.

"Of course," he murmured, "of course." He leaned forward. "Take me to Twainmere," he told Tom Prattle. "I'll put up at the inn there and let the doctor splint this leg properly."

Tom thought that a peculiar request. He turned around to argue. "Don't have no regular doctor in Twainmere," he protested. "It's clouding up to rain and there's plenty doctors at Chipping Campden." He was thinking that he could have himself a bit of gin at a tavern in Chipping Campden whilst he waited for the doctor to splint his passenger's leg and then take off on the profitable journey to Cirencester.

"Never mind," called his passenger firmly, leaning back against the pile of blankets and catching hold of the side of the cart to make the jolting ride over rutted roads more comfortable. He cast a tranquil took upward at the great thunderheads forming overhead. "Take me to Twainmere."

Claremont Court, Kent

Chapter 29

A summerlike warmth had descended upon Kent that spring and the lush scented air had beguiled Letiche Wyndham and her guest and kinsman the Marquis de Vignac out of the great paneled halls of Geoffrey's stately mansion and into the gardens. Now they were strolling through a maze of tall clipped boxwood which had been laid out in old King Henry's time and was now taller than a man. In places the dense box had grown so close together that sometimes the Marquis stepped aside, pressing his sky blue coat and orchid satin breeches against the hedge so that Letiche's wide creamy satin skirts might swish by.

The marquis was looking down from his greater height upon his kinswoman's complicated auburn coiffure and meditating that with so much pale shimmering embroidery and such a froth of creamy lace at her bosom, Letiche looked innocent as a bride. But—and his brows lifted in amusement at the thought—never had a bride been less innocent!

Now he studied Letiche's small arrogant figure and pondered how he could make use of her.

A great master criminal had been lost in de Vignac. Had he been born in a hovel instead of a tall chateau, he might have masterminded extortions that would have been forever celebrated in the annals of crime.

As it was, his early advantages, his great inherited wealth—now mostly vanished for the marquis lived as extravagantly as a prince of the blood—had enabled him to perfect more intricate intrigues. In France he had by his machinations brought a duke to suicide and a marquise to the madhouse. These ventures—whispered of but never affirmed—had earned for him the name the "Black Marquis" and a wary respect tinged with fear.

But careless Letiche cared nothing for that. Had she not always flirted with danger? Had she not always toyed with such wickedly attractive and unstable playmates as Andre Malraux? And was the Black Marquis not her kinsman and, back in the days of her wanderings among the apple orchards of her uncle's estates, briefly her lover? And did she not hold Geoffrey tightly bound by the invisible bonds of memory of their shared sorrow in the death of their children? Honor would not let Geoffrey desert her! What had she to fear from any of them?

So Letiche had schemed away the idle days in Kent, while the Marquis de Vignac played a more dangerous game in London.

Now, frowning as they strolled together beneath blue skies through the garden maze of Claremont Court, de Vignac reached a decision. He decided to put to use a talent of Letiche's which he had used before, in his mousetrapping of the unfortunate marquise, who had scorned him and ended in a madhouse for her temerity.

That talent was forgery.

Letiche's clever, ever-moving hands could write with delicate tracery or bold scrawl. As a child she had loved practicing her penmanship and had enjoyed copying signatures and other people's handwriting. She had tried a dozen different styles before she settled on the elegant sweeping strokes with which she penned her own notes.

She had entered into de Vignac's schemes in France with the enthusiasm of a wicked child. She was still like that child—just a little older, a little harsher in her judgments. So when de Vignac asked thoughtfully, "Letiche, have ye practiced your penmanship lately?" she turned to him with a roguish smile.

"I have lost none of my skill. Why do you ask?"

"And could you"—he coughed delicately, one eyebrow quirked, looking at her—"contrive a reasonable facsimile of your husband's signature?"

"I can duplicate it absolutely," cried Letiche, who had done so on more than one occasion without Geoffrey's knowledge when she wanted some trinket, had not the cash, and Geoffrey was not readily available. Geoffrey was aware of his wife's talent and that she had several times signed his name, but always it was for small things like a fur muff or a pair of gloves embroidered with seed pearls, items she could not resist. He had overlooked this fault in her just as he overlooked her wayward tongue and her insistence on importing French furniture and French friends. It was all part of Letiche.

It had never occurred to Geoffrey that Letiche would use his name fraudulently in any but the most trivial matter. That she would put his life in jeopardy he had not even considered.

Now de Vignac leaned forward, for here was the important part, the item on which all the rest depended. "And can ye get his signet ring so that ye might stamp the wax with his seal?"

Letiche hesitated. That would be more difficult for Geoffrey *wore* that ring and seldom took it off.

"If ye could arrange to 'borrow' it, I could have it duplicated," he suggested.

She met his eyes, her own sparkling. "What is it ye have in mind, Raoul?"

The revolutionary business had gone ill of late. The king of France sat even more securely on his throne in spite of the attempts of a handful of disgruntled expatriate nobles to unseat him. But de Vignac had recently been faced with an unpleasant shortage of funds. The inexhaustible well of resources that had been his to squander since birth seemed to be drying up.

He needed money.

"I have thought of a way for you to go to Whitehall," he said with a thin smile.

"Whitehall?" Letiche's curiosity was aroused and her taffeta petticoats beneath her creamy satin gown stopped rustling as she paused to consider him. "And how will you manage that, Raoul?"

"With some very damning letters that will link Geoffrey will Nell Gwyn. Love letters. If they reached the king, Geoffrey would be the worse for it. He will pay a price to have them returned—even though he knows he did not write them. I will say my informant chose me because I am known to be close to his family—meaning you, Letiche—and because I would be a "safe" person to make the exchange, the letters for a sum of money."

Letiche's laughter bubbled. "You are short of funds again, Raoul!"

De Vignac sighed. "It seems I am always short of late, *ma petite*. But your Geoffrey is never short."

"*Now,* you mean." Her voice was rueful. "I remember other days—leaner ones."

"Ah, yes, my poor Letiche. I do remember how you put up with him during those lean years. Ah, well, you have won through handsomely. Except to Whitehall," he added negligently, taking a pinch of snuff from a handsomely enameled gold box.

No pangs of conscience at the wrong she would be doing her husband influenced her as she said, meditatively chewing the tip of one finger, "I would be afraid to 'borrow' the signet ring, even for a night. Geoffrey would guess who had taken it."

"Then on the night we arrange, you must put something in his drink."

Letiche looked apprehensive. "You mean, *drug* him?"

"That is a coarser way of putting it," sighed de Vignac. "I will be waiting with the letters and together we—"

"You mean I am not to write them?"

"The more words written the more chance of error. We do not want Geoffrey to decide he can have them declared a forgery." He lifted a quelling hand to her protests. "I am aware of your skill, Letiche, but your husband is a dangerous man and not easily cozened. If I am to arrange this jaunt to Whitehall for you—"

"*And* a nice bit of coin for yourself as well, Raoul! Don't forget that," she added tartly.

De Vignac paused and considered her, his face a calm mask. She had become thoroughly detestable, he thought idly, since those long-ago days when they had strolled through the orchards of her uncle in France and he had delved under her ruffled skirts beneath the apple trees. Then she had had a delightful young wickedness about her. Now she was merely base. Still—he needed her. "Of course, *chérie,*" he agreed smoothly. "But the letters will appear to have been written by a scribe. I will write them myself—and you will sign them, with Geoffrey's signature." He fished about for a small vial with some white powder in it. "On the night I tell you, you will put this in your husband's drink at supper."

"What is it?" Letiche asked suspiciously, sniffing it.

"A harmless drug. Geoffrey will sleep soundly through the night. You can slip the signet ring from his finger and sign and seal the letters, and then return the ring. He will be none the wiser."

"You will be here?"

"Yes, of course, *ma petite.* So that all this incriminating passion committed to paper will be swiftly spirited away and not found in your possession. You see, I am protecting you."

"Geoffrey will vow that he neither wrote nor signed those letters."

"Of course he will. And I will agree that they are

undoubtedly forgeries. But I will show him one of the
letters and tell him it is the only one given me by the
go-between for the blackmailer, and I will ask him if the
King would believe them to be forgeries? That will give
him pause, for Geoffrey is as aware as the rest of us that
a man comes between a king and his mistress at his peril.
I will explain that my informant tells me that the letters
were never delivered to Mistress Gwyn and she knows
nothing of them, that they were bought from a former
chambermaid at the Hart, who obviously was acting for
some third party."

"Will not Geoffrey seek out this chambermaid?"

A crafty smile broke over de Vignac's cynical face.
"Indeed he will. He will inquire after her at the Hart and
discover she is missing."

Letiche stared at him. "You didn't—?" she asked in
an altered voice, for murder was not yet in her reper-
toire.

"No, of course I didn't," said de Vignac haughtily.
"She simply became one of 'Lady' Bennett's girls and has
since left her employ and dropped from sight."

"After visiting the Hellfire Club! Is she not the one?
It is rumored two chambermaids from London inns are
missing. Drowned in the Thames, some say."

De Vignac shifted his heavily brocaded shoulders
and frowned. Letiche was too damned well informed.
Both chambermaids were indeed at the bottom of the
river—he had had it from Andre who had been a guest of
Lord Wilsingame's at the Hellfire Club's last meeting.
Surely Andre had not been so rash as to tell Letiche a
story which might involve him in murder charges if it
came out! Of course it had not been *deliberate* murder,
but both women had refused hysterically to participate in
some especially nasty rite to be held in the converted
chapel. One of them had become violent as Wilsingame
tried to drag her toward the chapel. She had broken free
and struck him in the face. With a drunken howl, he had
leaped for her. She had lurched backward to avoid him
and tumbled into the river, dragging with her the other

chambermaid who had been bound to her by a length of chain. Wilsingame had teetered on the bank, too drunk to assist, and both the screaming wenches had been swept away by the current before anyone could reach them, borne to the bottom by the heavy chain—and drowned.

It would indeed be a nasty scandal if it came out.

"The plan is foolproof," he told her coldly.

Indeed it seemed to be. As were all of Raoul's plans. Letiche remembered a certain beautiful marquise in France, a woman of wealth who had scorned young impoverished Letiche d'Avigny—and who had paid a terrible price for it, was paying for it yet if she still survived in the madhouse outside Boulogne in which her enraged husband had incarcerated her. Letiche had been a part of that scheme too, although no one but a madwoman to whom no one would listen knew that. She, Letiche, was *safe*. She smiled at the memory and gave the poker-faced de Vignac a slanted, appraising look.

She well understood what de Vignac was offering her—Whitehall, at a price which would be "a sum of money" extorted from her husband, money said to be for the blackmailer as indeed it was, and a visit to Whitehall for herself as a favor to her kinsman who had been so helpful to Geoffrey in this "unfortunate matter." She never doubted de Vignac's ability to bring the scheme to a successful conclusion.

Best of all, it would not involve her. For the marquis wanted no estrangement between herself and the now rich and powerful Geoffrey; he would be careful to arrange it so that Geoffrey would never know his wife had had anything to do with it.

"That it should be Nell Gwyn . . . " she murmured in discontent.

"Would you prefer it to be Louise de Keroualle to whom we direct Geoffrey's affections?"

"No, I suppose not."

"It was Nell Gwyn," he said, watching her like a cat, "whose enmity cost the Frankford woman her place in the King's Company of Royal Players."

Letiche's auburn eyes widened. This was news indeed. So it was Nell Gwyn who had removed Lenore Frankford from the London stage "Letters to Mistress Gwyn then."

"Besides, to use Louise de Keroualle would be to involve the French, and I prefer to keep this little intrigue as far from home as possible."

"Of course." Letiche stuffed the vial containing the white powder into the cleft of her creamy lace bosom. She turned with a little rustle of scented taffeta petticoats. "Geoffrey is in the West Country now, on king's business he told me." She began to pout. "He is gone so much— can it all really be king's business, Raoul? Or is it that orange girl?"

"It is really king's business," de Vignac laughed. "I have had him followed."

Letiche blinked. Could there be more to this, that Raoul would go to so much trouble? She dismissed the thought. Raoul was always careful with his intrigues, which was why they were so successful. She need lose no sleep over this one. "Will you take a note to Andre for me when you go back to London, Raoul?"

"Of course, but hurry, *ma petite,* for I must be off. I would prefer Claremont Court to see little of me now that we are about to advance our small endeavor."

Letiche gave him an understanding smile and when he was mounting his horse she hurried out with a warm note to Andre scolding him for his neglect of her and urging his swift reappearance at Claremont Court. She gave it into de Vignac's hand. "Thank you, Raoul." She pressed his hand. "Except for Andre, I feel you are my only true friend." She batted her lashes and favored him with her bright insincere smile.

Masking the triumph that rose in him at his easy victory over Letiche's few remaining scruples, de Vignac bore her little hand to his lips and kissed it, a graceful gesture, then straightened up smiling and took his leave.

As he rode away from Claremont Court, the great branching oaks of the park shading the path for his horse, he thought of what he would put in those letters and smiled to himself. Geoffrey would pay for them all right—or go to the block. And Letiche would never dare to admit her involvement.

It was indeed a foolproof plan—but only for the Marquis de Vignac, whom men called uneasily the "Black Marquis."

Twainmere, The Cotswolds

Chapter 30

Fierce thunderstorms lashed the Cotswolds that summer, ripping slates from the steeply slanted roofs and sending dislodged stones rumbling down cottage chimneys. On one such night, while the thunder rolled, Flora awoke to a flash of blue-white lightning and clutched her hand to her mouth.

She had had a terrible dream.

In her dream Lorena had come into the house and her lips had been moving, she had been talking, saying terrible things that caused Flora to clap her hands over her ears in an attempt to shut out the girl's voice. And at the end Flora had been screaming and crying herself, her whole life destroyed.

Now Flora, who dreamed so seldom but whose dreams always seemed to portend something, clutched a shaking hand over her mouth and tried desperately to remember, *remember* what Lorena had been saying. It seemed to her in a confused way that Lorena had simply *appeared* and her happiness had been shattered forever.

Another flash of lightning lit the room with an eerie white glow and the thunder rolled again, reverberating through the dark house. Flora jumped up and managed to close the windows before the rain came pelting down, huge drops that crashed angrily against the windows.

Troubled and shaken, she climbed back into bed. It had been a very long time since she had had one of *those* dreams, and always they had a meaning, although that meaning was not always immediately clear to her. Before the Battle of Worcester, she had dreamt of an England soaked in blood—and Jamie had died in that battle. And now this . . .

Her sleepless thoughts fled back to the night when Maude and Lorena, soaked to the skin, had come back from the Games through a driving rain and poured out an excited story of a giant gone berserk who had pursued Lorena down Dover's Hill, shouting that her mother had stolen his horse. Flora had not slept that night either, for might not the giant learn where Lorena lived? He might appear on their doorstep and overpower them all as he dragged a screaming Lorena off by her hair. Early the next morning Flora had packed Lorena off to stay with Maude until she felt it was safe for her to return.

The angry giant had not appeared on the doorstep but just thinking about him had made Flora uneasy about being alone at the isolated smithy. She was jumpy and started at shadows. It had seemed the answer to a prayer when Mercy Meadows' new lodger had limped over and asked if he could take his suppers with her, since Mercy could only give him bed and breakfast now that her married daughter was ailing and she must go to their croft every day and prepare supper.

"I'm from up near Cirencester," Mercy's lodger had explained when Flora seemed to hesitate. "I'm searching for property around Twainmere," he went on smoothly, "and Mistress Meadows has told me ye're the best cook in the Cotswolds." His bold gaze had been admiring as he

spoke and he had leant against the doorjamb, exhibiting a
fine leg in a good russet stocking. Beneath the pressure of
that gaze, Flora had felt a little flutter. She had bridled,
admitted she was proud of her cooking—and told herself
the extra money would come in handy.

Lonely Flora, who had found herself a vicar's widow
without ever having been in truth a vicar's wife, was a
ripe goose for the plucking. She had hung on every word
the newcomer said, laughed at his jokes, flushed at his
compliments. At first she had missed Lorena dreadfully,
but lately—under the heady spell of a man's bold eyes
searching hers, and a man's deep-throated chuckle over
something she'd said—she had felt young again and full
of dreams. She had found herself looking up from weed-
ding her herb garden and wondered with a start if it was
not time to prepare supper—and felt a blush rising in her
cheeks at the thought that *he* would share that supper
with her. So Flora had let the time slip by, enjoying her
suppers with her gentleman boarder, and telling herself
that it was best Lorena stay secreted at the Cardwells in
case the menacing giant from the Games came to the
smithy and tried to harm her. For Flora's fear for Lorena
was very real; she had been careful to keep Lorena's
hiding place a secret, not even telling the new boarder,
although he had jovially tried to pry the girl's whereabouts from her, saying he'd like to view this maid Flora
described so warmly.

Now, lying in bed listening to the thunder roll and
the rain pour down, Flora wondered if Lenore really had
stolen the giant's horse. Lenore . . . all these years Flora
had lived in dread that Lenore would suddenly appear
and snatch her beloved Lorena from her. Instead "tinsel"
letters had arrived, for that was the contemptuous way
Flora had categorized them in her mind, letters that
described elegant gowns and jewels and balls, letters of no
substance. Of late, Flora admitted grudgingly, there had
been some coins enclosed in the letters, especially the last
one, which was from Oxford and sounded strangely sad.
With these coins Flora had bought new shoes and lengths

of dress material for Lorena, whose lovely young figure turned the simplest frock into a queenly gown.

Still it was strange, thought Flora, that Lenore had never come to Twainmere herself. She knew something must be holding her back.

* * *

Things had gone badly for Christopher and Lenore. After they rode out of Oxford, things were never the same for them again. They still made love—lightly, casually. But for Lenore something was gone from it and Christopher's lips no longer held their delicious tang.

I am become a wanton, she told herself in alarm. *I have taken a lover and now I am tiring of him!* But in truth Christopher seemed to her a changed man—driven, harsh. Like a pendulum he swung from anger to a fierce tenderness, a tenderness which was never lasting, and always tinged with bitterness.

But in London he changed again. There they plunged into a wild round of gaiety. Christopher found for them fashionable lodgings and hired a coach and six to take them everywhere. He bragged to Lenore that he had found a group of young bucks, adrift in London, who were so deep in their cups when they gambled that they never even missed the gold they lost—no need to hazard *her* sweet body trying to drum up a game with strangers, he'd struck the mother lode! She could almost believe it when he gave her lordly instructions to go out and buy anything her heart desired. Lenore hesitated, uneasy at the reckless need she sensed in him—a need to spend money?

"If ye're afraid ye'll run into Geoffrey Wyndham, there's no need," Christopher told her sharply. "He's in the West Country on the king's business, I'm told."

Lenore did not ask Christopher how he came to be so well informed about Geoffrey. She knew too well his jealousy. She took him at his word and went out and bought herself a wide-skirted gown of silver tissue over pale green silk, with rustling taffeta petticoats of a deeper emerald—and another of violet velvet that matched her eyes, which she wore over amethyst silk petticoats.

"That silver-green gown becomes ye well, Lenore." Christopher, resplendent in a newly bought doublet of shot silver, amethyst silk breeches and princely boots, lounged against the window, watching her as she modeled it for him. "Ye must have a cloak made to match it." His voice was casual but he was watching her closely as he spoke.

Lenore caught her breath. "I thought I had overspent," she confessed. "Are we really then so rich?"

"Aye, and will be as long as my friends' money holds out!" Christopher seized her and whirled her around so that her emerald skirts billowed.

"When will I meet them?"

He set her down and frowned. "They're a rough lot, Lenore. Country gentry with gold in their pockets. I've no mind to see one of them pinch you or plant a kiss on your cheek."

"You've no need to be jealous," she told him affectionately.

"Have I not?" For a moment there was desperation in those crystal eyes and she knew that he was thinking of Geoffrey.

"No, Christopher," she said gravely, lifting her arms in their slashed silver-green sleeves and putting them around his neck. "No need at all."

But when he looked down penetratingly into her face, she could not quite meet his eyes. For Geoffrey was an old ache in her heart. Like an old wound that had not healed right, the memory of him sometimes hurt. Perhaps it would always hurt but ... what had that to do with Christopher? No matter that he would not let her meet his gambling friends! They would ride out in their coach and six, a glittering couple for the populace to stare at and envy.

Lenore never dreamed that Mistress Potts was in London. She imagined her in Newcastle, living a revolving life as a perpetual houseguest of each of "the two Abbys" in turn. And she shunned the George and all her old haunts for they reminded her of Geoffrey and her wasted life.

So she could not know that old Mistress Potts, whom Geoffrey had set to watch for her and who had been seeking her so faithfully all this time, had come down with her old distemper and had been confined to her bed at the George ever since Geoffrey had gone to the West Country. Lenore, trying to forget, sought new faces, new places. And although she was sometimes recognized as "Geoffrey Wyndham's orange girl," no one thought to go and tell Mistress Potts that they had seen her, and that lady continued restfully in her bed, having enormous meals sent up, and promising herself that she would go abroad to look for Lenore as soon as she was able.

In the meantime Lenore was enjoying to the fullest Christopher's newfound wealth. They slept late on sheets of the finest linen and were roused to make ready for their evening festivities by a dimpled maidservant in apron and cap, and later handed into their coach by a footman wearing Christopher's livery of green and silver.

They boated on the Thames and dined at famous inns—places Lenore had never seen. They strolled about the shops and Christopher bought her anything that caught her fancy. It was such fun being wealthy! Lenore's only regret was that their frivolity could not include plays for all the theaters were closed for the summer. When fall came, Christopher promised her, he would buy them a box and they would attend all the wickedly immoral new plays that were the fashion in Restoration London. Lenore smiled at that and daydreamed of sitting in her very own theater box clad in scented silks with her hair dramatically arranged and asparkle with brilliants, looking down on Nell Gwyn as she performed on the boards below. How the Court dandies in the pit would nudge each other as they muttered how well the former orange girl was doing these days! How Lord Wilsingame would squirm! She was grateful to Christopher for making it all possible and shared with him wild nights of wine and laughter and romantic moonlit boat rides when they drifted beneath London Bridge and Lenore sighed and let her fingers dangle in the darkly silvered waters of the Thames.

Their whirlwind existence in London lasted some two months before it came to a crashing conclusion. They had been living, Lenore learned with shock, entirely on borrowed money. Contrary to what Christopher had told her, the gambling had not gone well. On his first night in London, a Cheapside rake, pretending to be very drunk, had palmed Christopher's dice and exchanged them for his own. That night Christopher had lost most of the money he had won in Oxford. Without his dice, in desperation Christopher had visited the loan sharks, whose exorbitant interest was now long overdue. Unable to win back enough to make good his losses, he had run up huge bills with shopkeepers who were impressed by his handsome garments, his coach-and-six—and his casual admission that he was the son of the Sheriff of Nottingham. He knew the game must end sometime, but in the meantime, he would give Lenore the time of her life.

The look on Christopher's face when he came pounding in and told her hoarsely that they must flee London before the constable came to impound their possessions was one that she would never forget. But his warning came too late, for the constable's men were already at the door.

Now, loaded summarily into a high-sided cart, they were being transported through London's winding streets in a drizzling rain that brought strands of Lenore's bright hair down around her shoulders and reduced the silver tissue of her gown to a sodden mass that stuck to the green shimmer of wet silk beneath.

She rode with her head bowed, thinking. It had all happened so fast, but now she remembered with a pang the night she had wakened to find Christopher, leaning on one arm, watching her with a tender wistful smile. "Are ye happy, Lenore?" he had asked her huskily, tracing questing fingers across her breast. "Does this life we're leading make ye happy?"

She had said sleepily, "Yes," and snuggled with a sigh of contentment into his arms.

Now she cursed herself for a fool. Christopher, head over heels in love, had done it all for *her*. Wild with jealousy over Geoffrey, he had borrowed from the money lenders, run up bills he could never pay, encouraged her to spend money they didn't have—and all so he could strut before her and win her favor. Poor Christopher . . . he was only trying to give her the kind of life she could have had with Geoffrey Wyndham.

And now, because he loved her, he had come to grief. Dully she noticed that the rain was slackening, the sun was trying to shaft sudden gold through the torn openings in a leaden sky. Lenore blinked the raindrops from her lashes and turned soberly to look at Christopher. He stood rigid beside her, clutching the cart side to keep his balance, as did she. Beneath them the wheels grumbled over the wet cobblestones and splashed mud and water on angry passersby who paused to watch this fancy pair being brought to jail by the constable's men. Christopher's jaw was hard and clenched beneath his carefully trimmed golden beard, but she could see the suffering in his eyes. Poor Christopher—his love for her had brought him low! Impulsively she reached over and squeezed his lace-frothed wrist. He winced as if the touch hurt him and turned his face abruptly away from her toward the tipsy half-timbered buildings careening by.

It was her fault. She had brought him to this!

A sob caught in her throat as the cart jolted to a halt and through a sudden shaft of bright sunlight Lenore blinked up at the forbidding walls of Newgate Prison.

Their folly had brought them here—and here, she knew without a doubt, they would rot.

Claremont Court, Kent

Chapter 31

Geoffrey Wyndham rode in from the West Country exhausted. Two long months he had been away on the king's business and he hated to think what condition affairs at Claremont Court must be in, for when he was gone Letiche always interfered with his estate manager's good practices and snarled everything up. All night Geoffrey had slogged along muddy roads, imagining the worst. He arrived at dawn, grimly intending to take at least this one day for his personal affairs before repairing to Whitehall and an audience with the king—that could wait until tomorrow.

He greeted Letiche civilly, but paused only to change his dusty riding clothes and eat a hasty breakfast before calling for his estate manager's report. All that day he spent riding around the estate with his manager, a Welshman named Glendower. Things, he discovered to his relief, were no worse than usual. Letiche had insisted the grooms received too much money but somehow mutiny had been avoided, and she had driven away one of the maids—but that was all.

"If ever ye do as ye once mentioned and buy yourself a holding in Virginia," sighed Glendower, after reciting the affair of the grooms, "I'd appreciate the chance to run it for ye."

Geoffrey shot Glendower a keen look. In point of fact he already had holdings in Virginia, a great rolling plantation with a new brick manor house near Williamsburg that he had purchased but recently. He wondered if Glendower knew that. Probably not, for the plantation had been bought secretly under the name of Daunt. He had used that name so Letiche would not hear of the transaction and try to block it, and before he had left for the West Country he had sent a great sum of money to his agents in Williamsburg to stock the place and employ suitable help. Four months ago in a rash moment he had even ordered furniture and a vast amount of silver and pewter and cutlery and linens and ironstone ware. He knew that it was foolish to expend so much of his wealth on these things but the Colonies had become to him a dream, for his life at Claremont Court was unhappy and Whitehall with its jostling sea of fops and dandies and wantons irritated him.

He was starved for something else, something that was missing from his empty life—that sense of home and hearth that he had had in Oxford with Lenore. But now as he rode about his great estate with the Welshman by his side, he felt that he would never go to America; King Charles would always find ways to keep him here and his meaningless life with Letiche would go on and on. Even now all that silver, all those carpets and draperies and goblets and mirrors and fine saddles were being unpacked and marveled over at the plantation near Williamsburg— things he would never see. He sighed and almost told Glendower that he would arrange for his passage, but desisted. Letiche, if she heard, would clamor for everything to be brought back or sold so that she might bedeck herself in jewels to rival the Queen of France—and besides Glendower was needed here to hold Claremont Court together, since he was away so much on the king's business. He sighed and turned his horse's head back toward the handsome west front of his manor house. Williamsburg had been for him a lovely impractical dream—but that dream had been woven around Lenore and now he knew gloomily that he would never have her either, for he had heard no word of her since they had parted so violently in York.

Such despondency was not natural to him; he told himself it was because he was tired. Two dawns had passed since he had slept and now the sun was setting in the west again and another soft summer night was beginning. He parted company with Glendower and rode back to his great shadowy house unaware that no sooner had he arrived this morning than Letiche had sent a message in haste to London.

"Geoffrey is back," her note read. "He leaves again in the morning to report to the king. Who knows when he will be back? You had best come tonight. Come when I pass a light three times across my window."

In his London apartments the Marquis de Vignac read the unsigned note and sneered. Pass a light across her window! Letiche had always had a flare for the dramatic. But he hastened to bundle up the letters which he had written with so much care and which he kept hidden in a secret drawer of the small French writing desk in his bedchamber. Languidly he ordered his horse brought round and rode out into the summer afternoon. Evening found him at Claremont Court hidden among the trees of the extensive park and watching the house from behind low-hanging branches for the signal.

Inside the great house the supper dishes were being cleared away by liveried footmen who padded back and forth in stately fashion across the long dining room. The gold braid of their livery sparkled in the light from the enormous crystal chandeliers that cast long golden streaks through the tall windows and across the sloping lawns, for Letiche was extravagant with candles as she was with everything else.

Geoffrey, a little refreshed by the excellent French dishes he had just enjoyed—for Letiche had imported her cook from France along with all of the other servants except George, whom she was afraid to dismiss because Geoffrey favored him—leaned back and studied his wife cynically across the long gleaming board. His gray eyes were underlined with fatigue but he was not too tired to notice that Letiche was obviously sporting a new gown—a bouffant creation of tissue of silver over changeable silk that muted from mauve to pale olive. The peridots and seed pearls that encircled her short neck and dangled from her shell-like ears brought out the olive hue of her gown—her emeralds might have been more spectacular, but last week she had given them to Andre who would sell them to pay his debts. For Andre Malraux had ever leeched off of women and his relationship with Letiche was no exception. Andre had had the grace to wonder if such a valuable necklace would not be missed and Letiche had laughed and said she would tell Geoffrey that she had lost it. Geoffrey knew nothing of her affair with Andre, of course. He did not dream his wife had a lover for it was a secret Letiche guarded fiercely. Still, tonight he gazed into that bright insincere smile and wondered how he had ever been fooled by it.

"I'm to bed," he said abruptly, rising and stretching his long legs. "I rode hard to get back, for tomorrow I'm due at Whitehall."

"You rode hard to get back—yet you did not spend the day with me." Letiche's voice had an edge to it.

Geoffrey gave a short laugh. "No, I spent the day with my estate manager that I may continue to keep a roof over your head."

She was pouting, but as he turned to go, her expression grew alarmed. "Oh, ye'll go to bed right after supper with no words for me? I'm so lonely in this big house I could die, with you gone all the time!"

Lonely? He had thought her all but mobbed by her French friends. As he hesitated, Letiche pressed her advantage. "Ah, Geoffrey, stay a while," she coaxed. "Drink a toast with me." She picked up a wine bottle that stood almost hidden in a forest of silver but within her reach. As a watchful servant stepped forward to pour the wine for her, she waved him away. "You may all go; I will call you when I need you," she said carelessly. "But this glass of good claret I will pour myself and take it to my husband in my own hands that we may clink our glasses together companionably now that you are at last back from the West Country." As she spoke, she poured out the wine, sloshing it a little in her nervousness. "A toast, Geoffrey. A toast to the old days in France!"

If Geoffrey was surprised by his wife's sudden change in mood, he did not show it. His dark face was impassive but his gray eyes were alert, wondering what had brought on this unusual show of nostalgia in the usually heedless Letiche. "To the old days?" he echoed ironically. "I thought you hated their very memory, Letiche."

"Not so, Geoffrey." Letiche heaved a great sigh. She was half turned from him, and now she bent over the wine glasses, quickly emptied the paper containing the white powder de Vignac had given her into his glass. "I often remember those days and wish we could live them over again." That she would have lived them over in other arms, she forebore to add. That she often remembered those days was true enough, but she remembered them with chagrin.

Smiling that bright false smile, she advanced on Geoffrey. With a swish of her wide changeable silk skirts, she bent forward coquettishly so that her husband might get the full effect of her shockingly low décolletage that almost spilled her plump breasts out of her bodice.

Geoffrey's eyebrows lifted as he accepted the glass from her small plump hand, but he was not to be beguiled by this aggressive display. "To the old days, Letiche," he echoed ruefully, but even as he spoke he found himself thinking of the old days in Oxford and the cheap cozy lodgings he had shared with Lenore off Magpie Lane.

Letiche was quick to catch that sudden softening of his hard gray eyes. *He is thinking of that orange girl!* she thought angrily. With trembling fingers she lifted her glass to her lips.

"To the old days, Geoffrey."

They drank.

"Have you no toast to make me, Geoffrey?" she asked in a deceptively wistful voice as she quickly refilled his glass.

Geoffrey studied his wife's flushed face. She looked feverish, he thought—or perhaps merely earnest. He wondered if there was hope for them after all. Could Letiche be tired of that conniving crew of displaced French aristocrats with whom she had kept herself insulated from everything English? Could it be that she had divorced herself from them and really wanted to change? If so, he would give her her chance, he decided soberly.

"Aye, I will toast the future, Letiche. May we not lose our way as we have in the past."

Geoffrey *would* say something like that, Letiche thought scornfully. Something irritatingly sincere, when all the world knew he didn't love her—nor she him. Raoul now would have said something witty and risque with a double meaning. Andre would have passionately toasted her lashes lying long upon her delicious cheeks and gone on to toast her supple hips—and more. Ah, these Englishmen—even their gallantry had no flare, no *éclat*. In the suddenly awkward silence she drained her glass again and returned to her seat at the other end of the table, wondering how much time would elapse before the drug she had put into his wine would take effect.

She did not have to wait long. Geoffrey got up suddenly and shook his head as if to clear it. He began to walk around the room.

"What is the matter?" she asked.

"I don't know," he muttered. "There is a great

buzzing in my head, as of a million bees. Letiche, did you notice anything wrong with the wine just now? I thought the first glass tasted strange."

Cold fear gripped her. "No, perhaps the glass was not clean. I will speak to the servants."

"No matter," he said, and wavered on his feet, then crashed, like a giant oak of the forest, to the floor. His head struck the table edge as he fell and Letiche gave a small shriek, for she could see blood oozing out of his dark hair.

A manservant, hovering in the pantry, came running at the sound.

"We must get him to bed," cried Letiche, her voice sounding thin and hysterical to her own ears. "The wine must have gone to his head! He—he toppled over and his head struck the table."

The manservant, whose name was George, gave her a brief impenetrable look. If there was one thing the master could do, in George's opinion, it was hold his liquor. George doubted if the master could have consumed enough wine at supper to make him stagger, much less make him fall. Still that scalp cut looked a bit nasty.

"D'ye wish me to summon a doctor, my lady?" he wondered.

"No!" The note of hysteria was clear in Letiche's voice now. "Just wash the cut out yourself, George, and put him to bed." She peered down at the blood clotting in Geoffrey's dark hair. "It does not look too deep," she said with a shudder. "If when he wakes he desires a doctor, we will call one then."

"Just so, my lady." George was not one to question his plain duty. Panting a little with the effort, he and another footman lugged the long body of the master upstairs, washed his cut—which, as Letiche had suggested, was not deep after all—and bandaged it.

"Don't bother to undress him," shrilled Letiche, for she was half afraid that any activity might waken

Geoffrey. " 'Tis better he lie quiet. There. Take off his boots but leave him lying on the coverlet."

"Do you want me to stay with him, my lady?" George asked impassively after this was done and the other servant had gone.

Letiche had not foreseen this eventuality. "No, no," she said in a hurried voice. "I will stay with him myself until he wakes. Light a candle, George; I may decide to read and the chandelier is so high up. No" —as George was about to set it down upon a table to the right of the window—"bring it over here. On the writing desk. And open the casements, George—it's suffocating in here." With a silken rustle she moved to the window George had just opened. "The candle will blow out from this breeze," she muttered, and set it back where George had originally placed it. "No, perhaps it will not." She put it back upon the writing desk. George blinked at this capricious moving of candles, but Letiche was satisfied. She had managed to pass the light across the window three times; if de Vignac was watching, he would surely have seen it. "So hot . . ." she murmured, standing before the window and dabbing at her face with her kerchief. She leaned forward suddenly to peer out. "I think I see a rider coming up the drive, George. Go downstairs and see who it is, arriving at this hour. If it is a stranger, tell him we are not at home. If it is anyone I know, bring him upstairs, I will receive him here in Geoffrey's bedchamber. For my husband may awaken, and I would be here by his side when he does."

George did his best to hide his astonishment at this sudden urge of Letiche Wyndham's to be by her husband's side.

Minutes later he ushered the Marquis de Vignac into Geoffrey's bedchamber and was imperiously waved away by Letiche, who left her husband's side abruptly and swept forward toward the marquis.

"Raoul, what brings you here?"

"I was in the neighborhood," said de Vignac in a noncommittal tone. Quickly he closed the door after

George discreetly left. "What has happened here, Letiche?" he demanded, staring at the bandage wound about Geoffrey's head.

"Geoffrey sensed there was something wrong with the wine and rose from the table," Letiche told him tensely. "He said his head was buzzing, and then he fell—and struck his head on the table as he went down."

De Vignac frowned; the stupid woman had bungled it. Now there would be questions. Why had she not arranged for a last drink in the bedroom before retiring? Of course that might have been difficult to manage since they were in effect estranged. He thought rapidly. "You will tell him when he awakens that there was something wrong with one of the meat courses, it was foul. Blame it on what he ate rather than on what he drank. Tell him you became sick yourself and passed the night in retching, and that you believe it was a form of food poisoning which struck you both down."

"I will dismiss the cook," Letiche agreed, relieved at this suggestion but still uneasy. "Have you brought the letters, Raoul?"

"Right here." He pulled them out, eight in all.

"So many?" She was surprised.

"Yes, I may have to feed them to him one by one, to make him believe that there are more, always more, where they came from. Your husband is a strong man, Letiche—and a violent one. He will seize the first letter, I've no doubt—and perhaps the second as well—and destroy them before my eyes. I would not dare to return to have you sign more and attempt the signet ring again. It would be too dangerous. "Here"—he was hurrying her to the little writing desk which stood by the window. "Is the light good enough for you to see well?" Already he had thrust a quill pen into her hand.

Letiche peered down at the first letter. It was hard to see in this light and she did not wish to call for another candle—that might be noted and remembered later.

"My adorable Nell," she read. "Since first I saw you

on stage, I have been enamored of you and now that you have deigned to notice me, my passion knows no bounds."

She tapped her quill against the parchment. "That is too flowery for Geoffrey," she objected. "No one would believe he had written it."

"*Any* excess would be believed of a lover," sighed de Vignac.

Letiche sniffed and lifted the page. "And this second one," she complained. " 'My Nell, I kiss your eyes, your lips, your breasts, your hips, your—' Geoffrey would *never* say that, Raoul! He is too restrained, too—too *English!*"

"And who will know that?" demanded the marquis coolly. "Has your husband written so many love letters to so many women that his style is known to all? Come, *ma petite,*" he urged, pretending to grow impatient for he was uneasy that she might riffle through all of them and find what was in the rest. "We must be quick for every moment that I stay endangers us both."

Letiche sighed. After all, what did it matter what Geoffrey said in these fake love letters to Nell Gwyn? None of them would ever surface anyway. They would be used and destroyed. By Geoffrey himself. "Very well." She dipped the quill into the inkwell. "Remove his signet ring while I sign these."

De Vignac hastened to the large bed where Geoffrey's long form lay stretched out upon the coverlet. Delicately he lifted one of Geoffrey's eyelids—still unconscious. He seized Geoffrey's left hand, but turned to keep his eyes on Letiche as he endeavored to drag the signet ring off Geoffrey's finger. The ring was surprisingly difficult to remove, he almost thought he must call for soap, but with a final tug it came off in his hand. With relief he noted that Letiche was not reading any of the letters. Her quill pen flew and she flipped each sheet over promptly as she scrawled "Geoffrey Wyndham" with a masterful flourish at the bottom of each letter. Watching, de Vignac thanked God for having made her a fool—but such a useful one!

Crossing over to her, he snatched up the letters and hastily folded each just after she signed. "And now the wax!" He was melting the sealing wax in the candle flame as he spoke, letting it drip red upon the parchment. With satisfaction he pressed the signet ring into the hot wax. There—it was done! The two love letters—and those more incriminating letters beneath that were not to Nell Gwyn but to the Dutch Ambassador, offering certain information on the state of the British forces for a price to be agreed upon—and this on the eve of a new Dutch war! He counted the letters methodically and thrust them into his doublet.

Letiche was biting her lip nervously. "I feel I should have read them, Raoul," she said plaintively.

"But this way you can never be surprised into betraying a knowledge of their contents," he pointed out reasonably.

"I suppose you are right." But she sounded doubtful.

"I am. Trust me, Letiche. Have I ever failed you?"

"No, Raoul." But she was gazing at him somberly as he kissed her hand and departed with a small insouciant wave.

Left behind, Letiche studied the long figure of the man on the bed. She did not dream he knew of her talent for forgery or that she had ever signed his name. He was busy, too busy, he would have paid the bills that came from the shops for fripperies for her without question. Such was his nature.

But if he found out about this—! A sudden feeling that she was in very deep overwhelmed her.

With great care she disposed of everything that might show that anything had been written here, cleaned the pen.

The ring! She had forgotten the ring!

In panic she snatched it up, a signet ring in plain

heavy gold set with a bloodstone in which was deeply etched the Wyndham arms. With a frightened sob that she had almost forgotten it, she flew to the bed, tried to remember on which hand Geoffrey had worn it, for he sometimes wore other rings. It was a day in which everyone who could afford it wore rings, often several to the finger, so many indeed that they could not use their sparkling hands for anything but display.

She thought he wore it on the middle finger of his left hand—no, it did not fit there, she could not shove it over the second joint of his finger. It must be the index finger then. Yes, it went on easily. Letiche gave a great sigh of relief and sank down for a moment upon the edge of the bed. She was trembling and now she pressed a hand to her temple.

When George knocked softly on the door, she gave a violent start.

"Yes, what is it?" she cried in a hoarse voice so unlike her own that even the unflappable George was taken by surprise.

"The Marquis de Vignac makes his regrets that your worry about your husband prevented you from receiving him for more than a moment," George told her, wondering mentally at the idiocy of such a message from a man who was often closeted with the mistress for hours while the master was away.

"Oh, yes—thank you, George," she said jerkily. And then, her hand still pressed to her temple: "I have a headache, George. Will you stay with my husband and ask him, when he wakes, if he feels the need of a doctor?"

"That I will, madam." Cheerful George took up his post and Letiche swept from the room to her own bedchamber. She sat for a long time staring into the French mirror above her dressing table before going to bed. Something cold seemed to be constricting her throat. She tore off the peridot necklace and thrust it away from her, began to rub her throat. When she summoned her maid to prepare her for bed, she really did have a headache.

When he arrived home at his luxurious apartments, the Marquis de Vignac put aside the first two forged letters with a contemptuous laugh. These were the ones to Nell Gwyn. Ridiculous! Charles would not have believed Geoffrey to be intriguing with Nell—indeed his majesty might even be relieved to hand over the burden, for Nell and Charles had been bickering much of late—some said they were no longer speaking. Gossips whispered that Nell had thrown a glass of port at his majesty and shrieked that the royal allowance was a pittance and the royal housing a hovel—for Charles had not set Nell up as magnificently as he had his titled mistresses: Louise de Keroualle, whom he had created Duchess of Portsmouth, and Barbara Villiers, who had now become Duchess of Cleveland. Letiche apparently had not heard that Nell had sworn she had bolted the royal stable and was going back to the London stage to look for a new saddle!

For the marquis had shrewdly guessed that Andre would not tell Letiche much about goings on among the theater folk now that he himself was dangling after a young actress from Suffolk who had recently become the rage. The marquis could but hope that Andre's new passion, if Letiche heard of it, would not evoke such a storm as might upset his plans. Letiche was very useful to him; he did not want her running off to France to sulk.

De Vignac left out the two letters to Nell Gwyn but hid the remaining six in a secret drawer of his delicate French writing desk. With those six he would draw Geoffrey Wyndham into a web from which he could never extricate himself. For those six precious letters at which Letiche had not bothered to glance outlined a scheme that even such a broad-minded monarch as Charles could hardly be expected to ignore.

Those letters—which were addressed not to Nell Gwyn but to the Dutch ambassador—contained a terse but rather complete plan for the taking of the ports of Newcastle and Hull, a feint on the Tyne and an invasion up the Humber—ancient invasion route of the Norse— and a detailed listing of the present strength of the British land and naval forces in the area around the Humber and throughout the North Riding. The information was accurate; it had cost de Vignac dear to procure it. But he preferred not to sell that information directly to the Dutch, for that was riskier—although he might do that later, of course. Better by far, he reasoned, to use it to blackmail Geoffrey Wyndham out of an enormous sum of money! And incidentally toss a crumb to Letiche in the form of an invitation to Whitehall, which Geoffrey could doubtless, under pressure, arrange.

Now in the candlelit room, de Vignac poured himself a glass of wine from an expensive crystal decanter and drank it, feeling his future was assured. He was about to burn the pair of love letters in the candle flame when suddenly a new thought occurred to him and he slapped his thigh and laughed aloud. He had long admired Nell Gwyn, who had had the effrontery to snub him. Now just by waving a scrap of paper he could summon a king's mistress to his bed! Never one to hesitate, de Vignac rang for his manservant and sent him off, stumbling with sleepiness, carrying a hastily penned note to the house of Mistress Gwyn. The message the note bore was cryptic. But not so cryptic that Nell would not understand it and hurry post haste to de Vignac's apartments even at this late hour to see what axe was poised over her pretty head!

Having dispatched his manservant, de Vignac changed to an elaborately cut dressing gown of rose shot with gold threads and sat down to await developments.

* * *

At dawn Geoffrey Wyndham awoke to find himself staring up into the face of a solemn-eyed if sleepy George.

"Ye're awake, sir."

"Yes, I'm awake, George." A pain shot through Geoffrey's head as he spoke and he groaned and grasped his head with his hands. "I don't remember coming to bed last night. What happened, George?"

George gave him a solemn look. "Ye fell in the dining room, sir, and struck your head. My lady thought"

—George hesitated delicately—"my lady said ye might have had too much to drink."

Geoffrey snorted, and then winced as another pain went through his still groggy head. "Ridiculous. I must have slipped, George." He thought back. The wine . . . it had tasted strange. He had remarked on it to Letiche and she had insisted it seemed all right to her.

He sat up and stretched, determinedly shook his head to clear it. Now he flexed his strong fingers—and felt a change there. He looked down at his hand. His signet ring, so tight it had almost grown to his middle finger, had somehow removed itself and now reposed on his index finger. Automatically he slipped it off his index finger and forced it back on the middle finger where it belonged. It took some effort to get it there, and his brow furrowed in thought. Abruptly he remembered Letiche's facility with penmanship, how easily she had signed his name on at least two occasions that she probably thought he didn't know about!

He turned to regard the manservant who was rising stiffly. "George," he said softly. "Who was here last night?"

George blinked. The master had slept sound all night—George had even managed to catch a few winks himself; how could the master know there'd been a visitor? "There was only one visitor, sir. The Marquis de Vignac. But he didn't stay long."

"Was he brought up here, George?"

Again George blinked. "Why, yes, sir, he was. My lady did receive him here in this room, since she had said she'd stay with ye until ye woke—in case ye needed a doctor."

"Very thoughtful of her," said Geoffrey grimly. "And were you here all the time, George?"

"Oh, no, sir, not while the Marquis was here. After he left, my lady told me she had a headache and that I was to stay with you."

"I see. Thank you, George, that will be all."

Geoffrey lay back and stared at the ceiling. There

was no use asking Letiche, she would only deny everything. But he wondered what new intrigue was afoot and what paper now bore his signature.

After he had drunk some coffee, when his head felt a little better, he determined that he would go to London and throttle the truth from de Vignac before going to Whitehall.

After that he would deal with Letiche.

Twainmere, The Cotswolds

Chapter 32

It was at Maude Cardwell's that Lorena learned of Flora's impending marriage.

Toothless old Goody Woodsall had come hobbling into the Cardwell's cottage on her cane, and seemed surprised to see Lorena there. Goody Woodsall had been a widow these twenty years and more, and she lived in a tiny out-of-the-way croft and hardly ever went out. But today she had had to talk to somebody.

"Wind took it, it did," she said without preamble. "I stayed under a tree all night and now I'm off to my married daughter's—can't live there no more. Yesterday when the sky clouded up I was out picking berries and I took shelter in that grove of beech trees. You know the place, Jane." She was speaking to Mistress Cardwell, who was busy pouring her a tankard of cider. "I could see my house from there but couldn't reach it—rain came pelting down like driving pegs. Soaked to the skin I was, and big forked lightning all around."

Jane Cardwell shuddered, and Lorena remembered

yesterday's thunderstorm. A big one it had been, for a while she had thought the house would be struck.

"And all of a sudden"—Goody Woodsall leaned forward and banged her cane upon the floor for emphasis—"there was this awful thundering noise and a big dark cloud seemed to reach down and stab my house. Everything flew about and I could see part of the roof being sucked up into the sky!"

She had their full attention now. They gaped at her.

"And after the storm was over, I hurried back and my house was *gone*. It had just vanished up into the sky!"

That rocked them. They knew Goody Woodsall's tiny house to be a flimsy wooden structure, but it had certainly survived many a storm.

"Lorena Frankford, what are you doing here when your Aunt Flora's getting married tomorrow?" added Goody Woodsall into the astonished pause that followed.

Lorena gasped. "Married? Oh, she can't be!"

"Well, she is. I heard it on my way over, from Matt Ungersoll who picked me up and took me part way in his cart. The banns have all been read and tomorrow she's to marry, and she'll be going to live on her husband's farm over near Cirencester."

Lorena looked wildly at Maude and Goody Woodsall smiled at the spectacular effect she had had on her audience. They were almost too engulfed with what she had told them to speak.

Maude and her mother both spoke at once. "I think you should get right back there, Lorena."

"I'm going." Lorena snatched up her things, thanked them for their hospitality, said good-bye and almost ran out the door.

"Wait, I'll go with you," cried Maude, wild with curiosity. "Mistress Silby promised Ma some herbs from her garden and I was going into town after them tomorrow, but I might as well go today."

"Hurry then," called Lorena impatiently. She must

get to Twainmere, she told herself. For now she did not know what she would find there.

*   *   *

In the cottage behind the smithy, Flora sang as she scrubbed the already spotless floor. Tomorrow was her wedding day! She had not been so happy since she was a young girl. A whirlwind courtship—and at her age.

She straightened up and beamed down at the clean-scoured floor. There! It would look wonderful when Alger Pye came by tonight. And to think, she'd hardly liked the look of him when he'd hobbled up on his injured ankle to her door. She'd thought him evil-looking with that big V-shaped scar etched prominently on his forehead. Evil! Flora dissolved in mirth. Why, Alger was the kindest of men. Hadn't he promptly offered a job to that old no-good Tom Prattle, when Tom came over and rapped on the cottage door and asked to see him outside. They had talked while Flora cleared away the dishes—Flora presumed the talk had been about Tom's urgent need for a job for it was common knowledge that the sheriff was about to evict Tom from his cottage—and then Tom had gone his way whistling and Alger Pye had come back in and announced in a loud cheerful voice that he was of a mind to help that fellow because he was a relative of the family. Flora had said promptly that Tom was Lorena's uncle by marriage and no kin of hers. "Nevertheless." Alger Pye's teeth had flashed although his eyes weren't smiling. "Tom needs a job and I'm going to give it to him. As soon as we're married, we'll stop by and pick up your young niece Lorena and we'll take Tom Prattle with us too. There's a mint of things he can do about the house."

"I suppose so," agreed Flora in a doubtful voice, but she was pleased by Alger's kindness to his less fortunate fellows.

Only once during their brief courtship had Flora wavered. And that was the night she had the terrible dream. In her dream she was in a strange house and

Lorena rushed in wild-eyed and said terrible things, things Flora could not remember when she woke up. But she *did* remember that those things Lorena said had all been about Alger Pye.

Thinking of the dream now made her bite her lips for a moment. Then she pushed back her hair with a wet hand and told herself she was being foolish. She was just starting back to the kitchen with the scrub pail when she saw Lorena hurrying up the path.

"Aunt Flora." The girl burst into the room. "What's this about your getting married?"

"It's true, Lorena," Flora said, setting down the pail and drying her hands on her apron. "Only I was planning to surprise you. We were going to have the service, and then come and pick you up in the cart and take you with us over to his farm near Cirencester."

"But you *can't* have been meaning to marry this man without telling me about it first!"

Flora's brows lifted a bit at that. "I didn't know I needed to ask your permission," she murmured. "Oh, there he comes now—and me still with this apron on! No, I'll let him in myself."

Lorena turned to the window as her aunt hurried to the door. Up the path to the cottage was walking a big heavyset man with heavy jowls and a very confident look on his squarish face—and a big V-shaped scar on his forehead.

All of Lorena's breath seemed to be expelled suddenly. She leaned against the window, hardly believing her eyes. This man whom Aunt Flora had just announced happily that she was going to marry tomorrow was the man who had attacked her last summer at the trout pool. There was no mistaking those heavy jowls or that V-shaped scar.

Suddenly she remembered that she had never told Aunt Flora about her naked outing, she had managed to slip into the house without being seen. Indeed she had waited a whole week before going back to the trout pool for her clothes, and had found them there, intact. Although she knew the story of her naked encounter with Watt Demming in the Demming's barn that day must have made the rounds—the ribald whistles and catcalls that greeted her red-faced passing of village swains had told her so—the gossip had apparently never reached Aunt Flora. Nor was it likely to, for since she had so abruptly shed her mourning after Robbie's death, Flora had been shunned by the village women, who deemed her conduct scandalous.

So Aunt Flora couldn't know what this man had done. And now she'd announced that she was going to marry him! Something must be done—and quickly.

Flora brought Alger Pye in and introduced them. Lorena stood with her hands twined tightly together, hardly acknowledging the introduction. Her eyes were brilliant blue spots in her pale face.

If she had expected their visitor to betray surprise at sight of her, she was disappointed. Instead he leaned down and peered at her, as if he had seen her before and was puzzled as to where it might have been. Lorena considered his gaze insulting, for she had no doubt at all that Alger Pye had recognized her—something familiar in his manner told her that—and she reddened angrily.

"Why, 'tis the little girl I thought was drowning and scared from the pool when I tried to rescue her," he said, neatly bringing up the incident before she could. "Don't tell me, Flora, that this is your niece!"

"I was *not* drowning," corrected Lorena in a tight voice. "Nor did you think I was. I was coming out of the pool to dry off when you leaped at me."

The heavy-jowled man's laugh was easy enough, although for a moment his gaze was threatening, and Flora said sharply, "When did all this happen?"

"Last summer," replied Lorena heatedly. "And I was *not* drowning. I—"

"I frightened the girl, Flora," Alger said smoothly, his big voice conveniently drowning out Lorena's. "And I'm sorry for it, but I saw the girl in the pool and I knew it to be deep and I thought her to be in trouble. Child, ye should not think the worse of a man for trying to help ye!"

Flora's face, at first suspicious, cleared. "That will be enough, Lorena," she chided. "Ye know I wouldn't have countenanced your swimming somewhere alone. Indeed ye could have drowned. Ye should thank Alger here for trying to save ye, even if ye didn't *need* saving." Her tone said clearly, *Surely if somebody had tried to pounce on ye, ye'd have told me long before this!*

Lorena dropped her eyes; she felt suffocated. Alger Pye's story certainly sounded very plausible; he was in complete control of the situation. In silence she served them cider and little cakes, but she refused to look at Alger Pye, answered his questions in monosyllables and kept her expression wooden.

But for once Flora did not seem to notice. Her whole attention was centered on the man with the V-shaped scar. Fondly she watched him consume three tankards of cider and a quantity of the good little cakes that she had baked earlier.

"Ye do be a fine cook, Flora," Alger complimented her, wiping his mouth with the back of his big hand when he had finished. "Your good meals will certainly brighten up my lonely bachelor life. And ye've done a fine job of bringing up young Lorena here."

Flora bridled at this compliment and looked pleased. But when Lorena winced, he turned to her coolly. "Ye're right to be suspicious of men, girl—isn't she, Flora? There's many a man as would do ye an injury in such a situation. 'Tis not right that ye be riding around alone like a hoyden. When I take ye both over Cirencester way, ye'll be riding to town in the cart with us."

Lorena flashed him a look of pure hatred. "No, I won't," she said, "for I won't be going to Cirencester."

"Lorena!" reproved Flora in a warning voice, and Lorena subsided.

But Alger Pye had hardly cleared the door before Lorena turned impetuously to Flora. She *must* make her Aunt understand the kind of man she was about to marry. "It was just the way I said it was," she cried. "That man jumped out of nowhere and tried to grab me and if he hadn't slipped and fallen back into the pool—"

To her surprise, Flora held up her hand regally for silence. "Don't say any more, Lorena," she said in a stern voice. "For I don't want to hear it—any of it." She walked over and sat down heavily and her face seemed to change imperceptibly, to age, so that she looked very old. "'Tis just as it was in my dream," she murmured sadly.

"Dream? What dream?"

Flora gave her a haggard look. "I dreamt you'd spoil my marriage for me, Lorena," she said dully. "I dreamt you'd come back and say something that would spoil it all for me."

Lorena recoiled. Everyone knew that Scottish Flora had the Sight. When Flora dreamt something, it came true.

"I thought if you didn't know I was getting married, it would all come right," Flora murmured forlornly. "I thought to be married first and then just to stop by the Cardwell's and pick you up and take you with us to Cirencester. I thought to get around the dream that way. But you knew, somehow you knew—and you came back."

So that was why Aunt Flora hadn't told her—she'd dreamed she was going to spoil her marriage! "Goody Woodsall came by," faltered Lorena, hurt to the quick by the look of pain on her aunt's face. "She'd had it from Matt Ungersoll."

"Ah, that would be the way of it," sighed Flora. "And I suppose this is just the beginning, that there'll be other stories and I'll half believe them, like I do this one. 'Tis a curse having the Sight, Lorena. It spoils your life."

"Oh, Aunt Flora." It was a cry wrung from the girl. "I'm just trying to tell you what happened."

"I know, I know," said Flora. When she looked up, her face was pinched and drawn. "But can't you see, I don't *want* you to tell me? I *want* to believe Alger. I want to believe it all happened just the way he said it did. And how can you be so sure it didn't? You were swimming—alone, you thought. Somebody coming up suddenly would certainly have frightened you, and *he* could have thought you were drowning."

"Yes, of course!" Hastily Lorena backed away from the subject, now that she saw how infatuated with Alger Pye her Aunt Flora was, how all this doubt was destroying her. "I suppose it *could* have been that way."

"And after all, if he'd really *attacked* you, you'd have come home and told me about it first thing, you wouldn't have waited a whole *year* to tell me. So please, Lorena, don't try to blow this thing up out of proportion. I never thought to have a man of my own again, much less a man who would love me—" She stopped, for she had almost said, *As Robbie never did.*

Lorena saw fully now what she had done. "I—I must have been wrong about it," she muttered. "I'm—I'm sure I'll learn to like him."

Flora gave her a wan look. "Alger is a fine man, a generous man," she said wearily. "He's promised you can live with us after we're married, and he'll buy your clothes and take care of you. And he's even offered your uncle, that no-good Tom Prattle, a job on his farm. Which is kindness itself, since Tom is due to be turned out of his house by the sheriff any day!"

Lorena swallowed. How she wanted to be convinced that she'd been mistaken about last year's incident at the trout pool when Alger Pye had leaped out at her from the brush. But in her heart she knew there'd been no mistake about it. There had been naked lust in his eyes then and his clutching hand had slid along her wet back—Lorena shuddered inwardly. Still, for Aunt Flora's sake, she'd have to pretend she was wrong. "I promised to meet Maude," she muttered.

"Back to the Cardwell's *today?*" Flora was astonished. "But you just came from there!"

"Maude's at Mistress Silby's picking up some herbs

for her mother. I promised I'd stop by and tell her if there was going to be a wedding or not. You see, we—we didn't believe it."

Flora bit her lip. That showed how much over the hill they all thought her! "Mistress Silby lives way the other side of the village," she observed. "You'd best take Snowfire if ye're going there. And tell Maude I hope she and all the Cardwells will come and attend the wedding tomorrow."

"I'll tell her," promised Lorena. She could hardly wait to get out of the house, for she felt she couldn't breathe.

On her way to the broken-down stable to get Snowfire, she was arrested by a voice. Alger Pye's voice. "A word with you, Lorena."

Lorena whirled. Alger Pye was standing in the bushes—ready to jump out, she thought, with a prickling scalp, just as he had done last year at the pool. And this time there was naked lust in his brown eyes too.

"*Mistress* Lorena, if you please," she said in a stiff voice and backed away from him warily.

"Come now," he wheedled. "I'm not going to hurt you."

"That's right, you're not. I won't let you."

His smile turned a bit nasty. "So that's the way it is, is it? You weren't so brave back at that trout pool without your clothes on!"

Lorena felt her face reddening. "If you ever touch me again," she warned, "I'll tell Aunt Flora."

"And what good would that do, little wench?" he mocked. "Think you that she'd believe your word against mine? Ye had proof of that just now, didn't you?"

Lorena sighed. "She *wants* to believe you."

"Aye, and she'll *keep on* wanting to believe me." His big hand seized her arm in a vicelike grip. "I waited here to tell you that if ye put any stones in the way of this marriage, I'll make it harder for ye later. Tomorrow we'll be on our way to my farm near Cirencester. Ye'll like it

469

there, Lorena, and"—his face became ingratiating and his free hand began to stroke the girl's forearm—"and ye'll learn to like me."

"I won't," gasped Lorena. "I'm not going with you!"

"And where will ye go?" Again his voice turned mocking. "Ye've no choice and ye should face up to it. Come now, ye won't have to work. Flora will do the cooking—she's a sight better at it than the housekeeper I've got now."

"Is that why you want her? For her cooking?" gasped Lorena, really startled.

"Why not? A good quiet wife cooking the meals and *you* with me up in the bedroom whilst she's preparing them!" It was a reckless statement, but he'd been driven to make it by the lure of the girl's tempting young body and the scornful look in her steady blue eyes.

So *that* was what he intended! He was marrying Aunt Flora, but only as a way to get to *her*. A shock wave went through Lorena even though she knew she had suspected it all along.

"I couldn't live like that," she told him through clenched teeth. "And neither could Aunt Flora."

"Oh, but ye will," he mocked. "Both of ye. For I've hired Tom Prattle to keep ye both in line. He drinks, but he has a heavy fist."

Lorena felt the color drain from her face. So Cirencester was to be their jail, and Tom Prattle, a brute who hated her, their jailer.

"Anyway," Alger Pye gave a harsh laugh, "once I get Flora pregnant, she'll have other things on her mind and you and I will have it all our own way."

"*Your* way, you mean!"

"Oh, come now," he chided. " 'Twill be an easy life. I'll buy you pretty clothes and take you to fairs. And I'll take care of any little bastards ye have, and once the old woman dies I'll marry you and admit they're mine."

Lorena felt she was going to be sick. "I'd rather die," she muttered, tugging away from him.

His laugh was brutal. "Oh, you won't *die*," he said.

"Tom Prattle will see to that. You're going to live a long, long life and please me in the bedroom every night." He let her go then, and her slender wrist slipped like water through his big fingers. She flung away from him and ran to the stable.

This on the eve of Aunt Flora's-wedding!

Alger Pye watched Lorena go with malice glinting in his brown eyes. What a splendid lass she was, so well set up in face and figure—but the wench needed a bit of taming. It would be a pity to bruise that luscious white flesh or mar that peach-bloom skin, but if he had to, he'd let the girl feel the flat of his heavy hand or the weight of his knuckles—or even a taste of the whip. For bend her to his will he would, no matter how hard she fought!

In the stable, Lorena threw her arms around Snow-fire's neck. She was shaking, but she took courage from the great white stallion who was so glad to see her he nuzzled her gently and whinnied to her in a soft welcoming way. She murmured to him and petted him and after a while peeked out the stable door.

Alger Pye had disappeared—gone, no doubt, she thought angrily, to gloat over all the things he would do to *her*, once he was safely married to Aunt Flora!

She led Snowfire out, stroked the long column of his shimmering white neck and mounted him. Slowly she rode, pondering what to do.

People stared at Lorena as she rode through the village, wondering where she'd been, for Flora had kept her secret well and none knew Lorena had been staying at the Cardwell's. But Lorena, usually so alert, did not return either their stares or their occasional greetings. She was lost in thought. Forgotten was the angry giant of the Games, fear of whom had driven her to hide at Maude's. Forgotten was her lovely mother-of-the-letters, gleaming like a star in the distance. All she could think of was the dreadful impending wedding, and what it would mean—to *her*.

She rode across Twainmere and on out a winding lane to Mistress Silby's, and found Maude out in the herb garden. Maude heard the clip-clop of hooves and straightened up at Lorena's approach. She waved a handful of basil and marjoram and tansy at Lorena and hurried forward. "Mistress Silby told me to take what I wanted," she said. And then, peering at her friend's pale pinched face, she said in an altered voice, "Why, what's the matter?"

"I've met him," she told Maude bitterly. She slid down off Snowfire's back and beckoned her friend over to the shadow of a hawthorn hedge where they both sank down, fanning themselves with their hands from the heat. "His name is Alger Pye and it's all true. They're being married tomorrow and—oh, Maude, he's the man who leaped out at me that day at the trout pool!" And she choked out the whole bitter story.

"That's terrible," breathed Maude. "But"—she looked distressed—"I don't know what you can do about it. If she insists on *believing* him—!"

Lorena had been thinking the same thing, but now that Maude was saying it, her combative nature was aroused. "I can refuse to go with them," she said energetically.

"Oh, no, you can't! They'll *make* you go."

"I can run away! I can ride to some nearby town and get myself apprenticed as a—a dairymaid. I know how to milk a cow!"

"It wouldn't work," sighed Maude. "If Alger Pye wants you bad enough to marry Flora to get you, then he'd come after you and buy up your articles of indenture. Once he owned your papers, he'd own *you* and the law would bring you back to him any time you ran away." She shook her head. "I don't see why Alger Pye didn't ask for you direct. As a wife. Instead of all this."

"Perhaps he knew Aunt Flora would never let me marry a man his age. And took this way instead."

"That could be," sighed Maude. "But whatever's the way of it, 'tis bad, I can see that. Still maybe you won't have to face it, any of it. Maybe you won't have to go to Cirencester after all."

"Why not? You just said—"

Maude gave her a sidewise look. "Tabby's back."

"Tabby?" Lorena breathed the name almost prayerfully.

"He's been away to sea. Mistress Silby told me he came back three days ago. He didn't know his father was dead and it took him real bad, finding the mill abandoned and vines running over it and his father under a stone in the churchyard. She says he's going to sell the mill and go to America."

"To America?" echoed Lorena wonderingly.

"And that he's already had an offer on the mill. If you hurry, Lorena, you can catch him before he starts out for the tavern because she says he's a drinking man these days. Hasn't been sober since he got back."

"Oh, Maude—thank you." Impulsively, Lorena hugged her friend.

Forgetting how distant Tabby had been before he left, remembering only how she loved him, how she'd missed him, Lorena rode through the village with her head high and her bright hair blowing out behind her in the long light of the late summer afternoon.

Tabby would help her! He always had!

*   *   *

Tabb Aylesbury had not liked the sea. The wooden merchant ships of reality were a far cry from the romantic galleons of his imaginings. His own ship had been full of hardship and drudgery and scurvy, made horrible by frequent floggings and other punishments. Once he had even seen a man keelhauled. He had had nightmares about it for weeks.

But his ship, the *Mary Ann,* had touched at Virginia and Tabby had fallen in love with the green Virginia countryside. He liked the freer atmosphere of the Colonies—made to seem even more attractive by being released from the ship to put his two feet on land for a while—and he saw great opportunities in this new land.

He had come back to tell his father about it, and to

say good-bye properly, for on his long voyage he had accepted the fact that his father and Lorena would be wed by now, with probably a baby on the way. Besides, this might be the last time he would ever see his father, for Tabby meant to sail to the Colonies and cast his lot there, never to return.

It had been a rude shock to find the yard around the miller's empty cottage overgrown with weeds and the deserted mill, now only a nesting place for swallows, collecting rats and spiders and overgrown with fast-growing vines that were creeping in the windows and across the dusty floor.

It had been a ruder shock still to learn that his father was dead these many months.

But it took Kate to tell him that it was all Lorena's fault.

Kate had lain in the hay with one lad too many and her mother, Lizzie Tilson, unwilling to let her ruined Kate marry the lad without prospects who had fathered her unborn child, had promptly given her to Abner Kilgore, whose young wife had died in childbirth the year before. Abner could provide handsomely for Kate and Lizzie—who had, after all, done the same thing in her youth, save that she had married a man near ninety to give *her* unborn child a name—thought Kate ought to be grateful that her mother had engineered such a neat arrangement.

But rebellious Kate was not grateful.

Abner was dull and had a host of tiresome relatives. Although he accepted the coming babe as his own—it would be born "premature" but he did not know that yet—Kate was fuming. Fuming over her suddenly ungainly body, fuming over the loss of the lads who had courted her so ardently.

And in a twisted way, she blamed Lorena. For it was a competitive spirit with Lorena that had driven her to such excesses.

When she saw Tabby coming out of the mill that first day, Kate's blue eyes sparkled. Here was Tabby, the wild young rogue who had played fast and loose with half the village girls, home again! Doubtless *he'd* provide her with some entertainment.

Kate crossed the road with an arch flirt of her skirts and intercepted him. She smiled seductively into his eyes as she told him how sorry she was about his father.

"Aye," said Tabby soberly. "I'd thought he and Lorena would be married by now, for they were betrothed when I left. I'd thought to come home and find a pot steaming over the fire and hear the mill wheel grinding."

Kate remembered hearing something about Lorena being betrothed to the miller, and the engagement being broken off after the vicar's death. She had dismissed it then as wild gossip, but now, seeing Tabby's stricken face, she knew it must be true. And Tabby, his mind filled with that hateful Lorena, was impervious to her charms.

" 'Twas Lorena was the death of him," she said spitefully, mindful that Lorena still walked free while she must go home of nights to confinement in what she considered a marital prison.

"What do you mean?" demanded Tabby, frowning.

Tossing her head, Kate told him a fanciful tale of a lovers' quarrel, how Lorena had run across the footbridge with Lyle Aylesbury in full pursuit. " 'Twas on the footbridge your father slipped and fell," Kate added regretfully, blending fact with fancy. "And 'twas said Lorena made no effort to get him out, that she wanted out of the betrothal and said afterward she took a sure way to end it!"

Tabby's face seemed hewn of stone. When he spoke, it was with a kind of killing restraint, as if he locked in devils. "I thank ye for telling me, Kate. D'you know where I can find her?"

Kate saw then that she had gone too far, but she was afraid to undo her mischief. She had only meant to exorcise Lorena from his mind, to make Tabby hate her rival so that he would turn his full attention on *her*. But now she saw a warlike gleam in his gray eyes and knew he would go seeking Lorena.

"Nobody knows where she is," Kate said in sulky confusion, hoping Tabby never found Lorena for then *she* might be caught up in her lie and called to account for it. "Lorena hasn't been seen since she came back after making some great commotion at the Olimpick Games. Flora won't tell anyone where she is."

"I'll find out where she's gone." Tabby's voice had murder in it. He took a quick leave of Kate and went down to inquire at the local tavern.

Nobody there had seen Lorena.

The next day Tabby got an offer for the mill. He was tempted to take it, but the need for revenge against the girl who had driven him from his home and destroyed his father ate at him. He wasn't ready yet to leave Twainmere. He could hardly swallow his ale for hating Lorena.

So when a bright-faced Lorena dashed up to the mill on her white horse and dismounted, it seemed to this new vengeful Tabby that providence had brought her to him—for punishment.

"Oh, Tabby!" Lorena ran toward him joyfully, for it was so wonderful to see him again. She had missed him so, and now he seemed to her taller, broader, older from his year at sea. She drank in the sight of him there in his leather jerkin and worn trousers with his legs wide apart, his arms folded, regarding her unblinkingly from the mill door. "Tabby!" She was flushed and breathless as she reached him: she had to hold herself back from throwing herself impetuously into his arms. "I'm so glad you're back, Tabby. I don't know what to do. Aunt Flora is getting married and—" Her voice faded as she saw the expression on his face. "What—what's the matter?" she faltered, taken aback.

"D'ye not know?" he demanded sarcastically.

"No, I don't. I—oh, Tabby," she remembered belatedly. "I'm so sorry about your father."

But Tabby was bearing down on her like a frigate on a light sailboat. "Tell me no more lies, Lorena!"

Lorena backed away a step in dismay. "Lies? I've never lied to you." Her voice sounded hurt. At his sudden snarl, she would have turned away in panic, but as she spun around her foot turned on a rock, her body twisted trying to right itself, and she sat down suddenly on the grass.

Undeterred by this mishap, the tall fellow swooped down on her and seized her hand in an ungentle grip. He would have preferred to grasp her by the hair but he didn't think of it in time. Roughly he hauled her to her feet and dragged her toward the mill.

"I should drown you!" he panted, almost overwhelmed by his intense emotions.

"Drown me?" Lorena, skidding along as best she could, gave him a look of pure horror. "Oh, Tabby! 'Twas you who saved me that day in the millrace."

"And I regret it!"

They were through the mill door now. The smell of rats was strong in the place. Lorena was sobbing from fright and Tabby's expression was wild. He flung her down upon a low pile of grain that waited patiently to be ground into flour, and stood glaring down at her.

Lorena cowered back. For a moment she thought he was going to kill her.

But he did not. A mixture of violent emotions played over his rugged young face—but uppermost was desire. "What kind of a woman are you?" he cried wildly. "I ought to kill you!"

She shrank back, but he was upon her, the weight of his lean body forcing her down upon the pile of grain. Through her light dress those grains dug into her back as she squirmed and tried to wrench free.

But escape was not to be.

Overcome with the miracle that at last Lorena, for whom he had longed so fervently, was pressed close against him, Tabby grasped her convulsively. Some of the grain cascaded down with a light rustling sound as Lorena struggled, panting, to free herself. Stunned by the sudden violence of his assault, she was quiveringly unaware whether he did not indeed intend to kill her and she fought him silently like a young wildcat.

But Tabby dug his toes into the yielding grain and held on grimly. One of his hands was locked in her hair behind her head, holding her head so that she must face him, and he held her legs down with his knee while with his free arm he jerked up her skirts, thigh-high.

Compulsion drove him. A burning compulsion to possess her, to press her young shuddering body close to his and savor all its sweetness. Gone was his desire to punish her. This was Lorena in his arms, and now, looking into those wide terrified blue eyes so near his own, he knew in the depths of his reckless heart that he loved her, had always loved her, had never stopped loving her. But the bitter thought flared up that she had proved herself a temptress and a wanton. He need have no regard for her, he could take her as he pleased.

And now with her skirts hiked up hip-high, Lorena divined his intention with certainty and gave a mighty lurch to free herself of him. She tried to cry out, but her cry was only a gurgle in her throat as Tabby's warm lips closed over hers and his strong tongue burst through them, probing, seeking, sending new shudders through her slight frame.

Torn between wild emotions herself, Lorena felt little tongues of flame, fierce in their intensity, run along her senses. Her heart, already pounding, seemed about to burst from her chest and take flight. How she had dreamed of some starry night when Tabby would take her to some bed of violets beside a shimmering stream and they would murmur as lovers do and slowly, slowly she would melt into his being and they would become one at last—*but not like this!* Not in an abandoned mill full of bats and spiders! Not with violence, ripping her skirts up to her waist and—! Her breath sobbed in her throat as she managed with a wrench to free her right arm. She beat upon his chest with her fist but Tabby seemed impervious to pain.

Dimly she was aware that Tabby had torn open his trousers now; shrinking back, she felt him moving against her bare skin. And Tabby felt a shockwave strike him with the force of a blow as his masculinity brushed her silken skin, evoking a violent shudder from Lorena.

Blood pounding in his temples, Tabby told himself he ought to hate her, she with her velvet wiles! Yet with every touch he could feel for her only tenderness and compassion. And he knew he could not drive into her like a spear and reduce her to a sobbing broken mass in his arms.

So, like a wild bird he held her now, stroking, soothing. And when she was quiet as some wild thing becomes quiet, frozen into a hypnotic waiting stillness born of confusion and dread, it was with gentleness that he made his first thrust. He felt the agonizing quiver that went through her slight young body, the instinctive recoil of her smooth stomach muscles bare beneath him—and felt his heart miss a beat that he had hurt her. He might have desisted then out of a fear of giving her further hurt, might even have fought back this torrent of wild unleased emotions that held him in thrall, might have let her go.

But now the message of his love for her had passed between them, borne on the soft relentless pressure of his lips, the determined yet delicate entrance he had made. For with that first thrust something sleeping within her had awakened and now in a burst of awakened response, Lorena flung herself against him with a wild sweet cry.

Dimly, through the blood that pulsed and roared in his ears, Tabby realized that Lorena had stopped fighting him, that her slender arms were wrapped tightly around his neck—and he could feel her tears, wet upon his cheek, as she pressed fiercely closer, ever closer.

Tabby caught his breath. She was no longer resisting him! She wanted him as much as he wanted her! And miraculously, she was not afraid. She was welcoming him, accepting him!

Confident now, Tabby thrust with more force.

At the sudden sharp pain in her loins as his surging masculinity knifed through her, Lorena choked back a scream and sagged against him. Then, as the leaping sword was withdrawn, she rallied. This was Tabby, this was her lover. Whatever madness had driven him to accuse her, whatever senseless anger had driven him to fling her down upon the grain and leap upon her, at this moment his masculine body could not lie to her. If love had made her defenseless before him, then love had struck down whatever it was he blamed her for. For all her innocence, as his flesh touched hers, burrowed so urgently, met its sweet response and lingered, then retired to plunge again, she was instinctively aware of the tenderness with which he held her, of his consideration for her virginity. Even through the bright haze of pain that seared her, she felt his fire—and his compassion. His torch kindled the latent fires within her youthful body so that the woman in her—for all that had befallen Lorena this past year had made a woman of the child—responded to him, welcomed him, held him, loved him, caressed him, murmured breathless endearments into his ear as he strove rhythmically now to bring her to match the soaring heights of his own reckless passion.

With fierce abandon and consummate skill he maneuvered the delicate body of the girl beneath him. Along uncharted seas he swept her, cresting mighty waves and dipping down into deep glistening hollows, only to surge again toward the sky.

Lorena forgot the grain that was scratching her back through her thin dress, she forgot the desperate trouble that had brought her here, she forgot everything but her lover, proving his love with every thrust.

She closed her eyes. Gone were the ancient heavy beams lost in dimness above her in the old mill. Instead she had ventured into a warm and pulsing darkness, a starlit world, half-seen but of unreal surpassing beauty, where everything blossomed and the rivers ran wine, a world lit up fitfully by the pulsing lightning bolts of her own flaring emotions.

On, on he swept her until at last the sudden tightening of her arms, the sudden fluttering of her body, the sob that rose in her throat, told him she had crested the last wave with him and was flying with him along bright distant shores. Not till then did Tabby let the floodgates on his own passion burst through and together they surmounted the last tall wave of passion and Lorena soared with him into the shining splendor of a burst of fiery beauty before they drifted down together onto a glass-smooth ocean that became once more the mill.

Panting, Tabby slid away and lay back upon the pile of grain. Lorena was sighing beside him.

In Lorena's arms, Tabby had dizzily lost his grasp on his world, but now, with force, that world came back to shame him. He could not love her—*not the girl who had driven his father to his death!*

He leaped to his feet and angrily adjusted his trousers, stood looking down on her with burning eyes.

"Get up," he said hoarsely. "Go home."

Lying there in the scooped-out hollow their threshing bodies had made in the grain pile, Lorena heard him with disbelief. From her prone position she stared up at him, towering above her.

"You took me by force," she whispered, "and now you're telling me *to go home?*"

" 'Tis what my father should have done!" The words were torn from him, but each one struck her a hammer blow. "What I did, I did in his name!"

None of this made sense to Lorena, but she could see that Tabby's expression had altered. The gray eyes were suffering, but that rugged jawline might have been hewn in stone. She could not know the churning emotions that drove him. She could only see his face—and that face was cold and hard.

Numbed by his words, she told herself that she had been mistaken. Love had not driven him, but only a desire for her body. Lorena gathered up what shreds of dignity were left to her. Shakily she scrambled to her feet, swiftly smoothing down her skirts with trembling hands, so that her bare legs might be hidden from his sight. Her heart hurt so much that she could hardly breathe. She was fighting back tears. In that moment she was proud that she could manage to control her voice.

"We are even, Tabby," she said bitterly. "You saved my life once when I would have drowned in the millstream —and now I have paid for it. I owe you nothing. Nothing!" Her angry voice rose in a sob. "Be damned to you, Tabby, you'll never see me again!" She whirled and stumbled away into the summer dusk.

In stony silence Tabby watched her go. Rigid, his strong chest heaving with the effort not to call her back, fighting to control his legs that wanted to run after her, he stood in the mill door and watched her scramble aboard Snowfire and disappear around a bend in the road.

She was gone.

Around him all was still, save for a tiny rustle as a winging swallow landed among the rafters. Pain banged dully in his head. He could not love a maid who had destroyed his father, brought him to dust! By God, he *would not!* And yet his loins ached with wanting her, his heart was breaking in his chest.

With a strangled sob, tall Tabby brought his clenched fist with force against the heavy hewn timbers of the mill door. The door shuddered under that assault and banged against the building, but Tabby felt the leaping pain of his bruised knuckles almost with gladness. He leant his hot forehead against that door and closed his eyes.

Leaning against that door, for the first time in his life, Tabby wept. Wept for his lost love who had betrayed him, who had betrayed them all . . . and yet he loved her still.

With drooping shoulders, poor Tabby, undone, took the familiar path to the tavern.

* * *

Proud and stiff-backed, Lorena did not go far. Once out of Tabby's sight, her slight frame was wracked by sobs. Her tears fell down unheeded upon Snowfire's gleaming white mane. At the first patch of trees she turned off the road and slipped off Snowfire's back and sank to the ground, shuddering and crying. In the space of one day her whole world had fallen apart, and for that lost world Lorena wept.

For a long time she lay there. The moon had risen when at last she rose. Pale but no longer weeping, she had come to a decision.

She could not return to Twainmere, for Alger Pye would seize her, find a way to hold on to her. She dared not appeal to Flora for that would break her heart. And perhaps if she were gone, Alger would show Flora his true colors and Flora would see him for what he was and reject him herself. Now Tabby too had failed her . . .

Hurt in mind and body, she climbed stiffly aboard Snowfire's back. She would ride for London, that was what she would do! She would leave them all behind her and never come back!

Silent now, on a proud old horse who seemed to understand, Lorena made her way to Maude's. On the hill above the Cardwell's croft she paused, looking down on the moon-silvered roof of the tiny cottage. She had dismounted and led Snowfire through the woods with its low-hanging branches, and now she stood there gravely for a long time, for she felt that she would never see the cottage or Maude again. Then quietly she led Snowfire down the hill, left him eating hay in the Cardwell's rickety barn.

No one in the moonlit cottage had stirred.

Lorena knew Maude slept in the loft above the room where her parents slept, which indeed comprised the whole of the downstairs. Cautious not to wake the elder Cardwells, Lorena cautiously threw pebbles at the tiny upstairs panes.

After a while Maude peered out, and almost fell through the open window when she saw Lorena.

"Bring the ladder," Maude whispered, and Lorena went to the barn and dragged a ladder back.

Carefully, with her chemise hiked up, Maude descended. She took one look at Lorena's disheveled hair and torn clothes and woebegone expression. "Alger Pye did that to you?" she whispered indignantly.

"No. Tabby."

Maude looked stunned. "I can't believe it," she muttered.

"Neither can I," admitted Lorena dully. "Maude, I can't go home. I don't have any money, and this dress isn't decent the way it's torn. I'm going to London, Maude."

Maude caught her breath. "To find your mother? Is she back in London then?"

"No. She was in Oxford last time I heard from her." Lorena couldn't bring herself to say it, but as she had lain on the ground weeping for Tabby, she had faced the truth about a lot of things. Among them, she had faced the truth about her lovely mother—a woman of tinsel and smoke and empty promises, a woman who had never loved her, who was never coming for her. "I'm going to work for that woman we met at the Olimpick Games—Lady Bennett."

To Maude, it seemed the best solution. "Wait," she said. "I'll draw some water from the well so you can wash, and I'll get you a dress of mine. 'Twill be too big, but perhaps that's just as well. You'll have to ride a long way alone and 'tis just as well if every curve doesn't show! And watch out for highwaymen—you haven't any money, so they might decide to take something else!"

Lorena shuddered at the kind of attention Maude felt she might attract.

"And I'll pack you something to eat," said Maude, very businesslike now that the first shock had subsided. "Let Snowfire eat all the hay and grain he wants in our barn. I'll tie a couple of big bundles of hay over his back so that you'll have something to give him if you have to stop where there's no food for a horse—and take these."

She rummaged and produced a few coins which she handed to Lorena with a look of pity. "I'm sorry—about Tabby."

"Thank you, Maude." Lorena took the coins. "It's all over between Tabby and me. I don't want to talk about it. Don't let anyone know where I've gone, Maude. Alger Pye would come after me."

Maude nodded.

Before the hour was out, Lorena had set out on the moonlit road to London.

The wedding next day did not come off. When Lorena was found to have been gone all night, Flora abandoned her wedding plans and set everyone to looking for her. Most of the searchers converged on Oxford, for Flora told them Lenore's last letter had come from there. But Alger Pye volunteered to lead the search in a more northerly direction, for he thought Lorena might have gone that way to lose herself at Banbury Fair.

The wedding was postponed—indefinitely.

Flora, whose dreams had never lied to her, had been right again: Lorena had come home and all her wedding plans had gone up in smoke.

Twainmere To London

Chapter 33

Having been stirred to life by the toe of the tavern keeper's boot, Tabby was making his way back to the mill the following morning when five mounted men passed him. Behind them ran Flora, calling out in a distracted way, "Now I remember! Lenore did say she had once stayed with a Mistress Watts in Oxford in a house off Magpie Lane—ye might inquire there."

"Aye," called back their leader. "We'll do that."

Tabby, who had paused to watch, turned as Flora hailed him. "I did not know ye were back, Tabby. 'Tis good to see you. The town has not been the same without your father, but now you're back to take his place. Will ye be opening the mill, Tabby?"

Tabby, who wished himself anywhere but here, admitted he was selling the mill.

"Too bad," sighed Flora. She gave Tabby a wistful look. "I suppose ye've not seen Lorena?" And when he shook his head, "I know now how your father felt,

Tabby. Now that Lorena is gone, I know how he must have felt when you left."

Lorena gone? Tabby felt a stirring of alarm. "Where has she gone?" he wondered.

"None know. Those men"—she nodded at the horsemen down the road—"and others are off to search for her. Ah, Tabby," she sighed, "I did wrong not to tell Lorena that Robbie had betrothed her to your father. 'Twas *my* doing that it be kept secret, for I knew she loved you, and I had hoped that you and she ..." Her voice trailed off before the look of dawning horror on Tabby's face.

"She did not know?" he cried hoarsely. "But all the town knew—even Kate."

"About that, I'd not be knowing," said Flora. "But Lorena did not know, for she was so young we kept it from her. And after Robbie died, I spoke to your father and he agreed to break it off—and Lorena did not know about that either. I thought it best not to—"

Flora stopped. She had never looked into a wilder pair of eyes. Tabby had fallen back a step as if he had been shoved backward, and his face was ashen. He felt as if the sky had fallen on him. Lorena had never known about any of it! In her innocence, she had been but trying to show him how she felt about him, hoping that he would make some move. *And he had. Oh, God, he had!* He had read evil into her innocence, guile into her girlish laughter. He had made Lorena pay a terrible price for his vile suspicions, and now she had run away!

He felt sick.

Flora watched in pity as he stumbled away from her. Poor Tabby, she thought with compassion. He is taking this hard. If only he had come back sooner.

For it never occurred to her that Tabby's return had anything to do with Lorena's departure.

Obsessed with a desire to find Lorena, to make amends—at least to grovel before her and beg her forgiveness—Tabby went straight to Maude.

He found her at the washtubs outside the Cardwell cottage, unwilling to speak to him. Her face was flushed and her hands red from the steaming water in the big wooden tub, but her eyes flashed resentfully at sight of him. "I've naught to say to you, Tabby," she said tersely. "Not after what ye did to Lorena!"

So she had seen Lorena afterward. "I've come to make amends, Maude."

"And how'll ye be doing that?" Maude's voice was tart. "Lorena went to you for help when Alger Pye told her he was marrying Flora only so that he could bed her, that he'd keep Flora for a housekeeper and Lorena to warm his bed! And you—"

"He did what?" cried Tabby. "I'll kill him!"

Maude leaned forward. "What you did was no better!"

"You're right," sighed Tabby. "I've no excuse. I should be shot."

Maude blinked; this was an about-face indeed! "Why did ye treat her so?" she asked in an altered voice. "Didn't you know she loved you?"

A tremor shook Tabby's big frame. Ah, that he had not known, not till Flora told him! "Kate lied to me," he muttered thickly. "She told me—ne'er mind what she told me. I blamed Lorena for my father's death and now I know I was wrong."

"Indeed you were! Your father got drunk one night and fell into the millstream and drowned, that's all there was to it! Lorena was home in bed, same as I was!"

"Maude," pleaded Tabby. "I'm half daft with worry. Tell me where she went."

"Ah, that I won't. I promised her I wouldn't and I won't." Maude wrung out a kirtle so hard she nearly pulled the seams apart. She flung it onto the grass and put her hands on her hips. "Nor can you beat it out of me!"

A groan rose from the depths of him. Lorena had come to him in her hour of desperate need, and he had mocked her, rejected her—raped her! And sent her away!

"Help me ye may not, Maude, but I'll spend the rest of my life looking for her if I have to." He stalked to his horse and flung a leg over the saddle.

"Wait." Maude almost knocked over the washtub as she ran after him. "I believe you, Tabby. Lorena's gone to London. Ye'll find her working for a grand lady who offered us jobs in her household as servants at the Olimpick Games. Her name's Lady Bennett."

All the color drained from Tabby's face. "Are ye sure of this, Maude?"

"Certain sure. Lorena told me herself when she left last night."

"My God, Maude," Tabby cried hoarsely. "All in London know that 'Lady' Bennett is no lady at all, but a brothel keeper who lures virgins into her establishment and then sells them to the Hellfire Club!"

"Oh, no!" wailed Maude. "Lorena doesn't know that!"

"I'm to London, Maude—I'll find her!" Tabby wheeled his horse toward a shortcut that would join the road up farther and left the croft at full gallop.

As he rode, Tabby lashed himself with the bitter whip of conscience. Lorena, his sweet trusting Lorena, was on her innocent way to the hands of that monstrous woman who'd turn her over to that evil pack at the Hellfire Club and then, broken in body and spirit, launch her on a career as a London whore—*and it was all his fault*.

Forgotten was the selling of the mill, forgotten was his dream of settling in the Colonies and establishing a mill there. Tabby wore out three horses on the road to London. He overshot Lorena, who was sleeping in a copse by the roadside as he charged by, and reached London four days before she did.

In London he burst into "Lady" Bennett's establishment and demanded loudly that she turn over Lorena Frankford to him. "Lady" Bennett gave this country lad a distasteful look and had four of her brawny huskies throw him into the street.

Tabby got up off the cobbles and collected himself. He would make the rounds of the inns. Perhaps Lorena had heard about "Lady" Bennett's profession in time and had put up at some inn whilst she sought gainful employment. He combed London for her, but he was at Moorfields seeking her among the laundresses there when Lorena, tired and exhausted, rode through the gates of London.

Unused to these twisting alleys, she got lost in the city and had a difficult time finding the address. But at last she tumbled wearily off Snowfire in front of "Lady" Bennett's plush establishment, left Snowfire in the street with a boy holding him—she'd promised him a coin which she must get from her shoe, for she was down to her last penny—and announced herself.

The man with the black patch who opened the door looked her up and down with cold reptilian eyes. He turned to see his employer rustling down the stairs in candy-striped taffeta.

"Lady Bennett." Spying her behind him, Lorena made a tired but dignified little curtsy. "I'm Lorena Frankford."

"Lady" Bennett stared at her in disbelief.

"You do remember me?" Lorena pursued anxiously. "Lenore Frankford's daughter?"

London

Chapter 34

It was a stern-faced Geoffrey who shortly after dawn mounted his big chestnut stallion and took the road to London. Alongside him on a dappled gray gelding rode a sleepy George, whom Geoffrey had routed out of the bed he had just fallen into, with a "Come on, George. You're the only English house servant I've got—all the rest are French. Ride along with me today. It may be I'll have a message to send back to Claremont Court." George had struggled up, vaguely aware that by the word "English" Geoffrey meant "trusted." Like estate manager Glendower, George was fond of Geoffrey and had withstood all of Letiche's attempts to unseat him. Entirely unflappable, George intended to remain in Geoffrey Wyndham's service for life, if that French termagant who ruled Claremont Court did not trump up some grounds to dismiss him.

On any other day George might have attempted light conversation with the master, but on this day Geoffrey's lowering brows gave off a warning. As the exercise of riding along country roads gradually woke him up, it was borne in on George that his master had not buckled on one of his light dress swords but was sporting instead his favorite weapon: a scarred but serviceable basket-hilted sword that he had carried during England's Civil Wars and that was his favorite for dueling. George's eyes widened and he sat on his horse straighter; it could be that today he would witness some of the master's justly famous swordplay!

They reached London in a light drizzle, and the horses' hooves rang plaintively on the wet cobbles as they wound through laden carts and hawkers making their rounds, through hurrying servants and tradesmen and bankers and brokers, all starting their day in the wet.

Ordinarily he might have avoided these crowds, but a tight-lipped Geoffrey was this morning headed for de Vignac's apartments and a confrontation with the "Black Marquis." For Geoffrey intended to give Letiche's kinsman a lesson he would never forget.

Unfortunately, someone else had already done that.

The night before, when Nell Gwyn had received de Vignac's threatening note, she was tempted to tear it up and throw it into the face of the manservant who had brought it. Incriminating letters indeed! Who would write her "incriminating" letters?

But reason triumphed over fury and Nell sat down to think. The "Black Marquis" had an evil reputation. It was said he had ruined a noblewoman in France—done such a thorough job of it that she'd ended up in a lunatic asylum. Nell did not fear any such fate for despite her lightsome ways, few in London had such a level head on their shoulders. Still, whatever de Vignac was threatening, it would be a bad time for a scandal to come to the attention of the king. For Nell had quarreled violently with Charles—indeed she had ended up throwing a goblet of wine at her monarch. Had she flung the wine into his face in private, Charles might have disciplined Nell personally—and ended up in bed with her at the end of a tearful struggle. But Nell had thrown the goblet in full view of half a dozen courtiers. Charles' long dark face, dripping with claret, had gone ugly, his black eyes had glared murderously at Nell and before she could apologize—for in her panic at what she had done, that was indeed her intention—he had brushed her aside and slammed out. Within the hour she had been cleared out of Whitehall with orders not to return. That had been several weeks ago, and Nell was scheming to get him back. She was sure his French favorite, Louise de Keroualle, had poisoned his mind against her with some unfounded tale of infidelity—for gossip to the contrary, Nell had never been unfaithful to her royal lover; it was, she felt, the best hold she had over Charles, who had not been so lucky with others. Even now, she was sure, he was reassessing his accusation which had prompted the throwing of the wine—and possibly regretting it. But if this Frenchman, de Vignac, were somehow to *reinforce* Charles' halfhearted belief that Nell had been having an affair, she might never get him back! Indeed he might revenge himself upon her by removing her from the King's Company of Players and wreck her career on the London stage!

Nell jumped up and ordered out her coach. She would confront that damned Frenchman tonight!

The marquis was expecting her. His hard eyes raked Nell up and down as she was ushered into his bedroom by his manservant, stripping her of vizard mask and satin petticoats and chemise. Before him in his mind stood the lovely naked Nell painted by Lelys. It was but a step to imagine her in his bed, lying stretched out nude on the satin coverlet with her arms wide to receive him and pleading placating words on her full red cupid's bow lips.

For de Vignac had been very successful with women. He viewed Nell contemptuously as a street girl come to prominence through the capriciousness of royal favor. Just another London whore, he told himself, only more beautiful.

But the Marquis de Vignac had underestimated Nell Gwyn. Child of the brothel she might be, brought up on the London streets and a prostitute before she was thirteen, but Nell had had many lovers and she was a superb judge of men.

Now she sized de Vignac up: treacherous, cruel, scheming. The letters would be real.

She must get them back.

She asked to see the letters, and when de Vignac saw that uneducated Nell was having trouble reading them, he smilingly offered to read them aloud to her. His smile deepened when she became very upset on hearing the first letter, twisting her hands together and walking in a distraught manner about the room. When he read out the signature she tottered against the writing desk, but managed to right herself with an obvious effort. By the time he was halfway through the second letter she was pacing about him in a circle, sobbing into her petticoat which she had brought up to hide her tearful face.

But before he read the signature on that one, a heavy paperweight Nell had snatched up when she "tottered" against the writing desk crashed into the back of his head and the "Black Marquis" sank senseless to the floor.

Nell stopped crying in mid-sob and stood looking down at him calmly. Fine actress that she was, it had been an easy thing to display a convincing hysteria; she had done what de Vignac expected her to do—broken up and wept. Now she bent and removed the two letters from the Marquis' limp bejeweled fingers and stuffed them into the bodice of her gown. She was shrewd enough to realize that Geoffrey Wyndham, who had never shown her anything but cold civility—naturally enough, since he was in love with her old enemy, Lenore Frankford—had not written these letters. Nell did not doubt her charms, but such sudden passion in one who had always regarded her with distaste was inconceivable to her. So if these letters had been forged, there might be others. And where would they be hidden? Why, here in the marquis' bedchamber, of course, where he could watch over them.

Casting her keen gaze about the room, she quickly eliminated the bed—servants might discover the letters there. And the bureau as well—his valet would be constantly into that, as well as the great armoire. That left the dainty pair of French commodes and the writing desk. Hurriedly she searched the commodes and found nothing. As she advanced on the desk, her eyes gleamed, for it had its mate in Whitehall. With ease she found the secret compartment and pulled out the six letters de Vignac had secreted there.

She tore open the first one and scanned it, and then the next. Nell did not need to read any more to see what was afoot. She stuffed them all into her bodice and rang for a servant.

"Your master has had an accident," she told the servant dryly, indicating the Marquis' prone but now stirring body, and swished past him down the stairs to her waiting coach.

As the coach took her home over the cobbled streets she patted the thick packet in her bodice and began to laugh. The two love letters she would burn in the fireplace, but those letters to the Dutch ambassador were the stuff that brought men to the block.

Nell smiled as she peered into the tiny ivory-framed mirror she always carried with her. Lord, she looked as if she'd been tussling in the gutter all night—circles under her eyes, puffy! She'd just catch a few hours' sleep, and in the morning she'd dress in her newest gown—a honey-colored satin that did wonderful things for her hair—before she confronted the king with this distressing news about his trusted friend, Geoffrey Wyndham! Nell's bright eyes sparkled with malice as she envisioned how touchingly she would tell Charles how his beloved Nell had risked life and virtue to procure these damaging letters from the "Black Marquis." She knew Charles' character well—he'd need some good excuse to forgive her, and these letters, which implicated one of Charles' friends in a treason plot, would be proof of her fidelity, of her love for the royal person.

Nell sighed and savored it all. This damning packet of letters, whether forgeries or not, would bring her all she wanted. She would bring Geoffrey—and thereby Lenore, she reasoned—down with a single blow, and before the candles were lit at Whitehall tomorrow, she would be back in the king's favor. Nell settled her full skirts about her in the bouncing coach, leaned back, and recrossed her pretty legs.

A little sleep—and then Whitehall!

*   *   *

Had Geoffrey continued in his present direction, he would have intersected the route of peppery Nell Gwyn, who was at the moment on her way to Whitehall with letters that could send him to the block. But the drizzle was slackening and Geoffrey guessed if the sun came out, he would find Charles on the tennis courts. There he could cut short the formalities and give his report verbally to his monarch between games—and deal with the "Black Marquis" at his leisure. It occurred to him that he might want to do that, for the urge to feel his knuckles crash into the Frenchman's jaw had long been with him. Indeed it would be a pleasure to pound the truth from de Vignac blow by blow—and if the Marquis objected, they could always settle the matter with steel.

He wheeled his horse around. "We'll to Whitehall first, George."

George was disappointed. He had hoped Geoffrey would challenge de Vignac to a duel; it would have pleased George thoroughly to watch Geoffrey cut the odious marquis in half. For Geoffrey had told George at the city gates where they were going.

But for Geoffrey the changed course was a fateful decision, for his path now led him directly in front of Newgate Prison.

As he approached, he saw the high-sided cart pull up at the entrance but paid little attention to it. It was merely another cart delivering its doleful burden of wrongdoers to the jaws of the infamous old building. Then just as they came alongside the cart, the rain stopped and the sun came out, shafting down on the head of a woman who stood in the front of the cart staring up at the building. The man beside her had just shifted his position so that Geoffrey was afforded a full view of her strained but lovely face, the defiant set of her shoulders. And even wet, her tumbled hair streamed down over those shoulders in burnished red-gold beauty.

Geoffrey's heart seemed to stop. He reined in his chestnut stallion so suddenly that the great beast reared up and pawed the air. The blood left his face as he stared at the woman. For a moment George, who had come to a hasty halt too, thought the master had had some kind of seizure. Perhaps they should have left the bandage on that cut! George moved forward but Geoffrey did not even see him.

She was here. Lenore. After all this time. And some fool was taking her to jail!

"Hold, there!" he called. "You in the cart! Of what crime does this woman stand accused?"

Lenore spun around, violet eyes widening, lips parted. By what miracle had Geoffrey found her?

The cold authority of Geoffrey's tone made the surly fellow who drove the cart turn and stare in the direction of the newcomer. "For debt, yer lordship—she and the fellow with her." He indicated Christopher.

Geoffrey ignored the crystal eyes and golden-bearded face that swung toward him. "There is some mistake," he said flatly. "This woman is under my protection. I'll pay her debts."

George leaned forward, fascinated. The beauty of the woman in the cart was unmistakable—this must be the orange girl of whom the staff at Claremont Court whispered!

But Lenore, standing white and still and feeling herself snatched magically from doom, was thrilled by that calm pronouncement. Through Geoffrey's words had seemed to toll a great bell: *she belongs to me.*

But Geoffrey was intent on dealing with her captors. "What are these debts?" he demanded.

"I've a list of them here, yer lordship."

"Good. Hand it over. I'll see they're paid." Geoffrey thrust the list at George, along with a purse of gold. "See to it, George, and when it's done, join me at the Hart."

With one more delighted look at the orange girl, so that he might remember and describe her later to all who would listen, George cantered away across the slippery cobbles.

Geoffrey was leaning forward, his hard gaze fixed on the driver of the cart. "Mind she is treated well," he warned. "For I'll be back for her."

"She'll have to see the magistrate—"

"Bother the magistrate. 'Tis a king's pardon I'll get for her! And if so much as a hand is laid upon this lady's flesh, I'll exact blood for it!" Geoffrey touched the basket hilt of his sword meaningfully.

The cart driver was taken aback. "Aye, yer lordship," he agreed meekly. "I'll pass the word along the wench is to be well treated."

"Not 'wench,'" snarled Geoffrey. "*Lady!*"

"Lady!" gasped the driver, mentally feeling the point of that wicked blade at his throat.

"Lenore." Geoffrey turned to her at last. "Be of good heart. 'Twill not be long."

"Oh, Geoffrey." Weak with relief, Lenore leaned over the side of the cart. "You must get a pardon for Christopher too."

George was around the corner by now, but all present could see the tremor that went through Geoffrey Wyndham's tall frame. He seemed to grow taller in the saddle, his wide shoulders seemed to broaden. Unbelieving, he gazed into those pleading violet eyes. "What, ye want me to plead for your lover's release?" he demanded silkily.

His tone should have warned her, but Lenore, overcome with joy and relief that she had found him again in this hour of need, cried heedlessly, "Yes—oh, Geoffrey, you must do it!"

She had not seen his face so pale or his expression

so terrible since he had come upon Christopher embracing her in York. That look staggered her. But she could not leave Christopher here in this terrible place. Her fingers tightened their hold on the cart's high side. "Geoffrey, I will not go unless Christopher goes also," she whispered.

"Then be damned to ye!" Geoffrey shouted. He almost crashed into the cart as he wheeled his horse around and galloped recklessly away over the slippery cobbles.

Lenore's body sagged as she watched horse and rider recede from sight. Escape had been so near . . . Tears filled her eyes that Geoffrey should be so unjust. And yet, she should have known this would happen, for she knew so well his jealousy. He would leave her here, just as he had in York.

But even as Lenore seemed to shrink, beside her Christopher Dorn stood straighter. His chest expanded and he suddenly squared his shoulders. He looked down upon her bowed head with tender concern. *I will not go unless Christopher goes also.* Every thrilling word of that utterance had gone right through him. Now he gazed upon this woman he loved so much, and understood why Geoffrey Wyndham could not get her out of his blood. Not only her beauty but her valor, her bold spirit and her bright loyalty bound him to her.

And he had been convinced she would throw him aside for Geoffrey Wyndham if ever they met! Yet she had lifted her small determined chin and defied Geoffrey for him. She had condemned herself to prison *for him!* In that moment Christopher Dorn knew that given the chance he would gladly lay down his life for her.

"Ye should not have done that, Lenore," he muttered, when he could speak for the lump in his throat. " 'Twas your chance to escape this place!"

Lenore's knuckles were white. Filled with despair, she was staring at the glistening empty cobblestones where Geoffrey had disappeared. But as Christopher spoke she rallied and lifted her head high. " 'Tis no matter, Chris," she told him bravely. "We'll find our own way out."

But Christopher knew they would not. Not from Newgate. His arm went round her protectively for the cart was moving again, and now the damp gray walls of Newgate Prison closed around them.

Through endless echoing corridors where daylight never really struck, they wound, led by a jailer who carried a huge ring of keys, until finally they arrived in a common room where male and female felons mingled with debtors and there was a great clamor going on.

Instinctively Lenore pressed close to Christoper, who felt even his hardy brow break out in perspiration as he surveyed the scene around them.

"Have ye money?" they were asked. When they replied they had none, they were told contemptuously that here only those with money would survive for long, for everything must be bought—linens, a bed, even food. Then their jailer left them.

"Would ye like to sit down over there, Lenore?" Christopher asked, indicating a stone niche in the dripping wall that was at the moment unoccupied.

"No," she shuddered. "It looks so—dirty."

His heart went out to her. "We'll just stand here a bit and get our bearings," he agreed.

"Yes." Her head was high but her heart was somewhere down near the toes of her shoes. She had heard terrible reports of Newgate, but the truth was worse. Inside the prison on this damp day, even the walls wept. But Lenore, standing with her hands clenched together beside Christopher Dorn, was oblivious to the sweating walls and the stale prison stench about them. In one corner a dead rat was being attacked by flies. Down the corridor someone was screaming drunkenly and there was the sound of blows. Lying on the floor, a thin girl, hardly more than a child, coughed incessantly. But Lenore's attention was focused on a half-clothed madwoman with bony clutching hands and long, straggly, gray hair. Bent over and chuckling insanely to herself, the woman was circling her, coming ever closer. Lenore, steeling herself to meet the expected onrush, the clawing hands and maniacal laughter—and perhaps even the crunch of teeth, for the hag had a fang or two left—met the bleary gaze of a big woman with unkempt dark hair.

"Pish, pay old Bonnie no mind," said the dark-haired woman carelessly. "She's only scouting now. 'Tis after dark she'll come at you. 'Tis your finery she wants."

An involuntary shudder shook Lenore. She turned to look at Christopher and saw him grimly studying a whispering group of burly thugs who were eyeing them, for this was the common room and male and female prisoners mixed freely during the daylight hours. Lenore guessed that ugly group was studying Christopher's fine clothes and planning to pounce upon him and steal them as he slept. There were others milling around eyeing them too: unclean wenches and evil-looking men, all the worse for the filth and sores that were everywhere apparent. Many of them were staring at Lenore with a hard unblinking gaze. *Waiting for night, waiting for us to fall asleep,* she thought, and felt herself trembling.

For she had no doubt that before morning both she and Christopher would be overcome, stripped naked for the expensive, though sodden, clothing on their backs, and then—she closed her eyes, only to have them fly open again with a start as Christopher squeezed her hand.

"I'll find us a corner," he said.

"But how will we eat?" asked Lenore. "You heard the jailer say that prisoners must cook their own food, and provide it too." That meant the impoverished must beg . . . or sell themselves for bread.

"My doublet will bring something. We can live for a while on that."

And after that? Lenore gave him a sad look.

"Ye should not have demanded that Wyndham free me too." Christopher's face was tormented. "Though I bless ye for it, Lenore."

Lenore managed what she hoped was an indifferent shrug. "We arrived in this place together, we'll leave it together, Chris."

For a moment Christopher Dorn could not speak. He had brought her to this hellhole, and yet she had not a word of reproach for him. In that moment he regretted to the full his wasted life. He should have spent all his days in a mighty effort to be worthy of this woman—and here he was in Newgate Prison. And by his folly he had brought her down with him.

Christopher is right, thought Lenore in panic. From outside, I could have arranged for his release. In here nothing is possible. We could even—her heart wavered at the thought—*we could even die here.* She clenched her hands the tighter and tried not to let him see the terror she felt at being caged with this terrible collection of human filth that had been dredged from the London streets.

Luckily for her sanity, Lenore did not know that her daughter Lorena, reeling with fatigue, had arrived in London and was even now knocking on "Lady" Bennett's door, hoping to find "domestic employment." Even as Lenore gazed hopelessly around her at the human dregs of Newgate, "Lady" Bennett, her eyes widening in surprise and her wide smile flashing to reveal two missing teeth, was lisping a welcome to the girl and ushering her to an upstairs bedroom.

" 'Tis—'tis very fine," Lorena said doubtfully, looking around her at the red damask draperies and the gaudy coverlet on the big bed.

"Yes, well, I treat my domestics well," said "Lady" Bennett hastily. "You can rest a while, my dear. You won't be disturbed."

Lorena's voice was blurred with fatigue. "No, I've got to go attend to Snowfire. He's out in the street."

"Snowfire? Oh, your horse. I'll see that he's stabled and cared for. You didn't just leave him wandering about out there?"

"A boy came up and offered to hold him for me.

He'll expect a coin for it." And that coin was in her shoe—her last. She took off her slipper and proffered the coin to "Lady" Bennett.

"Lady" Bennett stepped back in distaste. These country girls and their coppers! Why just to view this wench stripped, with her hair fluffed around her like moonlight and the candleglow gleaming on her pale body, would bring a storm of guineas! "Keep your coin," she said, waving the money airily away. "We'll take good care of your horse. I can see you need rest, child." For there were dark smudges of fatigue under Lorena's big expressive blue eyes, and "Lady" Bennett wanted this prize package who had arrived unannounced to look her best when presented to her avid clientele. What would Lord Faltrop not pay for this one?

"I hope," she said severely, "that you're a good girl, Lorena. No lying beneath the gooseberry bushes with young men!"

Lorena blushed deeply. It was a strange question, but she supposed an employer who was taking someone into her household had a right to ask. "Oh, no," she murmured. "I have no young man at all." That last was true, she told herself, and a pile of grain was certainly not a gooseberry bush. She was *almost* a virgin.

"Lady" Bennett sighed with relief. Still pure! Oh, what wonderful luck—it was so difficult to find a young girl like that these days! "Just rest," she crooned. "There'll be plenty to do later." Indeed, she chuckled inwardly, that would be true!

Lorena looked gratefully at the big bed. Now that she was here, really in London at last, past all the terrors of the road, she felt fatigue stealing over her like a warm cloak. "Lady" Bennett's voice seemd to buzz in her ears and drift away. Lorena fell across the bed and was instantly asleep.

How lovely the girl looked lying there with her fair hair spread across the pillow and one dainty white arm outflung! In her thin dress the sweet line of her young back, the soft rise of her buttocks, were appetizingly apparent. "Lady" Bennett tiptoed out and carefully locked the door behind her. She was very deft and made not a sound with the well-oiled lock, for she had done it often before, and for the same purpose.

So her offer made at the Cotswold Games had borne fruit after all. The girl had found her way to London. Lenore Frankford's daughter! What a sensation that would create! She went and peered out into the street. No white horse was in sight—obviously the lad who'd offered to "hold" him for Lorena had stolen the beast! "Lady" Bennett sighed. These country girls were so trusting! Ah, well, a horse would bring nothing compared to the price of the girl!

She smote her striped taffeta-clad thigh, and called softly to the cutthroat with the black patch. He appeared with alacrity. "We've just received a priceless piece of merchandise, John," she told him. "Hurry to Lord Faltrop. If you can't reach him, Wilsingame will do. Tell him I've a beautiful virgin for sale for tonight's meeting of the Hellfire Club. Say the price will be five hundred pounds —for she's Lenore Frankford's daughter!"

Upstairs, Lorena slept peacefully.

The Royal Palace
of Whitehall, London

Chapter 35

Since her most recent row with the king, Nell Gwyn had
been denied entrance to Whitehall. Now, having slept and
donned her new honey-colored satin gown, she hurried
her coachman through the drizzling rain, enduring the
bumps and teeth-jarring halts necessitated by the uneven
roads and morning traffic—and when the rain stopped,
the raucous, good-humored calls of passersby, for Nell's
pretty face was well known in London.

It was difficult for her to force an entrance at Whitehall, for the king's orders on the subject had been specific.
But by dint of ravishing smiles, the exhibition of a very
deep décolletage, and the whispered urgency of her "mission," she managed to arrive in an antechamber of the
room where the king was at present seated at breakfast
among his courtiers and court ladies.

Nell was announced just as Charles, his plumed hat
by custom clamped squarely upon his head, lifted to his
mouth a bite of the excellent spiced capon before him. At
the sound of her name, Charles put down the capon and
said in a voice that carried clear into the anteroom where

Nell was waiting, "Tell Mistress Nell I am still annoyed with her. Since I did not summon her to my presence, she will leave the palace at once."

In the anteroom Nell winced, but around the king's breakfast table knowing looks were exchanged. *So his majesty was still at outs with Nell Gwyn, those looks said. Doubtless Louise de Keroualle or Barbara Villiers was in better case—best hew to them.*

"She says it is a matter of some urgency, your Majesty," Charles was told by the unhappy fellow who had announced her, and who took this liberty only because he had been well tipped by Nell. "About some letters."

"What?" quipped a splendidly dressed courtier who sat nearest the king. "Has the wench learned to read?"

Charles frowned. He had always been touchy about his women. "Tell Nellie I will receive her at supper," he said in a quelling voice. His dark eyes raked the company around him; they had always been against Nell because of her low beginnings. It would amuse him tonight to make them bow and scrape to her. But in the meantime, exuberant Nell must be disciplined; there must be no repetition of the goblet throwing. "But she must go home now," he added coldly, "for I've a tennis game to play, now that the rain has stopped. And her talents lie in another direction."

A polite titter greeted this sally; the group was wary now for saucy Nell might yet return to favor.

From behind the door in the next room Nell heard it all. Her cheeks were stained red because the courtier's words had touched a sore spot—Nell had learned to read but not to write. She rushed away and as she left White-hall, her coach, its windows prudently covered lest it rain again, was mistaken by the crowd for that of the King's French mistress, Louise de Keroualle, whom the Londoners hated. They pelted the coach with eggs and vegetables until Nell, enraged by the cries of "French whore! Go back to France!" leaned out the window and shouted, paraphrasing the words of her famous predecessor, Anne Boleyn, "Ye stupid dolts! Can't ye see I'm not the French whore? I am the *English* one!"

A wave of laughter greeted this angry utterance, and the crowd fell back, some of them cheering, for Nell Gwyn was popular in London.

"Go faster," she screamed to the coachman. "Damn them all!" She was almost crying, for she had set her heart on making a grand entrance and thrusting the letters into the king's face so that he could read them before all the company. But as the coach bounced along the cobbles, buoyant Nell began to feel better. Tonight that slight puffiness under her eyes would not be so apparent; she would brush her hair into a shining mass, her gown would be aglitter with brilliants All evening she would tease and tantalize Charles about the contents of the letters. Then, when the royal interest was piqued both by her plunging décolletage and by her quips, she would show him the extent of her devotion by handing him this packet of incriminating letters!

Nell's eyes took on a mercenary gleam. She had a suspicion she was pregnant by the king. Bringing these letters to the king's attention should reward her unborn son—if it were indeed a son—with a dukedom!

So Nell retraced her route, with the seeds of Geoffrey Wyndham's downfall as yet unplanted. On such small things do the fate of men and nations hang.

*   *   *

At Whitehall, athletic King Charles was upon the tennis courts as soon as he finished breakfast. He was about to serve the ball when he saw Geoffrey Wyndham come striding through the crowd of court hangers-on, most of whom looked a little seedy from last night's debauchery. He waved his racket at Geoffrey but tossed the ball aside when he saw Geoffrey's grim determined face. What the devil was afoot? Had the Dutch invaded and was Geoffrey here to bring him the news?

In silence, he heard Geoffrey out.

"So it is not some West Country devilment that brings ye here so hotfoot!" A smile quirked the corners of the king's full lips. "Did I hear ye aright, Geoffrey? Am I to understand that ye wish a King's Pardon for your wench—*and her lover?*"

Geoffrey's teeth ground slightly at that humorous inflection, swiftly echoed by a faint ripple of chuckles from the agog onlookers, but he nodded. "Aye, ye heard me aright, Sire. Ye have my word that my man George is even now making good those debts. I would go forthwith to Newgate and have them both released into my custody."

The quirking smile had become a grin, and now a shout of laughter broke forth from the royal mouth, and the royal shoulders and great black periwig shook with mirth. "Then a pardon for them both ye shall have," gasped the king, slapping his thigh. "God's teeth, Geoffrey, but ye never cease to amaze me. I can understand your seeking a pardon for the woman, but why do ye not leave your rival to rot in jail?"

"Because," grated Geoffrey, "I could not get at him in prison. 'Tis my aim to rid the world of him."

"Ah-h-h." Understanding gleamed in the king's dark eyes. "I could not think ye meant to become a threesome. Perhaps 'tis the best way. Direct—and permanent. Well, then." He clapped Geoffrey on the shoulder. "We must hasten the moment when ye splatter the ground with your rival! You there!" He waved to a scribe who scuttled over and began to write industriously, using a stone balustrade for a desk. While the court looked on in wonder, Charles leaned upon his tennis racket and grinned at Geoffrey. Never had a Royal Pardon for two culprits been secured so speedily, for when Geoffrey left he bore it with him, complete with the King's Great Seal. When he was half a dozen steps away, the king, with mirth still uppermost in his voice, called after him, "Ye must let me know how it comes out, Geoffrey."

Geoffrey turned and his gaze swept the avid faces of the courtiers and court ladies. "Sire, ye'll have word of it in Whitehall, I don't doubt, before ever I can bring ye the tidings!"

Charles gave a roar of laughter. "Aye, that's God's truth, Geoffrey. How the gossips here do it is a wonder." But his gaze at that broad departing back was rueful. For it was gossip after all that had rent Nell Gwyn from him; and perhaps unreliable gossip at that. He had been hard on her this morning. Ah, well, he would remedy that tonight. For Nell's wit amused the King. Hadn't she once saucily said that to all of England he might be Charles the Second, but to her—since she had had two lovers named Charles before him—he would always be Charles the Third? As he turned to resume his game, he shook his dark head and said aloud, "I would love to see today's foolishness when Wyndham and his rival meet at Newgate!"

A laughing feminine voice reached him over the general clamor. "Then I will watch it for ye, Sire, and bring ye a report on it!" Louise de Keroualle, that beautiful temptress who had been sent from France to seduce the English monarch and had succeeded all too well, glided forward. Her gown of ripe cherry red silk rippled, and there was the intimate rustle of taffeta petticoats as she made the king an elaborate curtsy. Charles' hot dark eyes followed her as she ran lightly away.

But Louise knew the populace hated her. She left discreetly by sedan chair with curtains drawn even in this heat and hurried the panting men who carried her, lest she miss the forthcoming scene at Newgate.

* * *

Inside Newgate Prison, Lenore was listening, stiff with horror, to a stooped old man querulously asking Christopher if he was under sentence of death. When Christopher shook his head, the old man sighed regretfully. "If ye were," he confided in a singsong voice, "ye'd be seated in the 'condemned pew' at chapel—them as is condemned to death, they sits around a coffin at chapel to prepare them for the next world. 'Tis a pretty sight."

"Half these people belong in Bedlam," Christopher muttered when the old man limped away.

That hellhole? Lenore shuddered, then asked herself if even a lunatic asylum would be any worse than Newgate when night closed down. And night was surely coming.

"I'll send word to Geoffrey at the Hart," she announced desperately. "He can't leave us here."

And then I will lose you, thought Christopher. *All I will ever have of you will be these short hours in jail, for Wyndham would be a fool ever to let me go—my freedom would threaten him. He will see that I am kept here for life.* "You must do that at once," he said. "For I like not the idea of your spending the night here."

"Yes." Lenore started and almost screamed aloud as a heavy hand fell upon her arm. She whirled to face a heavyset slattern in a dirty apron who dangled a large ring of keys. "Ye're to go with me, Mistress Frankford," she instructed. "And you too, Mister Dorn."

Silently they padded after the heavyset woman though the tortuous corridors and once again found themselves blinking in the sunlit courtyard outside Newgate's thick walls—where Geoffrey waited.

"This gentleman has paid your debts and brought ye both a pardon from the king." Her voice broke into a supplicating whine. "Ye can see for yerself, yer lordship, ain't no harm befallen either one of them; they's good as new for they's been took good care of—by me." She cast an acquisitive look at Geoffrey, who was standing with his booted legs far apart, studying Christopher and Lenore from beneath straight lowering brows.

In silence he tossed her a coin, but Lenore reached out and caught it angrily. "It's filthy in there!" she cried. "This money would be better spent on fresh water and candles—and food for those poor wretches!"

The heavyset woman leaped forward with a murderous expression but Christopher Dorn stepped hastily between them, taking the coin from Lenore with a warning look. "This coin is for the child with the dreadful cough," he said sternly. "See that she's fed and cared for. If I hear ye have not done it, I'll have ye removed from your position here for, as ye can see"—he nodded impressively toward Geoffrey—"I've friends in high places."

The heavyset woman seized the coin and stomped away muttering. Geoffrey scowled at Christopher and jerked his head toward the entrance. "I've a coach waiting."

Meekly, Lenore accompanied the two men. Her heart was in a turmoil. Furious or not, Geoffrey had come for her; he had brandished a King's Pardon, he had paid all their debts!

Geoffrey came to a stop beside the coach, his boots planted firmly on the cobbles. He flung open the door. "I've taken rooms for you at the George, Lenore." He had in fact sent a boy round to the George not only to take rooms for Lenore but to inform Mistress Potts of Lenore's imminent arrival.

Lenore was about to let herself be boosted into the hired coach when she turned impulsively to Geoffrey. " 'Twas a terrible place, Geoffrey. Thank you for setting us free."

"The *king* has set ye free," corrected Geoffrey coldly. "I but paid your debts."

"I too thank ye," murmured Christopher, still amazed by this turn of events.

"Do not bother to thank me, Dorn," said Geoffrey pleasantly. "I'm told ye're a gentleman, the son of the Sheriff of Nottingham, to be exact?" And at Christopher's puzzled nod: "And thus undoubtedly you have some skill in swordsmanship?"

Christopher clapped his hand to his hip in a philosophic gesture. "They took my sword," he admitted, "and have sold it for my debts by now, I would think."

"I thought they might have." With a sardonic look, Geoffrey reached into the coach and tossed Christopher a sword he had bought on the way. "Defend yourself."

"Geoffrey!" cried Lenore.

But Geoffrey was in a towering rage and not to be stopped by her or any other.

"Why?" cried Christopher wildly, stepping back. "What quarrel is there between us?"

"Need ye ask?" Geoffrey shed his coat and flexed his powerful arms.

Christopher took one look at that deadly pair of gray eyes boring into his and gasped. He saw death coming. This tall fellow had not wangled him a pardon to set him free, but to pry him out from behind the protective jail bars so he could kill him!

Lenore seized Geoffrey's arm. "Geoffrey, *I went with him willingly*. He did not take me by force!"

"I could see that in York."

That remark stung her and Lenore aimed a slap at Geoffrey's face. He swept her aside impatiently, and she staggered against the coach.

From across the street came a titter, instantly stifled. Louise de Keroualle was peering at them avidly from her sedan chair.

"And now I think we can dispense with the formalities." Geoffrey tested the edge of his blade with practiced fingers. "You who thought to take what was Geoffrey Wyndham's—*on guard!*"

His blade sang through the air, not so close as to actually endanger Christopher, but close enough that Christopher instinctively brought up his own to parry it. The golden-bearded man's expression was wild. He was no swordsman—that was readily apparent with his first thrust—but he *was* a gentleman. And a gentleman must at all times defend his honor.

Christopher was prepared to die for his.

From her position against the coach, Lenore could see that. Already she could envision the next few minutes.

Geoffrey, in jealous rage, would play with his prey, would lead Chris into the belief that he could actually conquer the redoubtable Geoffrey Wyndham. And then that mighty swordarm—whose work she had seen often enough in the days when they fled across England together—would suddenly slash out with savage precision, and Christopher's confident expression would change to one of surprise as he wavered, mortally hurt, and finally crashed to earth—there to bleed out his life beneath the walls of the prison from which he had so lately been set free.

She could not let it happen!

Out of the corner of her eye, through the open door of the coach, she could see Geoffrey's coat, where he had flung it—a handsome coat of dark red velvet. Too heavy for the weather. She saw too that the coachman had his eyes riveted upon the uneven contest between the two swordsmen.

Lenore reached out an arm and seized the coat. Then without stopping to think that she might be slashed from both sides by the singing blades, she swung the coat out in front of her and leaped between the combatants.

Geoffrey was just making a lunge and his face turned pale as his blade slid by her, missing her by a breath.

Christopher was desperately trying to parry and at the advent of coat and woman plunging between himself and Geoffrey's on-reaching blade, he slipped and fell awkwardly on one knee. He scrambled to his feet gasping, "Lenore, for God's sake, keep out of it!"

But Lenore stood determinedly between them, still holding the coat. She was facing Geoffrey and her expression was desperate.

"Geoffrey—I cannot let you kill him."

The words rang like iron tears on Geoffrey's heart. *I went with him willingly.* And now: *I cannot let you kill him.*

He knew now where he stood and the taste of defeat

was bitter in his mouth. But he could not let it rest here. His love for Lenore was so great that it kept him there, enduring yet one more turn of the screw.

"Then choose between us," he said hoarsely. And some perversity made him add, "And if ye choose Dorn, I will kill him anyway!"

Lenore leaned forward. Her violet eyes were dark spots in her white face and her red-gold hair was a fiery halo around her head. Across the street Louise de Kerouaille almost fell out of her sedan chair in her excitement.

"You cannot kill him, Geoffrey. He is the man who threw me the whip in Wells, and then blocked the pursuit. We owe him our lives, you and I. You *cannot* kill him!"

Geoffrey's stern gaze flew to Christopher. "Is this true, Dorn?"

Christopher nodded, but a bit of the old insouciance flared up. "But don't let that stop ye, Wyndham," he drawled. "For I'd fight ye for Lenore any day!"

"No, Christopher, no!" Lenore was tearing the sword from his grip.

Geoffrey turned a haggard face to Lenore. "Choose anyway," he said dully.

Lenore gave him a bitter look. "I have already chosen."

He took a deep breath, waiting for the blow to fall. "So who is it to be?"

"Neither of you!" cried Lenore, tears breaking through her voice. "I am through with you both!"

Across the street, Louise de Kerouaille gave a shout of laughter.

Lenore turned and would have run, but Geoffrey seized her in a rage and flung her into the coach. "Take her to the George!" he roared. "I will not have her walking the streets!" He slammed the door, the frightened driver snapped his whip, and the coach rumbled away. He turned a thunderous face on Christopher. "For what ye did for us in Wells, I give ye your life," he cried. "But if ever I see ye again—!"

"You won't!" Christopher flashed his charming smile and hurried away lest Geoffrey change his mind and decapitate him.

In the coach Lenore covered her face with her hands. At the moment she did not care where the coach took her, to the George or to the devil. Her heart was wracked and torn. She loved Geoffrey—but *her* Geoffrey, kind and generous—not this sword-brandishing madman who had arrived with a treacherous pardon that was meant to be a sentence of execution for her friend!

In the speeding coach, she quickly reached the George.

It took Christopher somewhat longer.

Lenore was lying listlessly on the bed staring at the ceiling, but her head lifted at his knock. At first she believed it was Geoffrey returned to her and her heart leaped.

"Come in," she whispered.

But it was Christopher who stood in the doorway.

"I'd have leaped into your coach," he told her cheerfully. "But your tall fellow would only have jumped in and tossed me out again."

Lenore gave him a hopeless look. "Better you hadn't come here, Chris," she sighed.

He was taken aback and his face showed it. "You can't mean that!"

"I do mean it. I don't know what I'm going to do, but I'm not going back to the old life, Chris. Ever. We haven't been lucky for each other—and today I nearly got you killed. Is that the kind of woman you want?"

Christopher gave her a long tortured look. The words almost rushed out that she was the only kind of woman he would ever want. But looking at her distraught face told him something, for she had never looked that way before. Their relationship had been light, playful. But her feeling for Geoffrey was something else—fixed, unchanging. He had sensed it in Oxford and *known* it from the time he had seen them together, known it, but denied it to himself.

Now she sat with her head bowed, her face in her hands.

"Oh, Chris," she whispered. "What am I going to do? I love him so! But I'm not cut out to be the London mistress of a man who has a wife in Kent!"

"I know." The words were wrung from him for it was then he knew that he had won the battle but he had lost the war. Lenore had never stopped loving Geoffrey Wyndham. She would love him until the day she died.

And who, he asked himself, was he to stand in the way of this towering passion? He would make one last unselfish gesture. He would step aside.

"Are you expecting your tall fellow then?"

"I don't know." Lenore was staring dismally down at her hands, but if she had looked up she would have seen Christopher studying her with infinite tenderness in his crystal eyes.

"Take heart," he said cheerfully. "It may all turn out all right."

"I don't know how you can say that. It never has."

"But this time ye've Christopher Dorn, miracle worker, on your side."

Lenore looked up at him and tried to smile. It was a smile that did not quite come off. Christopher carried that smile with him as he left. He would always carry it.

London

Chapter 36

For the Marquis de Vignac it had been a night to remember. He had awakened on the floor of his bedchamber, robbed of the two forged love letters, struck down by that strumpet Nell Gwyn. As he struggled to his feet, aided by his manservant who was vainly attempting at the same time to stanch the flow of blood from the head wound Nell had inflicted on him with the paperweight, he looked around for Nell.

"You let her go?" he raged.

"But of course," responded the manservant, dazed. "I dashed past her to your side when she told me you had had an accident."

"Fool!" roared the marquis. "She attacked me!" He clutched his aching head and groaned, then launched into a flow of French profanity that had his manservant rolling his eyes and wondering if his master had not secretly frequented the dockside brothels of Marseilles.

When his wound was cleansed and court plaster applied, de Vignac fell back with a groan into the pillows of his bed and prepared to spend the day in fuming and serious drinking. It was some hours later that his now fuzzy mind suddenly focused on his writing desk. A terrible thought occurred to him, and he struggled up and staggered toward it.

What he found brought sobriety back with a hammer blow and he sank shakily into the delicate chair before the writing desk.

The letters were gone! Nell had undoubtedly taken them. And now she would be at Whitehall exhibiting them to the king. There would be no blackmail money, for Wyndham would be arrested and charged. De Vignac did not care if Geoffrey went to the block, but Nell would tell where she got the letters, and he too would be arrested, questioned, tortured, a confession wrung from him!

A cold sweat broke out on de Vignac's brow. He jumped up, struggled into his coat, and sank back down to think.

At that moment Geoffrey Wyndham pushed past the marquis' protesting manservant, strode into the bedchamber and confronted the distraught marquis.

"Letiche has told me everything," he told de Vignac crushingly and watched the other man's face change color. "And now—" He reached the Frenchman in a bound, struck de Vignac a stunning blow first on the right side of his face and then on the left, and jerked him to his feet with a cruel twist of the lace about his neck. "Now *you* tell me what I signed or I'll crush your gullet for you, and ye'll ne'er speak lies again!"

Strangling, de Vignac put up a desperate struggle and tried to signal his manservant to bring a pistol. But his manservant had recognized the dashing Englishman and prudently retired to his own quarters below. There was no one to help him.

"Plans—for a Dutch invasion—up the Humber," he gasped in agony when Geoffrey slackened his grip a little.

"Signed by me?" roared Geoffrey. "Produce the documents!"

De Vignac's anguished howl was cut short by a painful twist of the lace. "I've not got them," he gasped. "Nell Gwyn took them."

"Nell Gwyn?" echoed Geoffrey in disbelief.

"Aye," croaked de Vignac. "Two of them were love letters—to her. She came over to get them—and pilfered the rest. I'm to Holland—and so should you be!"

Geoffrey glared murderously down at the man he still held by the throat. It was all abundantly clear to him. De Vignac was blackmailing Nellie for her ripe body, and himself for his gold. And Letiche had lent herself to this! But the plan had gone awry, and now undoubtedly the treasonous papers were with the king, brought by Lenore's old enemy, Nell Gwyn. He could expect no help from that quarter, there'd be a warrant out for his arrest soon enough. Nor could he drag the "Black Marquis" to Whitehall for a retraction, for that might put Letiche's auburn head on the block as well, and however richly she deserved it, a man could not do that to his wife. Geoffrey had only one consolation; they'd arrest this conniving Frenchman as well—if they could find him.

"Tell Letiche," he said clearly, "that she had best join you in Holland. If you reach there. For she'll see no more of me!" He crashed his hard fist into de Vignac's gasping mouth. There was the sound of breaking teeth and the marquis crumpled, sliding inert to the floor. Geoffrey stood staring down at him and then his eyes focused on something bright and glittering that had slid from the fallen de Vignac's pocket. He bent and picked it up.

In his hand was the emerald necklace he had bought Letiche when they moved into Claremont Court. It was one of the most valuable pieces she owned.

"So Letiche has been funneling funds to you to finance her revolutionary friends," he muttered, glaring down at the unconscious marquis. For he knew nothing of

Letiche's affair with Andre. "Well, here's one bauble that will not find its way to France!" He stuffed it into the pocket of his dark red coat, turned on his heel and left.

He must move fast now, for there was little time. He'd lost Lenore to that damned Christopher Dorn, he could afford to take long chances. Letiche was out of his life at last; now that she had brought ruin on them all, he would never see her again. She could live by selling her jewels; they would keep her in style for several lifetimes!

Where would they look for him first? He guessed the king's men would go first to the Hart and then to Claremont Court, for he had seen Louise de Keroualle's chair at Newgate and knew by now that word must be all over London that Lenore had rejected him and he had gone storming off.

He went directly to the bank. It was a bold move, but he thought that word of his downfall might not yet have reached the banking community. He cleared out his account on the pretext that he was purchasing a large estate in Lincolnshire. On the same pretext he mortgaged Claremont Court and its furnishings for a vast sum, and took it all with him, in gold. Geoffrey was mindful that what a king had given, a king could take away—land could be confiscated, belongings seized, heads fall beneath the headsman's axe. Carrying the gold in a cheap and hastily purchased canvas bag, he hastened to the docks. The *Enterprise* sailed on the morrow for the port of Philadelphia, her captain an honest Quaker named Jervis who had had a late cancellation and was glad enough to let "Mister Daunt" have the ship's last private cabin.

"Good. I'll just stow my things here till we sail. Have ye a key?" Geoffrey asked casually.

The captain nodded and produced one. Having left a fortune in gold on board the *Enterprise,* Geoffrey took one more long chance.

He returned to the Hart, where George was waiting.

The Hart's common room was uncommonly empty and Geoffrey's swift passage through it went unnoticed. Upstairs he gave George terse orders. George was to proceed at once to Claremont Court, taking with him Geoffrey's chestnut stallion. He was to say nothing to the mistress but to give a letter—which Geoffrey swiftly penned and stamped with this signet ring—to Glendower, the estate manager. That letter told Glendower the location of Geoffrey's strongbox, instructed him to empty it and to drive all the livestock, including the horses, to Southampton (for the king's men, finding the livestock gone, would believe them driven to the nearer port of London and search there). In Southampton, Glendower was to load the stock aboard the first ship bound for Philadelphia, for he had sold them to a Mister Daunt, who would meet them on the dock upon arrival there. He suggested that Glendower accompany the livestock to America for he thought Glendower would relish employment with Mister Daunt.

George was watching him gravely. "If there's some sort of trouble, sir, ye can count on me."

Geoffrey considered him. "Are ye married, George?"

"That I'm not, nor likely to be unless some wench's father catches up with me!" George grinned.

"Then go with Glendower to America," suggested Geoffrey, "and seek employment with a Mister Daunt."

"But I've no desire to leave yer service, sir!"

Geoffrey hesitated. "I think things will turn out to your liking, George."

A great light seemed to dawn on George. So the master was leaving that French parcel at last—perhaps for the orange girl! "Indeed I will go to America," he cried. "So long as I can work for ye—Mister Daunt."

"Not so loud, George. I'm a wanted man now. Mind ye make haste, George. You and Glendower make the move quick—and quiet. And"—he clapped George companionably on the shoulder—"God willing, I'll see ye in Philadelphia."

Delighted at the prospect of this splendid adventure on which he was about to embark, George dashed out. Geoffrey heard the clatter of his boots on the stairs.

Now he looked around the room. He would leave

everything exactly as it was. Then perhaps those who came looking for him would believe him still in London after they came away empty-handed from Claremont Court. Letiche, he was sure, would take off at the first breath of treason, and the fortune in jewels he had bestowed on her would carry her fast and far.

And Charles was an easygoing monach. At first he would be hot for Geoffrey's blood, but he would forget in time. And perhaps even laugh at his old friend who'd been seduced into his folly—as Nell Gwyn would probably tell it—by a faithless orange girl.

Which brought him back to Lenore.

He would leave for America, he would arrive in the Colonies with most of his wealth—but he would carry with him forever an ache in his heart.

London

Chapter 37

Andre Malraux had spent a night of debauchery at Lord Wilsingame's house on London Bridge, slept late, eaten a good breakfast, and lolled around with his host for an hour or two laughing over last night's revelry, when he and Wilsingame and two others had dined on roasted pheasant and later spent a pleasant evening deflowering a sobbing fourteen-year-old laundress who had had the misfortune of bringing the washing late. The poor girl had been dragged from the kitchen to the dining room, enjoyed by all—and then pushed callously into the dark street with a handful of coins and the words "Ye aren't pretty enough" ringing in her ears.

Coming home now, a bit bleary-eyed, through the winding crowded streets, Andre dodged the contents of a chamber pot being emptied by a chambermaid from an upstairs window and stopped to swear at her in angry French. Both her head and the chamber pot swiftly disappeared from the window and Andre, who had to jump back smartly again to avoid a darting hawker carrying a load of smelly fish, found himself looking into the wickedly lovely face of the king's French mistress, Louise de Keroualle, seated in a sedan chair.

Louise was having a delightful day. Already she had told six separate chance-met friends about what she had witnessed in front of Newgate Prison, and now she was about to return to Whitehall with the tale, where she had no doubt she'd have the full attention of the king. Louise's friends were notorious gossips. By afternoon, word of the aborted duel would be all over London and the wags at Whitehall would be convulsed with laughter and composing couplets deriding the fabled duelist, Geoffrey Wyndham, who was so besotted with love for his errant orange girl that he must needs spare her lover to please her!

Now Louise studied her handsome swaggering countryman who was so brazenly stripping her with his eyes before he bowed in courtly fashion, and pondered whether to share her amusing tidbit with him. With a sigh she decided she would not because Andre was after all in the "other camp." He was a revolutionary, mixed up with the "Black Marquis," who was trying to unseat the king of France—and Louise was passionately loyal to that king. Had she not proved it by seducing in his interests a foreign monarch?

So with a regretful nod she passed on in the crowd, speculating what it would be like to bed Andre.

Andre's gaze followed the chair until something suddenly dug into his ribs. His head swung round with a curse and he found himself looking into the apologetic hazel eyes of a country lass, carrying a brace of dressed fowls hung from a kind of wooden harness that she wore across her shoulders. It was one end of this wooden harness that had poked him.

Andre grinned and leaned over, giving the girl's right breast a painful squeeze. With an indignant squeal she stumbled away from him and into a long-robed banker, perspiring in the London heat. Laughing, Andre let the crowd flow around him and continued on home, wondering if he might find a message waiting for him from de Vignac about the emerald necklace he wanted to sell. Ordinarily Andre would have sold the necklace himself. His career as a kept man was well established and he regularly disposed of items that came his way from clinging feminine hands, but this particular necklace came from Letiche Wyndham. It was of a distinctive design and Andre could think of no plausible excuse to be selling Letiche's necklace if news of the transaction should reach Geoffrey's ears. With de Vignac it would be another story: he was Letiche's kinsman, he could always tell some smooth lie about Letiche wanting to buy Geoffrey a valuable present and, being short of cash at the moment, having given the necklace to de Vignac to dispose of.

Andre hoped the marquis would have other news for him as well, for de Vignac had been hinting of late that their plans were coming swiftly to fruition, and that they would soon be able to begin their long-awaited overthrow of the French king. Andre hoped so; he had long had his eye on a handsome estate near Paris, which he believed would fall to him like a ripe plum if his swordarm were to assist in bringing a new king to the throne of France.

Now as he shoved his way impatiently through a crowd of gesticulating foreign seamen, he pondered the delicious bit of information that had come his way just before he left Wilsingame's. A messenger had arrived from "Lady" Bennett, saying plaintively that he had been unable to find Lord Faltrop and that "Lady" Bennett was offering the Hellfire Club a rare treat tonight: a young virgin fresh from the Cotswolds with a beautiful face and a body pale as moonlight. But "Lady" Bennett insisted on getting five hundred pounds for her. Lord Wilsingame had laughed at the price and snorted that he could get ten virgins for that! But when he heard that the girl was the daughter of Lenore Frankford, his face had taken on a wolfish look, and he had instantly accepted in Faltrop's name. He had promptly invited Andre to join in tonight's festivities at the Hellfire Club. It would be a debauch to remember, he promised. All of them would ravish this

Cotswold virgin. Lenore Frankford's daughter . . . He savored the phrase and thumped Andre on the back—the pity was they could not have the mother to ravish as well!

When he arrived back at his own lodgings, Andre was startled to find Letiche Wyndham waiting for him at the door and tapping her foot dangerously.

For that same morning, feeling restless and uneasy about her clandestine activities of the night before, Letiche had ordered out her coach and journeyed into London. She knew she could safely spend the day with her lover and be back before Geoffrey missed her, for it was his custom to stay the night in London when he went to Whitehall.

But Letiche had passed another private coach just leaving as she herself entered the city. The ladies inside had recognized the Wyndham arms on the side of Letiche's coach and leaned out the window to hail her. They were three of Letiche's expatriate friends and they had just spoken to Louise Keroualle, whose sedan chair they had passed outside Whitehall. Louise had been malicious enough to tell them all about the happenings outside Newgate Prison, for Letiche had publicly called her "a whore and a discredit to France," and she wanted to make sure Letiche heard all about her husband's latest encounter with the orange girl.

Letiche heard—from her tittering female friends, who watched her brightly for the expected outburst.

None was forthcoming. Splotches of color appeared on Letiche's pale face and her breathing became erratic, but otherwise she seemed unmoved. She arrived at Andre's lodgings in a blind rage.

" 'Tis all over London!" she stormed.

"What is?" Hastily Andre unlocked the door and held it for her. She came storming in while he looked around him wildly to see if there were any ladies' stockings or torn lacy chemises strewn about. For Andre had entertained his new paramour, the actress from Suffolk, here night before last, and since he was two months behind in his rent, no one had come to clean up his rooms.

Breathing hard, Letiche whirled about dramatically to face him. She was standing in the middle of the floor fairly sizzling with wrath. Andre thought with sudden distaste how her face always grew splotched of late when she was angry. "That damned orange girl was flung into debtor's prison," she cried, "and Geoffrey went to the king and *publicly* sued for a King's Pardon for both the woman and her lover!"

"*And her lover?*" echoed Andre stupidly. At first amazed, he was suddenly convulsed with laughter and fell against the door, rocking with merriment.

"How dare you laugh?" From splotchy, Letiche now turned crimson with indignation. "Think what it is like for *me*. I am made a laughingstock!"

"Of course you are right," he gasped, trying desperately to control his laughter. "It is terrible for you, *ma petite.*"

Letiche gave him a cold look. "Indeed it is. I would ask you to call Geoffrey out—except that he would probably kill you."

The touch of ridicule in her voice sobered Andre. Nettled, he asked in a loud voice, "Would you like a glass of wine?"

She gave him a sulky look. "I would *rather* be avenged."

Andre did not like her in this mood. In fact, he had been increasingly disenchanted with Letiche of late, for except for the gift of the emerald necklace—which she had supposed would pay his rent and keep him in wine—she had not been so forthcoming with gifts recently. "Well, perhaps this will appease you," he said. And he told her the delicious news that the orange girl's young daughter now reposed at "Lady" Bennett's awaiting her delivery to the Hellfire Club tonight. "Wilsingame has promised Faltrop will pay five hundred pounds in gold for her," he finished.

Letiche's auburn eyes took on a feverish glitter and she brought her palms together sharply. "At 'Lady' Bennett's, you say? Ah, and has the orange girl heard of this?"

"I doubt me anyone has acquainted Mistress Frankford of her daughter's fate."

"Good. Then let us be the first."

Andre looked at her, astounded. A frown line appeared between his eyes. His reckless lady had proposed many things, but this——!

"That will surely draw your husband into the thing," he said slowly.

"Not if we handle it properly! She must learn of it—and yet be able to do nothing."

Andre looked into those glittering auburn eyes. Callous as he was when he drank, for a moment even he was revolted. "You want me to garnish the tale of what will happen to the daughter?" he asked distastefully. "To what purpose, Letiche?"

Again Letiche struck her little hands together. "No, no, you do not see the possibilities here, Andre. A mother loves her daughter, *n'est ce pas?* She will value her daughter's life, no?"

Andre returned her gaze a trifle sourly. *One* mother of his acquaintance had not valued the lives of her children: Letiche herself. "None has said the girl will die," he demurred. "Only be deflowered."

"Ah, but you and I both know that *someone* will die there tonight."

Andre knew the Hellfire Club's excesses grew worse with each meeting. "Some old street bawd perhaps," he muttered.

"Precisely." Letiche pounced on that. "A woman whose disappearance would not be remarked."

Andre moved his shoulders uneasily. What was Letiche getting at? Did she want him to persuade Lord Faltrop to sacrifice this Cotswold virgin to Satan at the climax of their bloody rites?

"Perhaps," he admitted.

"You see?" cried Letiche triumphantly. "You are not my only informant. Renée de Paulet went there last time in a vizard mask. I have heard all about it—not only how they debauch virgins *en masse,* delighting in their screams, but how the select few in their devil's chapel march about in white robes and plunge a knife into the heart of some naked woman even while she is in the throes of—"

"Yes, yes." A few beads of sweat appeared on Andre's forehead. "I have heard of it. 'Tis said they do it on occasion, but it has never been proved against them."

"Come now, Andre, *you have been there.*"

"Not in the chapel," he muttered. "That is reserved for the members, not their guests. No more than a dozen, I believe, march into the chapel."

"With a woman." Andre nodded his head. "And they march out without her. *What happens to that woman, Andre?* I am told she is never seen again."

Andre was perspiring freely now. He'd no mind to be mousetrapped into a murder charge in this barbarous country, this England!

"*I will tell you,* Andre. All of them violate her and at the last they drive a dagger through her heart and annoint their foreheads with her blood. After that, her lifeless body is tossed into the Thames. Talk of it is all over London."

"So?" Andre's voice had roughened. He drew a hand over his perspiring forehead. "What do you want me to do about it?"

"Nothing! Nothing at all. I merely want you to carry a message to the Frankford woman that her daughter is to be debauched by all of them." Her high-pitched laughter rang out. "Yes, by Lord Wilsingame even! That should spur her, for 'twas at Wilsingame's house on London Bridge that Geoffrey so nobly dashed in and rescued her!"

"And then?" Andre was following this new train of thought, fascinated.

"Tell her you are from 'Lady' Bennett, and that

'Lady' Bennett offers her a trade. Herself for the daughter."

"But Lenore Frankford is not a virgin!" cried Andre. "They are virgins who are brought in for the night's entertainment."

"All but the bawd who is to be sacrificed," corrected Letiche, rubbing her white hands together gleefully.

Andre's eyes widened. His lady had depths that even he had not plumbed.

"She will rush to 'Lady' Bennett's and exchange herself for the daughter," predicted Letiche. "You will see."

"Even though she knows it to be her death? For, as you say, word of these 'sacrifices' is all over London." Such an exchange was incomprehensible to Andre, who valued his own handsome body above all things.

"Even so. Our Mistress Frankford holds herself higher than her station and pretends to the sense of honor of a lady!"

Andre gave Letiche a wry look. He could think of at least one lady at the moment who had no sense of honor at all; he was facing her.

"*And then we will have her,* Andre." Letiche's low tone dripped venom and sweetness.

"But what is to keep her from rushing to your husband and demanding he take the girl from 'Lady' Bennett's by force?"

"Bah! I am told they quarreled at the jail and that Geoffrey flung her into a coach and rode off in the opposite direction!"

"But he might ride back."

"Not before tomorrow. His temper will need time to cool. And by then it will be too late. His orange girl will have vanished beneath the waters of the Thames."

Andre frowned. It was very risky. "I don't know where Mistress Frankford is," he grumbled. "So how can I take her a message?"

"She is at the George," supplied Letiche promptly. "Geoffrey has taken lodgings for her there. I suppose that was to save her reputation since all know he usually stays at the Hart when he is in London." Her voice was tinged with irony.

Andre moved restlessly. He felt hemmed in. "But suppose she—"

"Hush." Letiche had anticipated his obstinance. In the final analysis Andre was always moved by gold. "Here." She unclasped from her neck the necklace of amethysts and diamonds that Geoffrey had given her the Christmas before and handed it to him. "This should be enough to bribe anyone needed to get the job done."

The diamonds and amethysts moved like water through his greedy fingers. "It should be enough," he murmured. "Still—I would prefer not to contact her. I am told this orange girl reads and writes."

Letiche nodded. "I will write a note." She was thinking that Andre's very well founded fear of Geoffrey might cause him to bungle the message. She sat down and tersely penned a note, signed it "Lady" Bennett with an almost illegible scrawl. The Frankford woman would believe "Lady" Bennett had employed a scribe to write the note but had given it her own wavering signature.

Andre accepted the note from her hand.

"Hurry." Letiche gave him a little push. In her impatience she did not even bid him good-bye. But as he started down the stairs she called, "Wait!" and ran up to him. "I would see it!" she breathed.

"What?" Andre looked at her, astounded.

"You could arrange it," she wheedled. "Oh, Andre, do this for me. Other ladies—not only Renée de Paulet but court ladies as well—have attended the doings of the Hellfire Club in vizard masks to hide their identities. Why could not I? You could take me there. Who would be the wiser?"

" 'Lady' Bennett would have to know," stuttered Andre. He was starting to perspire again. "The only way I could get you there would be if we arrived with her party. For it is too late to reach Wilsingame—he is spending the afternoon dicing at Cheapside, and Lord

Faltrop is out of the city. He will be rowed to the island just in time for the festivities."

"Arrange it." She gave his arm a little hug and stepped back, waving him away. "Arrange it, Andre, and I will give you the matching earbobs." She touched her ears.

From the head of the stairs Andre's brown eyes glittered with avarice. As a set, the three pieces were much more valuable. "I will arrange it," he told her hoarsely, and clattered down the stairs and out into the street.

Her eyes shining in triumph, Letiche watched him go.

"I will see Lenore Frankford humbled," she whispered to herself. *"Yes, and her daughter too."* For she had no doubt that once Lenore had turned herself over to "Lady" Bennett, that enterprising madam would arrange to net the daughter again. Letiche laughed scornfully, deep in her throat. *A woman nobody would miss—except Geoffrey.* She laughed again.

Andre Malraux was too wary to deliver the note personally to Lenore. Indeed, had Letiche not foiled his plans by insisting on attending the Hellfire Club's debauch tonight, he would have simply crumpled it up and thrown it into the gutter, waited a reasonable time and sauntered back to her.

As it was, he had to deliver it. He entrusted it to a chambermaid at the George, gave her cheek a playful pinch and whispered rougishly, " 'Tis a *billet doux, ma petite.* Be quick, the lady waits!"

Giggling, the little chambermaid had skipped upstairs with the note, handed it to Lenore with another giggle and run back downstairs.

Lenore's violet eyes had widened with horror as she read the note and she had sagged into a chair. Lorena here with "Lady" Bennett, about to be debauched by the Hellfire Club this very night? Surely it was not possible! Yet the note was very specific: "If you will exchange your body for hers, I will let the girl go, as Lord Wilsingame and others are very eager to see you again." Like a distant scream, Lenore remembered a night in Wilsingame's house when she had held a pair of scissors to her breast in despair. Geoffrey had saved her then—he would save her now! For Lorena was *his* daughter as well as hers, whether he cared to acknowledge it or not!

She was about to hurry over to the Hart to tell Geoffrey when an ominous thought struck her. Lorena was in the clutches of that cruel woman, terrified and alone, believing no one would save her from her fate. Suppose there was a pair of scissors handy?

Lenore's hand gripped the newel post. Lorena was her mother's daughter, she would have pride and cold courage—*she would do it, she would take her own life to prevent them having their way with her!* Oh, God, she could not afford to waste another minute, she must send word to Geoffrey and go as fast as she could to "Lady" Bennett's. Wilsingame could have nothing against Lorena—it was herself he wanted. Lorena would be set free and—God willing—Geoffrey would come in time to save her. For once on that accursed island, there would be no escape. Its shores were guarded by savage dogs who were let loose to prevent outside interruption once all the guests were assembled and not leashed again until the revelers were ready to be rowed back to the mainland.

In the common room to her right she saw a serving lad, and she thrust the folded note from "Lady" Bennett into his hand. "Quickly, take this to Geoffrey Wyndham at the Hart. He will reward you. Tell him I have gone to 'Lady' Bennett's and will await him there."

The lad took the note so hastily thrust upon him, but once Lenore was gone his lips twisted in a sneer. Take a note to someone at another inn? With a message that the writer would be waiting at a brothel? He'd been on this job long enough to know that gentlemen in London had a way of dropping unwanted ladies at inns and not coming back to claim them. And this woman made no bones that she was one of "Lady" Bennett's "girls"! The last time he had delivered a *billet doux* for a lady, he had been rewarded by a lusty kick in his posterior region by the recipient and a warning not to return.

He looked up as a strident voice called to him from the kitchen; he had work to do or he'd be let go. With a surly shrug he ambled to the kitchen—and tossed the note into the fireplace where a big brass pot held a simmering stew.

"What was that?" demanded the cook sharply.

" 'Tweren't nothin'," he muttered. "Bit of paper a lady gave me to throw away. How's about some of that stew? I'm fit to starve."

The cook gave him a keen look. He reached down and would have fished the bit of paper from the fire but the flames had already taken it and it blazed away merrily, curling into black and gray ash that was lost upon the big log burning below.

Outside, Lenore had already leaped into a hansom cab and hoarsely given "Lady" Bennett's address. Hands clenched, praying she would be in time, she spilled out of the cab almost before it came to a halt and called to the driver to wait, he would be paid when he took her daughter to the Hart.

"I should be paid now!" roared the driver indignantly, "not at the Hart!" But Lenore had already lifted the boar's head knocker and banged it loudly.

When a man with a black patch opened the door, she backed warily away. "Tell 'Lady' Bennett I am here to trade myself for Lorena."

Behind Black Patch, "Lady" Bennett's head appeared. "What's this?"

"You sent me a note," shouted Lenore, trying to make herself heard over the clamor of the driver, wanting his money. "I am here to exchange myself for Lorena."

"Lady" Bennett blinked. She was unable to read or write, and it sometimes made her calling difficult. "Pay the driver," she told Black Patch, and muttered as he edged past, "Work around behind her."

Black Patch gave a barely perceptible nod. He came out, pulling out coins for the driver, and Lenore retreated. "Bring out Lorena!" she cried.

"Lady" Bennett frowned. "She don't want to come out. She's been one of my girls for two weeks now."

"One of your—" For a moment the horror of "Lady" Bennett's lie threw Lenore off guard. It was enough. Black Patch swooped down on her and fairly threw her through the door, where "Lady" Bennett stepped nimbly aside to avoid the woman catapulting past her as if it were something she did all the time.

Several people had stopped to watch, muttering. Even the cab driver looked uncertain now.

"Go away, all of ye!" cried "Lady" Bennett, shaking her fist at them. "This is one of my girls returned and makin' trouble. You don't want no part of it!" Black Patch ran past her and she slammed the door even as Lenore's scream rent the air.

Atop the hansom cab the driver sat irresolute. Suppose that screaming woman's daughter really was a prisoner in there? Still, if she worked for "Lady" Bennett . . . And didn't the daughters of these London bawds usually grow up to become whores themselves? And sometimes courtesans—look at Nell Gwyn! Still an honest workingman shouldn't concern himself with an argument between bawds. He was still hesitating when a plump lady leaped out of a sedan chair that had come to a halt across the street to watch.

"Is this cab free?" she panted as she reached him.

That decided the driver. Whatever was happening inside that house was no affair of his. He pulled away even as the screams from within were suddenly shut off, as by a large hand clapped across a mouth.

"These two months past I've lain sick in my bed," wailed his passenger. "And to see such a thing on my first day out—one's not safe in London even in a chair! *Drive faster!*"

The driver cracked his whip in the air and silently agreed. He reminded himself that "Lady" Bennett was known to employ half a dozen husky cutthroats to maintain order at her place of business, and they would have mauled him and left him in the gutter had he interfered. Abruptly he realized that his excited passenger had not yet told him where she wanted to go. He leaned back to ask her, then wended his way into a broad street and through the tangle of London traffic.

*　　*　　*

Andre Malraux, still edgy as he strolled back to his lodgings from delivering the note to Lenore, decided to detour by the Marquis de Vignac's apartments and see what progress had been made in selling the emerald necklace.

He was astonished to find a cart in front of the marquis' apartments and all of de Vignac's belongings being loaded into it, helter-skelter.

His own interests being always uppermost in his mind, Andre's thoughts immediately flew to the necklace. What, was the marquis decamping with it? He took the stairs three at a time and burst in upon de Vignac, who was holding a wet cloth to his mouth and rocking back and forth, moaning.

"What the devil—?" In full charge, Andre came to an amazed halt.

"Wyndham was here," croaked the marquis, displaying a set of broken teeth. "He near killed me—and I think he would have killed Letiche had she been with me."

"Merde! Why?"

"He's about to be arrested for treason, and he blames us."

"Wyndham arrested? For treason?"

"The cart is loaded," announced a voice behind Andre.

"I'll be down directly." De Vignac staggered to his feet. "I've no time to explain." He pressed the wet cloth to his mouth again. *"Mon Dieu,* my mouth hurts! But when this net closes, it will embroil us all. I'm for Holland. There's a ship sailing within the hour, and I mean to be on board. You and Letiche should follow."

"Holland!" Andre's head was whirling. Somehow they had been involved in Wyndham's treason? But de Vignac was pushing past him now. "I must go," he muttered indistinctly.

"Wait! The emerald necklace, what have you done with it?"

De Vignac felt in his coat pocket. "It was here," he muttered. "Wyndham must have taken it. These thieving English!"

"But it was mine!" cried Andre.

De Vignac smiled grimly through his broken mouth. "Try telling Wyndham that." He brushed past Andre and hurried down the stairs.

In impotent fury, Andrew stood on the street and watched the marquis throw a leg up over his horse. "Ye'll have to make good the necklace!" he cried.

"In Holland," de Vignac promised vaguely and rode off, hastily following the lumbering cart that contained his possessions.

In a torment of mixed emotions, Andre strode back to his lodgings. Whatever was afoot, if it involved Geoffrey, it could also involve Letiche. She might be arrested and himself as well. By God, he would throttle the truth from her!

But by the time he reached his lodgings, he had become quiet and thoughtful.

He had had another idea. If Wyndham fled—and who would not, with a treason charge against him?—then Letiche would be at loose ends. She had a fortune in jewels. Together they could ride back to Claremont Court and she could slip in and remove those jewels. They could sell the gems and sail to Holland or wherever fancy led them. They would be rich! But they must hurry.

He opened his door, deciding to suggest they not attend tonight's Hellfire gathering.

"Letiche!" Andre called impatiently, for he did not see her. "I have delivered your message but I—"

His words were abruptly cut off as one of his shoes, flung through the bedroom door, struck him full in the face.

"There is a woman's stocking tangled in your laundry!" Letiche screamed. "And a lace chemise stuffed under your pillow! They are not mine, Andre!"

He opened his mouth in a wild attempt to explain as the other shoe hit him.

Reunion

Chapter 38

At "Lady" Bennett's, Lorena was awakened by the screaming downstairs. She jumped to her feet and was standing tensely by the bed when the door burst open and a woman with red gold hair was suddenly thrust inside.

"Ye're screeching for yer daughter—here she is!" roared Black Patch. And as suddenly, the door was slammed and locked.

Frozen to stillness, the woman and the girl stared across the dim room at each other.

For a moment neither could speak: this was the meeting for which they both had longed.

"Lorena," whispered Lenore. "Is it really you?"

"Mother?" Lorena's voice was uncertain. "What is happening? How did you find me?"

Lenore couldn't tell her—not just yet. Overcome by emotion, she crossed the room and enfolded her daughter in her arms, resting her cheek against that fair young head so that her own glorious hair spilled over them both like a protective, shimmering shawl. For several golden moments, it was not a meeting in a brothel under the shadow of death, but a reunion, a special time of laughter and tears.

Even with Lenore's slender arms wrapped tight around her, Lorena couldn't believe it. She had found her elusive mother at last!

"Lorena, oh, Lorena, let me look at you." Lenore clasped the young girl's face in both her hands and studied it tenderly. "You do not look like me, Lorena," she decided. "Not even in this dim light." She cocked her head on one side the better to study the smooth planes of that lovely young face. "Nor yet like your father."

"My father? But Aunt Flora says—"

Lenore's voice was gentle. "I mean your real father—Geoffrey Wyndham. No, and you do not look like Jamie MacIver either, although you have his coloring."

"My—my real father?" Lorena gasped.

"I did not want to tell you in a letter, and it could only have hurt you in Twainmere. But though Jamie MacIver and I were handfasted, your father was a cavalier who saved my life in Worcester the night Jamie was killed. We fled across England together." Her voice soared. "We were lovers." *Ah, Geoffrey, we are lovers still, together or apart . . . we will always be lovers. Across time. Across eternity.* "In Oxford I bore his child. You are that child, Lorena. He is here in London. And now he has saved me once again"—her lovely lips had a wry twist—"for earlier today he plucked me from Newgate Prison. I have sent for him, Lorena. He will not fail us."

That they needed saving went unheeded by a bewildered Lorena. "But"—the question came tumbling out— "if he is indeed my father, then why did you never marry him?"

"He was already married when I met him. To a girl in France. It was an empty marriage, made for convenience, but he honored it. I was young and proud, and I refused to take second place."

"Were you ashamed of me?" Lorena was looking down at her hands. "Was that why you never came back to Twainmere?" she asked in a low voice.

"Ashamed?" Lenore gazed at her daughter in shock. "Oh, Lorena, I loved you more than anything else in this world! I killed a man who would have harmed you!"

Lorena did not seem to hear that. She edged away from the yearning hand Lenore would have placed over hers. Her voice sounded forced. "But you had so much—the stage, beautiful clothes, a wonderful life. While in Twainmere we had nothing."

So this was what her letters had wrought!

Lenore swallowed. "I was wanted for murder. Flora must have told you. I made my way as best I could."

"But *afterward*. After the king pardoned you, why did you not come then?"

"I had no money, Lorena."

"But—but you were an actress," burst out Lorena. "The greatest actress on the London stage! You performed for the king! Your letters—"

Lenore's voice was husky. "All lies, Lorena. I could not bear for you to know my circumstances. Nor could I face Flora's pity."

Lorena caught her breath and her blue eyes widened. *Pity?* She looked again at her beautiful mother, saw a torn dress with part of the lace ripped away. She had assumed that had happened in the struggle when Lenore was thrust unceremoniously into the room with her but . . . her mother had mentioned being saved only today from Newgate Prison!

"Are you a criminal then?" she asked, fascinated, her rebelliousness forgotten.

"A debtor," sighed Lenore, feeling that she had deserved that question. "Debtors are cast in with felons at Newgate. Cast in to beg or starve."

Imprisoned for debt! Lorena's eyes were round.

"And did *you* beg for your bread?" she asked, enthralled.

Lenore's face went cold; her proud heart told her

she had not deserved *that* question. "I never begged for anything," she said harshly. "Except once—for your life."

Lorena did not seem to hear that. Like revolving colored lights, new truths were crowding in upon her. "But my father," she asked resentfully. "If you could not come, why did *he* never come to see me?"

"We quarreled in Oxford and he left me." Lenore could not bring herself to say: *He did not believe you were his child.* She could not tell this young vulnerable face that. Not yet. Instead she answered the question she had so far ignored. "You asked me what is happening, you wonder why we are locked in here. Let me ask you—how did *you* get here?"

"I came seeking domestic employment. I met Lady Bennett at the Olimpick Games and she—"

"You have been lured into London's most notorious brothel by London's most notorious madam who styles herself 'Lady' Bennett although she is no lady at all, but a bawd from the streets," Lenore interrupted brutally.

She saw Lorena's face go white. "Then it was all lies?" she faltered. "What Lady Bennett told me at the Games? She did not want to hire Maude and me as maidservants at all, but as . . . ." Her voice trailed off in dawning horror.

Lenore nodded. "The world is full of liars, Lorena." Her tone was rueful.

"But we must get away from here!" Lorena started up, but Lenore's strong fingers clasped firmly over her daughter's hand and pulled her back down.

"We will," she promised Lorena firmly. "We will. They will not harm us until tonight when they intend to deliver us to the Hellfire Club. But your father will be here before then. I sent him 'Lady' Bennett's note."

"Her—her note?"

"She told me she had you and offered to release you if I would take your place. I was afraid for you, and my fear made me reckless. I rushed in heedlessly, not realizing that it was but a trap and that they would seize me too."

"What—what do they intend for us?" asked Lorena fearfully.

What did they intend? Lenore looked away. *Mass rape for innocent Lorena, and for her who was no virgin—?*

"Don't think about it," she told Lorena quickly. "Your father will come. He has never failed me." It was not true, but it was a lie well intended, as so many of her lies had been. Lenore could not bear to feel that she herself would not be able to shield her daughter from this terrible fate that was fast bearing down upon them.

"But if he does not?"

Lenore gave her a long slow look. Lorena was no fool. Her gaze traced the outlines of that sweet young face. *Her daughter* . . . the baby she had left in Flora's arms, whose childhood she had missed. Other arms had rocked Lorena to sleep, other voices comforted her, never Lenore's. And now this bittersweet reunion on what might prove to be the last day of both their lives, for Lenore knew her own proud blood coursed through this child of hers. She was heart of her heart. Lorena would never submit—as *she* had not submitted to Lord Wilsingame and his devilish crew. *What if Geoffrey did not come?* For a moment she closed her eyes to blot out the memory of the scissors she had poised ready to strike into her breast had Geoffrey not saved her that night on London Bridge. For Lorena perhaps it would be a knife or a dress sword snatched from a scabbard.

But of course Geoffrey would come. No matter how angry he had been when he had flung away from her at Newgate, he would read the note 'Lady' Bennett had sent to her and instantly comprehend the situation—he would come!

But when? Suppose he missed the messenger, missed the note? He would come but—she cast a silent frantic prayer to heaven: *Dear God, let him come in time to save our child!*

Lorena deserved an answer. Lenore took a deep breath. "If Geoffrey should not come, if anything should go wrong, if we should become separated, do not let them take you to the island. As a last resort, throw yourself overboard into the Thames, let the current take you, sweep you away. You do swim, don't you?" And when Lorena nodded: "You will have a better chance in the water than with Faltrop or Wilsingame."

Lorena felt a long shiver go down her spine. "I will remember," she promised numbly.

"And now in the time before we are—saved, let us talk." *For this may be the last chance we will ever have.* "There is so much I would know, Lorena. About your life in Twainmere, all the years we have been apart."

Lorena told her as words bubbled forth. They had a lifetime to catch up on, to share. And Lenore interrupted, laughing, giving her daughter an occasional hug. Their words tumbled over each other as they confided and reminisced. They came to understand each other, these women of the same proud blood, and to find not only mutual affection but respect as well.

And all of it beneath the shadow of the sword.

For on sundials all over England the shadows lengthened. And every lengthening of those shadows brought them nearer to hell.

The Assault

Chapter 39

At the Hart, unaware that Lenore and Lorena were prisoners at "Lady" Bennett's, Geoffrey Wyndham was taking one last look around the room before leaving for the dock and the good ship *Enterprise*. When he opened the door to leave, he almost collided with Christopher Dorn—a jaunty Christopher, minus his doublet, who carried under his arm what appeared to be a large roll of canvas.

At sight of him, Geoffrey stiffened and his ironic tone was laced with menace. "I am surprised ye'd care to test my temper again, Dorn."

"Oh, I'm the sort to try anything." Cheerfully, Christopher barged past him into the room. "Besides, ye'll thank me when ye see what I've brought ye."

Geoffrey doubted that, but to pitch this impudent fellow summarily down the stairs could hardly fail to attract attention, and right now attention was what Geoffrey Wyndham least desired. He watched in silence as Christopher unrolled the canvas to reveal a painting of a richly dressed lady clad in a luxurious dark green velvet gown trimmed in ermine tails and surmounted by an elegant lace ruff.

In haste to leave, Geoffrey gave the portrait but a cursory glance.

"Aren't you curious who this lady is?" Christopher asked softly. "Come now, don't you see a trace of her when you look into the mirror? She's your mother, Wyndham." He watched Geoffrey's face intently, for this portrait was surely the lure that would drag Geoffrey back to Lenore, and Christopher Dorn was now determined to bring that about. For once in his reckless life he was making a purely unselfish gesture—against his own interest. "I thought I owed ye something for saving me—for whatever reason—from a debtors' prison. So"—his arm described a sweeping arc—"I make ye a gift of this."

"How came ye by it?" Geoffrey asked calmly.

In point of fact, Christopher had acquired the portrait a few minutes before at a flea market, trading his silver-shot doublet for it. But his crystal eyes met Geoffrey's stern gray ones with bland clarity. "A servant of your mother's, a woman named June Rowe, left your father's employ at the time he drove your mother away from the house," Christopher lied smoothly. "Being from Nottinghamshire, June Rowe returned north to her people, and there became my nurse. When I was in my teens, she went to live in London with an older daughter. And she took with her her most precious possession—this portrait of your mother. Having heard from Lenore that you'd never seen your mother's face, I sought out June Rowe and procured the portrait for you."

Now Geoffrey scanned the portrait with more interest. The painted face that looked back at him with just a trace of hauteur was very fair, the hair so blond as to appear hemp-white, the eyes wide and vividly blue. It was not lost on him that this was Lorena's coloring.

"And why would ye go to so much trouble?" he wondered.

It was on the top of Christopher's tongue to retort

glibly, "To repay ye for your kindness," but something in that intent gray gaze made him blurt out the truth. "Because Lenore loves you," he said simply. "And I hoped by this method to bring you back together."

His words jarred through Geoffrey as if a horse had kicked him. "It cannot be true," he said slowly. "She was in your arms in York, she has lived with you, she refused even to leave prison without you!"

"I was there to save her in Northumberland when you were not. She is grateful to me, she even has a fondness for me—but that is all. 'Tis you she loves—and she is crying her eyes out at the George this minute in fear that you will not come back to her."

Geoffrey swung around, impelled to dash immediately to the George. He had so nearly taken ship without her! He found the open door blocked by the stout, panting form of Mistress Potts.

"Lenore is not at the George!" she wailed. "Not twenty minutes ago I saw her dragged into the house of that terrible woman—that "Lady" Bennett!"

* * *

On "Lady" Bennett's notorious establishment, men now converged from two directions:

From the alley to the west came Geoffrey and Christopher, both heavily armed. In order to conceal the pistol and the short sword which Geoffrey had thrust upon him, Christopher was now wearing the dark red coat which Geoffrey had hastily stripped off. Geoffrey himself was wearing the serviceable sword with which he had done battle with Christopher earlier, plus a brace of pistols, all concealed by a short black cloak trimmed in silver.

And from the direction of the docks, unseen by either, strode Tabby, leading a group of burly sailors recruited from a dockside tavern. Riding by "Lady" Bennett's on his way back from Moorfields, Tabby had spotted Snowfire. Hastily he had spilled a handful of coins into the hand of the startled boy who held the horse, seized Snowfire's bridle and headed determinedly for the docks. There he had persuaded—by dint of buying them half a dozen drinks apiece—these tough men to accompany him to "Lady" Bennett's to effect a rescue.

"I can bring two down with my pistols," Geoffrey said grimly as he and Christopher neared "Lady" Bennett's front door. "But I'll have no time to reload for at the first shot they'll be on us in a pack. How good are ye with a pistol?"

"Better than with a sword—ho, what's this?"

They almost collided with a group of burly sailors, walking with a rolling gait, and led by a determined young fellow with russet hair who stopped as he saw them. "Gentlemen," he said courteously, "my name is Tabb Aylesbury. I know not who ye be but the madam who runs this place"—he nodded his head toward "Lady" Bennett's front door—"has abducted my betrothed. I mean to get her back and I've brought these lads to help me do it, for I saw I could not hope to take the place alone, and my lady would have been spirited away before I could swear out a warrant. If ye'll help me I'd be much obliged—and so would Lorena Frankford."

Christopher shot a stunned look at Geoffrey, but he didn't notice. He was staring at the tall, young man whose eyes shone with fierce determination that, with or without their aid, he would save the girl he loved.

"Ye've found the right company, Tabb Aylesbury, for she's my daughter." His voice was rough with emotion. It was the first time he had ever acknowledged Lorena as his daughter—even to himself.

"Your daughter, sir?" Tabby said, stunned. "But she's—"

"I know what you thought," said Geoffrey sternly. "Ye were wrong. And if you gentlemen will accompany *us,* ye'll meet her *mother,* for Lenore Frankford was seized and dragged into this building, and we're here to rescue *her.*"

From this second piece of startling information, Tabby recovered swiftly. This was no time for questions. He was reaching for the knocker when Geoffrey calmly stepped in front of him and took hold of it.

"Follow me, lads," he said in a tone accustomed to command. He drew out his pistol. "We'll surge in over whoever opens the door, and I'll shoot the first man who tries to stop us. After that 'twill be everybody's fight." He brought the knocker down resoundingly against the wooden panels of the door.

After a moment it was opened a crack, and Geoffrey promptly set a boot inside it. Tabby's shoulder struck the door and they spilled into the hallway like a dam bursting. While the sailors held the downstairs, smashing their big fists into any strange face, Geoffrey and Christopher and Tabby ran from room to room upstairs, smashing down doors and setting anyone free who wished to go. Before they were finished, half a dozen released virgins ran into the street and scuttled for home while the sailors cheered.

At the first eruption of sound downstairs, followed by shots, Lorena sprang up.

"My father has come for us!" she cried joyfully.

"Perhaps not." Lenore cautioned her daughter. "Remember what kind of a place we are in. There are fights here all the time." *A man had been killed here only last week*. She did not want to tell that to Lorena!

Now she cast about for a weapon—any weapon. But there was none. Only the big bed and a cupboard too heavy to move.

Feet pounded on the stairs. Quickly, Lenore thrust a pillow at Lorena. "If the door should be opened by other than Geoffrey, throw this pillow into his face and I will throw this over him." She snatched up the coverlet from the bed. "While he grapples with it, run past him down the stairs. I will deal with any others." She prayed she would be able to! "Then, go to the Hart and tell your father what has happened. He will come for me!"

There was fighting outside in the hall now. Lorena protested, but Lenore bade her sharply to be still. Lorena could but obey the tone of command in her mother's voice. With a pounding heart, she waited before the door with her foolish weapon, while Lenore stood at one side with the coverlet poised to strike. Lorena thought fleetingly that her mother had the poised, feline grace of a hunting cat.

Outside the door they heard the clash of steel, doors crashing open, oaths and screams. Once in the clamor Lenore thought she heard the laughing voice of Christopher Dorn but she could not be sure. But not Geoffrey's or Tabby's, for they went about their work in deadly silence.

A big body landed on the hall floor with a thud that shook the house. Lorena shuddered.

Outside, Tabby took a running start and now he crashed against the heavy door panels with both boots. Beneath his assault, the iron hinges broke and the door crashed inward. Tabby sailed in, riding atop the falling door like a flying carpet. Lorena leaped back with a shriek as the door fell in upon her, and instinctively upraised the pillow before her like a shield. Tabby's surprised face plunged into that pillow's suffocating depths. The enveloping feathers effectively stifled any greeting he might have had for her. Lenore swung the coverlet like a net over his head and body in one lithe, confident motion. As that heavy cloth descended over him, Tabby wavered and lost his footing. Like a thunderclap, the door crashed down upon the floorboards. Tabby skidded off it and went down, bearing Lorena with him in a tangle of cloth and feathers.

Lenore, aware only that their room had been invaded by a stranger with a smoking pistol, was tugging urgently at her daughter's arm.

"Lorena, run!"

But Lorena was not to be separated from her fallen rescuer, now netted like a fish and floundering. She pulled away. "No! This is Tabby!" she wailed, clawing to free him and to untangle herself from the coverlet which had trapped her legs.

With a mighty effort, Tabby fought free. This slight buffeting from his lady he took as only his just due. By the Lord Harry, he felt he deserved more than that, a blow at the least! But even as Lorena struggled to free her trapped legs, he seized her by the shoulders, and his tormented face was thrust close to hers.

"Lorena," he cried hoarsely. "Have they hurt you?"

To Lorena, even though she was desperately glad to see Tabby, the memory of his treatment of her was still fresh. Well she knew what he meant.

"Suppose I told you they'd all raped me?" she flashed.

She had never seen a pair of eyes so wild. "Then I'd kill them all—and marry you after!"

Marry her?

Lorena's world did a triumphant somersault and came up roses.

"They didn't hurt me," she whispered, managing to free her legs and trying to shrug him off. She mustn't act *eager!*

But Tabby kept his grip upon her. "Lorena, Lorena," he groaned. "Will you ever forgive me?"

Geoffrey, who had just wrested another door open and let two screaming young girls run past him to safety, had turned to help Tabby. He reached the door just as Tabby's flying body sailed through it.

There he was faced with the stunning spectacle of Lorena and Lenore at bay, and attacking with what they had: a pillow and a coverlet. For a breathless moment he watched as his lady—his brave, beautiful lady—stepped into full view and tossed the coverlet over Tabby's astonished head. How could she know Tabby had come to save them?

It caught at Geoffrey's heart to see Lenore so fearlessly attack an armed man with naught but a coverlet—and not to save herself but to save *their child.* For hardly had the fair-haired young girl within crashed to the floor with Tabby, than Lenore was trying to free her, calling her "Lorena."

And then he knew without a doubt. This beautiful girl struggling with Tabby and the coverlet was his daughter. *His daughter,* as daring and as lovely as his splendid Lenore! For a moment he filled his eyes with her flushed young face and felt a peculiar tug in his chest that was like nothing he had ever experienced. A wave of exaltation coursed through him that he should have produced this wonder.

At that moment Geoffrey was fiercely proud of both his women. Indeed his heart was near bursting with love and pride as he surged into the room. Lenore spun around to face this new danger—and saw him. However long he lived, Geoffrey would never forget the sight of her at that moment, whirling toward him in fighting stance like a tigress protecting her young—or how her lovely eyes melted to glory as she recognized him.

"Oh, Geoffrey," she whispered. All the nights they had spent together flooded back to her and throbbed in her low vibrant voice. Her confident words shook him clear to his boots. *"Geoffrey, I knew you would come. I told Lorena we could count on you!"*

Geoffrey's smoking pistol went into his belt in one fluid motion. He reached Lenore in one long stride. The serviceable blade in his other hand described a flashing arc as he swept his woman into his arms, holding her in a fierce embrace against his thudding chest.

"I've little to offer ye," he murmured against her bright hair, "for I'm a wanted man again. But I seem to remember ye liked me once before in that condition. Will ye have me now, Lenore?"

Lenore did not know what he was talking about, but she did not care. She leaned back and looked up into that dark, saturnine face, and all the love she had felt for him all these years glowed to splendor in her violet eyes. "I will have you, Geoffrey. *In any condition.*"

"Even though"—he was looking at her steadily—"every man's hand be against me?"

Lenore nodded and there could be no doubting the set of her delicate jaw. "Even so."

"Then you're my lady," he said softly and bent his head to kiss her. His long dark hair poured over her shoulders to mingle with her own shimmering locks. But before their lips touched in a kiss that sealed their bargain, they looked long and steadily into each other's eyes, and all the unspoken words they might have said were carried in that long searching gaze: *From this day forward ... forsaking all others ... yours to have and hold ... through all eternity.*

Beside them now—and quite unaware of her embracing parents, so absorbed was she with her own tall lover—Lorena was looking at Tabby with her head tilted to one side. Would she ever forgive him? Men asked such foolish questions!

But her answer did not come quickly enough for impetuous Tabby. "You should strike me down with this pistol for what I did to you," he said earnestly and gestured with the smoking gun barrel.

Lorena gave him a long, level look from beneath golden lashes. There was a wicked light in her shadowed blue eyes. "I'd rather let you make it up to me," she said. "For years and years and years."

Transparent relief and dawning hope flooded Tabby's honest face. "You mean you don't hate me?" he demanded.

"I thought I did," Lorena said slowly. "But I guess I never did. I guess I loved you all the time. Even though," she added crisply, for she meant to make him suffer a bit longer, "you didn't deserve it."

Tabby nodded eagerly. Caught in the grip of crushing emotions, he almost wished she would strike him. He felt he could never atone for his lack of faith, for the wrongs he had done her.

"Lorena." He seized the girl's shoulders in a grip so fierce she flinched. "I will spend all of my life making it up to you." The intensity of his voice thrilled her. "If only you will let me," he added humbly.

A great joy surged through Lorena. She still did not understand why Tabby had used her so vengefully in Twainmere, yet had pursued her all the way to London to beg her pardon. At the moment she did not care. She was riding high on a sense of exhilaration that made everything that had happened to her seem worthwhile.

Tabby loved her! At long last she was making him admit it!

"Join the fun!" Christopher Dorn called from the doorway. Even as he spoke, he was parrying a blow and careened out of sight down the hall. "Ho!" they heard him roar. " 'Lady' Bennett must keep her own army quartered here! I've found two more of them!"

Geoffrey swore and thrust Lenore away from him. Both Geoffrey and Tabby sprang forward, surging through the door to Christopher's aid. Lenore and Lorena ran to the doorway and stood peering down the hall, calling out encouragement as their men subdued the opposition.

After their raid was accomplished and they all swept out into the street, it was Christopher Dorn—bringing up the rear guard as he had that day in Wells—who brought a pistol barrel down squarely on the head of the pursuing Black Patch. It was a neat piece of work, for Black Patch's big form crumpled up in the doorway, tripping up the pursuit as the laughing sailors scattered.

Geoffrey seized Lenore's hand and, carrying her with him, tunneled through the crowd of curious onlookers who had collected in the street at the sound of shots from within. Tabby, holding on to his precious Lorena, had paused to call his thanks to the departing sailors, and now Christopher grasped his arm and urged him to follow Geoffrey. Together they all raced toward the docks where the *Enterprise* lay at anchor.

Halfway there they came to a skidding stop for they had almost run head-on into a troop of the king's horsemen. Christopher would have darted on through but Geoffrey—knowing they might be looking for him— prudently checked their flight and motioned them into a deserted alley. As they swerved, Christopher would have taken Lorena's arm to guide her in, but Tabby stayed him with suddenly flashing eyes. Christopher gave Tabby a knowing grin and desisted. Young lovers were always jealous. He moved back beside Lenore, and waited for the king's men to pass, their horses slipping on the cobbles. Standing on Lenore's other side, a picture of studied casualness, Geoffrey guarded the alley's entrance, ready to sweep up his lady and run with her.

Behind them Tabby and Lorena had retreated for privacy beneath the bulging overhang of a timber-and-wattle building—and they were quarreling.

"I have no mind to be your mistress, Tabby!" Lorena told him in a severe tone vaguely suggesting Lenore's. She airily ignored the fact that he had already mentioned marriage. Well, let him ask her again!

Tabby winced. "I'd not ask it of ye. We'll go to the church as soon as the banns can be read!"

Lorena's blue eyes gleamed. But she was determined to torment him yet a little longer. "How do you know I'll accept when you have not yet asked for my hand? I want to be courted, not assaulted like some fort!"

Tabby cast a desperate look around him. He would court her! It was in his mind to go down on his knees right now and beg for her hand—but how could he do it in this public place? "I do ask ye, Lorena," he said hurriedly. "I ask ye most humbly to be my wife."

He was hanging on her answer.

Lorena gave him a slanted look, "Well—I might consider it."

Tabby's face lit up like a burst of sunlight breaking through the clouds. With a shout he swept Lorena up in his arms and both Lenore and Geoffrey turned to stare.

"She's promised to marry me!" he cried.

Lenore felt her heart lurch. Her little girl . . . married. But Geoffrey, who remembered that Tabby had already referred to Lorena as his betrothed, quirked a quizzical eyebrow at Tabby. Plainly the lad had stretched the truth a bit.

"Geoffrey!" Lenore's voice rang with pride. "You have not yet been properly introduced. This is my daughter, Lorena."

Geoffrey stepped forward. *"Our* daughter," he corrected gravely. "Lorena, I am your father."

Lenore felt her heart would burst. *He had acknowledged Lorena at last!* Her vision blurred so that she could not see them, but she heard Lorena's shy halting words as father and daughter took stock of each other.

Lorena felt shy with this tall, resolute stranger who gazed at her so searchingly. But Geoffrey, looking into that sweet face, felt again that peculiar tug in his chest that he had experienced when first he had seen her savagely lifting a pillow to smash it into poor Tabby's onrushing face. His spirited daughter, flesh of his flesh, this beautiful young girl who was so like and yet so unlike her lovely mother—*his daughter.*

A pang of regret went through him. Once he could have done so much for her. He might have arranged for her a great marriage, a liaison befitting his position and her beauty. But no longer. And this tall young fellow might do well enough. At least she'd found a lad who was willing to fight for her. In his heart he could not but approve of Tabby.

"I am not surprised you are a beauty, Lorena," the girl heard Geoffrey say. "For Lenore has always swept all before her. But"—he turned half humorously to Tabby— "I am not sure this young buck is good enough for you."

For a moment Lorena felt a lively tug of fear. She had always known she had a mother, beautiful and unattainable like some distant star blazing through the heavens. But a father? She had thought him long asleep under some unmarked grave in Worcester. And now this dark commanding stranger claimed her. Would he forbid her to marry Tabby? she wondered in sudden fright.

Tabby bristled, for the same thing had occurred to him, and Lorena cried hastily, "Oh, yes, he is!"

"I'll never be good enough for her, sir," Tabby told Geoffrey earnestly. "But—will anyone else be?"

"A good point," Geoffrey agreed with a smile. "Lorena, I give ye freely to this lad who will have ye anyway. 'Twas obvious from the way he stormed 'Lady' Bennett's at the head of his hastily recruited army!"

Lorena felt it best to be silent about the fact that Tabby had already stormed *her*. There were some things parents had no need to know—and she was *almost* a virgin, she told herself. Maude could keep her mouth shut. Lorena was going to wear white at *her* wedding!

"Though I dare say he will sail away with ye, and we will never see ye again," Geoffrey added ruefully.

"He will not! For he is not a sailor but a miller—and a good one!"

Geoffrey gave Tabby a thoughtful look. Mills were needed in Virginia. He'd thought to establish one himself, but now there'd be a son-in-law to do it! He turned to Lenore. "It would seem we have not only acquired a daughter, but a son as well."

Before Lenore could speak, Christopher, impatient with this sentimental reunion which he had helped to bring about, said briskly, "The king's men have gone. We'd best away!"

They resumed their hurrying footsteps to the dock where the *Enterprise* lay at anchor.

The Reckoning

Chapter 40

Ten minutes later when the bulk of the milling crowd around the brothel had dispersed and "Lady" Bennett was wringing her hands and moaning that her virgins were all gone and that now Lord Faltrop would surely take his custom to "Mother" Moseley, a hansom cab drew up at her front door and presently Andre Malraux alighted.

He was sporting a bruised mark under his right eye where the flung shoe had hit him and a cut alongside his ear where a raging Letiche had slashed at him with a paperknife. His expression was sulky, but aside from that he was his usual dapper self. From the cab behind him, a pair of snapping auburn eyes peered out from behind a vizard mask. For it was with difficulty that Andre had made any kind of peace with Letiche. All the way here she had not spoken to him, keeping her lips tightly pursed and her head turned away, for she refused to look at him as well. It boded ill for their future together, and Andre had not thought it a propitious moment to acquaint Letiche of her husband's imminent arrest.

Watching her in the cab, Andre was certain Letiche would repudiate him and break off their relationship the moment this night was over. Tomorrow morning she would take her jewels and promptly leave for Holland—and de Vignac. He would be left in London—penniless. And when the king's men learned—as he had no doubt they would—that he, Andre Malraux, had spent all these hours with Letiche just before she fled, he might find himself in jail or on the rack.

Like de Vignac, his mind inclined to flight, perhaps to some faraway place like Amsterdam. Unfortunately he did not possess de Vignac's resources.

Still—he was not without assets.

Through narrowed eyes he considered Letiche, the lower part of her face flushed beneath her vizard mask, her auburn eyes glittering through the slits.

He would sell her.

Arriving at "Lady" Bennett's, Andre was surprised to find people milling about the front door, which stood open. Obviously there had been some kind of trouble, for that door was now slammed.

Andre sat there watching while the curious drifted away, one by one. He could only catch bits and pieces of their remarks as they passed: "Thought I heard gunfire, I did." "Ought to close that place down, did you see all those young girls come running out into the street? Looked scared to death, they did!" Now he too was curious as to what had happened here. He sprang down from the cab and banged the heavy boar's head knocker.

When nobody answered, he tried the door. It was not locked. He went in and found "Lady" Bennett moaning on the stairs, Black Patch getting unsteadily to his feet, and two other burly but battered fellows trying to help up a third who was bleeding profusely from a wound in his chest. From another part of the house came masculine curses and a howl of pain.

"Lady" Bennett's face contorted as she saw Andre. "I am ruined!" she cried. "All my virgins are gone—and all of them promised to the Hellfire Club tonight. Where am I to find more on such short notice? Worst of all, I've lost my two prize pieces—Lenore Frankford and her daughter."

"Wyndham was here," murmured Andre.

"Everyone was here! The whole street poured in on us—sailors, strangers, 'twas a madhouse." She gave him a sharp look. "How did ye know 'twas Wyndham?"

Andre shrugged. " 'Twas an easy guess. Where the orange girl goes, he follows."

"Lady" Bennett got up and dusted off her skirts with her hands. "Well, if ye're seeking an evening's frivolity, all my regular girls are upstairs hiding under their beds, what with all the noise and the guns going off. 'Twill take them time to settle down!"

"I've not come to buy, I've come to sell."

"Lady" Bennett gave him an astonished look. "Pish, ye overrate your charms. Who d'ye think would want ye? Some duchess?"

"I am not offering myself. Ye would have been paid handsomely for the Frankford women."

"A thousand pounds," mourned the famous lisp, deepened now by another broken tooth, for Lenore had snatched up a heavy decanter and hurled it into "Lady" Bennett's face on her way out.

"Half of that was for Lenore Frankford, because she was a choice piece that Wilsingame and the others wanted to humble. Come." He led her to the front door and cracked it. "Look at the lady peeping out of the hansom cab."

"Lady" Bennett peered out. "I cannot see her face for the mask," she complained.

"Behind that mask is a beautiful face—and a notably sharp tongue. The lady has speared half of London with that tongue. She is the wife of Geoffrey Wyndham. Would Wilsingame and Faltrop—both of whom she has insulted—not give a thousand pounds between them to humble *her*? After today's raid on your place and the loss of your virgins, would *you* not give a thousand pounds to humble Geoffrey Wyndham's wife?"

"Lady" Bennett gasped. "But what is she doing here?"

Andre's lips curled. "She is here at her own insistence. Letiche Wyndham thinks she is going to watch Lenore Frankford set upon by a mob and then dragged into the chapel to die."

"Revenge?"

Andre nodded and "Lady" Bennett's gaze upon that masked face, half-visible in the hansom cab, grew thoughtful. She had seen Letiche Wyndham riding by in her coach many times, elegantly gowned. A beautiful woman certainly—not so beautiful as the Frankford woman, but still outstanding. A woman with many enemies—some of them members of the Hellfire Club, for Letiche had always been careless with her biting tongue. Her brows drew together; it was too risky. "But would this not bring retribution from her husband? A powerful man."

"A man at present on the run." Andre's mouth split into a conspiratorial grin. "And not likely to return this way. He has fallen from favor, he is being hunted by the king's men for treason, and he has left his wife. At least, she does not desire to accompany him into his dangerous exile."

"Lady" Bennett's crafty eyes widened in admiration. She gazed into the Frenchman's dissolute countenance and grinned broadly. "A woman who would not be missed," she breathed. "All would believe her fled with her husband."

"Even so. And at a bargain price. Say—five hundred pounds?"

Her bargaining instincts were instantly aroused. "Two hundred. 'Tis all I have at hand."

"Two hundred and fifty."

"All right," she muttered grudgingly.

"Close the door. The lady must not see you give me money."

"Lady" Bennett gave a little contemptuous laugh. She had had many dealings with men like Andre in the past and would doubtless have many more in the future, but she could never respect them. She knew his kind; gentleman he might pretend to be, but one day he would end up working for her, or someone like her. She paid him.

"Done." Andre made the coins seem to disappear into the cuffs of his satin coat. Again "Lady" Bennett looked at him with grudging admiration. He had talent, this one! "I wish you joy of her," he said grimly.

"Bring her in," said "Lady" Bennett, mindful that he already had her money.

But Andre wanted to get rid of Letiche Wyndham— before she could talk, before she could tell all she knew about him, about their revolutionary plotting—almost as much as he wanted the money. He hurried to hand Letiche down from the cab.

"Must we go in?" she wondered, wrinkling her nose in distaste.

"Oh, come, 'tis very attractive inside," said Andre in a bored voice. "And we do not leave for another twenty minutes. We cannot wait in the street all that time, someone might come along and recognize you."

"Yes, you are right." She dropped his arm as if it were hot, swished her satin skirts away from him disdainfully and went into the house to be greeted by a broad smile from a woman with missing teeth.

"If your ladyship will just follow me?" lisped "Lady" Bennett, hurrying Letiche toward the stairs. "There's a private waiting room upstairs that I reserve for persons of quality."

Not noticing that Andre had slunk back, Letiche ran lightly up the stairs after "Lady" Bennett. She had dismissed Andre from her mind—by tomorrow he would be an ex-lover with no claim upon her. All her gleefully vindictive thoughts were upon the spectacle she would witness this night: Lenore Frankford humiliated, debauched, dishonored; and at the end of it, although regretfully she wouldn't see that, killed. She would make sure Geoffrey heard of it, Letiche promised herself, bringing her small teeth together with a snap. *And suffer*.

At the head of the stairs two huge figures suddenly appeared and pounced upon her before she could scream.

It was the first inkling Letiche had that Andre had "sold" her to "Lady" Bennett, although a moment later that famous lisp informed her that she was to take the escaped Lenore Frankford's place at the Hellfire Club tonight.

A little moan of terror rose in Letiche's throat and was lost in the gag that was thrust suddenly into her mouth. That terror became a raging river of fear that washed over her like an avalanche of melting snow as the lisp callously informed her:

"You are an ideal replacement. *A woman who will not be missed*."

The Daunts
of Williamsburg

Chapter 41

On the London dock, where the good ship *Enterprise* was but one among a flotilla of tall-masted merchant ships silhouetted against the red glow of the evening sky, Christopher Dorn bade them a jaunty good-bye.

"Ye may keep those trinkets, Dorn." Geoffrey indicated the dark red coat Christopher wore, the sword and pistol Christopher now carried. "For ye may have need of them—especially the pistol, if you should run across any of those cutthroats from 'Lady' Bennett's."

"Am I always to be thanking you?" laughed Christopher.

Geoffrey's voice rang with sincerity. " 'Tis I who thank you—for bringing Lenore back to me."

Smiling, Christopher turned to go, but cast one more lingering glance toward Lenore. Lenore was not fooled by his debonair manner; she caught the anguish that flared for an instant in those crystal eyes.

"Oh, Christopher!" She ran forward and flung her arms about him. "Thank you for everything!" In his ear she pleaded, "Chris, try to understand. I love him so."

"Don't look so sad," he chided, pushing her away from him regretfully. "Ye were born to have a big house and a dozen children round your knee. And as for me, I'll have a new wench before the week is out!"

His grin flashed and he left them, swaggering slightly. He cut a dashing figure, Lenore thought, with his golden hair and his dark red coat glowing like a ruby in the crimson light. Her eyes grew moist as she thought of the friend she had had in that man. She stepped back and leaned against Geoffrey as she watched him go.

Just before he disappeared into the dockside crowd that was thinning out, now that night was falling, Christopher turned and looked back. He could see her there, her shoulders encircled by the strong right arm of the man she had loved for so long, and nearby—with Tabby's arm wrapped firmly around her waist—her newfound daughter Lorena. Lenore would have a family now, he thought wistfully, protection, love—all the things he now realized he had wanted for her all along. She would be all right.

It was hard for him to tear his gaze from her, and he would always remember her the way she looked at that moment. Standing there proud and erect against the backdrop of the tall-masted ships with their great white sails, with her glorious red-gold hair an ember against the evening sky, a valiant woman who had won through at last.

To Christopher Dorn—before his vision blurred and he plunged blindly into the dockside crowd to be lost from view—she had a shining splendor that was all her own.

"Dorn loves ye," murmured Geoffrey, his thoughtful gaze upon the spot where Christopher had disappeared. "Else why would he bring me a cheap copy of a likeness of the Duchess of Devonshire and pass it off as a portrait of my mother?"

Lenore caught her breath. "But why would—?" Then suddenly she understood. This was what Chris had meant when he said "Christopher Dorn, miracle worker, is on your side." He had loved her enough to try to trick Geoffrey into believing that Lorena was his—for her sake. "He did not tell me," she said soberly.

"I guessed that. And I guessed *why* Dorn did it. But he need not have gone to that trouble. For it has come to me with force that if ye tell me Lorena is mine, then she is mine. You are not the woman to live a lie."

"No," sighed Lenore, "I am not. And she *is* yours, Geoffrey."

His arm tightened about her. "Will ye miss Dorn?"

Lenore hesitated. "I'll *remember* him," she said carefully. "And wish him well. And I'll always be grateful to him for all that he did for us this day. He knew how I felt about you, Geoffrey. He couldn't stand it; it drove him into debt."

"I misjudged Dorn. I thank God I didn't kill him." Geoffrey bent over, looking down into her somber eyes. "Don't try to hide it, Lenore. You're *worried* about him."

Lenore sighed. "We forgot he had no money. We let him go without even a farthing. He hasn't eaten since yesterday. Where will he sleep tonight? How will he live?"

"Ye need not worry about Dorn's keep," Geoffrey told her in a wry voice. "For when I told him to keep my coat, I clean forgot that I had stuffed into it Letiche's emerald necklace that I had taken from de Vignac. We've endowed your Christopher right handsomely. 'Tis enough to put him up at the finest inns and carry him back to Nottingham if he's a mind to go there."

"He'll not." Lenore laughed ruefully. "He'll spend the money buying a horse and a fine saddle and a pair of loaded dice—and be off to the fairs, as blithe as before. I hope he has found the necklace by now. Chris always said he was born lucky."

His luck was knowing you, thought Geoffrey, gazing down at her tenderly. *Just as my own greatest good fortune has been finding you again—and learning that you still love me.* But even he found himself wishing luck to reckless Christopher Dorn, who had it anyway.

"We'd best go aboard," he told Lenore. "'Tis conspicuous, standing out here on the docks with two such beautiful women." He smiled at Lorena, and Tabby grinned broadly back at him.

That first night before sailing, a celebration was held. In the cabin of Geoffrey Daunt aboard the good ship *Enterprise,* there was a family reunion to warm the heart. The rude table in the center of the room was heaped with food, for the ship's captain had sent down a roast goose and half a dozen side dishes and bottles of wine when he had learned that Mister Daunt's wife would accompany him on the voyage and that therefore the captain would pocket double passage money.

Lorena was starving and ate hungrily. Across the table Geoffrey and Lenore gazed fondly at this wondrous daughter whose childhood they had missed.

Lorena looked up from her heaping trencher and met her mother's violet gaze, and a look passed between them that made Geoffrey swallow and look away quickly, for it was like a binding promise given from woman to woman: *We will be mother and daughter now; we will abandon lies, bind old wounds; we will start anew.*

For when she had been trapped in that room at "Lady" Bennett's and Lenore had been suddenly thrust inside, Lorena had shrunk back from this woman who claimed to be her mother. But when she had learned that Lenore had come to trade her own body for her daughter, so that Lorena might be set free, all the barriers between them had come tumbling down. In that moment all the resentment Lorena had ever cherished against Lenore for leaving her alone had melted away, and she had flung her arms about her mother and wept.

Smiling on them both, Geoffrey now proposed a toast.

"To my daughter." His voice rang with pride. "I drink her health."

Lenore had thought she would never live to hear him say that. Tears glimmered on her lashes as she drank her wine.

It had been bewildering for Lorena to learn that Jamie was not her father, that Flora was not her aunt, and that Kate Tilson had hated her all these years for nothing. But in that locked bedroom at "Lady" Bennett's, she had listened to what Lenore told her and asked—not about Geoffrey Wyndham, whom she had never seen up to that time—but about Flora who had loved her, brought her up. "How—how did you fool Aunt Flora?" she had faltered.

"She fooled herself," Lenore said. "She took one look at you and decided you were Jamie's. For your sake, I let her believe it. Not that she wouldn't have taken you in anyway—but the law was pursuing me and I couldn't take any chances on your future." She hesitated. "It was one of the reasons I never came back to Twainmere, I suppose, the fact that I'd tricked Flora. But the main reason was that I wanted you to believe me a success, someone you could be proud of—and I was not."

"Oh, mother," Lorena had whispered. Her tears had spilled over and run down her cheeks, and before her eyes, the vision of her mother—this warm beautiful woman who had come without question to give her life for her daughter—blurred into a dream come true. "Mother, I *am* proud of you."

Lenore knew she would never forget that either.

Now, under the table, Tabby found Lorena's hand and squeezed it, and Lorena turned her happy gaze on him. In all the excitement since her rescue, she and Tabby had had scant time to talk although Tabby had asked her forgiveness several times. Now the look she gave him was all the forgiveness anyone could ask. Tabby's heart melted and he silently thanked God for giving him a second chance with Lorena.

Later there would be explanations between them, heartfelt apologies, warm forgiveness. But for the moment they were two young lovers about to embark upon a great adventure, a new life. Blissfully Lorena considered her newfound lover, her strong newfound father, her beautiful and staunch newfound mother. All of them had cared enough to come to save her, she marveled. And she knew with the warmth breaking in her heart that the future was going to be very wonderful indeed.

Lenore wanted Lorena to make the trip with them so they could get to know her, but Lorena was adamant.

"I'm going back for Aunt Flora," she said stubbornly. "I know now that she isn't really my aunt and never was, but that doesn't make any difference to me, and it won't to her. She brought me up and I love her like—" Her eyes fell away from Lenore, and Lenore knew with a pang that Lorena had been about to say "like a mother."

"We're very close," Lorena went on. "Aunt Flora was so lonesome she almost made a terrible mistake, but I'm sure Alger Pye will never come back for her, and she'll be all alone." Almost apologetically, she turned to her newfound parents. "*You* have each other, but Aunt Flora has no one but me. But once we get her to America, I'm sure the place is full of bachelors who'll be jostling each other aside to win her hand in marriage! And she'll have a *good* man, who'll love her, and not someone like Alger Pye."

Lenore gave her daughter a fond misty look, for it was loyalty, loyalty to those she loved, that had torn her own world asunder and now magically had woven it all together once again. But the message was clear: Lorena's first loyalty was to Flora.

"You're right to go back, Lorena," she said gently. "Neither of us can ever thank Flora enough for all she has done. And there'll be lots of time for us to get to know each other—in America." In America, she promised herself humbly, she would *earn* her daughter's love.

But Tabby, who was already imagining what it would be like to make love to Lorena aboard a ship in harbor, a ship that would take wings and sail away before they waked, protested, "Let's not go back, Lorena. The captain can marry us as soon as we're on the high seas, and we can send for Flora later."

Lorena shook her head. "Her heart is breaking *now*. We can be married in Twainmere and jump over the stile together. And Maude can be my bridesmaid. I owe her a new dress, for the one I'm wearing is hers; you can see it's too big for me. And then after you've sold the mill, you and I and Aunt Flora can take ship and join— mother and father"—she tripped a little over the words but came up smiling—"in America, where you can set up a new mill like you've always wanted. Besides," she added, to clinch her argument, "if we took a later ship, we could have a private cabin instead of your being crowded into common quarters with the men while I bunk in with the women. We could have more—privacy."

A private cabin, a bed of their own instead of borrowing a cabin for stolen moments of love . . . Tabby's broad grin broke like sunshine.

Watching her slim lovely daughter wind the big russet-haired lad around her fingers amused Lenore. How like her in spirit Lorena was, she thought, and fought back a yearning desire to go over and stroke that fair head and murmur a mother's endearments to her young. Lorena had grown up apart from her and it would take time to bring them together. But now they would have that time—all the time in the world.

"Geoffrey." Lenore turned her lovely face toward him. "Could we not send Flora something? Some gift?"

Geoffrey, who had been casting about for a suitable wedding present for his daughter, nodded. He rose, found pen and parchment and an inkwell, and wrote swiftly. "Go back to the Cotswolds by way of Claremont Court in Kent," he told Tabby over his shoulder. "Here is a bill of sale for my coaches and other equipage there, for I clean forgot to mortgage them. Present this document to my estate manager, Glendower—he will not have left yet— and he will honor it. Ye can sell enough of it to buy six horses to pull the coach and ye can travel back to Twainmere in style." He melted sealing wax and pressed his signet ring into the hot wax, swung around and handed the document to Lorena with a smile. "This is my wedding gift to ye."

A coach! She'd be going back to Twainmere in a coach-and-six—with Snowfire ambling along comfortably beside them like the pet he was! Lorena's eyes sparkled. The entire town, friend and enemy alike, would never forget her return! Just wait till Aunt Flora saw them riding up!

Tabby was thinking about that too. "There'll be questions about this new father who gives away coaches," he grinned.

Geoffrey gave Lenore a thoughtful look. "Perhaps ye'd best say it came from your mother, who has had some success in London."

Tabby's grin widened, thinking what the gossips would make of that, but Lenore leaned forward, misty-eyed. "I have nothing to give you, Lorena—only my love and hopes for your future."

"Wrong," Geoffrey firmly disagreed. "Ye have already given her the greatest gift—life." He looked critically upon his winsome daughter, smiling back at him. "And the gift of beauty. Your gifts, Lenore, are richer far than mine."

Unable to speak, Lenore gripped his hand and pressed it. Had Christopher Dorn been watching, he would have shaken his head and been forced to admit that they were indeed well suited to each other, the resplendent lady in torn lace and her dark and dangerous cavalier.

"I have been seeking a way to repay Flora, this woman who took care of ye when I did not," Geoffrey told Lorena soberly. "With part of the gold ye realize from the various equipage, buy her a new gown and passage money to America. Tell her she will always be welcomed as an honored guest in my house."

Lenore murmured in a choked voice, "Well spoke, Geoffrey. Well spoke."

"And I will tell her also that you know many fine

men there who are in urgent need of wives!" added Lorena eagerly.

Geoffrey's lips quirked. "By all means tell Flora that I am sure to know many men of substance who would be improved by taking a wife." He was thinking specifically of Glendower. The Welshman had never married, never found a woman to his liking, he said. Geoffrey suspected Glendower was afraid of women. Scottish Flora might do just fine.

Lenore was gazing at him proudly. *Geoffrey, Geoffrey,* she thought from a full heart, *truly we can count on you . . . for always.*

* * *

Later, much later, when the *Enterprise* had sailed majestically down the Thames and spread its white wings to skim out upon the open water, when another night's moon shone down on the English Channel and the rugged coast of Cornwall raced by on the starboard bow, Lenore leaned on the taffrail beside Geoffrey and looked out over the moon-drenched waves. Above them on the tall masts the white sails billowed and a fine fresh wind bore them toward the land of dreams—America, where old wounds would be forgotten, where they would start a new and wonderful life together.

By now Lorena and Tabby would have left Claremont Court with their coach-and-six—and Lenore guessed that her shining-eyed daughter would not be riding, as a lady should, inside the jolting coach, but rapturously up on the box beside Tabby as he drove, bound for Twainmere. And picking his dainty way along beside them would be Snowfire with his white silky mane tossing in the sunlight. Snowfire—he'd been *her* horse and she'd loved him. Lorena had promised to bring Snowfire to America too, so there would be yet another reunion to look forward to in the green Virginia countryside.

Now as the fresh salt wind blew her red-gold hair, Lenore turned a blissful face to Geoffrey. "We are lucky,

Geoffrey," she murmured, leaning close against him. "So very lucky."

Geoffrey's dark face looked down at her, the gray eyes tender. At her words his strong arm tightened convulsively about her trim shoulders, for his heart was too full to speak.

He told himself that Charles was not a vengeful sovereign. He had not even given England the bloodpath they expected for beheading his father. Only half a dozen culprits had paid for that crime after he reached the throne. Just now his minions would be hot on the heels of Geoffrey Wyndham, but by the time these strong winds blew them to American shores, Charles would have more pressing matters to think about and Geoffrey, old friend of his exile, would be forgotten and perhaps even forgiven by the cynical young king. Charles might even chuckle wryly if he learned that Geoffrey and his orange girl had become planters in the Colonies; he might mutter that Geoffrey Wyndham—whether he called himself Daunt or the devil—would be a bastion in the West for England, a good man for the Crown to lean upon.

Tenderly Geoffrey looked down upon Lenore's bright head in the moonlight, seeing the rich gleam of her thick lovely hair. In de Vignac's apartments he had divorced Letiche in his heart, divorced her forever when he learned of her treachery. No matter what transpired, he knew he would not return to her.

Lenore sensed this, sensed that she would never have to fight a rival for him again, never tremble over losing his love.

And later still, when she lay beneath him in the bunk in their cabin, when she felt his dear hard body gathering her to him with all the love and tenderness a man could ever give a wife: when his demanding lips, his gently searching hands, his fierce masculine hardness sealed the bond between them and she was fully and forever his: she opened her long lashes with a sigh and saw a white moon riding in the velvet dark beyond the cabin's porthole and listened to the music of the great ship's creaking timbers as it cut a moonpath through the waves and *knew*.

For her the long journey was ended. She would have Geoffrey beside her and at long last her courageous daughter—they would be the Daunts of Williamsburg after all!

Then the towering passion that had driven them like straws before a great wind engulfed them once again. And the world was forgot and time stood meaningless as the lovers melded into each other's arms.

OUTSTANDING READING FROM WARNER BOOKS

PASSION STAR
by Julia Grice   (91-498, $2.50)

The sapphire was called the Passion Star. It was stone-mined by men and polished to brilliance—but to Adrienne McGill the six-spurred Passion Star was both magic charm and mystic curse. It transported her out of the slums of Glasgow to training and stardom on the stage. But the girl with the radiantly pale blonde hair had stolen the treasure in the throes of rape. Now she must pay for her deed with her heart...

AMERICAN ROYAL
by Anne Rudeen   (81-827, $2.50)

They had loved each other once... but with a youthful passion that consumed them; now Selena, more beautiful than ever, was a rich widow whose husband nearly had become President of the United States. And Hank was now a racing car magnate who had agreed, without knowing his parentage, to let Selena's son Blair race for him. For a race that may be the beginning or the end.

THE BEACH CLUB
by Claire Howard   (91-616, $2.50)

Have fun in the sun with... Laurie: a smouldering redhead whose husband, down from the city only on weekends, brings along a teenage babysitter bursting out of her bikini and out of bounds; B. J.: sharp-tongued rich girl who trapped her husband into marriage and herself into a swinging scene; Sandy: the loving wife whose husband has so much love in him it just overflows—to other women; and Jan: the plain girl whose husband lost interest in her as soon as her father took him into the business. It's hot in the sun and getting hotter for the four couples exposing bodies, secrets and passions under the umbrellas at THE BEACH CLUB.

CARVER'S KINGDOM
by Frederick Nolan   (81-201, $2.50)

Sarah Hutchinson, married to an irresponsible wanderer when Theo Carver, the merchant adventurer, first met her, loved her and lost her. Sarah Hutchinson, who irrevocably changed the lives of the ruthless brothers who had wrestled riches and power from expanding America... the men of CARVER'S KINGDOM.

IF YOU LIKE ROMANCE...
YOU'LL LOVE VALERIE SHERWOOD

THIS TOWERING PASSION
by Valerie Sherwood   (81-486, $2.50)

They called her "Angel" when she rode bareback into the midst of battle to find her lover. They called her "Mistress Daunt" when she lived with Geoffrey in Oxford, though she wore no ring on her finger. Wherever she traveled men called her Beauty. Her name was Lenore—and she answered only to "Love."

THESE GOLDEN PLEASURES
by Valerie Sherwood   (95-744, $2.75)

She was beautiful—and notorious and they called her "That Barrington Woman." But beneath the silks and the diamonds, within the supple body so many men had embraced, was the heart of a girl who yearned still for love. At fifteen she had learned her beauty was both a charm and a curse. It had sent her fleeing from Kansas, had been her downfall in Baltimore and Georgia, yet had kept her alive in the Klondike and the South Seas.

THIS LOVING TORMENT
by Valerie Sherwood   (82-649, $2.50)

Perhaps she was *too beautiful!* Perhaps the brawling colonies would have been safer for a plainer girl, one more demure and less accomplished in language and manner. But Charity Woodstock was gloriously beautiful with pale gold hair and topaz eyes —and she was headed for trouble. She was accused of witchcraft by the man who had attacked her. She was whisked from pirate ship to plantation. Beauty might have been her downfall, but Charity Woodstock had a reckless passion to live and would challenge this new world—and win.

WARNER BOOKS
P.O. Box 690
New York, N.Y. 10019

Please send me the books I have selected.
Enclose check or money order only, no cash please. Plus 50¢ per order and 20¢ per copy to cover postage and handling. N.Y. State and California residents add applicable sales tax.
Please allow 4 weeks for delivery.

_____ Please send me your free mail order catalog

_____ Please send me your free Romance books catalog

Name_____

Address_____

City_____

State_____ Zip_____